**"Hugh?" she murmured in a daze.
"What do you plan to do with me?"**

"I've something on my mind," he said, setting her on his bed, following her down. As he leaned above her, his dark hungry gaze flickered over her, and his voice broke low. "Something I need tae see."

He rubbed an unsteady hand over his mouth, looking like a man in agony. His body seemed to thrum with tension. Frowning, she brought her palms up to cup his face, but he groaned and shuddered, even at that slight touch. What was happening here?

For all the books she'd read, for all that she'd heard from her cousins and learned in London, she'd never imagined a man behaving like this—as though he were about to die from desire, pained with a need so great he could scarcely speak and could barely stand to be touched.

Hugh slowly reached forward to brush her nightdress straps down her shoulders, then dipped a kiss to her collarbone. Just as she felt cool air on her breasts and belly, he hissed something in Gaelic, and sank back on his haunches to stare. She felt his gaze on her bared skin like a touch and arched her back for him.

Leaning forward once more, lowering his head, he rasped, *"Mercy. . . ."*

If You Desire

KRESLEY COLE

POCKET BOOKS

New York   London   Toronto   Sydney

An *Original* Publication of POCKET BOOKS

POCKET BOOKS, a division of Simon & Schuster, Inc.
1230 Avenue of the Americas, New York, NY 10020

This book is a work of fiction. Names, characters, places and incidents are products of the author's imagination or are used fictitiously. Any resemblance to actual events or locales or persons, living or dead, is entirely coincidental.

ISBN-13: 978-1-4165-0360-6
ISBN-10:   1-4165-0360-9

This Pocket Books paperback edition May 2007

10   9

POCKET and colophon are registered trademarks of Simon & Schuster, Inc.

Cover illustration by Craig White
Handlettering by Dave Gatti

Manufactured in the United States of America

For information regarding special discounts for bulk purchases, please contact Simon & Schuster Special Sales at 1-800-456-6798 or business@simonandschuster.com.

Cheers to the very real "sensation seekers,"
a virtually unrecognized breed of Victorian,
wild enough to imbibe, partake, and
cavort with reckless abandon
—and wily enough never to get caught by history.

Discipline is nothing more than avoiding consequences.
Ultimately, disciplined men will always prevail.

—Hugh Logan MacCarrick

Bringing a strong man to his knees is simple.
It's keeping him there that's the tricky business. . . .

—Jane Farraday Weyland

Prologue

———◆———

The Kingdom of Morocco, North Africa
1846

"*Take the shot, MacCarrick!*" Davis Grey ordered yet again. His tone was harsh, but low enough not to give away their vantage, concealed high in the desolate headlands of the Atlas Mountains.

Hugh ignored him. This was to be his first kill, and he knew that once he committed this deed, there was no going back—a weighty decision for a man of only twenty-two years.

He would do it when he was bloody ready.

Taking his eye from the telescopic sight, Hugh released his rifle with one hand and ran his forearm over his face, wiping away the sweat and sand that stung his eyes like needles. Summer was upon them, and the surreal blue of the sky stretched relentlessly, unmarred by clouds. Hugh squinted against the light of a white, indistinct sun.

"Why in the hell are you hesitating?" Grey bit out. "It's noon." The sun was directly above, casting the fewest shadows of the day. Shadows mocked a gunman's truest aim.

Hugh didn't want to disappoint the older Grey, his mentor of sorts. Grey was Hugh's only real friend outside of the MacCarrick clan, and the only person Hugh would spend time with, apart from his brothers. And apart from an auburn-haired lass Hugh would kill for. He gave a bitter laugh, adjusting his rifle against his shoulder.

In a way, he *was* killing for her.

To take out a stranger in cold blood was to cross a line. Which was what he wanted.

"Goddamn it, MacCarrick!" Grey yanked his own rifle and its detached refractor scope from his leather holster, assembling them. "It'll take us four more weeks to get a shot like this again."

That was true. The traitor knew he was marked for assassination for his treason and had been running for a month, before holing up in the abandoned Berber farm far below them. In this part of the world, even a battered, flat-roofed hut like the one below had a courtyard for a private oasis, and the man sat within it. He faced the courtyard's only entrance with a pistol in his lap and a shotgun by his side, yet he was unguarded from above.

The shot was clear, but both of them knew Grey could never hit a target so far away. Where Grey's preferred weapon was a blade, Hugh had been hunting and target-shooting since he'd been old enough to lift a rifle. Besides, Hugh wanted to act soon while the man was still alone. "I'll do it," Hugh grated, sliding a glance toward Grey. He refused to believe he saw excitement there in the man's expression. This was a job, a foul task. Grey couldn't enjoy this.

Hugh turned back and took a bead once more. The wind was light, but the target was more than a quarter of a mile away. The glare of the sun was an environmental factor, and the nearly four feet of his gun barrel were heated, as was the single bullet inside the chamber. He took all of this into account.

He stroked his forefinger over the trigger guard before placing his sensitive fingertip at the trigger, beginning a ritual he performed with every shot, almost unconsciously. With his other hand gripping the forestock, he rubbed his thumb twice over the wood, then froze halfway through an exhalation of breath.

The press of the trigger was smooth; the report was like a cannon boom in his ears, louder, for some reason, than all the times he'd shot while hunting.

Nearly two seconds later, the bullet pierced the man's forehead and cast him to the ground. Blood seeped out from the back of his head, soaking the gravel, and his legs twitched in death, stirring a cloud of dust at his feet.

It's done, then.

Hugh was done.

There again, he saw something like pleasure in Grey's eyes. "I've never seen anyone shoot like you, Scot." Grey slapped him on the back, then took a swig from the flask he always kept near, grinning against the opening.

All Hugh felt was disgust and a strange sense of relief.

They mounted up quickly, then rode hard down winding mountain trails. An hour after they reached the valley, they neared a village and slowed.

"When we get back to London," Grey began, still jovial, still excited, "I'm going to tell Weyland that you're ready to go out on your own."

Hugh's expression must have revealed his uneasiness with Grey's buoyant mood.

"Don't look at me like that, MacCarrick. You do this for as long as I have, and we'll see if some part of you doesn't come to love it."

Love it? Hugh shook his head and quietly said, "It's a job. Nothing more."

"Trust me." Grey's smile was knowing. "It'll be something more—when it's all you have. . . ."

One

———•◆•———

A hardened killer, denied his obsession for a decade.

That was what Edward Weyland was bringing back into his daughter's life with one cryptic message: *Jane is in grave danger.*

Since receiving Weyland's missive in France two days ago, Hugh had read and reread it with fingers gone white from clutching it in fury.

If anyone had dared to hurt her . . .

Now, after days, and nights, riding like hell was at his heels, Hugh had finally reached the Weyland town house. He slid down from his saddle and nearly toppled over, his legs gone boneless from so many hours on horseback. His mount was as winded as Hugh, its coat lathered and its barrel chest twitching.

As Hugh approached the side door, where he always entered, he encountered Weyland's nephew, Quinton Weyland—who also did *work* for Weyland—sprawled along the stairs.

"Where's Jane?" Hugh demanded without preamble.

"Upstairs," Quin said, seeming preoccupied and even somewhat dazed. "Getting ready for . . . for her night out."

"She's safe?" When Quin nodded absently, relief sailed through Hugh. Over the hours alone on the road, his mind had conjured too many ways she could be in *grave danger*. He'd prayed she hadn't been hurt, that he wasn't too late. Now that Hugh had been assured of her safety, the hunger and thirst he'd ignored for two days began to gnaw at him. "Who's watching her now?"

Quin answered, "Rolley's inside, and I'm trailing her tonight."

Rolley was Edward Weyland's butler. Most butlers in the exclusive enclave of Piccadilly were older with a hint of grandeur about them, denoting experience and the longevity of a family's fortunes. Rolley was in his mid-thirties, wiry, his nose shapeless from being broken so many times. His fingers were scarred from his incessant use of steel knuckles. Hugh knew the man would die for Jane.

"Is Weyland here?" Hugh asked.

Quin shook his head. "Not getting in till late. He said if you somehow managed to get here tonight, to tell you he wants to see you in the morning to give you all the details."

"I'm going in—"

"I wouldn't do that if I were you."

"Why the hell no'?"

"For one thing, your clothes are covered with dirt, and your face looks like hell."

Hugh ran a sleeve over his cheek, remembering too late the jagged cuts marking his skin.

"For another, I'm not sure Jane would want to see you."

Hugh had ridden nonstop for days, and his body was a mass of knotted muscles and aching old injuries. His head was splitting. The idea of being near her again had been all that kept him going. "That does no' make sense. We used to be friends."

Quin flashed him an odd expression. "Well, she's . . . different now. Completely different and completely out of control." He caught Hugh's eyes. "I don't know that I can take another night of it." He shook his head forcefully. "No longer. Not after what they did last night. . . ."

"Who? Did what?"

"The Eight. Or at least, three of them. Two of whom are my sisters!"

Society's notorious Weyland Eight consisted of Jane and her seven female first cousins. Remembering the brazen antics they'd encouraged Jane to take part in, Hugh felt his irritation building.

"But this is no' what I've been brought here for?" Hugh had abandoned his injured younger brother Courtland in France and nearly killed his new horse, a fine gelding that had been a gift for a service he'd rendered. "Because Weyland needs someone to rein her in?"

Surely Weyland wouldn't be so foolish as to call Hugh back for this. Weyland knew what Hugh was, of course. He was Hugh's superior and dispatched him to deliver deaths in the name of the Crown. But then, Weyland had no idea how badly Hugh coveted Jane. Nor for how long.

An obsession. For ten bloody years . . .

Hugh shook his head. Weyland would never have exaggerated the danger in his missive.

"Weyland didn't tell you what's happened?" Quin's brows drew together. "I thought he sent you a message."

"With little information. Now, what in the hell—"

"Bloody hell!" Rolley came barreling through the doorway. "Bloody, bloody hell! Quin! Have you seen her?"

"Rolley?" Quin shot to his feet. "You're supposed to be watching her until she leaves."

The butler cast Quin a scowl. "I told you she knew we'd been following her. She must've gone out the window. And got that saucy maid of hers to walk about, tryin' on dresses in her room."

"She's gone?" Hugh lunged for Rolley and fisted his hands in the man's shirt. "Where's she going and who's she with?"

"To a ball," Rolley said, but immediately glanced at Quin.

Hugh gave Rolley a shake, knowing he was risking Rolley's swift uppercut, usually accompanied by those steel knuckles.

"Go ahead," Quin said. "Weyland tells him everything anyway."

"She's goin' to a masquerade with Quin's sisters and one of their friends."

"What kind of masquerade?" Hugh asked, though he had a good idea.

"Libertines and courtesans," Rolley said. "In a warehouse on Haymarket Street."

With a grated curse, Hugh released Rolley, then forced his legs to cooperate while he crossed to his horse—which seemed to eye him with disbelief that their journey wasn't over yet. Gritting his teeth at his tightened muscles, Hugh mounted.

"You're goin' after her?" Rolley asked. "We're just supposed to follow her. Weyland doesn't want her to know yet."

"MacCarrick, rest," Quin said. "I'm sure they took a hansom, and the traffic will be mad. I've got time to saddle up and beat them there—"

"Then follow, but I'm going now." Hugh reined around. "Best tell me what I'm up against."

Quin's grave expression made Hugh's fists clench around his reins.

"Not what, but *who*. Weyland thinks Davis Grey's on his way to kill her."

Two

───◆───

At his first sight of Jane in nearly ten years, Hugh forgot to breathe. The pain in his body, the hunger and fatigue went unnoticed.

He strode headlong after her, shadowing her group from a parallel alley as they strolled down Haymarket after alighting from their hansom.

At the mere mention of Grey, Hugh was determined to take Jane from this place—

A massive hand clamped on his shoulder and yanked back. "Could've planted a knife in your back a dozen times these last ten minutes," a deep voice intoned from behind him. "Losing your touch?"

"Ethan?" Hugh wrenched his arm back, throwing off his older brother's grip, then swung a lowering glance at him. "What are you doing here—"

"Christ, what happened to your face?" Ethan interrupted.

"Explosion. Falling rock." Hugh had been caught in a shower of slate in a battle down in Andorra just days ago—the same battle Courtland had nearly lost his leg in. "Now answer the question."

"Went by Weyland's. Caught Quin just as he was

readying to leave," he replied. "And lucky thing I did. It's no' like you to be so careless in a place like this. What are you thinking?"

"I'm thinking I'm taking Jane home."

"Weyland only wants her followed. Stop shaking your head—Grey has no' made England yet." When Hugh remained unconvinced, Ethan said, "And he might no' make it here alive. So just calm yourself and take your nursemaid duty like a man."

"Is that what I've been called back here for? Why would Weyland want me?"

"He seemed to think I would unnerve Jane while protecting her," Ethan said casually. His scarred face had been known to scare women. "And that Quinton is only qualified to divest certain foreign ladies of certain critical secrets. No, Weyland needed a gunman. And you know Grey best."

Hugh returned his attention to Jane, who was at that moment passing the cross-street where he stood concealed, so close he could hear her throaty, sensual voice, but couldn't make out the words. She was clad in a rich green dress with a plunging neckline that bared her alabaster shoulders and revealed how much fuller her body had become. Her face was partially covered by a mask of dark green feathers that fanned out to the sides, like the wings they'd been plucked from.

In that dress and that mask, she looked . . . wanton.

He wasn't even surprised when cold sweat dotted his forehead. He'd always reacted physically to her. He remembered well the symptoms he'd endured that last summer he'd spent with her—the thundering heart, the need to swallow half a dozen times a minute, the stifled shudders of pleasure at her lightest touch.

One of her soft whispers in his ear could make him bite back a groan. . . .

"Is Courtland back in London with you?" Ethan asked.

Without looking away from her, Hugh said, "I had to leave him behind when I got the missive from Weyland. Court injured his leg and could no' ride fast enough."

"Where did you leave him?" Ethan snapped. "Far enough away from *her*, I hope."

Hugh had been charged with more than just seeing Court back to England—he was supposed to make sure that Court didn't have second thoughts and return for his woman, Annalía Llorente. "I left him in France. Court will no' go back for her. He understands what he'll do to her if he returns," Hugh said confidently enough, though he had to wonder. Court yearned for his lass so badly it was palpable. But Hugh hadn't had a choice except to abandon him, not after learning Jane was in danger. "What the hell is this I'm hearing about Grey?" Hugh asked. He had counted the man a friend until the last couple of years.

"Weyland sent him on a suicide mission. That failed."

That got Hugh to face Ethan. "Were you a part of that?" Sometimes, most times, he wished Ethan had never been recruited with himself by Weyland.

Ethan gave him a chilling half smile—distorting the whitened scar winding down his face—the sneer that now seemed to say, *Brother, had I been, there would be no failure.* Then he replied, "I was no', but I did volunteer to take him out. Weyland seemed to think I was personally too involved, and declined."

"You volunteered?" Hugh asked in disgust.

Ethan shrugged, unconcerned. "Well, go on. Doona let me stop you from overtaking their little coterie once more so you can see her from the front."

Hugh scowled, but Ethan was well aware of his desire for Jane—there was no use denying it. "Have no' seen her in years," he bit out defensively as he strode down the side lane with Ethan following. "Curious about her."

"It's like a carriage wreck I can see coming from a mile away," Ethan muttered. "First Court with his lass and now you with Jane—again. Thankfully, I remain immune."

Hugh ignored his comment, settling into another dark spot farther up the street. "Why is Weyland so certain he'll target Jane?"

"Grey wants revenge," Ethan said simply. "He'll destroy what's most precious to the old man."

Just then, Jane laughed at something one of her cousins said, and Hugh returned his gaze to her. She had always been quick to laugh—a quality that was foreign to him, but one that had beguiled him. She'd told him once, while cupping his face with her delicate hand and gazing up at him solemnly, that she promised to laugh enough for both of them, if need be.

"So now Grey plans to kill Jane," Ethan murmured over his shoulder, "seeks to slit her throat like he's done with other women. Only now it seems he's got a real taste for it. Likes to make it last."

"*Enough*," Hugh grated, still staring at Jane's soft smile. The idea that Grey needed to be taken out permanently had never sat well with Hugh, even as he understood it might be the only course. No longer would he be reluctant.

"I wager that right about now, you wish my offer to kill Grey had been accepted," Ethan said, easily reading him. "But no' to worry, little brother, it certainly has now. Weyland will do anything to protect her."

Ethan jerked his chin at Jane, faced Hugh, then did a double take back to the girls, only to stare. A disquieting interest flickered in his eyes, then flared—all the more unsettling to Hugh because it was completely unfamiliar. *Interest? In Ethan's deadened eyes?*

At once, Hugh's fists clenched. Was Ethan casting that hungry look at Jane?

Hugh had him shoved against a building wall, his forearm lodged against Ethan's neck, before he'd even realized his own intention. They used to fight constantly when younger, and had mutually called a truce when the two determined they were getting better at it and could easily kill each other.

Hugh was ready to resume hostilities.

Unaffected by Hugh's ready violence, Ethan gave him a weary look. "Rest easy. I'm no' ogling your precious Jane."

After a long moment, Hugh released him, believing him, although it was hard to understand how any man would *not* be battling lust for her. "Then what held your attention?" *Still* he was looking over Hugh's shoulder, and Hugh followed his gaze. "Claudia? The one in the red mask?" That would fit Ethan. Hugh remembered Jane telling him Claudia possessed a wild and wicked nature.

When no answer came, Hugh turned back. "Belinda? The tall brunette?"

Ethan shook his head slowly, never taking his eyes from the object of his attention—the third girl, a short blonde wearing a blue mask, whom Hugh didn't recognize.

Since the injury to his face, Ethan had seemed to lose interest in so many things—including chasing skirts, as he'd once been wont to do. Now, it was as if years of *something*, some kind of need, rushed to the fore.

Ethan, it seemed, was *not* immune.

The unusual notice shocked Hugh. "I doona know her, but she must be one of Jane's friends. And she looks young, no' more than twenty. Too young for you." Ethan was an old, *old* thirty-three.

"If I'm as bad as you and Court and all of the clan believe, then I'll find her that much more enticing for it, will I no'?" In the blink of an eye, Ethan's hand shot out to snare a passing masquerade-goer's domino. The man opened his mouth to object, took one look at Ethan's ominous expression, and darted away.

"Doona toy with her, Ethan."

"Afraid I'll ruin your chances with Jane?" Ethan asked as he donned the mask. "Hate to remind you, brother, but they were ruined before you even met her. And you've got a book to prove it."

Shadowed to walk with death . . .

"Your fate is just as grim as mine," Hugh reminded him, "yet you're going after a woman."

"Ah, but I'm in no danger of falling in love with her"—he turned to stride into the masquerade, tossing over his shoulder—"so it's no' likely my dallying will get her killed."

With a grated sound of frustration, Hugh followed him in.

Three

---•◆•---

A brick dropped into a reticule was a necessary evil when touring Haymarket Street, Jane Weyland knew, but the drawstring strap was murder on her wrist.

As Jane and her companions—two intrepid cousins and their visiting friend—waited impatiently in queue for admission to the Haymarket warehouse, Jane shifted the bag to her other hand yet again.

Though tonight was by no means their first foray to *tickle* a bit at London's dark underbelly—their decadent haunts included the east-end gaming dens, the racy stereoscopic pictorial shows, the annual Russian Circus Erotisk—the lascivious scene that greeted them gave even Jane pause.

A horde of courtesans fronted the warehouse like a painted, and aggressive, army. Masked, well-dressed patrons, in clothing that screamed stock-exchange funds or old-money tweed and university, perused the wares, physically sampling before deciding which one, or ones, they would sponsor and escort inside.

"Janey, you've never told us what brought about this change of heart about attending," her cousin Claudia said in a light tone, no doubt trying to relax the others. "But I've a theory." She must dread that the others would back out. Raven-haired "Naughty Claudie," tonight sporting a scarlet mask, lived for thrills like this.

"Do tell," said her sister Belinda, a heads-and-tails opposite of Claudia. Belinda was brilliant and serious-minded, here tonight for "research," and not euphemistically. She planned to expose "egregious social inequities," but wanted to write with authority on the subject of, well, the other side of inequity. Already, Jane could tell, Belinda was eyeing the scene in terms of reform from behind her cream-colored mask.

"Did we need a reason to come," asked the mysterious Madeleine Van Rowen, "other than the fact that this is a courtesans' ball?" Maddy was a childhood friend of Claudia's who was visiting for a few weeks. She was English by birth, but now lived in Paris—a seedy Parisian garret, if rumors were to be believed.

Jane suspected that Maddy had journeyed to London to call on an old friendship and see if she could snare Claudia's older brother, Quin. Jane was not at all perturbed by this. If Madeleine could get Quin to settle down and marry, then she deserved him and all his money.

In fact, Jane genuinely liked the girl, who fit in with their set perfectly. Jane, Belinda, and Claudia were three of the Weyland Eight—eight female first cousins notorious for adventures, pranks, and general hijinks—and were the only ones born and bred in London. Like all young Londoners who had coin in their pockets, they spent their days and nights recklessly pursuing all the modern pleasures to be had in this mad city, and all the old sins still on offer, within reason.

Jane and her cousins were moneyed, but not aristocratic. They were gently bred but savvy, ladylike but jaded. Like Jane and her cousins, Maddy knew how to take care of herself and seemed perfectly at ease in the face of this risqué masquerade.

As if revealing a great secret, Claudia said, "Jane's finally going to accept that gorgeous Freddie Bidworth's proposal."

Guilt flared, and Jane adjusted her emerald green mask to disguise it. "You've got me all figured out, Claudie." She and Freddie Bidworth were an item of sorts, and everyone assumed Jane would eventually marry Freddie—including him. But Jane had yet to accept the rich, handsome aristocrat.

And she feared she never could.

That conclusion was what had brought about her change of heart tonight concerning the masquerade—she needed something to get her mind off the conundrum she found herself in. At twenty-seven, Jane *knew* prospects like him would only become more and more scarce. And if she didn't marry Freddie, then whom? Jane *knew* the train was leaving the station, yet she couldn't board.

She'd told her cousins she wavered because of Freddie's horrid mother and sister. In truth, she'd hesitated because, her upstanding father excepted, she didn't trust men.

Over the last couple of years, Jane had begun to realize she'd been ruined. Not socially ruined. No matter how badly the Weyland Eight behaved, they never could seem to manage that coup, since her unassuming father, a mere businessman, had an inexplicable influence with the aristocracy and powerful government figures. Invitations continued to arrive, even as the cousins shook their baffled heads.

No, a black-haired Scot with a deep, husky voice and intense eyes had ruined Jane—though he had never touched her, never even kissed her, no matter how much she'd teased and tempted him.

Belinda frowned at Jane. "You've come to terms with Bidworth's family?"

"Yes, I believe so," Jane replied carefully. "I've just been moving slowly with something so important." Slowly? Freddie had asked her the first time nearly a year ago.

"Are these wild oats we're sowing, Jane?" Maddy asked, making Jane wonder how wild any oats would seem to a woman from the not-nice part of Paris. Sometimes on their nightly thrill-seeking adventures, Maddy had appeared . . . *bored*. "A last hurrah?"

"Did we need a reason to come," Jane said wryly, repeating Maddy, "other than the fact that this is a courtesans' ball?"

Luckily, they'd reached the bottleneck of the entrance, where a burly attendant with a pig mask and a shining pate accepted the steep admission price, so the subject was dropped. As the four labored to keep their skirts from being dirtied in the crush, Jane tendered a guinea apiece for everyone—mainly to pay for Maddy and not hurt her pride.

Though Maddy was attired in a lavish sapphire gown, Jane had seen the girl's trunks in Claudia's room and knew her stockings and underthings had been mended and remended. Her jewels were paste. Maddy spoke of French mansions and elegant parties, but Jane suspected she was nearly destitute. Sometimes the girl had a back-against-the-wall air about her.

Once the attendant waved them through, Jane blithely crossed the threshold with the others close behind. Inside the warehouse, masses of perfumed bodies swarmed around the edges of the central dance floor, or waltzed to the jaunty music of a seven-man band. Legally, this place was termed an "unlicensed dance hall."

Those in the know called it "the Hive."

If the outside of the Hive had been rough and unassuming, the interior was lush. The walls were silk papered, and expensive-smelling incense burned, oozing a flat layer of smoke that floated just over the heads of the crowd. Along the walls were massive murals, hanging from shiny brass chains and painted with nymphs and priapic satyrs in lurid poses. Beneath the murals were Persian rugs with pillows cast about. There, women kissed lechers and fondled them artfully through their breeches— or were fondled in return.

Anything more, Jane surmised, was taken to the rooms lining the back wall.

Happily married Belinda murmured, "Just look at what these women are forced to do to earn their coin."

"Earn *coin*?" Claudia breathed, feigning ignorance. "You mean you can . . . ? Ah! And to think I was doing it for free!"

Belinda glared, because twenty-eight-year-old Claudia was, in fact, carrying on a torrid affair with the family's groom. "Claudia, you might try doing it *while married*."

An exhibit, of sorts, silenced all of them—halting yet another sisterly row.

Men and women with shaven bodies covered in a layer of clay posed as statues, motionless even when admiring patrons cupped and weighed body parts.

"This was so worth attending," Claudia said with a quirked eyebrow, gaze riveted to the well-endowed and muscle-bound men.

Jane had to agree. Nothing like naked, real live statues to distract the mind from thoughts of marriage, ticking clocks, and rumbling-voiced Scotsmen who disappeared without a word.

Their group had little time to admire the scene as the crowd, circling the warehouse like a current, pushed them along. When they passed a table where a half-naked debauchee in a fox mask served punch, they each eagerly swooped up a glass, then made for the wall to get out of the traffic.

Jane drank deeply. "Well. No one told us coverage from the waist up was optional—for both sexes," she observed as another half-clad woman sauntered by, breasts bouncing as she smiled flirtatiously up at her. Jane gave her a saucy wink back, as was polite. "Otherwise," Jane continued dryly, "I might have opted for a lower-cut bodice and a bigger brick."

Maddy sniffed her glass with a discerning expression, then took a hearty drink just as Claudia raised her own and said, "I'm just glad to be at a ball with punch *I* don't have to spike." Having seen her older brother Quin doing that once and noted the raucous results, Claudia never failed to bring flasks to staid gatherings.

When a middle-aged roué exposed himself to the Persian-rug women and they laughed, Belinda harrumphed. She shoved her glass at Jane so she could surreptitiously take notes, like a first-year plebeian might write up boys' school demerits. Jane shrugged, placing her own finished glass on a tray, and started on Belinda's.

She nearly choked on the last sips as she spied a towering man in a long black domino pushing through the crowd, clearly searching for someone. His build, his stride, the aggressive set of his lips just beneath the fluttering veil drop of his mask—everything about him reminded her of Hugh, though she knew it couldn't be him. Hugh wasn't in London.

But what if it had been him? Sooner or later, he would have to return to the city, and they would run into each other. It was possible she might see *him* on the carpets, with his knees falling open and eyelids growing heavy as a woman's skilled hand rubbed him. The thought made Jane drain Belinda's cup. "Going for more punch," she mumbled, suddenly longing to be away from the warm throng of bodies.

"Bring us back some more," Claudia called.

"A double," Maddy added absently. She was watching the tall man wending through the crowd as well.

As Jane made her way toward the punch table, she recognized that the restless feeling in her belly that she continually battled had grown sharply worse. Ever since she could remember, she'd been plagued by an anxiety, as if she were missing something, as if she were in the wrong place with greener grass calling to her. She felt an urgency about everything.

Now, after regarding the man who was so like Hugh, and imagining Hugh being serviced by another woman, she felt an *urgency* for fresh air. Else she'd lose her punch.

Once she had glasses in hand, she returned to the group to see if they wouldn't mind going outside—

But Maddy wasn't there.

"I turned around and she was gone," Claudia said, sounding not too concerned. Maddy had a habit of slinking off whenever she felt like it. The more she did it, the more Jane realized Maddy didn't find environments like the Hive threatening.

"Shall we start looking on the dance floor?" Jane asked with a sigh.

The three began maneuvering through the crowd. Unfortunately, Maddy was short and had an uncanny way of blending in. A half an hour passed, and they still hadn't spotted her—

A shrill whistle rent the din; Jane's head jerked up. The band whimpered to a lull.

"*Police!*" someone yelled just as more whistles sounded all around them. "*It's the bloody peelers!*"

"No, no, that isn't possible," Jane said. These dance halls always paid off the police! Who in the devil had forgotten the "payment for protection"?

All at once, waves of screaming people clambered toward the back entrance, jostling them. The Hive was suddenly like a bottle turned upside down with the cork pulled out. The entire building seemed to rock as people fled, colliding with Jane and her cousins until a current of bodies separated them.

Jane battled to reach them, but was only forced back. When Belinda pointed to the back door, Jane shook her head emphatically—that way out was choked with people. They would be crushed to death. She'd rather get nicked and have her name printed on the page of shame in the *Times*.

When Jane lost sight of her cousins completely, she backed to the wall—stunned to find herself separated and completely alone. The wave of people continued to swell until Jane was engulfed again. Unable to find a clear spot or an empty corner, she felt the world spinning out of control.

Two hands shoved against her back, sending her careening. She whirled around, swinging her reticule. She garnered a split second's worth of room but connected with nothing, and the momentum tore her reticule down and off her wrist. Gone. Her money, her makeshift weapon . . .

The next push didn't take her by surprise, but someone else was standing on her dress hem. Jane flailed her arms, helpless to stop herself from being pitched to the ground.

At once, she attempted to scramble up, but her skirts had spread out over the floor like the wings of a framed butterfly, pinned there by the stampede. Over and over, she fought to rise, but always new boots trapped her skirts.

Jane darted her hands out between ankles, yanking at the material with desperate strength, struggling to gather her dress about her legs.

She couldn't catch her breath under the press of people. How had this night gone so wrong—

A boot came straight for her head. To dodge it, she rolled toward the wall as far as she could, but then, even over the commotion, she distinctly heard the eerie ping of metal.

Looking up with dread, she saw one of the hanging murals directly above her, swaying wildly. The brass chain holding it had an opened link that was straightening under the massive weight.

Like a shot, the link popped, and the chain lashed out like a whip. The mural came crashing down.

Four

———•◆•———

When Davis Grey chased the dragon, he had no dreams.

In that hazy twilight of opium, the pain in his body ebbed; no longer could he see the faces of the men, women, and children he'd killed.

Chasing the dragon, Grey thought with a weary exhalation, staring at the paint chipping across the ceiling of his hidden east London loft. What an appropriate saying to describe the habit—and his life.

In the past, the smoke had quelled the rage in his heart, yet finally his need for revenge had overpowered even opium's sweet pull.

He rose in stages from his sweat-dampened bed, then crossed to the basin to splash water over his face. In the basin mirror, he studied his naked body.

Four crusting bullet wounds riddled his pale chest and torso, a constant reminder of the attempt on his life. Though it had been six months ago since Edward Weyland, for whom Grey had killed faithfully, had sent him to his own destruction, the wounds still hadn't healed completely. Though half a year had passed, Grey could remember perfectly the order in which he'd taken each bullet from a trio of Weyland's hungry, younger killers.

Yet somehow Grey had survived. He'd lost much muscle, but he still possessed a wiry strength—enough to enact his plans.

He ran a finger down his chest, skating around the wounds in fascination. Perhaps Weyland should have sent his best man for the kill. But then Weyland always spared Hugh MacCarrick the *altering* jobs, the ones that changed a man forever.

Those tasks should have been split between Grey and Hugh, but Weyland carefully meted out each one. Hugh was dispatched to kill people who were out-and-out evil, dangerous people who often fought for the lives Hugh sought to take. Grey executed the variables, the peripherals. Toward the end, Grey hadn't been very particular if children got in the way.

In dreams, he saw their glassy, sightless eyes.

Weyland, that bloody bastard, didn't even send Hugh to kill me.

That galled Grey more than anything, scalding him inside.

Soon Grey would deliver his retribution. Weyland treasured only one thing in this world—his daughter, Jane. MacCarrick had loved her from afar for years. Take away Jane, and two men would be destroyed, forever.

A little work had ensured that Weyland and his informants knew Grey was stirring. Cunning and two deaths had ensured that they thought Grey was still on the Continent. Weyland would already have sent for his best gunman to protect his precious daughter.

Good. Hugh should be there to see Grey end her life. Both MacCarrick and Weyland should know the searing purity of grief.

There was power innate in having nothing left to lose.

Years ago, Weyland had said that Grey was suited for his occupation because he possessed no mercy, but he'd been wrong then. Years ago, Grey wouldn't have been able to happily slit Jane's pretty throat. Weyland wasn't wrong now.

With a shriek, Jane rolled out of the way just as a corner of the mural hammered into the floor directly beside her. She didn't have time to gape at how close it had been because more charging people overwhelmed her. She couldn't breathe. With a cry, she ducked her head down, raising an arm over her face.

Seconds later, Jane lowered her arm, brows drawn in confusion.

The crowd was parting around her instead of treading over her.

At last, she had room to maneuver, a fighting chance....

She'd be damned if she'd be killed by the very spectacle she'd come to leer at! Finally able to gather her skirts, she made another wobbling attempt to rise, and lurched to her feet. Whirling around, she lunged forward. *Free!*

No! Brought up short, she dropped to her front with a thud. She crawled on her forearms, but realized she was crawling in place. Something still anchored her. More people coming in a rush—

The middle-aged roué she'd seen earlier dropped bodily to the ground beside her, holding his bleeding nose, staring up horrified at something behind them. Before she could even react, another man went flying over her, landing flat on his back.

Suddenly, her skirts were tossed up to the backs of her legs, and a hot, calloused hand clamped onto her thigh. Her eyes went wide in shock. Another hand pawed at her petticoats, ripping them.

"Wh-what are you doing?" she screeched, her head whipping around. With her mask askew and her hair tumbling into her face, she could barely see the man through the shadows of a jungle of legs all around them. "Unhand me this instant!" She jostled the leg he held firmly.

With the back of her hand, she shoved her hair away, and spied another flash of her attacker. Grim lips pulled back from white teeth as if in a snarl. Three gashes ran down his cheek, and his face was dirty.

His eyes held a murderous rage.

The visage disappeared as her attacker bolted to his feet and felled another oncoming patron, before dropping down beside her once more. His fist shot up at intervals as he ripped again at her petticoats.

She realized he'd finally stopped—when he swooped her up onto his shoulder.

"H-how dare you!" she cried, pummeling his broad back. She vaguely noted that this was a bear of a man who'd lifted her with the ease of plucking lint from a lapel. The body she was looped over was massive, the arm over her heavy and unyielding. His fingers were splayed, it seemed, over the entire width of her bottom.

"Don't go this way! Put me down!" she demanded. "How dare you paw at me, ripping at my undergarments!" As soon as she'd said the last, she spotted the remains of her petticoats pinned beneath a mural with a jaunty satyr covering a nymph. Her face flamed.

With his free arm, the man sent patrons careening. "Lass, it's nothing you have no' shown me before."

"What?" Her jaw dropped. *Hugh MacCarrick?* This murderous-looking fiend was her gentle giant of a Scot?

Returned after ten years.

"You doona remember me?"

Oh, yes, she did. And remembering how she'd fared the last time the Highlander had drifted into her life, she wondered if she mightn't have been better off trampled by a drunken horde.

Five

———•◆•———

Outside, instead of following the general flight down Haymarket, Hugh immediately ducked down a back alley behind a gin palace, then set her on her feet.

Before she could say a word, he began pawing her again. "Were you injured?" he barked. While she could only sputter, he pulled up her skirts again to check her legs, then rose to fist his hands around her arms, dragging his palms down them from her elbows to wrists to fingers, checking for breaks, sprains. Amazingly, she felt herself to be unharmed.

"Jane, say something."

"I . . . Hugh?" Somehow he was here for her, though she scarcely recognized him. It was Hugh, but it *wasn't*. "I-I'm all right." Soon, yes, *soon*, she would catch her breath and stop gazing up at him.

How many times had she imagined their first time meeting after so long? She'd envisioned herself coldly sighing and spurning him as he begged her to marry him. He would plead for forgiveness for abandoning her without a word.

How different reality was proving. *Of course*, Jane would be quite foxed and capable of little more than dumbly staring. Oh, yes, and fresh from a police raid and near death by stampeding.

As he lightly tweaked her crooked mask, he exhaled a long breath. "Ah, lass, what in the hell were you thinking, coming here?" Though his looks were altered, his voice was the same—that deep, rumbling brogue that used to make her melt.

Buying time to collect herself, she drew back and brushed off her torn skirts. "This would have been perfectly safe if the proper bribes had been paid."

"Is that so?"

"Quite." She nodded earnestly. "I'm writing a letter to management." She could tell he couldn't decide if she was serious or not. Jane did have a tendency to joke at inappropriate times.

When she began untying her mask, he said, "Keep that on for now. Till I get you in a cab—"

More whistles sounded, and a harsh horn trumpeted the arrival of a police wagon. Hugh took her hand and strode forward, quickly putting distance between them and the warehouse—and her group.

"Hugh, you must stop. I have to go back!"

He ignored her.

When she tried to dig in her heels, he easily pulled her along. "Hugh! My cousins and my friend are still back there."

"They're fine. But if you go back in your condition, you'll get arrested."

"In my condition?"

"Drunk."

"Well, since you've addressed it, I will tell you that, in my *condition*, the idea of going back to save my friends feels imperative and quite achievable."

"Will no' happen."

The alley finally ended, and they reached a cabstand. So Hugh was sending her home for the night? Perfect. She'd let the cabbie go a block, and then she'd get out and return.

As ever, a score of drivers geared up to jockey and wrangle for the fare. But Hugh held up one finger with a look that subdued even this lively bunch, then pointed to the nicest-looking cab. The chosen cabbie eased his vehicle over, all obliging.

Hugh tossed Jane inside, then turned to direct the driver to his mount on the next street over. When she realized Hugh was accompanying her, Jane opened the opposite door and heedlessly climbed out.

"Damn it, Jane." He loped around the carriage after her, swooping her to his side with his arm around her waist.

She was being carried again and could do little more than drunkenly blink behind her mask.

"Your friends are safe," he repeated as he tossed her back in, keeping a fist in her skirts as he joined her. He slammed one door, then reached over her to slam the other. Once they'd begun to roll along, he finally relaxed a fraction.

He'd never forget catching sight of her inside, then seeing her disappear in that swarm of people. Never, not as long as he lived.

"How do you know they're safe?" she demanded.

"I saw Quin go in, no' five minutes before me. And trust me, Quin will no' let his sisters stay to look for you."

Jane's eyes narrowed. "What was he doing there?"

"He suspected his sisters would attend."

She quirked an eyebrow, glancing out the window in the direction of the warehouse. "Really?" When she said the word slowly like that with her proper English accent, it always sounded like "raaaally."

Oh, yes, she was very suspicious. She hadn't climbed out her window tonight for no good reason.

She suddenly gasped, facing him. "B-but we were separated from Maddy!"

"Is she the blonde in the blue dress?"

"You noticed her?" Jane stilled. "I didn't think blondes were your type."

He frowned at her tone. "Apparently, they're my brother's. Ethan is intent on the lass and went in to . . . talk to her." Even after Hugh had followed him inside and warned him yet again not to seek out the girl, Ethan was undeterred. "Your friend Maddy—"

"Madeleine. Madeleine Van Rowen."

Van Rowen. The name hit him. His brother could not be lusting after that one. What in the hell would Ethan do when he discovered whose daughter she was?

"Your friend will be fine." *At least from the crowd and the police.* "Ethan will no' let her be hurt." *By anyone else.* "But when you see her again, you might want to warn her about Ethan. He's no' the most honorable of men."

Another understatement. Hugh would like to say Ethan had changed after he'd received the injury to his face. Or when his fiancée had died the night before their wedding. But Ethan had always been a rough, roguish sort, showing a marked indifference to feelings and forming few attachments even as a young man.

"Oh." Then she frowned. "Actually, Hugh, you might

want to warn your brother about that one. Little Maddy's not as sweet and helpless as she looks. I'd worry more about Ethan." He cast her a doubting expression, but she ignored it and said, "So, both Quin and your brother were there. I wonder, what were *you* doing in a place like that?" When Hugh simply shrugged, her lips thinned. "No need to answer, I can imagine. Curious, though, that you're not scandalized that *I* was there."

Did she want him to be? Of course, he hated it, hated that she was in a place so rife with danger. "Nothing you do could shock me, Jane."

"No comments on my behavior?"

"You're a woman grown, are you no'?"

"Hugh, you don't have to interrupt your night's revelry just to take me home." Her tone was almost cutting. "And there's another establishment very like the Hive, not too far away. I could give you directions. Much amusement for a man to have inside."

"I dinna go for that," he answered quietly.

"Then why on earth were you there?"

He studied the window beside her as he muttered, "Heard you might be." He glanced back at her. Her sudden smile was as baffling as it was devastating to him. Never taking her eyes from his, she untied her mask. Somehow she made that small movement sensual—as if she were undressing her body for him alone.

Want tightened his every muscle, and he leaned closer to her, even as instinct screamed for him to ease away.

She dropped the mask; he stifled a curse. Goddamn it, how could she have grown *more* beautiful? He'd hoped he might have imagined how lovely she'd been. He'd thought she would have lost the first blush of youth, the fire in her personality diminishing. Seeing her again now, he knew these qualities would *never* fade.

An old question arose for the thousandth time: Would he have been better off never having met her?

Right now, he believed so, yet he was still greedy for the sight of her, studying her face at leisure, savoring.

Her eyes were that changeable, intoxicating green. Her cheekbones were high, her nose slim and pert. In the cab's flickering lamplight, her loosened hair appeared dark, nearly black, as it curled all around her face and shoulders, but it was actually a deep auburn. Her lips were plump, and on the one occasion he'd dared stroke his thumb over them, he'd been amazed at how soft and giving they'd been—

"Do I pass muster?" she murmured breathlessly with a slow, easy grin that made his heart punch the insides of his chest.

"As ever." He fought not to touch a curl that teased her cheek, taunting him.

"You, however, are quite dirty," she said with a disapproving glance at his clothes. "And your face is cut up." Were her words slurring worse? "Hugh, whatever have you gotten into?"

"I've ridden for days on end." He hadn't taken time to heal and sure as hell hadn't stopped for ablutions when he'd believed she was in danger. But how badly he wished he looked successful, as wealthy as he'd finally become. Any man would want to appear rich and powerful to the woman he desired. Instead, Hugh was injured, his clothing covered in road grime.

Appear *successful*? Right now, he'd accept clean.

"And what brings you to London?" she asked.

You. Finally, I've permission to see you. Hugh had never lied to her before. Yet the last time he saw her, he'd been a decade younger and still concerned with honor. No longer.

He opened his mouth to speak, but the facile lie he'd prepared refused to escape his lips. So, he told her the truth. "Your father sent for me."

"Important business?" she asked, gazing over at him with an understanding expression.

Staring at her, he searched for his voice, finally grating, "*You canna imagine.*"

Jane had been quaking with jealousy at the thought of Hugh sampling the pleasures of the Hive—and at the possibility of his interest in Maddy. Jane had no objection to Maddy snagging her cousin Quin, the only male in Jane's entire Weyland generation, solely for his money.

But the idea of Hugh together with Maddy had made Jane want to claw her eyes out.

Then came Hugh's quiet admission. His words had softened her, undermining her guard.

"How do you feel, Sìne?" he asked.

Sìne was the Gaelic form of Jane—he pronounced it *Shee-ah-na* and had never seemed to realize that he always said it as if it were an endearment. Her eyes nearly fluttered closed with pleasure at the name rolling from his tongue. That brogue would be the death of her.

"Lass, are you shivering?"

"Too much excitement," she said, though she knew that wasn't why she shook. Even if the crush hadn't scared her witless, even if seeing him once more hadn't stunned her, she'd still be reduced to shivers by the way he said her name in his language.

"Hugh, someone really ought to see about these." Before thinking better of it, she lightly touched the backs of her fingers to the three marks on his face, but he flinched as if burned.

"Did I hurt you?" She laid her hand on his arm, but he slowly shrugged away. "I'm sorry."

"No bother."

Then why had he shifted as far away from her as possible on the bench and turned away without a word? As he stared out the window, eyes subtly darting over the street as though searching for something, she took the opportunity to study him.

She couldn't decide whether the years had been kind or unkind to Hugh. He'd grown larger than he'd been at twenty-two, which was saying something, considering his strapping build even then. He was perhaps six and a half feet tall, still towering over her own five and a half feet, but now his body seemed packed with even more muscle. He was a man in his prime, and the years had honed the strength of his body.

Virile, masculine, rough. All the qualities she'd loved about him before had now become magnified—his heroic actions tonight were proof of that.

Yet if his body had benefited by the years, his face had not. Those three long gashes carved his cheek, and a furrow was etched between his brows. A raised scar marred the side of his neck. And his brown eyes seemed darker, as if the flecks of warm amber that she'd loved to stare at had been extinguished.

As she'd discovered tonight in the melee, Hugh looked . . . *dangerous.* The steady, grave Hugh she'd known had become an intense man—an *alarming* man.

But he also looked markedly unhappy. Wherever he'd been without her for all this time, he hadn't been content. She could have made the brooding Highlander happy these past years. That was all she'd ever wanted. Just a *chance* to—

"Do *I* pass muster?" he asked quietly, facing her.

Striving for politeness, she replied, "The years have been kind."

"No, they have no'. And we both know it." His gaze flickered over her. "At least they have for one of us."

Her hot blush of pleasure flustered her. Luckily, she was saved from having to reply when the cab stopped for Hugh's horse. The poor animal looked as road-weary and fatigued as Hugh, but Jane could tell that under the layer of dust the animal was exceptionally fine with an unusual build and markings.

After Hugh had tethered the horse to the back of the hansom, and he'd rejoined her, she said, "You're lucky someone didn't steal a horse like that. Why didn't you take it to the city stables a block away?"

"I dinna have t—" He broke off, seeming irritated. "I just dinna."

"Oh. I see," she said with a frown. After several moments of silence, she ventured to make conversation with him. Her home was only fifteen minutes away, but as the ride was filled with clipped, awkward exchanges—between two who used to be so at ease with each other—it seemed the longest of her life.

Mercifully, they arrived at last. When Hugh put his hands to her waist to help her down, he seemed to linger, then kept his palm across her back as he escorted her to the front door.

"I don't have a key." Jane patted her skirts as if she had pockets. "I lost my reticule tonight."

"Rolley will be awake," Hugh said, but he didn't make a move to knock. He looked like he was about to say something, but whatever he saw in her eyes made him fall silent.

There they stood at the door facing each other, each seeming to await something. Could he see how much she yearned for an apology, or, at the very least, an explanation? The moment stretched out interminably.

Hugh, if you were ever going to make things right between us, now would be the time. But he didn't. Instead, his eyes grew intent, and his brows drew together.

He's going to kiss me! she vaguely comprehended, her breaths growing shallow. *For the first time? Now?*

Anger simmered inside her. He didn't deserve her kisses. He could have had them freely for the last ten years.

He leaned in. . . .

Without even an apology? Her palm itched to slap him—

At the last instant, the door swung open. "Thought I 'eard something," Rolley said, standing tense in the doorway.

Hugh drew back and had to cough into his fist to rasp to her, "Go inside now. I'll see you in the morning when I return."

"See *me*?" She blinked up at him. "Whatever for?"

Six

———•◆•———

Jane's cousins called him Hugh "Tears and Years" Mac-Carrick.

Because she'd wasted an inordinate amount of each on him.

Now that the giddy rush of seeing him again—and the effects of the deceptively potent punch—had worn off, she stared into her dressing table mirror, combing out her hair after her bath. When her eyes glinted in the glass, Jane realized she was about to go wasting even more. She laid down her brush beside the message from Claudia saying they'd all gotten home safely, then put her head in her hands. She shoved the heels of her palms against her eyes, as if that would stem the tears.

Countless nights crying and years of her life she'd squandered. Jane—who knew how precious time was!

When Jane was only six, her mother had died from a lung inflammation, and since then Jane had never been *content*. Perhaps she knew too well that she could never take for granted a single second, and that was what made her restless. Perhaps she was simply never meant to experience a feeling of complete satisfaction.

She burned to travel, to experience exciting new places—but was it wanderlust, or the yearning to be wherever she *wasn't* at the time? Ten years ago, with Hugh at her side, that anxious feeling had dimmed to a point where she could ignore it. She couldn't explain why.

Then he'd left her behind without a word.

She'd grieved for him, longed for him, and had wasted nearly half of her life on him.

Damn him, no more, she swore to herself, and yet still she replayed their history in her mind, seeking, as usual, some answer as to what she'd done to drive him away....

"The Scotsman is mine."

Jane had made that declaration to her cousins with her very first look at him. Her heart had stuttered, and she'd decided then that she would be the one to make him happy so his eyes wouldn't be so grave. She'd been thirteen and he'd been eighteen.

He and his brothers had come down from Scotland to summer at their family's lake house, Ros Creag, which shared a broad cove with Vinelands, her family's. When she'd charged up to him to introduce herself, he'd chucked her under the chin and called her "poppet," and it sounded wonderful the way he said it with his brogue. He was kind to her, and she followed him everywhere.

At her urging, her father had also visited and befriended the reclusive brothers, though they seemed to want to have nothing to do with the rest of the merry Weyland brood. Somehow he persuaded them to come back down the following summer, delighting her. Since he had no sons, Papa was set on recruiting them to work in his import business.

By the end of the next season at the lake, whenever she got a bee sting or splinter she ran to Hugh alone.

Her fifteenth summer they returned again, but Hugh spent most of the time frowning at her, as if he didn't quite know what to make of her. When she'd turned sixteen, just when she'd started to fill out, he'd avoided her entirely. He'd decided to work for her father, and spent all his time with him at Ros Creag, discussing the business.

She'd cried from missing her big, solemn Scot. Her cousins told her she could have anyone and that they didn't want her pining over "that rough MacCarrick," but upon seeing she would not be dissuaded, they'd suggested she play dirty—and her cousins had known what they were talking about. Their saying was, "Man bows before the Weyland Eight. And if he won't bow, we'll make him kneel."

Claudia had said, "Now we scheme, Janey. By next summer, we'll make sure you have low-cut dresses, soft-as-silk hands"—she grinned a devilish grin—"and a shameless demeanor. Your Highlander won't know what hit him."

But he didn't come the next summer, leaving Jane devastated. Until that one night when luck was with her, and he'd arrived with an urgent message for her father. Whatever could be pressing about relics and antiques, Jane couldn't fathom.

Before he could ride off again, she made sure he saw her, and he gaped as if he didn't recognize her. A single night's stay had turned into two, then three, and he couldn't seem to spend enough time with her.

Her older cousins had taught her much in the previous year, and every day he was there, she teased and tormented him for the days he hadn't been.

She'd learned that whispering in his ear could make his eyes slide shut and his lips part, and that running her fingers through his hair as she hugged him could make him hiss in a breath. As often as she could, she'd coaxed him to swim with her—especially after that first time, when he'd frozen in the middle of shrugging out of his shirt to silently watch her removing her skirt and blouse, until she was in naught but stocking, garters, and a chemise. After they swam, Jane—never one for modesty—had slipped from the water in the transparent garment. She'd followed his rapt gaze on her body before he finally jerked his face away. "Hugh, can you see through?"

When he'd turned back to her and given her a slow nod, his eyes dark, she'd said, "Well, darling, if it's only you." She'd noted that it had taken him a very long time before he'd been able to get out of the water that day.

During what would prove to be their last afternoon, they'd been lying side by side in the meadow, and she rolled on top of him to tickle him. He despised it when she tickled him, and for hours afterward was surly and tense, his voice husky.

But that time, instead of shaking her off, he reached up and tugged her ribbon loose to free her hair. "So fair," he rasped as he ran his thumb over her bottom lip. "But you know that well, do you no'?"

She leaned down to kiss him, intending not the torturing little kisses on his ear before she whispered to him, or the brushing of her lips on the back of his neck that she'd been giving him all summer. She wanted her first real kiss.

But he took her shoulders and pushed her up, grating, "*You're too young, lass.*"

"I'm almost eighteen, and I've already had marriage offers from men older than you."

He scowled at that, then shook his head. "Sìne, I'm leaving here soon."

She smiled sadly. "I know. That's what you do when summer's over. You go back north to Scotland. And every winter I miss you very much until you return to me here."

He just stared at her face as if memorizing it.

Jane had never seen him or heard from him again. Not until this night.

She'd been so convinced Hugh would marry her—it had been a foregone conclusion for her—that she'd only been counting the days until Hugh deemed her *not* too young. She'd believed in him so much, certain they would be together. Yet he'd known he was going to work abroad for years, had known he was leaving her behind. It had been a conscious decision on his part, and he hadn't even told her why.

He hadn't asked her to wait for him, or given Jane her chance to make him happy.

And now, ten years later, she stared into the mirror, watching the tears roll down her face. . . .

Tonight, the women Jane had seen at the masquerade had hard eyes for all their swagger and flirting. They were bitter, but it wasn't simply due to economics or circumstances, as Belinda lamented.

Those hard-eyed women had been hurt *by men*.

Jane recognized it in them with perfect clarity, because this very mirror reflected the same quality growing in her own eyes every day. She could finally acknowledge that.

She would do whatever it took to avoid that fate. Bitterness was a life sentence, and it was one that was entirely avoidable.

She dried her tears—for the last time.

Early tomorrow morn, she'd accept Freddie's proposal.

Seven

———•◆•———

The side door to the Weyland home was unlocked the next morning.

Hugh's body went tense as he let himself inside the quiet house, striding directly to the second floor to find Jane, unholstering his pistol as he hurried up the carpeted stairs. Had Weyland even arrived home from the night before?

He finally heard movement in a room down the hallway and hastened to follow the sounds. Through a cracked-open bedroom door, he spied Jane on her knees, sweeping her hand back and forth under the bed.

He inhaled deeply, gathering control, then stowed his weapon behind him under his jacket.

Unable to help himself, he entered her room and approached silently, staring at her body clad in naught but a silk gown. She slowly gazed up to meet his eyes. She had the damnedest green eyes.

"Just what are you doing in my bedroom?" she demanded, rising to her feet. Though scarcely dressed, with her curves more highlighted than concealed, she sashayed around him, continuing to search through piles of lace for whatever she was missing, unconcerned by her state of undress.

He could see her nipples under the silk and swallowed hard. Why couldn't she have grown reserved over the years? Never had he encountered a woman so immodest. But then, that last summer with her, he hadn't complained whenever she swam with him.

"What do you want, Hugh?"

"Where's your father gone so early?"

When she shrugged, the threadlike strap of her gown skimmed down her shoulder. Typical Jane, she did not pull it back. "I don't know. Did you check in his study? That's where he is these days, twenty hours out of twenty-four."

Something was different about her this morning. From the time he'd left her last night, fighting not to kiss her, to now, she'd become colder. He felt it strongly.

"I dinna see him. The door was open, and Rolley's nowhere to be seen."

"Then your guess is as good as mine. Why don't you run down there and check again?" She turned, dismissing him.

"You're coming with me. Put on a robe."

When she ignored him, he scanned the room for a wrap. No wonder she'd been searching for something. Shoes, stockings, laces, and satiny corsets littered the room. Dresses were puddled where she'd dropped them. So much disorder. Hugh hated disorder, craved the opposite in every aspect of his life.

He finally spotted something that might cover her. "Put this on."

"I'm not going downstairs until I'm fully attired. I'm late as it is for an engagement." She chuckled as if at some private joke.

"We have a problem, then." For all he knew, Weyland and Rolley had been taken down. "Because I'm no' letting you out of my sight."

"And why is that?"

"Your house is empty with the door unlocked."

"Call down."

He strode to the doorway. "Weyland," he bellowed. No answer. "The robe, Jane."

"To hell, Hugh."

Why was she the one woman on earth he didn't intimidate?

"I've told you I'll go when I'm ready."

"Then dress yourself," he grated.

"Leave the room."

"No' going to happen."

"Turn around, then." When he didn't, she tapped her cheek and said, "But there's nothing you haven't sneaked a peek at before, is there?"

Stunned by the difference in her, he grated, "As I said last night, lass, there's little you have no' shown me."

Her eyes glittered with anger. "But just as you've changed, so have I." She put her shoulders back and pulled her hair behind her, clearly aware that her figure had become even more tempting.

He scrubbed a hand over his mouth, about to say something he shouldn't. "Just dress," he ordered. As he turned from her, he caught his reflection in the basin mirror and scowled. He was well aware that the years had *not* been kind.

One night's restless sleep had done nothing to alleviate his exhaustion, and for the last three days, his injuries had prevented him from shaving.

Was it only three days ago that he'd been in a war? That he'd killed?

Now her reflection caught his attention. He watched her in the mirror as she poised a dainty foot on a stool to roll her stocking up one long leg—

He found his jaw slackening in wonderment when she slid her gown higher to wrap the wickedest garter he'd ever seen around her thigh. As she tied it into a perfect bow, his hands clenched the edges of the washstand so hard he thought he'd break the marble.

That last summer, she'd always worn her garters high. Because her shifts were so short. . . .

He forced himself to look away. When he heard stiff material rustling, he asked, "Are you no' done yet?" He didn't recognize his voice.

"Be patient with me, Hugh." How many times had he heard that phrase?

He exhaled and answered as he always had, "I try, lass." *Think of other things.* He spied her bow propped up near the doorway and noticed fresh blades of grass affixed to the bottom of her full quiver. He was pleased she'd kept up with her archery.

He'd bought Jane her first bow, and helped her with her aim, and by the end of the summer, she could split a wand at a hundred paces. She'd taken to shooting as if she'd been born for it.

Perhaps she had. In the past, when she wasn't torturing him with coy smiles and soft words and touches, Jane had been a bit . . . fierce.

He glanced at her dressing table and saw a book entitled *A Gentlewoman's Apprentice*. Probably a scathing satire, knowing her. He picked it up, finding that the cover was a false one stretched over the real cover. Brows drawn, he opened it and scanned some pages, quickly comprehending the nature of the content. A swift perusal of one scene told him this was more lewd than anything *he'd* ever read.

The idea of her reading these writings didn't outrage him—it aroused him, and blood rushed to his groin with each word he skimmed. After swallowing, twice, he grated, "Where do you find books like this?" Without turning, he held it up over his shoulder.

In a bored tone, she said, "All the printers on Holywell Street sell them."

"Is this what young ladies are reading these days?"

"Very much so. Women patrons ensure that our favorite bookseller returns from his grubby little Holywell shop to his grand estate outside of the city each night. He can't print them fast enough. You can turn around now."

No . . . no, he couldn't.

At length, after getting his erection under control, he turned and found her holding out a necklace to him. "Hugh?"

He crossed to her and took it, and she gave him her back. Tendrils of dark red hair lay starkly against the alabaster skin of her neck. He wanted to press his lips there more than he'd wanted anything in his life, and was a heartbeat from doing so. Instead, he inhaled her perfume—so light as to be a mere tease of fragrance, but spicy.

Then his big hands, which had never been clumsy except around her, fumbled for several moments. Once he'd finished, he lost the struggle to keep from stroking the backs of his fingers over the soft, smooth skin of her neck.

When she shivered, he briefly closed his eyes.

"Hugh, did you just touch me?" she asked, her voice sultry. When he said nothing, she turned, gazing up at him. Her breaths were shallow—he doubted he breathed at all.

His eyes darted to her lips, and she saw it.

"Did you?"

"It happens, when you fasten a necklace, does it no'?"

Her brows drew together in puzzlement, but without waiting for an answer, he grabbed her hand, pulling her along the corridor and down the stairs.

They found Weyland in his study, gazing at his late wife's portrait, absently rolling a letter as one might roll a map. The man schooled his features immediately, but Hugh had always known how much he missed his lovely wife, whom Jane favored so strongly. Weyland faced them and forced a smile, but he appeared exhausted. He looked twenty years older than when Hugh had seen him just months ago.

"MacCarrick, it's good to see you, son."

Hugh didn't shake hands since he still clutched Jane's. "You as well, Weyland."

"Papa," Jane said, yanking her hand away, "please tell me why Hugh was allowed to walk in on me dressing."

When Weyland raised his graying eyebrows, Hugh gave her a baleful look. "No one was here and the door was unlocked. I thought that was . . . unusual."

"Oh, yes, well, Rolley was with me in the mews. The damned coal vendor was shorting us again," Weyland explained, as if he would ever worry himself over something so trivial. "Jane, I want you to wait outside my study for a few minutes."

"Can't, Papa. I'm supposed to meet Freddie at Hyde Park this morning," she said airily.

Hugh's stomach clenched. *Freddie?*

"Do give Frederick my regards."

Who the hell is Frederick?

She nodded and swirled out of the room without a backward glance at Hugh.

Hugh said, "I go with her, if you have no one else."

"Quin's got it. She's just going down the street," Weyland assured him, but Hugh continued to stare after her. "You know, all of Jane's beaus call her Plain Jane." Weyland gave a chuckle. "I suppose sarcasm passes for wit among these young bucks today. But who can keep up with them? I only remember Frederick Bidworth because he's lasted so much longer than most."

Now Hugh glowered at the door. Beau? Just how long had "Freddie" lasted?

"So I trust your moonlighting went well?" Weyland asked.

Hugh turned, frowning until Weyland pointed to the cuts down the side of his face.

"Aye, successful," he said, inwardly shaking himself. Just a casual suitor. An innocent meeting in the park. So why this sudden roiling in his gut?

"I expect you're wanting to know what the situation with Grey is." When Hugh nodded, Weyland said, "You knew he was becoming more unstable, but it finally got to the point that he was uncontrollable. We made an attempt to take him out. But a more cunning killer, I've never seen. He survived, and in retaliation, he's gone rogue, threatening to make public a list of all our people in the organization. He might already have done it."

Hugh's fists tightened. "Everyone?"

"I was just receiving word from a messenger out back when you arrived. From what we've been able to gather, it's the entire Network. If the list goes public, you'll be officially retired."

Hugh had never expected to end his career that way. "Does Jane have any idea?" he asked, trying not to reveal how much the idea disturbed him. "Any idea what I am?"

"No, she still thinks you're in business with me. And I plan to keep it that way until we know with absolute certainty that the list has gone public. After that, it won't matter—everyone will know."

Hugh exhaled a weary breath. "Weyland, you ken the danger you're in. No' just from Grey."

"I know." Weyland nodded gravely. "At last count, no man in England has more people who want him dead than I do. And they'll want more than that—the information, the secrets, the political prisoners. . . . It's about to be a maelstrom. That's why I need you to take Jane away for a time."

"And you?" Weyland had become like a father to Hugh, and he wouldn't allow him to be hurt. "I will no' leave you here to the wolves."

"This is the worst crisis in the history of our organization. I can't go to ground. But I'll call in help, and with luck, we'll bait Grey to come here. Stop shaking your head, son. Ethan has been spoiling for a chance at Grey. Quin and Rolley are itching for the fight. But my daughter must go."

The reminder that Ethan would be fully involved reassured Hugh, and he finally relaxed somewhat—

"And you will marry Jane first. That's why I brought you here."

Eight

Jane's soon-to-be fiancé was so much Hugh's opposite, he was like a foil to him.

As she gazed into Freddie Bidworth's cerulean blue eyes, Jane considered how perfect a man he was. He was the golden boy, the gentleman Adonis, and his looks made young women sigh whenever he strode by. If his blond locks caught the sun, swoons would be imminent.

When he laughed, and he laughed often, he threw back that blond head, giving himself up to it. Whereas Hugh was brooding and a loner, Freddie was merry and got along with everyone. Society loved him. And he loved it back.

Even after her unsettling encounters with Hugh, Jane couldn't help but smile at her good fortune that Freddie had waited so long for her. He'd joked that he would be the knight who tamed Plain Jane. He treated her as if they would be "partners in life," as he'd put it, and he'd promised that they would have a bloody good time of it. He let her be herself and even seemed to like her wild ways, since his personality tended toward . . . safe.

Not to mention that he was the *Earl* of Whiting.

"Freddie, let's go away together," Jane murmured. Since it appeared that Hugh was remaining in the city, she thought it best for her to vacate it. "Let's leave London for a holiday and get away from everyone."

"You're irrepressible, d'you know that?" Freddie sighed. "I can't be running off with you."

"No one would have to know. Besides, you like that I'm irrepressible."

"Now, that I do." He tapped her nose. "But I did want to talk to you about your wicked ways. Mother has asked me to coax you to be a bit more circumspect. Since everyone assumes we'll be wed, she says your behavior reflects on our family."

"To *coax* me, Freddie?" she asked, her tone gone leaden.

"Just until Lavinia finds a husband, you see."

His sister, pursed-lipped Lavinia, wed? As soon as waspish, sanctimonious prudes came into matrimonial demand.

Jane had no sympathy for the young woman, not after she'd found out that Lavinia and the dowager countess routinely did the unthinkable, the unforgivable.

They donated funds to the Society for the Suppression of Vice—the bane of most Weylands. The sodding *S.S.V.*

The society that received anonymous hate mail whenever Jane sat down at her escritoire.

Jane wondered what they would say if the new Lady Whiting formed the Society for the Expression of Vice. Just a thought.

"Well, if you'll ever agree to be my wife," Freddie continued, "countesses sometimes must make sacrifices. And it's just for a while."

For a while? No, it'd be a protracted sacrifice. So long as men shuddered at the sight of bitter females. Her face fell. Who was she to talk? *She* was becoming bitter. "Lavinia might not wed for a spell," she said carefully.

"Surely she will!" He gave her a boyish grin. "Could you do it for me, vixen?"

She smiled tightly, hating it when he called her that. Just last night, Jane had had a Scot with a body like a god's rasp "*Sìne*" to her. Compared to MacCarrick's husky brogue that set her blood afire, Freddie's clipped "vixen" was downright insipid.

Still comparing every man to Hugh, Janey?

"Kiss me," she said suddenly, placing her palms on his chest. "Give me a nice kiss, won't you, Freddie?" she asked almost desperately. They'd kissed hundreds of times before, but this would be the most important one of her life.

Be the man to make me forget him.

"*What?*" Hugh hadn't heard correctly. Surely he hadn't. "Something you should know—I'm no' marrying anyone. Ever."

"You must wed her," Weyland said. "If news of the list breaks, then I want her gone for at least a couple of months, out of the city. Away from the scandal and the danger. As her husband, you can take her away."

"I can do that without wedding her."

"No, Hugh, it must be—"

"You ken what I am. And what I've *done*." Weyland couldn't truly want his daughter married to a gunman with a broken-down body and blood on his hands? "How can you choose me for this . . . task?"

"It's because of what you are and what you've done that it must be you. Do you know what the marriage would say to anyone who would think to do her harm?

She'd become a MacCarrick. If the threat of your reputation failed to deter them, then what about Ethan's? She'd be his sister-in-law. And Courtland's as well. The only bride in the family. Who would risk your family's wrath to hurt her?"

Hugh's head was pounding as if a vise were tightening at his temples. "Goddamn it, did you ever think that I might no' wish to wed? When I made my first hit, I knew I would never take a bride—"

"There are several members in the organization who have spouses."

"And they put their families' lives in jeopardy because of it."

"Jane's life is already in jeopardy."

Hugh made a sound of frustration. "Then did you ever think I might no' want to marry *her* specifically?"

"No, I did not." Weyland gave him a sympathetic smile. "That thought never entered my mind."

Hugh hid his astonishment. Or maybe he didn't. Apparently he hadn't been able to hide his feelings for Jane before.

Weyland continued, "If there's a choice, you always opt for the jobs farthest afield, and you never come to my home unless Jane's out of town. It's telling how determined you are to stay away from her."

Hugh could deny nothing.

"I'd believed you would be more receptive, but if you're truly averse to the idea, then you can get an annulment after these difficulties have been resolved."

"No," he snapped. "It will no' happen."

"It must. I won't trust her with anyone but you." When Hugh still refused, Weyland clasped his forehead. "Son,

I'm tired, bloody tired, and I'm about to have the fight of my life. I can't win against the deadliest, most skilled adversaries on earth when I have one blatant vulnerability that would be like a red flag to them."

An unmarried, heartbreakingly beautiful, trouble-seeking daughter. No wonder Weyland looked like hell. "Weyland, you doona understand." Was Weyland forgetting that Hugh was uncomfortable around groups of people, unsociable and forbidding? Jane would slowly die around him. "I canna make her happy."

"Hugh, you can bugger *happy*!" He slammed his fist on the desk. "I want her *alive*."

Hugh was undaunted by his tone. "Let's talk scenarios. The most likely is that you apprehend Grey, and Ethan goes on the offensive and strikes out against a few of the worst threats so severely that he warns the rest away. Everything returns to nearly normal, except that we overreacted with this marriage when I should simply have taken her to lie low for a couple of months. And then Jane and I are stuck with each other for the rest of our lives."

"In that case, you can get an annulment after things die down. If the two of you are so dead-set against it, then don't have a marriage in truth." Hugh shook his head, but Weyland spoke over him. "Here's a scenario, Hugh. You know I might not make it through this alive." He put his hand up when Hugh opened his mouth to interrupt. "Before I die, I know that my daughter is married and could not have a more fearsome protector. I *don't* die wondering what will become of her. Can you comprehend what a boon it would be to me to know she's safe with you? *Finally* to have her settled? Would you not do this for me?"

"You doona know what you ask. She'd be safer without me."

"I hadn't wanted to bring this up, but Grey isn't targeting Jane only because of me. I know you beat him bloody years ago. And I know it was over her." When Hugh could only grind his teeth, Weyland said, "He wants revenge against you as well. I am letting her go—you too need to do what you must to keep her safe. We both owe it to her. She'll be the one to pay for our actions if we don't make sacrifices."

Hugh shoved his fingers through his hair. "This idea of yours has a serious flaw. Jane will never agree to it." Hugh had been only a summer diversion for a young lass of just seventeen years. Upstairs just now, she hadn't even wanted to give him five minutes of her time.

"Then I'll make you a deal. If she agrees, you wed her and take her into hiding until this dies down. If she refuses, you take her away temporarily with no bond between you, risking scandal at best and increased danger at worst."

Hugh scowled at that, but stubbornly insisted, "She will no' agree." Right now she was with her long-term beau, the one who'd lasted longer than the others.

Was Jane in love with this Bidworth? The possibility clawed at him.

"Then do we have a deal? Hugh?" Weyland added, when Hugh remained lost in thought.

Confident of Jane's refusal, Hugh faced Weyland and gave him one tight nod.

"Good. Now, I believe this must be done as soon as possible. This morning, even."

"You canna get a license that . . ." He trailed off at Weyland's mildly offended expression.

"If only everything was that easy," Weyland said. "So, if you'll just go fetch her from the park—she usually goes to the folly by the fountain. Tell her I need to speak with her at once."

Hell, Hugh wanted to go just to get her away from this Bidworth.

"And, son, if I may make a suggestion before she returns? A wedding ring for Jane might help smooth any ruffled feathers over the suddenness of all this."

Hugh glowered. "I would no' know the first thing about how or where to buy a ring."

"You've never bought jewelry for a woman?"

"Christ, no."

"You pass Ridergate's on Piccadilly on your way to your family's town house. They have her ring size on file."

Hugh raised his brows—even he had heard the name of that exclusive jeweler. "You must know more about my finances than I do."

"Don't poormouth me, Hugh. I do know you're truly wealthy now."

Hugh shrugged.

"And I think a part of you has always been saving up for a wife and family."

"If so, I dinna know about it," he muttered, turning to stride from the room.

Once outside, he realized his heart was thundering. Because within hours, he could be *wed to Jane.*

No. If Hugh wed her, if he said the vows and signed his name, he would be exposing Jane to his own doomed fate.

He could take her away without marriage. As soon as Jane had, as expected, scoffed at the idea of wedding him,

Hugh would prevail upon Weyland to allow them to go into hiding without that bond. The man couldn't know that there was a risk to Jane in marrying Hugh—one that might even outweigh the danger inherent in Grey. *Not to marry . . .*

What was he thinking? Jane would *never* agree.

But what if she does?

In the park, Hugh spied Quin lounging on a bench on one side of a whitewashed folly, admiring young women strolling in the sun. "MacCarrick, good morning," Quin said when he caught sight of him. Strangely, he stood to block the path around the folly.

"Anything happen last night at the warehouse?" Hugh asked.

"We lost Claudia's friend, Maddy."

Damn it, Ethan.

"I forced my sisters to return home while I searched for her. When I finally decided to check back at home to see if she'd come in, she had just arrived, pale and shaken but unharmed. I think the chit was so frightened, she might have learned a lesson," he said, then gave a long-suffering sigh. "My sisters, of course, remain undaunted."

Hugh was glad to hear that at least nothing *permanent* had resulted from Ethan's pursuit. His brother must have taken the girl home.

"The lot of my cousins should be married off to un-suspecting Yanks," Quin added in a grumble. "So, what are you doing here this early?"

"Come to fetch Jane for Weyland."

"I'll bring her back in a trice," Quin said quickly.

"No, I'll do it."

A flash of something like *pity* flickered in Quin's eyes. "She's meeting with someone."

Hugh immediately determined two things: Quin knew he'd wanted Jane. And she was even now being kissed—or worse—in her *meeting* with Freddie.

He shoved Quin out of the way, but the man followed.

"And how did you know, Quin?" Hugh asked in a seething tone.

Quin didn't bother pretending he didn't understand what Hugh spoke of. "Grey told me. Said you were . . . in love with her."

Who else had Grey told? Who else pitied the big, lumbering Scot his obsession with the exquisite Jane?

He stormed around the folly.

Nine

———— •◆• ————

"*H*ere, Jane?" Freddie asked, his voice breaking as he glanced around. "You want me to kiss you here?"

Nodding, Jane leaned forward. "There's no one to see us." She cupped his neck and tugged, and finally, he met her, brushing his lips against hers.

No, kissing was not new for them. What *was* new was Jane's recognition that his kiss felt as good as someone reassuringly patting her cheek. Last night, the feel of MacCarrick's big, hot hand surrounding her own hand had aroused her more than this.

Dismayed, she kissed Freddie more deeply, clutching his shoulders to provoke more from him, desperate to convince herself she could live with only this for the rest of her life. Even as she went through the motions, she remembered the books she'd read—the lascivious ones that were *suppressed*—and she knew there was more than what he was giving her. There was passion and aching and longing. Just not with *him*—

Freddie's body flew away from her.

Jane stared up in shock. "*Hugh?*" His wild eyes raked over her, his black hair whipping across his cheek. His jaw and fists were clenched. He shot her a disgusted look, then turned toward Freddie, looking for all the world like he would kill him.

Jane could do nothing but gape as she rose unsteadily. Freddie was stunned as well, struggling to get to his feet.

"No, MacCarrick!" Quin snapped, barring his way. In a lower voice, he said, "You could easily kill him."

"That's the goddamned idea," Hugh grated.

The next moments seemed to go so slowly. She watched, as if from a distance, Hugh shoving Quin far to the side. Freddie made it to his feet—just in time to catch Hugh's fist. Blood spurted from his nose as he went hurtling back.

Quin caught Hugh's arm behind him; Jane screamed and ran to Freddie. She grabbed him under his arms and tried to lug him to his feet, darting nervous glances over her shoulder. Freddie was big, yet Hugh's one blow had sent him flying.

"You'd best get out of here, before the constable shows up," Quin warned. "Don't know if you're aware, but you just broke the nose of a well-respected earl."

Hugh's look of hatred only seemed to deepen.

"You have to get Jane out of here," Quin insisted. "You hurt her more than you know with this insanity."

Hugh flung Quin off so readily that Jane realized he could have done so at any time, then he lunged forward, seizing her elbow to drag her away from Freddie.

This morning, Hugh's touch against her neck had been so gentle that she had scarcely felt it. Now his massive hand clutched hard, squeezing.

"Obviously, Quin's been spying on me," she said, her tone strident. "But what in the hell are *you* doing here?"

When he didn't answer at once, she pried at his fingers, trying to get back to Freddie. She gave Hugh's hand a withering glare when her efforts failed to loosen his grip. "I want to make sure you didn't kill him!"

Quin said, "He's fine, Jane. I'll stay with him, but you need to go."

"I won't do it—" She broke off with a gasp as Hugh dragged her along the walk toward her home, uncaring of the morning pedestrians staring or scrambling out of the way.

"Hugh, unhand me this instant!" she hissed. "What in the devil has gotten into you?"

"I ask you the same." Out of sight of the folly, Hugh stopped to grasp her shoulders, his hands shaking. In the minutes before, he had seen nothing but a red haze over his vision, felt nothing but the need to rip the man limb from limb. He knew what he must look like, but Jane stood her ground, chin up.

"Who is he?" Hugh bit out, trying not to notice that her lips were swollen. "Why're you kissing some man there for all to see?"

For me *to see.*

"His name is Frederick Bidworth, *Lord* Whiting."

Naturally, she'd be kissing a peer. One who'd never seen Hugh coming because he'd been too drugged by her kiss.

"And he's not just *some man* to me," Jane continued. "How can you react like this, when I was just at a courtesans' ball? This is mild! You told me I was a grown woman just last night!"

That was before he was expected to marry her. Before there was the possibility that he was to take her under his protection. Now everything felt different.

"Why are you behaving this way, Hugh? I demand an answer. Now!"

Because I wanted to kill him for touching you. The first man he'd ever *wanted* to kill. "Because the daughter of a close family friend was being compromised." Not a lie, an understatement. When she began to deny it, he said, "You ken he should no' have been risking your reputation by kissing you in the park."

"It's not as though any of this concerns you!" Her face tightened into a glare. "I do not have to explain my actions to you! This is none of your business."

"No? Perhaps no' *yet*," he said, making her frown at his words.

He knew that he was wrong to behave this way, but the idea of marriage to her, no matter how far-fetched, was like an opening wedge freeing every possessive instinct inside him. When he'd seen that bastard kissing her, a thought was seared into his mind: *Mine. He's taking what's mine.*

On the walk to the park, Hugh had been trying to determine what his move should be, wanting to make a cold, shrewd decision and ignore the fact that *everything* within him burned to possess her. *Is the sacrifice to marry her or not to marry her?* he'd asked himself with damned near each step.

Now he was so furious that there was no reasoning. All he knew was that he never wanted Bidworth to touch or kiss Jane again.

Hugh knew a fine way to ensure he couldn't.

Back inside the town house, Hugh yanked her into Weyland's office, ignoring her gasp and furious glare. "*See it done, Weyland,*" he bellowed to the unperturbed man.

Had Weyland known Hugh would find Jane in a compromising position? Of course. Weyland knew everything. And Hugh was responding just as predicted, being manipulated. "Just see it done."

"Consider it so." Weyland nodded solemnly. "Why don't you go round and pack a case, son, make any *purchases* you'll need? I'd like to speak with Jane privately."

Hugh strode out and shut the door, but listened for a brief moment.

"Papa," she began, "how can you stand by and let him treat me like this, manhandling me and ordering me? If you knew what he just did to—"

"I can and I must," Weyland interrupted, "because Hugh's about to be your husband."

"Have you gone mad? Married to Hugh MacCarrick?" Her sharp laughter grated. "Never! Never, on your life."

Ten

—————•◆•—————

"What is *wrong* with you?" Jane cried as soon as she heard Hugh slamming out of the house. "Have you sustained a blow to your head in the half-hour since I've been gone? Perhaps Hugh did it in his present state of violence?" She snapped her fingers. "Of course! Rapid senility!"

"If you will calm yourself." Her father's lined visage looked so serious. His kind blue eyes were now grim.

"How am I to be calm? Hugh just *attacked* Freddie." Hugh's face had been set so cruelly, she'd thought he would kill him. "Like some crazed man—"

"I trust there was no permanent damage?"

"—and you just told me I'm to marry him! You should know—I was accepting Freddie's proposal this morning!"

"Indeed?"

She gawked at his tone, at his utter lack of reaction. This man before her was somehow harder than the easygoing father she'd seen earlier this morning.

"I know this is difficult to accept," he said. "But I finally must put my foot down."

"Put your foot down? I'm twenty-seven! You can't force me to marry him."

He continued as if she hadn't spoken. "I have turned a blind eye to all your doings with your cousins."

When she peered at the ceiling, all but whistling to it with guilt, he went on, "I know that Samantha has *accounts* with the printers' shops on Holywell. I know Claudia is having an affair with her groom. I know of Nancy's penchant for dressing in men's clothing. And your cousin Charlotte is most likely even now waiting in line to get into the divorce court to hear every scandal firsthand."

"I get the point," she hastily said, wondering how he could possibly know all this. . . . Quin! Quin had told on them. It must be. But he should know better than to call down the wrath of the eight cousins.

"I've allowed these things because it seems your entire generation has gone mad."

She rolled her eyes. "This isn't the Regency, Papa."

"But I've also allowed them because on her deathbed your mother made me promise that I would give you the freedom she was afforded and never stifle your spirit."

"She did?" Jane gazed up at her mother's portrait. Lara Farraday had been the only child of a famous artist, and a gifted one herself. Lara's unique upbringing had been acceptable for a celebrated artist's daughter. "I never knew that."

"Already at six, you were so much like her. And I have kept my promise, even when I was stricken with worry for you."

Jane narrowed her eyes. "Is that why Quin was spying on me?"

"No. That's not why. He was doing that for the same reason I'm going to break my word to your mother."

"I don't understand."

"I've had ill dealings with one of my business associates. I made a decision that affected him and his fortunes critically. He wants revenge, seeks to hurt me in some way. Everyone knows you are what I hold most precious in the world."

She said slowly, "Hurt you?"

"He's afflicted with a hunger for opium. He hallucinates. There could be violence."

She nodded, adding sarcastically, "And who is this dastardly businessman who has struck fear in your heart? Who moves you to force your daughter into marriage—a marriage, I might add, that is much less advantageous *than the one she arranged for herself*?"

He ignored her rising tone. "Do you remember Davis Grey?"

"You're jesting?" she said, as a shiver of alarm ran through her.

"Not in the least."

"I-I had tea with him a couple of times while he waited here for you." Of all the men he could've mentioned . . .

Upon first meeting Grey, she'd been struck by his soulful brown eyes, boyishly handsome face, and open mien. He'd been extremely well dressed and had an urbane polish to complement his congenial air.

Yet he'd given her chills when she'd been forced to be near him.

She'd once caught him examining her with an eerie concentration. His expression had never been lustful. *That* she could have dismissed. She hadn't understood it, but for the first time in her life, and at the age of twenty-five, she'd wished for a chaperone. Now she said softly, "He gave me chills."

"Then you sensed that he could be capable of violence?"

"Yes," she finally admitted. "But why such drastic steps?"

"Hugh knows Grey from the past, knows him better than anyone does. He can protect you."

"Freddie could protect me."

"Jane, we are both pragmatists, realists above everything. And we both know that Frederick couldn't protect you from anything worse than committing a fashion mistake."

She gasped at the insult, and her father shrugged. "You know it's true."

"Why not just call the police?" she demanded. "With all your influence, you could get Grey on a prison hulk by teatime."

"I have called in favors and requested help with this matter. But we can't find him. We have no idea when or where he could strike."

She stood, then slowly crossed to the window. "So he could be out there watching me right now?"

Incredibly, her father didn't scoff and reassure her. "He could be. But we don't believe he is. He was last seen in Portugal, and there's been no indication that he's made England yet, only that this is his destination."

She stared out at two mothers pushing perambulators and tapping each other's forearms as they leaned in with gossip. A boy played at the edge of the park with a hoop and stick. So peaceful. She bit her bottom lip. Though this all seemed so far-fetched, she'd heard of madder scenarios.

After all, she lived in London.

As much as she loved this city, she could acknowledge its dangers and the violence that played out here daily. Just a year ago, Samantha had had a vial of vitriol splashed on her by a perfect stranger. Luckily, it only ate through her dress and scarred her leg—instead of her face, as other women had suffered in similar random attacks over that summer. There were grave robbers, or resurrectionists, who got *impatient* waiting for corpses to sell. And Jane had been mugged so many times that a lull in the offenses gave her cause to wonder if she was dressing shabbily.

She'd read of opium eaters like Grey who, in the grips of hallucinations, assaulted others.

As with a dazzling yet dangerous animal, one could admire London, but had to respect the risks inherent here. If her father said Grey was unhinged and she needed to flee the city, then very well. She'd certainly read stranger accounts in the *Times*—accounts she'd always cringed to see included not only the criminals' names and addresses, but the *victims'* as well. . . .

She shivered. "I'll agree to leave London for a time. But not with Hugh. There's no reason for him to do this. Why would he ever agree to a marriage?"

"As of ten minutes ago, I don't believe he was agreeing, I believe he was *demanding* your hand."

"That's correct. He was behaving like the crazed, ravening madman you want to protect me from."

What she said struck her father completely the wrong way. His face grew tight and his lips thinned. "They are nothing alike, Jane. Don't you *ever* say that again!"

She drew back at her normally placid father's furious tone. "Papa?"

"Hugh is a good man. An honorable man. He and Grey worked together and shared similar experiences. Hugh could have taken the same path, but he didn't."

She swallowed. "F-fine. Then I shall go with Hugh. But there's no need for marriage—"

"What have I ever done to indicate to you that I'd let my only child, my unmarried daughter, run off to travel with one of my business associates?" When she opened her mouth to answer, he cut her off. "Yes, well, that ends *today*. Besides, if you are so miserable, you can get an annulment as soon as this is over."

"You can't make me marry him. I'll simply go to Freddie and get him to take me away."

"Yes. I'm sure the dowager countess and her pinch-faced daughter will welcome you with open arms. Surely they won't mind that I won't be providing you with a dowry."

Her eyes went wide. "You wouldn't!"

He nodded gravely.

"Who *are* you?" she asked, blinking at him in bewilderment. Her father's personality had shifted utterly, just as Hugh's had. "I-I'll stay with my cousins. Samantha and Belinda and their families are going to Vinelands this week—"

"And how long will you flit from cousin to cousin? From estate to estate as a hanger-on?"

She crossed to him, determined to reason with him. "Father, you know I can't go back if I do this," she said with a light touch on his arm. "Once this is over, I will not be able to make another match."

"Certainly you will. John Ruskin got his marriage annulled just last year, and his former wife is already remarried. And think of all the girls who elope to Scotland. When their families find them and drag them back, the chits have their marriages annulled, and a couple of years later they marry again. If I had a pound for every time that happened during the last season—"

"Those girls are eighteen, nineteen. They have time to wait for another match." She lifted her hand from his arm and gripped her forehead. "I'm too old to wait! And you know my chances with Freddie would be ruined by this."

"If you still want him after all of this is over, then I would use all my influence to see it done."

She sank into a chair. "And why on earth would Freddie still want me?"

"He's waited this long."

She bit her lip at that, then said, "I still don't understand why Hugh has agreed to this. How can you make him take a wife he doesn't want?"

"Are you so sure he doesn't?"

"Of course he doesn't!"

"I believe he cared deeply for you when you were both younger. Don't you think he acted as if he did?"

"If he cared for me so much, then why would he leave without a word?" Looking back now, it was difficult to see him as anything other than a typical male, enjoying the attention she lavished on him.

"You know he told me to tell you good-bye. If you asked about him."

"*If?*" She gave her father the same expression she'd given him when he'd last voiced this nonsense. "It doesn't matter anymore. He's had a life of his own, and we hardly know each other anymore."

"Yes, he has had a life of his own, and in that time he's earned enough money to take care of you. I know that you two used to get along. Can't you charm him? Cajole him and win him over? It should be easy enough for you. Maybe you might *try* staying married?"

"Why would I ever choose Hugh over Freddie?"

"Because you never loved Freddie."

No, she didn't, but she cared for him, and they had fun together. And since she hadn't loved him, she'd known Freddie had no power to wound her. "Perhaps that's so—but Freddie's never hurt me."

"You don't believe Hugh purposely hurt you? I think you're forgetting all the times he took you riding, or the hours he spent helping you with your archery. He was patient with you, when I could scarcely be."

When she said nothing, recalling scenes from her childhood, her father said, "In the weeks to come, I want you to remember one thing. Remember that Hugh *tries*. He's going to try to make you happy."

"You're assuming I'm going to agree to this."

"Just think, Jane, he'll likely take you out of England."

"Where? Far?" she quickly asked, then flushed at her father's knowing expression. Transparent Jane, eager to travel. "To Carrickliffe?"

"Yes, possibly among his clan. It's up to him. But I do know that he'll go north. And that he won't travel more than a day's ride from a telegraph. I'll be able to contact you the minute you can return home. If at that time you still want an annulment, it will be done."

Self-preservation, Janey. What if you get attached to him again?

When she was still shaking her head, he said, "Jane, this is not up for debate. You will leave London, and you'll do it this morning."

She'd concluded that she didn't recognize her father, but just when she determined that she didn't care for this new stranger, his face and tone softened. "Ah, daughter, you're so brave about everything, and yet you're terrified of this, aren't you?"

"Well, if I am, it's because Grey looked at me in such a disquieting—"

"Not about Grey. You're afraid of getting hurt again."

Her lips parted, but she couldn't deny her apprehension. "Hugh left me once and never came back. And I know you invited him again and again."

"But, Jane, he came back when it counted."

Eleven

———◆———

*N*ever! Never on your life. . . .

With Jane's words running through his mind, Hugh rode for Grosvenor Square in a daze. There'd been too many developments this morning for him to digest. Simply seeing her kissing another man had nearly been his undoing.

And then, after so many years of fighting to stay away from Jane, to be forced to be with her—no, to marry her. He was shocked at how badly part of him wanted Weyland to succeed in persuading her.

Even as Hugh knew he couldn't keep her.

Did I truly just see Jane kissing another man?

When he arrived at the square, Hugh strode inside the MacCarrick family's mansion. They all called this place "the family's," though in truth it now belonged to Ethan. As the oldest son, Ethan had inherited all of the Mac-Carrick properties, as well as the Scottish earldom of Kavanagh—though he would likely pummel anyone who dared remind him he was a peer.

In the entry hall, Hugh ignored, as usual, his mother's messages to him, lying in the silver tray. He couldn't say he hated the woman, but she'd blamed her sons for their father's death, and that made it damned difficult to want anything to do with her. His brothers felt the same. All her messages to them were unopened as well.

Ethan hadn't banned her from the property, yet. By tacit agreement, she never stayed here when any of her sons were in London, though Hugh would bet she was still bribing the servants for information about them—everyone but Erskine, their butler. The dour-faced man was committed to his job of discouraging any and all visitors, and loyal down to his bones.

Hugh strode directly to the study, his boots drumming across the marble floor. He knew precisely where the *Leabhar nan Sùil-radharc,* the Book of Fates, would be—still laid out on the long mahogany desk, where Hugh had found Courtland, staring at it almost pleadingly just weeks ago.

As always, Hugh was amazed that such an ancient book could be preserved so well after countless years had passed. Of course, the only marking it had ever accepted was blood.

Long ago, a clan seer had predicted the fates of ten generations of MacCarricks and inscribed them in the *Leabhar*. The lines within foretold tragedies and triumphs that had all come to pass.

Although Hugh had long since memorized it, he turned to the last page, written to his father . . .

To the tenth Carrick:
Your lady fair shall bear you three dark sons.
Joy they bring you until they read this tome.
Words before their eyes cut your life's line young.
You die dread knowing cursed men they become,
shadowed to walk with death or walk alone.

Not to marry, know love, or bind, their fate;
Your line to die for never seed shall take.
Death and torment to those caught in their wake . . .

The last two lines were obscured by dried blood that could not be lifted from the page.

Tragedies and triumphs revealed? Hugh exhaled wearily. No triumphs were revealed to the brothers. No, they had sired no bairns among them, had killed their father by reading this very book, and continued to hurt everything they cared for.

Running his forefinger down the prediction on the crisp parchment, he felt his skin grow cold and clammy. There was something innate there, some palpable power in the *Leabhar*. The last person from outside the family who'd touched it had stared at it in horror and crossed himself.

Hugh turned away in disgust, then made his way to his bedroom. He forced himself to pack, though he wasn't convinced that Weyland could in fact move Jane to this measure, short of blackmail—

"What the bloody hell are you doing?" Ethan barked from the doorway. He glared at Hugh, who was dragging clothing from his wardrobe to a leather travel bag.

"Leaving London."

"With *her*?"

"Aye. Weyland's asked me to . . . wed her and take her away." His tone was defensive.

"No' again!" Ethan's scar was whitening. "We just got Courtland's woman away from him. Now you're running off with yours?"

"And what of you?" Hugh countered, snatching up

shirts. "I think you showed more interest in that girl last night than I've ever seen you show another woman."

"Ah, but I merely played with my wee blonde." He rubbed his scar unconsciously. Did he hate it anew after last night? Or had the chit slapped his face? Hugh hoped the latter. "But you and Court are always wanting more."

"I've agreed to wed Jane—*temporarily*. And only to take her away until you capture Grey and the havoc caused by the list dies down. I've made it clear to Weyland that this marriage will be annulled at that time, and he understood."

Ethan was shaking his head. "You're no' thinking clearly. You took one look at her after all that time away and bloody lost your mind. And the clan calls you the reasonable one?"

"I *am* reasonable," he grated, punching shirts into his bag so hard that the stitches in the leather strained.

"Running off with the woman you've been lost for, to *marry* her? Temporarily? Aye, the example of reason you are," Ethan sneered. "My God, you lectured Court about this verra thing. Rightly so."

Hugh glanced away. He'd been *smug* when he'd lectured Court, smug that he'd had the discipline to stay away from Jane all these years.

"Hugh, how can you ignore what's happened? Court made up his mind to marry Annalía, and within days, a bullet almost splattered her brain across our front doorstep. And then me. Have you forgotten my fiancée? It was *you* who found Sarah's broken body. Would you expose Jane to a fate like that?"

Christ, no. Never. "I will no' consummate the marriage. I will no' *keep* her," he said in a low tone. "It will no' be a marriage in truth. Besides, I've *already* jeopardized her. Grey will seize on her because of me. I know this. Grey will definitely kill her without me to protect her. I *might* hurt her."

"Even ill in the head, Grey will be deadly. As much as I hate to say it, he has unmatchable instincts." Ethan caught his gaze. "Why do you no' let me take Jane away?"

The thought made Hugh's blood boil. "Grey will never harm her while I live. Mark me, Ethan. Never."

Ethan raised his eyebrows. "Then you'd better hope I get to him before he gets to her. You think to protect her when you're no' cold about this? Certainly no' cold like Grey is. You're going to get both yourself and the girl killed."

"Damn it, I can take care of her—"

"*And* keep your hands off her at the same time?" Ethan gave him an incredulous expression.

"I have discipline. You ken that I do." Hugh strode to his wardrobe for a few essentials—a pistol as backup to the one he always wore holstered, and another rifle, second to the one he kept in his saddle holster. He also packed a good deal of ammunition for all of the weapons. "And I've stayed away this long, have I no'?"

"I also know you've got years of want stored up. You might seem calm on the outside, but I'll bet inside you're seething with it."

Seething. The perfect word for how he felt. "Does no' matter. She hates me." *Especially after this morning.* "Hell, she'll probably balk." Though he wondered. Weyland always got what he wanted. But then, so did Jane. Surely Weyland couldn't want him as a son-in-law as much as Jane wanted to have nothing to do with him. "I will no' keep her," he insisted again. "And she will no' want me."

Ethan studied him for long moments. Then he exhaled a resigned breath. "Aye, then. That, I can accept. Even if the old man forces her to wed, the chit will want out at the first opportunity."

Hugh scowled at Ethan's tone. As if he were reciting a fact.

"Is it so bloody inconceivable that she might want me as I want her?"

Ethan simply said, "Aye."

Hugh snatched up his bag, then exited the room to stomp down the stairs.

"Where're you taking her?" Ethan asked, following. "No' to the clan?"

Hugh shook his head. He'd considered taking her to Carrickliffe, but the people there all knew about the curse. At best, they would be wary around Jane, superstitious and treating her as though she were doomed. At worst, they would try to spirit her away from Hugh, seeking to save them both. He would only go there if there was no other alternative. "I'm taking her north to Ros Creag."

"Does Grey know about the lake house?"

"I never told him about it, but I canna be certain whether he does," Hugh answered. "If he hasn't reached England and I only keep us there for a few days—"

"I'm fast, but I'm no' that fast."

As Hugh reached the front door, he said, "Any suggestions among your various hideaways?"

"Grey knows of several, and I canna swear by the rest. You should take her to Court's."

Hugh slowed. He hadn't thought of Court's property, probably because his brother had owned it for so short a time.

"Court said the keep was old, but it's solid and only needs a bit of work," Ethan said.

He'd told Hugh the same, and that it was in the middle of *thousands* of acres. "I'll go to Ros Creag, and if I haven't heard anything from you in five days, we'll journey north to Court's."

"Good. I'll alert the staff to your arrival," Ethan said, referring to the skeleton staff that lived just off the property.

"If Grey follows us, I hope to God you'll be following him." Hugh skewered his brother with a look. "Much is in your hands, and you canna afford to get distracted. The sooner you kill Grey, the sooner this marriage is annulled."

"Then doona get settled in," Ethan said with a chilling smile. "And best take care with the marks on your face. You doona want them to scar."

"Go to hell," Hugh bit out, opening the door.

Ethan cursed under his breath, then said, "Wait a minute." He strode off, returning with the *Leabhar*, and offered it to Hugh. "Take it. It will remind you as nothing else can."

Hugh accepted the weighty book. "And what about you? What if you need it?"

Ethan's face was perfectly cold. "I've no heart to be tempted, remember?"

Hugh narrowed his eyes. "What did you do to the girl last night?"

He smirked, reaching up to rest his hand on top of the door. "Nothing she dinna want me to."

"Quin said she'd been afraid."

Ethan's brows drew together. "No. I dinna *scare* her." He touched his scar for the second time—something he *never* did. Either he'd never wanted to remember the injury, or had never wanted to draw attention to the mark. But this morning, he'd been mindful of it for the first time in years. "Goddamn it, I bloody had a mask on."

Hugh didn't think this was a good time to point out that his bearing and demeanor were as disturbing as his face. "Do you know who she is?"

"Was going by Quin's today to find out," Ethan drawled, "but now I find my calendar filled. Did you find out her name from Jane?"

Hugh saw an eagerness in his brother's eyes that gave him pause. Though Hugh didn't have the full details, he knew that Geoffrey Van Rowen was somehow responsible for Ethan's scar. Hugh also knew that the injury to Ethan's face had been deliberately delivered in a manner that ensured it would never heal seamlessly.

In turn, Ethan's revenge had been protracted and ruthless—and not particularly discerning between those in the Van Rowen family who deserved it, and those who didn't.

Hadn't he done enough to them?

Perhaps Ethan would lose interest in her over the coming days. "I know she's a friend of Jane's, so doona hurt that lass, Ethan, or you'll answer to me." He stuffed the *Leabhar* into his bag.

Ethan's cold expression turned menacing. "You think you can stop me if I feel like amusing myself? Go to hell, Hugh. You're smug about this subject, too," Ethan said. "But if you get Jane killed, you'll find you have a lot in common with me. Brother, you'll end up *just like me*."

Hugh cast him a disgusted look before turning away. As Ethan shut the door behind him, Hugh thought he heard him mutter, "*Just doona end up like me. . . .*"

Twelve

———◆———

*T*hough well over an hour had passed by the time Hugh returned to the Weylands', their muffled argument was still going strong in the study, so he sank down into a chair outside the room. He let his aching head fall back against the wall while he anxiously brushed his fingers over the small case in his jacket pocket.

Everything in Ridergate's whisper-quiet shop had appeared breakable to a man of Hugh's size, and he'd wanted to pull at his collar the entire time he was there. But when Hugh had found just the ring for her, he hadn't hesitated to spend a small fortune on it. What else was he going to spend his money on, if not her?

He'd known what to buy her because, that last summer, she'd told him exactly what she dreamed of receiving from her future bridegroom: "A gold ring with emeralds *and* an enormous diamond in the middle. It should be so heavy, I'll be forever knocking it into things, breaking shopkeepers' counters and accidentally unmanning pedestrians."

They'd been floating in a rowboat, her head in his lap as he played with her silky hair, fascinated as he lifted it to the sunlight, but he'd frozen at her words, tensing with anxiety. As a second son, he'd had no money to speak of and could never afford anything remotely like what she'd described.

Then he'd remembered that he could never have her anyway. . . .

Now, years later, he stared at the ceiling as round and round his mind played out the same scenarios and consequences.

Far too early in life, he'd learned about consequences, both avoidable and unavoidable.

The morning after he and his brothers had found and read the *Leabhar*—which was thought to have been destroyed—Hugh had woken to his mother's screams. She'd discovered her husband, Leith, the clan laird and a bear of a man in his prime, cold and dead in their bed.

And then she'd shrieked her blame. Hugh had been nigh on fourteen, far too young to be saddled with that guilt.

Years later, Ethan had scoffed at the curse, calling their father's death a freak coincidence, and found a bride from the neighboring MacReedy clan who would actually dare to wed a "cursed MacCarrick son." Sarah had fallen—or, as most believed, had been pushed by Ethan—from a turret at Carrickliffe.

Then Court had lost his heart to a foreign lass and intended to marry her, though he knew that he could never give her children and would only bring her misery.

Court had been defiant, daring to challenge their fate—until his Annalía had been a breath away from being shot in the head. Court had finally left her behind, safe at her home in Andorra, though it had nearly killed him. She'd become his entire world.

Consequences. The lines within that book said Hugh was not to marry or to bind. Hugh worked to convince himself there was a difference between *married* and *wed*.

Damn it, there would be no sealed union. If Jane agreed, they would be wed, but not truly bound together. As long as he didn't claim her, she'd be safe. Surely. And God knew, he had no intentions of keeping her.

He stood when Jane came out five minutes later, her eyes bright with either unshed tears or fury. A good wager said the latter.

What's it to be, then? What's the verdict?

Weyland was right behind her. "I'll just go send a note to the minister and pick up the marriage license. Jane, you need to begin packing immediately."

Then Weyland was gone, leaving Hugh so dumbfounded he nearly rocked on his feet. "You're going tae . . ." he began, but his voice broke lower. "We're tae . . . marry?"

"Yes, I am constrained to agree to this insanity—you are not. And you will ruin my life if you don't refuse to do this for him." Turmoil and emotion rolled off her in waves. She'd always been like that—volatile, like an explosive. Yet no one but Hugh seemed to understand just how *complicated* Jane was.

So Weyland had succeeded. Hugh hadn't expected her to be happy about the nuptials, but . . . "A temporary marriage to me counts as a ruined life?"

Every word she spoke was clipped with her proper English accent, and dripping with outrage. "Do you know *why* I was with Frederick Bidworth—*Lord* Whiting—this morning?" She answered her own question, "Because I was accepting his sodding *proposal* today!"

Hugh's vision swam. But why should he be surprised?

He'd wondered as each month went by, for years, why she hadn't married. *Wait.* How had Weyland not known about this? He had to have. She was about to be "settled" without any interference from them.

Bloody hell. This just kept getting better. Hugh had wanted to kill Bidworth for kissing Jane—whom the man had thought was his.

"However, my plans were interrupted when you *attacked* Freddie."

Jane was within her rights to be kissing her soon-to-be fiancé. Just because Hugh could think of naught but her didn't mean she was affected the same way by him. She'd had a life of her own these last years, and Hugh had just been dropped in the middle of it, swinging as he landed. "You were about to accept an earl, yet your father is still insisting on me?" It was a genuine question, but she took it as a retort and glared at him.

"Why, Hugh? Why is Davis Grey doing this? You know him—is he truly so dangerous that I have to flee my home?" Her face was drawn with confusion. "Why is Father so set on *you*? Did he blackmail you into this as well? Of course he did. Why else would you agree to such a lunatic idea?"

"I've no' been blackmailed, but I have promised your father. Just cooperate with me. The arrangement will no' be permanent as long as we doona . . . consummate the marriage." He lowered his voice. "Rest easy, this is temporary. I have no intention of remaining married any more than you do. And you know that if I dinna touch you before, then you're safe from it now."

"As if I'd let you," she hissed.

He pinched the bridge of his nose. His head was throbbing, his neck knotted with tension, but he tried to calm his tone. His ire never daunted Jane. "Did you ever think that this is no' something I want either?"

No, he didn't want this, was never supposed to marry. But now that he'd seen her once more, he didn't want anyone else to wed her either. And he was just selfish enough to agree to Weyland's machinations. Her father knew what was best for her, he reasoned, and Weyland had chosen Hugh. "Jane, I dinna come here thinking I'd leave with a bride."

"Then why did you tell Papa to *see it done*?"

"Because I can protect you."

She advanced until she was toe to toe with him, unflinching as she raised her face to his. "If you do this, Hugh, you have no idea how much I'll make you regret it. I'm giving you fair warning right now to desist from this."

When he said nothing, making his expression unbending, her lips parted in disbelief.

"Resolved, are we? Then so must I be." She made her tone soft when she asked, "Hugh, do you remember when I used to tease you?"

As if he could ever, *ever* forget.

"Darling, you're going to find that I've gotten better at it." She walked her fingers up his chest, and her voice grew breathless. "You'll see that I've gathered new arrows . . . in my quiver." Somehow she made that phrase sound wicked, and the customary sweat beaded on his brow.

"You've made it clear that you don't want this marriage," she said. "So before you go forward with this madness, consider—how much can you resist . . . day after day?"

He swallowed.

"Prepare yourself, darling." She turned, sauntering up the stairs with a hip-swinging gait that drew his riveted gaze. Over her shoulder, she said, "Because I'm about to make your life a living hell." Disappearing into her room, she slammed her door.

"More of the same," he muttered, wondering if his wedding might go smoother than his engagement.

Thirteen

————— • ◆ • —————

*T*he wily old man had done it.

Weyland had somehow convinced MacCarrick to marry his daughter. *Felicitations all around.*

Grey had been creeping around the house all morning, entertaining himself by dodging Quin and Rolley. Though Grey didn't blend as perfectly as he had in his prime, he'd been able to get close enough to gossiping servants to garner information.

Apparently, Miss Jane was having trunks packed for at least a month, but she couldn't provide a destination to help them select appropriate clothing to pack. And her lady's maid was being left behind, while her horse and her bow and quiver were not. Food preparations were being made—refreshments for the minister, who'd arrived early, but no wedding breakfast, as the newlyweds were setting off immediately after the simple ceremony.

The servants were sniffling at the news of the wedding and their mistress's departure. They all fawned over her. Not surprising. Weyland had told Grey and Hugh with obvious pride that Jane had always been generous with her wealth and her time, regardless of a person's station.

The servants were far from enamored of the groom, however. As one of them opined: "'E's frightening as 'oly 'ell and not near good enough for our Miss Jane."

This was true. Jane was so far out of his league it was laughable. MacCarrick was massive, stony, and intimidating; Jane was a celebrated beauty brimming with wit and charm.

And she was MacCarrick's sole weakness.

Grey had discovered that the night of Jane's coming-out ball—an event Weyland had insisted they attend. Grey had gotten MacCarrick drunk to lure him there, but Hugh had skulked outside, watching her through a window, his body tense. There'd been such longing in his eyes that Grey had realized the young Highlander was in love with the fair Jane.

A bear chasing a butterfly.

Grey had had to stifle a chuckle at the illogical match—even more so because Hugh had *known* he wasn't good enough for her, yet he'd been unable to let go of his feelings.

More shocking to Grey than Hugh's capitulation was that Weyland had somehow convinced Jane as well. How? Had he come clean about their occupations? About Grey's?

It had been years since Grey had felt genuine amusement, but this situation was boiling over with such rich irony. An assassin bade to protect a life, the life he held dearest in the world—his *wife's*. And to protect her from a *better* assassin.

All of them had to know that Grey was a much more accomplished killer than Hugh was a protector.

His amusement faded. He hadn't wanted this to be easy. . . .

With Quin and Rolley hovering about them, and a sharp-eyed coach driver who had "Network" written all over him on the lookout, Weyland escorted Jane to the coach. Hugh followed, close behind her, behaving as if she had a target on her back.

She did. Grey had a clear shot from where he lurked this moment. Unfortunately, his aim was . . . impaired at present. If he missed, he'd be doing nothing but alerting them that he was in England. No, he would have to get closer.

At the coach door, Weyland held Jane's head in both hands and put his forehead to hers. Her face went stark white, her expression stunned, when her father kissed her cheek good-bye. "*Papa?*" she said in a breaking voice, as if she was just now realizing she was leaving him and her home.

Weyland forced himself away, pausing only to squeeze her shoulder and to give MacCarrick a hard look, letting him know what he was trusting him with. Then he left them, his own shoulders sagging like an old man's—like the old man he was becoming.

As Grey watched their actions and interactions in a kind of dazed captivation, he wondered if Weyland had told MacCarrick about the list to convince him. Probably.

Grey *did* have the list, and had threatened to release it, but if that information went public, Weyland would be dead directly. In Weyland's clandestine service, he'd routinely had to make cold-blooded decisions, dispatching men like Grey, Ethan, and Hugh to carry them out. If those numerous decisions were traced back to Weyland, it would be over.

That wasn't Grey's agenda, not yet—

When a sudden cold clamminess broke out on his neck and back, dampening his shirt, Grey reached into his jacket pocket. He'd anticipated that smoking would be more inconvenient in England than in some other countries, and had had his "medicine" prepared differently. He needn't have bothered. In London, opium was proving easier to find than tobacco and cheaper than gin.

But he liked the alteration. He chewed it, relishing it. The taste was like almonds that were slightly off. The texture was gummy.

My medicine. He snorted. His body had been ruined from injuries sustained in his profession, and laudanum had made the pain bearable. Upon noticing that Hugh limped himself, especially in the mornings, Grey had offered him some. The bastard had shook his head firmly. *So bloody sanctimonious.*

As he chewed, Grey's heartbeat slowed to a ponderous rhythm, though he felt more excitement than he could remember. Luckily, with this dosage there would be no hallucinations. He hoped. . . .

Ah, and there went Jane, waking as if from a trance, beginning to gesture and fume even as MacCarrick was loading her into the coach. Stubborn Jane wasn't one to be led blindly, and she was no doubt demanding answers, ones that Hugh clearly wasn't providing. At the coach door, she stepped up, but turned to say something else to Hugh, putting their faces close. They both fell silent.

Grey had compared Hugh to a bear chasing a butterfly. The corners of Grey's lips tilted up. No, Hugh was better than that—he was like a wolf with a rabbit twitching her tail in front of him.

Sooner or later, the wolf would attack.

When Hugh shut the carriage door, he stood for just a second, exhaling deeply, as if getting his bearings. He ran a shaking hand over his face, no doubt disbelieving he'd wed the chit.

"Don't worry, Hugh," Grey softly assured him. "It shan't be for long."

In the past, if Jane had caught Hugh staring at her breasts, he'd always averted his eyes. In the coach for the last hour, he'd looked at her brazenly, studying her body, as if re-learning it, as if it was his *right* to do so. It galled her. He could have had unfettered access to her body. She would have denied him nothing in the past.

The fact that she reacted to his heated gaze only infuriated her further. Why couldn't she have found him less attractive than she had years before? She'd always thought him the most beautiful man she'd ever seen—even before she'd spied on him shucking off his clothes to swim naked in the lake and had gazed in awe at his magnificent body. And now this new hardness about him was nearly irresistible.

A living hell, she'd promised him. She'd sounded so strong, so determined.

Now she waffled.

Stay married, her father had advised. She didn't want that, couldn't have that. She'd been forced to accept the alliance, but Hugh hadn't been and could have saved them both from this.

He'd refused.

Because Hugh had left her no way out, Jane felt he might as well have pushed her off a cliff. Yes, a nice, big shove, sending her flailing and screaming right over the edge.

Inevitably, once she landed, it was going to be messy.

She was already livid with him over the past, before he attacked Freddie. Now she was wed to the very man who'd betrayed her, and this on the heels of the rawest show of fury she had ever seen. Hugh in the warehouse had been bad, but this morning he'd been worse. What she couldn't understand was why.

Had he become one of those men whose first reaction always tended toward violence? Or had her father already promised her to him, days, even weeks, before? Which would mean Hugh had thought his *fiancée* had been kissing another? She frowned. Recalling her conversation with her father, she realized he'd never asked her *why* Hugh had attacked Freddie. . . .

Hugh's own explanation had rung hollow, even as he'd uttered it. Yes, Hugh was a close friend of the family's, and, yes, perhaps she oughtn't to have been kissing Freddie in the park behind the folly, but nothing excused what he'd done.

Jane was angry and she wanted revenge. Her talent still lay in teasing and tormenting. In fact, as she'd pointed out to Hugh, her arsenal had only expanded, thanks to all the tricks she'd learned in her five London seasons among seven master cousins.

Hugh should know what he'd given up back then. He should have a taste of what he *couldn't* have now without risking a binding marriage to her.

For every hopeless day and night filled with tears, for every man she'd compared to him and found lacking, for his decision to leave her . . .

For all her pain, she would make him pay.

"Oh, Hugh, darling, it's close in here, is it not?" She unfastened the first few buttons of her blouse and drew it wide to fan herself. After opening the window on her side, she tugged up her skirts so she could kneel on the bench facing him. She reached past Hugh toward his window, resting one knee against his thigh, and placed her palm just above his own knee. His entire body went rigid.

With her other arm stretched out to the window, she turned her head so their lips were barely inches apart. "You don't mind, do you, darling?" she asked in a sensual whisper as she slowly rubbed her palm higher up his rock-hard thigh. His jaw clenched, and he swallowed hard. His brows drew together as though he was in pain.

Make him pay.

They hit a bump, and though his hands shot to her waist to steady her, she made sure she landed straddling him.

He hissed in a breath. "*Jane,*" he growled, tightening his grip. But he didn't raise her from her position—if anything, his shaking hands on her waist pressed her down.

"What is it, darling?" she murmured.

"Doona touch me, lass," he rasped. "Just . . . you canna touch me."

And pay.

"How clumsy of me," she purred. "Needing you to support me, or else I might *slide . . . slowly . . . inch by inch . . . down upon your*"—she leaned in close to his ear, making sure he felt her breaths before she enunciated—"*lap.*" He shuddered violently, lowering his head to her neck.

When she eased back, he faced her, appearing stunned. His normally clenched jaw was slack.

She patted his shoulder firmly—all business—then maneuvered and swished back into her seat to gaze casually out the window. "Yes, darling, now it's *much* better in here."

Fourteen

───────◆───────

*H*ugh violently rubbed his palms on his legs, struggling for a calm he didn't possess. His swift, bloodpounding erection strained against his trousers. His breaths came haggard.

After wanting her for so long . . .

She didn't understand just how tenuous his control was, and was even now gazing out the window, unconcerned. But he could see her coral lips curling without humor. She was playing with him, just as she always had.

He'd tolerate it no longer. *I saw her kissing another goddamned man.*

His hand shot out to grasp her arm, and her smirk vanished. She turned to him with a glare. "Hugh, release me."

He yanked her closer to him on the bench. "You'd do well to recognize I'm no' the same lad I was."

"And what are you now?" she asked airily, seemingly unaffected by what had just occurred and by Hugh's building anger.

"I'm a man with a man's needs." He would teach her, give her this lesson now so that she would stop these flirtations. Because she was right—she had gotten even better, somehow improving on perfection. He sensed it was critical to put her in her place now. His voice grating,

he said, "Doona expect to tease me like that and no' relieve me in some fashion."

Her eyes widened, then narrowed. "Some fashion? Enlighten me, darling." Her soft fingertips toyed with his
chest in the V of his shirt. Christ, she made him weak.
"How do you usually prefer to be . . . relieved?"

So she'd meet him measure for measure? He was a
man with more experience, he should be able to win this
handily. There had to be a line she wouldn't cross. But
could he pull back once they reached it?

"I'll have tae show you," he heard himself saying. In
one sweeping motion, he dragged her onto his lap, easing
her back against his arm until he was leaning over her.
She looked startled—after all, this was the first time he'd
ever touched her back when she'd teased—but then a
flicker of that stubborn look crossed her face. In the space
of a heartbeat, she was all seduction again, reaching out
to pet his neck even as she relaxed into his arm.

His blood pulsed in his groin, making it hot and
aching. When she gasped, he knew she could feel his erection throbbing under her arse. He was having difficulty
thinking. Didn't he have an agenda with this?

*Kiss her so hard she'll forget she was in another man's
arms this morning. . . .*

No. He was only doing this to push her, to startle her,
to win this battle of wills. They always used to have them,
and Hugh had lost as many as he'd won.

Her lips were parted, welcoming. Her body was so
damned soft against him. Just one taste. *Yes, get this out of
the way in the beginning. Of course.* He'd only imagined
how good kissing her would be, and when that was
proved otherwise, he could get past his obsession.

He leaned down, never taking his eyes from hers. He felt the lace hem of her skirt clenched in his shaking fist and had no idea how it had gotten there. No doubt he wanted to get to those wicked garters he'd seen her lace around her white thighs this morning.

Her open blouse revealed the swells of her creamy breasts above her corset, and he bent to brush his lips over them, stunned to find her skin was as soft as it looked. When she shivered, her playfulness gone, he kissed up to the base of her neck, realizing this was the first time his lips had ever touched her.

He inhaled the light scent of her skin and knew that he wouldn't rest until he'd tasted her. Just once. With a defeated groan, he opened his mouth and flicked his tongue over her flesh. He shuddered with pleasure, and she gave the sweetest little cry, making him want to wrench more from her.

"Is this what you want from me?" he rasped, drawing back to take in her face. She looked as dazed as he felt, staring at his lips, no doubt wondering how things had escalated so fast.

He cupped her nape and slanted his lips over hers. She hesitated as if startled by the contact, then parted her soft, giving lips in offer.

Her mouth was hot and wet as he slipped his tongue in, and when she met it, taking his strokes with hers, he stifled a groan. She moaned against him, the sound making his cock pulse painfully in reaction, and soon he was lost in the experience. At last he was tasting and touching her, dazed by sensation.

This wasn't a dream, not a scenario he'd envisioned in a lonely bed in some distant country. He was kissing her. And it wasn't as good as his imaginings.

It was *better.*

His hand had slipped up the outside of her thigh almost to her garter, about to slowly untie—

"Miss Weyland!" a voice called from outside the carriage. "I say, is Miss Weyland in there?"

Jane froze, then pulled back. "Freddie?" she gasped.

Not Bidworth.

"Hugh, we have to stop."

His gaze flickered over her chest, her neck, her lips. When he met her eyes, he shook his head slowly. Leaning in, he took her mouth once more.

She shivered, then pushed against him. "Stop!" She scrambled to sit up. "I am in deadly earnest, Hugh!"

He finally released her, though he struggled not to yank her back when he realized she'd just responded to *him*. Such a small taste, after such a long wait, and it was still worth it.

But as sanity returned, he disbelieved what he'd done—and been about to do. He had to cough to speak, and still his voice was hoarse when he said, "Never do that again. Never, Jane, or I vow tae you, I'll—"

"Stop the carriage," she said, inhaling and exhaling deeply as she fumbled with the buttons of her blouse. When he made no move to do so, she added, "We're setting off for a location so secret you aren't even going to tell me, but if you don't let me talk to him, he'll follow us all the way there."

"No' if he's unable to follow," he said quietly.

Her eyes widened, and she gazed at him as if she didn't recognize him. "You're crazed, aren't you? Have the years warped your mind? You listen to me, Hugh MacCarrick. You are not to hurt him again. Do you hear me? Or, so help me God, I will get in the middle and—claw—your—very—eyes—out." She gave him a glare to punctuate her threat.

"You told your father that you'd sent a message to him."

"Of course I did," she said, straightening her hair. He took the opportunity to pull his jacket edges together and furtively adjusted his shaft within his trousers. "Freddie must have ridden over directly upon receiving it, just missed us, and followed us north."

Biting back a curse, Hugh called to the driver to stop.

"I want five minutes with him—alone," she said, throwing open the coach door.

"No' a chance—"

"I'm telling him good-bye. He deserves five minutes of my time. Especially after your attack today." She met his eyes. "Hugh, damn you, *please*."

She always knew he couldn't deny her when she looked up at him like that and said please. When he bit out a curse, she quickly descended before he could assist her. Through the back window, Hugh watched as Bidworth dismounted. When she rushed to him, the bastard laid his hands on her shoulders, then pulled her to his chest.

Hugh couldn't watch this, not now. She was his wife now. Not for good, only temporarily, but for now, she was *his*.

His first impulse was to stalk out there, drag her away from him, then plant his fist in Bidworth's face again. That last hit had felt so sodding good, and the break at the bridge of Bidworth's nose was swollen and already blackening his eyes gruesomely. Hugh stifled the impulse, barely, but stayed tensed and ready to reach her in a hurry.

He half-expected Bidworth to snatch Jane up and toss her on his horse to steal her.

Hugh would have.

He would use this time to study them interacting, to determine what type of loss this would be for her. Jane stared up at Bidworth adoringly—but then, it made sense that a woman like her would want a man like him. He was an earl, tall and blond, and they looked rich and aristocratic together. A perfect Briton couple.

Hugh was a black-haired Scot with a menacing expression and gashes marring his face.

Not to mention his occupation.

Jane lightly brushed her fingers over Bidworth's cheek, and Hugh hated him for it. She touched Bidworth lovingly—as she used to with Hugh. Now she touched Hugh to hurt him.

Seeing this was hellish. Put Hugh in a sweltering marsh, force him to stand perfectly still with a rifle poised for a shot for half a day as the sweat stung his eyes and insects devoured his legs, and he would be happier than watching this. Jaw clenched, his hands in fists, Hugh watched as Bidworth refastened her top blouse button and suspected they were already sleeping together.

"Jane, you cannot tell me this is what you want," Freddie said. "I thought we had an understanding."

"I don't, and we did." She could *feel* Hugh's eyes on her and shivered, still affected by how rapidly things had escalated between them. In the past, she could always touch and tease him, and he *never* touched her back. Just then in the coach, he'd had her in his lap, her bottom pressed against his very sizable and insistent erection, in the space of a heartbeat.

His kisses had been scalding, devouring. Until five minutes ago, Jane had never known kisses could be like that. As though Hugh were branding her. . . .

As she and Freddie stood at the side of the road, she wanted to adjust their positions, so that Hugh couldn't see her flushed face—and could only burn holes in her back with his eyes.

"Your father said this MacCarrick has just returned after a long absence," Freddie began, "and that you two had been promised to each other years ago. Is this true?"

In a way. In her mind. "It's rather involved, Freddie."

"Is Weyland forcing you to do this, sweetheart?" He stroked her hair. "Jane, you poor thing. You're trembling." He looked as if he might kiss her to comfort her, and Hugh immediately descended from the carriage, unfolding his towering height. In a clear warning, he crossed his arms and leaned his muscular frame against the side of the carriage.

Freddie's expression was aghast. "My God, he looks more barbaric than before! I still cannot believe your father is letting *him* marry *you*." Then Freddie gave Jane a look that suggested he was amazed by her fortitude in surviving the marriage even this long. "What is Weyland thinking? This won't be tolerated! We will figure out some way to free you from this man."

Jane glanced at Hugh and had to admit that he looked fearsome. Unfortunately for her, she'd always liked that about him, when it was directed at others.

"I'll take you away from here this very moment," Freddie vowed.

In a toneless voice, she said, "It's done, I'm afraid." Yes, her father did have significant influence with persons of power, but even he wouldn't be able to smooth this one over.

In her letter to Freddie, Jane had broken it off with him—completely.

"This is probably for the best," she said with a sigh. "You know your mother and sister don't approve of me." She would have been Lady Whiting by the skin of her teeth.

"I hope that is not what has swayed you in this, because I say to hell with them."

Despite these heroic promises now, Freddie actually wasn't accustomed to taking stands or becoming involved in discord in any way. That was one of the reasons she'd liked him so much, because he was so opposite to Hugh, who'd always been so quick to roll up his sleeves and fight for her.

"I just don't understand this," Freddie continued. "I-I won't accept this!"

Yes, he would. Because the truth was that he wasn't in love with her, either. He'd lost his heart to Candace Damferre, their mutual friend and his childhood sweetheart, who'd been forced to marry a doddering old man who was, impossibly, richer than Freddie.

But Jane and Freddie had promised each other that if they did wed, they'd do their best to make a go of it, and Jane had known that Freddie was looking forward to a future with her. The entire situation was *wrong*.

"I'd be sending you off to your doom—" He broke off as Hugh stalked toward them, exuding menace. Freddie's voice scaled an octave higher when he said, "He's going to hit me again, isn't he?"

Fifteen

———— •◆• ————

$\mathcal{A}$s Hugh neared, Bidworth's face paled, making his bruises stand out. Hugh heard him murmur, "Jane, th-there are ways to amend this predicament, I'm sure. You're not inescapably his wife, not yet."

"Seems like she's more mine than yours," Hugh bit out, aggravated by Bidworth's statement, because it went to the heart of this whole situation. And the galled look the man was casting him tried his patience.

Why did everyone find it so unbelievable that Jane would wed a man like Hugh? She'd kissed him in the coach like she was bloody well wed to him. Hugh placed his hand on her nape, an obvious sign of possession.

Jane shot him a look that promised reprisal. "I wanted five minutes."

"Get in the carriage. Now." When she only gaped at his command, Hugh leaned in and told her in a low tone, "Do it, or he's going to get more than a tap this time."

In a rush, she took Bidworth's hand and briefly shook it. "I'll write, Freddie," she said, then hurried to the coach.

When she paused outside, Hugh told Bidworth, "Doona follow us. Doona come near her again. Forget you even know her."

"D-do you have . . ." Bidworth swallowed and began again, "Do you have a-any idea who I am?"

The miserable coward, Hugh thought with disbelief, grappling for control of his temper. He had expected a jilted suitor, especially one nearly engaged to a woman like Jane, would be a threat waiting in the wings.

Not a threat. Not even giving Hugh a serious argument.

"Aye, I ken who you are. You're the man who's letting a woman like *that* go without a fight." If Hugh had been in Bidworth's position—able to have a life with Jane without risking dire consequences—he'd have fought off a bloody legion before handing her over to another man. A real brawl, with mud flying and blood spraying.

For Jane as a prize, he would have spit blood with a grin on his face.

"You doona deserve her, and you sure as hell could no' have handled her," he snapped. Leaving Bidworth floundering for words, Hugh turned to the coach, scowling as Jane climbed in instead of waiting for him to help her. When he joined her inside and the coach began to roll along, she waved at Bidworth until he was out of sight. Long after, she continued to gaze out the window, her little hands in fists. If Hugh ever expected a woman to cry, it'd be now.

Jane had rarely cried when younger. On the few occasions when she had, he'd been at an utter loss. Seeing she was on the verge, he ran his hand over the back of his neck, realizing that hadn't changed. "If you wanted him so badly, why did you no' fight for him? You've always gotten your way in the past."

"This is your fault," she snapped at him, "this entire

situation. If Father hadn't been able to *order up* another lackey bridegroom so handily, he would have let me marry Freddie."

"You blame me more than your father, who arranged all this? More than yourself, who agreed to go through with it? Maybe you might blame Grey?"

"Why did Father pick you? You weren't even in London. I demand to know what is really going on! Is this some scheme you and he cooked up to get me to marry you?"

"As I said, I dinna go to your home thinking I'd be leaving with a bride. I never asked your father for you."

"So I'm actually supposed to believe that Grey might do violence to me. The business of imports must be spectacularly dangerous. And all this time I never knew the risks Father was taking."

Hugh said nothing.

"Look me in the eye and tell me Grey's unhinged and might hurt me."

Hugh met her eyes. "I can say with absolute certainty that Grey is soft in the mind and has dangerous intent, probably toward you."

"Grey was always nice to me," she muttered.

"I'll bet he was." When Grey became increasingly crazed, his taunts to Hugh always involved Jane. He'd known that she was Hugh's one weakness. "Did Grey ever say or do anything odd to you? Show an untoward interest in you?"

"No, I wasn't around him that often." She shivered. "Why would he want to do something so drastic?"

"He was becoming unstable. Your father broke off ties with him and ordered an action—something that was within his right to do—that furthered Grey's ruin."

"What do you mean by 'an action'? What kind of ruin? Where do *you* fit into this?"

Weyland had again stressed that he didn't want Jane to know anything about the Network until they'd confirmed that the list had indeed been made public. Until then, Hugh was supposed to brush aside her questions, or lie. As Hugh wanted to avoid telling her of his own role, he'd readily agreed. Unfortunately, he found it impossible to lie to her. He needed some time to get his bearings with her, to find a way to deter her questions. "You're keen on interrogating me, but I doubt you'd answer questions so readily."

"Ask me anything!"

"Why did you wait so long to marry?" She'd had plenty of opportunities, had had offers when she was still a young lass and a coming-out ball when she was nineteen.

"I hadn't found the right man," she answered in a that'll-show-you tone.

"*Bidworth* was the right man?"

"He has all the qualifications I'm looking for. Every single one of them."

"Like what?" he asked.

"He's gentle and kind and considerate." At Hugh's bored look, her eyes narrowed. "He's blond, with a face that makes women swoon, and he's titled and popular and rich."

If these were the traits she was looking for, Hugh had never had a chance with her, family curse or not. "Bidworth's cowardly," he said. After meeting the man, however briefly, Hugh knew Weyland had been right not to let her marry the earl—he could never protect Jane.

His comment got her going. "Just because he didn't

call you out over this doesn't mean Freddie isn't brave! He's a peer of the realm and a proper British gentleman— who's *above* issuing a challenge on the side of the toll road!"

Hugh supposed there were advantages to being a brutish Scot with no title.

"Freddie's a wonderful man, all around," she continued. "And your attacking him today? My Lord, Hugh, what has gotten into you?"

"He should never have kissed you in public—"

"*I* kissed *him*."

Twist that knife, Jane, he thought. *That's right, lass, from twelve o'clock to three.*

"And what about provoking him just now?" she asked. "He woke up this morning thinking I was his. Yet you threw this marriage in his face as if this means something to you."

"No worse than you throwing yourself at him on the side of the road."

She gasped. "I didn't throw myself at him! I *embraced* him in farewell. Which would be expected, since Freddie and I have been seeing each other for *years*!"

"Aye, but during those years, you likely were no' panting in another man's lap, returning his kisses, just moments before."

Her lips parted wordlessly, as if she'd only just realized she couldn't deny it.

"Jane, even if this marriage of ours is a farce, it's binding until it's ended. Never touch another man in front of me. Unless you want him dead."

She rolled her eyes at him. "Why, Hugh, you sound jealous, which we know can't be true."

It was undeniably true. In this one day, Hugh had felt more jealousy clawing at his gut than in his entire life before. If they'd been truly committed, perhaps he wouldn't have felt it to such a blistering degree just now—but there was no foundation for them. They were embroiled in a sham. He'd given her his name but could expect nothing back.

The situation was maddening. How had he found himself agreeing to it, when all his instincts screamed against it? He'd been well aware that he was being maneuvered—and yet, he'd allowed it.

Hugh had never been one to lose his temper or react impulsively. Now he felt he was losing control. What was it about Jane that made him feel primitive and possessive? He'd felt compelled to bare his teeth at Bidworth—or to hit him again, just for pleasure.

Men like Hugh could not afford to lose control. Grey wasn't the first of their kind to succumb to darker impulses. "And doona tease me any longer. Lass, you play with fire."

"If you can't stand my teasing, you never should have agreed to this. It's not as if you haven't experienced it before or didn't know what to expect when I *warned* you not to go along with this!"

"We both agreed to end this marriage when the situation is resolved," he grated. "I will no' be trapped into something I dinna want because you think to amuse yourself by playing with me."

A coldness seemed to settle over her. "Don't spend another minute's desperate worry that you might be 'trapped' with me. There is *nothing* that can happen between us that will bind us together in this marriage, I assure you." She opened her small traveling case at her feet and withdrew a book, turning from him dismissively.

If only he could turn away and shut her out as easily.

All morning Hugh had felt outside of reality, waiting for everyone to realize what a mistake his and Jane's marriage would be. Each minute, he expected Jane to back out.

In the back of his mind, he'd never thought it would truly be his decision as to whether they would move forward with this or not.

When she'd begun packing, Hugh had paced. *She's actually going through with this? Impossible.* What if the final choice came down to *him*? Time and again he weighed the risks, but before he knew it, they were all waiting for him to sign his name to the marriage certificate.

Hugh had heard Rolley mutter to Quin, "Never thought I'd see the day steady MacCarrick's hand would shake like that."

How could it not, when Hugh felt he walked upon a razor's edge between what fate would allow—or punish him for?

And when he risked the only woman he'd ever loved.

After an hour of silence in the coach, Hugh reached over and removed her book from her hands. Before she could gasp her displeasure, he presented her with a glass jewel case, offered in his big palm.

"And what is this?" she asked, though she recognized the *R* emblem etched in the crystal.

"Take it."

After a hesitation, she did, then opened it with a nonchalant air. Her heart flipped over like a cart's wheel.

Inside lay the most gorgeous piece of jewelry she had ever seen.

She stared, light-headed, then gazed up at him. "This . . . this is wholly unnecessary." She tried to hand it back, but he wouldn't take it, and the bewildered look on his face made her hesitate.

"Will you no' wear it, lass?" he asked incredulously.

He'd obviously never envisioned that she might not accept it. She finally set it on the bench between them. "Hugh, you didn't have to do this. I know many women who do not have wedding jewelry."

"You will."

"I also know many women who don't like to be given temporary jewelry."

"What do you mean?"

"We know this will be over soon," Jane said. "Jewelry, in this case, seems a bit . . . cruel."

He shook his head firmly. "You'll keep it. After."

After he left her. Again.

"So, did you have this lying around the house, in case of any impromptu weddings?"

"Got it this morning. While you were packing."

"Hmm." She tapped her cheek. "Now it all becomes clear. You got it after you guiltily realized that perhaps you shouldn't have bludgeoned Freddie and manhandled me. You rode out and bought me a *very* expensive olive branch."

"You've been slighted a grand wedding and all that surrounds it. This is one thing I can control. I wanted to give my friend something befitting her."

"Are we friends, Hugh?" she asked, her voice sounding sad, even to her.

He stiffened. "I've never doubted it."

She bit her lip at that, then surreptitiously glanced down at the ring case, her hands itching to pick it up. Her father had told her Hugh had saved some money, but Ridergate's was fantastically expensive, and that ring—classically set with a huge diamond amidst a cluster of emeralds—was oh-so-lavish.

With a sigh, she realized she ought not take it, because Hugh shouldn't be spending that money on her, no matter how badly she wanted it. Especially when they weren't to stay wed—

He swooped the case back, surprising her. But he did it only to pluck out the ring and capture her hand. "Wear—it," he grated.

Was he *nervous*? Jane could always tell when Hugh was uncomfortable or discomfited because his shoulders went back. They were presently jammed back. "This is what you wanted."

"Why would you think that?" Had he possibly recalled her description of her dream wedding ring? She nibbled her lip as she awaited his answer.

He muttered, "You told me, lass."

He remembered? If a man could recall such minute details all these years later, then perhaps they had at least been the friends she'd thought them.

When he slipped it on her finger, she shivered—she didn't know why. He appeared relieved that she'd accepted it. And now that he was at ease, she began to react to him, finding herself relaxing as well.

No matter how hard she fought it.

Damn him, they'd always been like that—able to settle in with each other in easy companionship. Now it came more slowly, little by little, like a feather wafting down, but in the end, the amity was the same. Damn, damn, damn. . . .

Could a woman *miss* a man who brought her pain? Then somehow ignore all that pain and be excited to be near him again?

A quick consideration indicated: *possibly.*

Maybe she was simply grateful that for a space of many minutes, she'd forgotten about her anxious feeling. Or, more likely, she just liked the ring. *Typical, typical Jane.*

She sighed. A near-acceptance of a proposal and a kiss before nine; a marriage, another kiss, and a ring before noon. She wished she could say that all these had occurred with only one man.

Sixteen

—◆—

"*B*e forewarned, Hugh," Jane said, when he held out his hands to assist her from the carriage. "I will now place my waist into your grip. Please don't take it as teasing or making merry with fire in any way."

Ever since she'd entreated him to stop at this inn, he'd been wearing a scowl, and at her words it deepened, a glaring contrast to her own jewelry-induced blithe mood.

When he grasped her waist and swung her down, she asked, "Hugh, why are you so averse to this place? It looks perfectly acceptable."

Hugh still held her. "It is. But you have to go through the common room to get upstairs."

"You've been here before?" she asked.

He gave a short nod, his dark eyes raking over her décolletage, and she reacted yet again to his avid gaze. All day in the carriage, she'd alternately relaxed and tensed under his stare. After that kiss—which she'd worked to convince herself was a fluke of perfection, a devastating anomaly—she'd felt her breasts grow sensitive, swelling against the lace cups above her corset.

And while he'd studied her today, she'd done so to him, though much more circumspectly. She'd noted that those gashes on his face and the scars on his neck and hands didn't square with the occupation he professed, nor had the way he'd struck Freddie. Freddie was a tall man, yet Hugh had sent him flying—and he'd done it with the ease of an afterthought.

Jane had been to pugilist matches before and had seen the great, hulking fighters with their meaty fists, yet she'd put everything she owned on Hugh against the lot of them. That didn't fit. Nor did the way his muscular body had been honed as though from hard labor.

She was convinced that he wasn't just a businessman. What he *might* be instead eluded her—

"Can you no' cover yourself more?" he grated, finally releasing her. "The patrons here have no need to see you."

"I don't have any clothing that's not in my trunks."

"No' even for your hair?" He frowned at the loosened tendrils.

She wasn't a bonnet type of woman, and a hat was impractical for carriage travel. "Hugh, I haven't complained about the rigorous pace you've set. But if you continue to keep me out here in this damp night, famished and weary, I shall begin."

He exhaled a long breath, took her hand, then dragged her inside as though they were in a race. The common room they entered was, well, common. Boisterous patrons swilled gin and lunged for barmaids. Jane watched, impressed, as one escaped capture with a swift swish of her hips.

Of course, Jane had been in much seedier places before with her cousins. If all of London seemed to be caught up with seeking thrills, then the Eight had made an art form out of successfully locating them. After disguising them-

selves in men's clothing and pasting on fake mous-
taches—which probably served no purpose other than to
make them chortle with laughter—they'd visited bawdy
wax museums. They'd gambled in the east-end gaming
halls. They'd gawked wide-eyed at lascivious pictorial
shows.

For Jane, this common room was a bit tame.

When Hugh had to slow to wend through a crush of
patrons, too inebriated to dart out of his way, a drunkard
approached Jane. He stumbled after her, leaning in, looking for all the world as if he wanted to lay his head on her
breasts.

"Here, Hugh," she said, squeezing his hand. "You might
want to—"

Hugh wheeled around, yanking her behind him, drawing back a fist in one fluid movement. Her eyes went
wide, just as the room grew quiet.

She touched his arm and murmured, "Hugh . . . don't.
It's hardly sporting."

Jane's cousin Sam had once described Jane's temperament as fierce, but even Jane was startled at Hugh's deadly
demeanor and swift aggression. An importer? And she
was the queen of Egyptian artifacts.

When Hugh lowered his fist, the drunk lurched back,
mumbling apologies—and, Jane feared, wetting himself a
bit.

Hugh kept her locked behind him in a vise-like grip as
he scanned the room slowly. It occurred to her that she
was with the biggest and most fearsome-looking man in
this place. And the patrons all seemed to know it, as they
peered at him warily and avoided looking at her alto-
gether.

When Hugh relaxed his hold and turned to offer her his arm, she proudly took it. As the room returned to normal, she and Hugh made their way to a salon off the common room. His body was still thrumming, as if not hitting that clod had taken much from him. She tried to make light of it. "My darling, the perilous world of imports has hardened you—"

"MacCarrick!" a lovely older blonde called as she exited a back room. Her eyes sparkled as she sashayed up to Hugh. "I couldn't believe it when they said you'd returned to my modest establishment," she all but purred as she took his hand. She was buxom, with a sexy French accent and a bodice more riskily low-cut than even Jane had ever dared.

Jane now fully comprehended Hugh's reluctance to stay here. She suspected he and this curvaceous French woman had been lovers.

Hugh extracted his hand from the woman's, then presented her to Jane. "Jane, this is Lysette Nadine. Lysette, this is my . . . wife, Jane . . . MacCarrick."

Jane thought of all those times she'd written her name as Jane MacCarrick, and sighed. Hugh could scarcely utter the words. The pleasure that used to warm her turned into an annoying jab.

"Wife?" The woman's lips parted, but she swiftly recovered. "Must be a recent acquisition. You were unwed six months ago when I last saw you."

Hugh shrugged without interest. So they hadn't seen each other for that long?

Lysette lowered her voice to say, "I'd heard you'd sworn never to marry."

"Circumstances changed," he replied, and Jane knew

she was only dipping a toe into the undercurrent of their conversation. *Sworn never to marry?*

This Lysette had big, ingenuous blue eyes—but she was actually very alert, taking in details, missing nothing. When Lysette rudely looked her up and down, Jane simply smiled at her as she might an unruly child seeking attention. She was confident enough in herself and, strangely, in Hugh's attraction to her over the voluptuous woman— even if they'd been lovers. However, this woman's misplaced possessiveness couldn't go unanswered. Though Hugh had warned her not to tease him, Jane sidled closer to him, rubbing her cheek against his arm. She felt him tense immediately.

Raising an eyebrow as if in challenge, Lysette asked, "How many rooms do you desire, Hugh?"

"One," Jane said before Hugh could answer. *A challenge?* Jane's hand traced up Hugh's back, passing a pistol in a holster she hadn't even known he carried, and her fingers settled about his neck, nails languidly scratching just above his collar. His body shot even tighter with tension. "And we'd like a bath and our dinner brought there."

Lysette looked at Hugh as if expecting him to naysay Jane.

Jane placed her other hand flat on his muscular chest, displaying her ring. "Have I overstepped, *husband*?"

He glowered down at her, but he did tell Lysette, "One."

Lysette gave her a tight smile. "I will show you up myself."

Once inside the surprisingly spacious room, Jane hopped on the bed and patted it. "Yes, darling, this will do nicely." She gave Hugh a lascivious look and a teasing growl in her throat. "And I wager we'll even sleep well on it, too."

He and Lysette both shot her looks. Hugh's was one of warning. Lysette's was one of promised retaliation.

Finally Lysette huffed out, with a halfhearted, "If you need anything . . ."

As soon as the door closed, Hugh asked, "More games?"

"Shouldn't we act as if we're married?" Jane collapsed back on the bed, raising her hands above her to sneak another glance at her ring. She'd decided she would definitely keep the ring, even if she wasn't keeping the groom with whom it was associated. "This is how I will behave with my final husband when he comes into the rotation. I'll be eager to flirt with and touch him. And I won't take it lightly when another woman tries to do the same."

"You'd be possessive of your husband?"

"Quite so." She eased up to her elbows. "Especially when it's obvious that you—I mean, *he* has some type of history with a buxom innkeeper who's intent on making me feel like an outsider in your—I mean, *their* little party of two." She raised an eyebrow. "Care to enlighten me about your history with the Frenchie?"

"No, no' particularly."

"Hugh, sometime soon you're going to burn to know something from me. I won't be inclined to answer you if you continue to brush aside my questions."

Before he could reply, a maid knocked and entered to set up a copper bathtub behind a dressing screen.

Under his breath, Hugh said, "Do you need her to help you undress before she leaves?" At her look, he added, "I thought you might be missing your lady's maid."

"Oh, since you wouldn't let me take her with us? It's no matter—anything I require, you can provide. Besides, I'm sure you're quite well versed in undressing women."

Behind the screen, the maid coughed. Hugh gazed at the ceiling, as if praying for patience.

Jane ignored him, studying the maid behind the flimsy screen, noting that she could see every detail of her form in shadow or clearly through the slim gaps between the panels. If Hugh stayed in the room while Jane bathed, he would see the same. Jane shrugged. She wasn't going to develop a sudden case of modesty when she was traveling and confined with a man indefinitely.

Once the red-faced maid had carried in several cans of steaming water to fill the bath and retreated from the room, Jane crossed to the screen, slipping behind it. Was she undressing a trifle slower than usual? She thought she heard a low groan when her petticoats dropped, and a louder one when she slid her shift up her body, over her breasts, then up over her head.

Oh, her poor, poor back was *so* travel-fatigued. She raised her arms above her and stretched.

Hugh paced the room like a caged tiger.

When she finally got in the tub, Jane softly moaned with pleasure—not feigned, as she adored taking baths. Then she lounged back to reflect on her insane day.

She recalled the disappointment in Freddie's eyes and immediately felt a pang. She'd been wracked with guilt over the way things had turned out, and his expression had nearly been her undoing. Adding to her guilt was the fact that just seconds before Freddie had overtaken them, she had been on the verge of forgetting why she'd teased MacCarrick in the first place.

Even as impulsive and impetuous as she was, she was still was reeling. And it was by no means over. Now she was setting off on a grand adventure with Hugh.

Jane believed he was finally taking her to Carrickliffe far in the north of Scotland. After he'd described it to her years ago, she'd always longed to visit it. Now she wanted to go there to experience the place that produced men like Hugh.

She'd been to Scotland, but never north of Edinburgh, never into the wild Highlands. Was Hugh finally going to make good on a promise?

She felt out of sorts—naturally she would, after the day she was having—but she was especially concerned about her burgeoning fascination with her new husband. After seeing Hugh so beautifully menacing downstairs, and after feeling the pistol holstered at his back, she was burning to know more about him.

When he paced by once more, she stretched her leg up and smoothed bath oil down it. He stopped pacing, and she knew he could see her. In the past, she never would have worried that he was the type of man who might yank down the screen at the sight and ravish her.

Now, she was forced to wonder.

Exactly who *was* Hugh now? If he wasn't in trade, why lie about it? Unless he'd been doing something illegal—perhaps with his younger brother, Courtland, the infamous mercenary? She raised an eyebrow. What if *Hugh* was a mercenary?

She sighed. The problem with this fascination was that fascination led to feelings, feelings led to love, and love led to misery. She'd endured this sequence before and would give anything to avoid it.

He was right. He wasn't the same lad. The quiet, steady Hugh she'd fallen in love with was gone forever. And she didn't know how to handle this new ruthless, intense man.

He'd warned her that toying with him would be like playing with fire, and her antics in the coach this morning had definitely earned her a nice singe.

She tilted her head to the side and frowned. *But then, when have I ever hesitated to play with fire?*

Seventeen

---

*H*ugh almost asked himself what he'd done to deserve this torment, but the answer would be too lengthy.

She was running her hands up and down her long, long legs. He suspected she knew he could see, though she was such a sensual person that he'd wager she rubbed her legs as lingeringly when she was alone.

What else did she linger over?

The thought of her running her fingers over her sex . . . He had to gnash his teeth as his erection stiffened even more. He'd wager anything he owned that she did indeed touch herself like that whenever the need arose. Did she ever think of him? He unfailingly did of her. After Hugh had seen her last night, even his beaten, fatigued body had hungered for her, and he'd taken himself in hand.

She had always been forward-thinking about sexual matters, and he knew she was filled with passion—passion that would need an outlet.

He remembered Bidworth buttoning her blouse. Had Bidworth fulfilled her needs?

Hugh should have killed him.

How long before he could escape this impossible situation? *Hurry up, Ethan. Else I'll go mad.* Striving to think of other things, distracting things, he paced to the window.

Hugh hadn't wanted to stay here. There were too many people he knew, and one who was privy to exactly what he was—Lysette, Grey's ex-lover. But they wouldn't have reached the next inn until nearly dawn, and once Jane had begun insisting, Hugh had thought he might as well try to extract some information from Lysette about Grey.

Lysette had always been partial to Hugh, and Grey had left her to be with a whore.

Yet the incident in the common room had proved this was a bad idea. Hugh should have had his arm around Jane's shoulders, but he'd been dragging her along to get through the crowds. And Jane had taken one look at Hugh's expression as he fought the urge to deal the drunkard a blow, and she'd known—not precisely what he was, but definitely what he wasn't.

He heard her rise from the water. Bounder that he was, he leaned back. When he caught a glimpse of her, he had to bite back a curse and shuffle his feet to keep his balance. In the space between the panels, he could see her damp back and hissed in a breath at the sight of the spot where her surprisingly generous arse met her long, slim leg.

He closed his eyes briefly, berating himself for looking—even as he imagined striding forward to palm that taut cleft as he ran his mouth down her neck.

He was stunned anew at how shapely she'd become. Her arms and legs were still slender, her torso as well, but her breasts and arse were plump and seemed to taunt his hands to cup them. *Pull her to the bed, cover her wet, slick body with mine, take her furiously—*

The maid knocked once more, possibly saving them from disaster, and entered to set out their dinner on the room's dining table. Hugh stayed facing the window since his cock was stiff as wood. When the girl left, he sat so Jane wouldn't notice. He found the fare was simple, but the wine appeared to be a tolerable vintage.

A few minutes later, Jane emerged from behind the screen, having donned a deep blue dressing gown and wrap. She wore the wrap open enough that he could see the pale tops of her breasts. When he could drag his gaze away from them, he saw that her shining hair was loose, with damp tendrils curling all about her face. Her flawless skin was pinkened, her eyes bright.

She was elegant and fine, the lines of her face and body so pure. For a moment he just wanted to pretend that he was a lucky bastard who'd somehow *truly* landed her as wife. He wanted to pretend he saw her fresh from the bath at his leisure, and dined with her every night before they went to bed together.

Here he was with a woman so lovely she'd make any man conscious of his words and actions, concerned about how she perceived him. She would unnerve most men. And yet she was still *Jane*.

And when she allowed it, it was so damned easy being around her.

"My wedding night." She sauntered to her seat. "Darling, it is *just* as I've always dreamed."

She wasn't going to allow it.

He felt a flare of anger. Everything he was doing was for her benefit. Now, if she would just allow him to do his job unhindered . . . "My wedding night as well. I'm just as disappointed."

"Disappointed in the circumstance—or your bride?" Never taking her eyes from his, she took a sip of the wine he'd poured, then dabbed her tongue to her bottom lip.

He shifted in his seat. "Any man would be proud to call you wife."

"Then, does this disappointment have anything to do with the fact that you'd sworn never to marry?"

"Partly."

"Partly? So why else. . . ?" She trailed off, eyes widening. "You have a lover, don't you? One you didn't want to forsake? That's it, isn't it? You already have a woman."

"I'm . . . between," he said, hedging. He had never formed an attachment with another woman—didn't think he'd slept with the same one twice. If he got angry enough at the world, he might drink and take a woman to try to forget, but it just worsened his resentment.

Court had once asked Hugh why he bedded so few. *If you felt like I did after, you would no' either.* "I just never had any intention of marrying—"

"Never?" she asked in a strange tone.

"It was not in my plans," he said.

She drank deeply. "*Between*, then, is it? I'll bet you've had a lot of women."

"I'll no' speak of this with you."

"You used to tell me your secrets."

Never the big ones. Though he'd burned to.

Hugh had often considered telling Jane about that terrible and weighty curse, but knew she would scoff. Jane could be irrational, temperamental, unreasonable—but she was never, *never* fanciful. He could just imagine her smirking and playing along: "*Then I must eschew your cursed company, darling, for I quite fancy being alive.*"

And now, why would he tell her? The closeness they'd shared was gone.

"So, Hugh, what do you *truly* do? You're not a businessman. Unless a nefarious import attacked your face?"

He raised his eyebrows at that. She was such a curious female, and one who had an infuriating habit of deducing and then deciding fixedly on her own theories. That could help him now. "Knowing you, you've worked out a theory as to what I am."

She put her hand out, palm up, motioning for him to give her his hand. Before he even had time to think better of it, he'd reached across the table. She captured his hand in hers, then ran the soft pads of her fingers over the calloused, scarred skin of his palm. Such a simple touch, but she made it sensual.

Glancing up, she met his eyes. "I believe you're a mercenary."

She was getting close.

"Is that what you do?" Increasing the pressure, she ran her forefinger down the center of his palm, then back up.

His voice was rough when he asked, "What makes you think that?"

"It make sense. Father said you'd just come from travels with your brother Courtland on the Continent. Court is a known soldier of fortune—we've all heard of him wreaking havoc down there with a band of Highlanders. You must be one of them."

Hugh *had* been in Andorra riding with his brother's men, but he'd only been there to help Court. They'd fought the Orden de Rechazado—the Order of the Disavowed, a band of fanatical assassins bent on killing Court and Annalía.

"That would be how you cut your face," Jane continued, with a feathery brush over the back of his hand. "And that's how you saved up some money."

Some money? Hugh had turned his earnings into wealth with meticulous planning and calculated speculation. He was rich by anyone's standards, with a grand seaside estate in Scotland. Her words sparked another first for Hugh—the unfamiliar need to boast, to impress her. Which was purposeless. "Why do you no' believe I work in your father's business?"

"Hugh, I'm not a complete imbecile." She tapped her finger against the worst scar on the back of his hand. "Look at your hands. And look at how muscular and fit you are. You did not hone a physique like that by working in *commerce*."

He checked a flush of pleasure at her inadvertent compliment and said, "I get outdoors a lot."

"I've been to pugilist matches with my cousins." Her wee hands worked his into a fist, and she studied it before meeting his gaze once more. "I know what those fighters are capable of, yet after I saw the way you hit Freddie, I'd put you up against them with stacked odds."

Another roundabout compliment. He thought. "I had two brothers. I received a lot of practice. You ken that I used to fight with Ethan more hours than no'."

Of course, she was aware he was being evasive, but he knew that was only making her dig in her heels. "Father covered for your career as a mercenary, didn't he?" She released his hand abruptly. "The youngest son gone bad would be met with a clucked tongue and a head shake. But two brothers? That would start to affect Ethan's reputation, and he has a title."

Ethan's reputation? She had no idea. How such a cold-blooded bastard could somehow keep his deeds secret amazed Hugh. Especially since Ethan had never bothered to try to. Still, he only shrugged.

She leaned back. "Hugh MacCarrick, the mercenary. Unless you want to offer another explanation."

"No, no' at all." *Take that one, lass, and run with it.*

"What do mercenaries do?"

"Mercenaries fight for money—professional soldiers."

"Have you gotten to travel all over the world?" she asked, her tone suddenly wistful.

"No' to many places you'd want to tour."

"It must be exciting at times." When he said nothing, she admitted, "I've always wanted to travel to exotic places. Quin has promised again and again to take Claudia and me on a grand adventure, but he's always so busy."

Quin, take them traveling? Only if the two lasses wanted a tour of the world's upscale brothels.

"Do you ever get scared?" she asked. "During the fighting?"

Hugh's objective was to avoid fighting. "Even if I did, men doona admit to things like that."

"So you've been in wars? How many people have you killed?"

He ignored her question. "You're no' eating, though you told me you were famished."

"I am." At his look, she amended, "I'm eating distilled grapes. Answer me, won't you?"

"I have no' kept a count." Grey had taught him that. He'd said, *One day, Scot, you'll wake up, and you won't be anything more than that number.*

"What *did* happen to your face?"

She would bring that up again. She was pale and perfect in her silk.

When Grey had begun sinking farther into the abyss, he'd loved to remind Hugh how far out of reach a woman like her was for a man like Hugh—a man with a beaten, pained body that made him feel so damn old and weary, a man who was awkward in social situations.

A man who'd crossed a line from which there was no going back.

"I was cut by falling rocks." After he'd exploded a mountaintop to blow up the Rechazado camp—while they were still in it. "There was an accident." True, he hadn't *meant* to be in the way of a shower of slate.

Hugh had killed thirty Rechazados, dead in an instant. *She has no idea what kind of man sits across from her.*

"On the job?" She looked as if she was truly curious about him. But it wasn't genuine interest. She only delved to gather what Hugh refused to give her—and *only* because he'd refused. Jane loved nothing more than fighting for something she wanted.

He took a drink of wine, remembering that he was the fool who'd encouraged that drive.

Once, when she was fifteen, Hugh and a grumbling Court had taken her to a nearby archery tournament. When the other female contestants discovered that she'd entered, none would compete against her.

Hugh had seen the sharp disappointment in her eyes, a glimpse of a vulnerability that was so rarely seen. It had torn at him, and he'd found himself telling her under his breath, "*Challenge the men, lass.*"

She'd brought a bloody medal home.

It hadn't been her first—there was a reason the women knew they'd be trounced—but Jane had stared at it as though it were, as if with that one came realization. She'd clutched it in two hands and met his gaze. "I want *more*."

"You've the skill for it," he'd said, hedging, saddened. He'd known there weren't many more for a young lass to go out and fight for—no matter how badly she *needed* that fight. . . .

"That's why you don't want to be married?" she asked. "Your job would prevent it."

"Jane, why is it that I'm always the one being interrogated?"

"At least tell me where we're going."

"If I'd told you this morning, would you have told Bidworth?"

"No," she said quickly, then admitted, "Well, I might have. But Freddie wouldn't have told a soul."

"Then no, I will no' tell you." When she opened her mouth to argue, he made his voice like steel. "No more questions."

She sighed, glancing around the room, visibly restless. She didn't seem to notice when her wrap slid from her smooth, pale shoulder, while every muscle in his body tensed. The thin nightdress beneath clung to her breast, and he found he couldn't drag his riveted gaze from it. The material was so stark against her fair skin, and he imagined brushing the silk down her shoulders, letting it whisper over her nipples and slide down her lithe body. He exhaled a breath and hoped it sounded exasperated instead of enthralled. "Put your wrap back on."

She glanced down with a frown, then studied his reaction. "I need to leave it off. Because it's warm in here, and I can't *ask* you to crack a window."

"Put it back on."

She quirked an eyebrow. "You stared at my breasts so much in the coach today, you should appreciate when more of them is displayed."

"I admit I take pleasure in looking at you." He wouldn't even bother trying to deny that. Even now, her small nipples jutted hard against the fabric, and he imagined taking one between his lips, feeling it swell and throb as he sucked it. He glanced away and said quietly, "You're a beautiful woman."

When he turned back, he thought she had blushed at his comment.

"But seeing you like this makes me desire to do more, a desire you doona share and one we canna indulge."

She tilted her head, seeming to weigh his words very carefully, then said, "What if I told you I did share that desire?"

"I'd answer that you're a merciless flirt, and then I'd remark on how easily you have forgotten Bidworth." *In the space of an afternoon. Inconstant woman.*

Her eyes narrowed at his words, but she didn't offer an answer.

Not even a *show* of loyalty. And to think Hugh had worried that he might have to see her pine for the man.

Hugh wouldn't want a woman like Jane, even if he could have her.

Didn't matter. He was only here to protect her, and her games would get in the way. In a deadly calm tone, he said, "I've given you warning. You know what will happen."

She made no move to cover herself. This was just another battle of wills with her. Yet another.

But he wasn't the same compromising lad he'd been. Couldn't be, even if he wanted to be. The things he'd seen had changed him. The things he'd done had tainted him.

He'd killed with his bare hands.

He shot to his feet and crossed to her, tossing her onto the table. He'd only planned to stand before her and yank her wrap up, yet he found himself grabbing her slender arms, pinning them to her sides. He could still back away; why was he drawing closer?

No good can come of this. Because he was a hardened killer, obsessed for the last decade with an inconstant woman. One who loved to provoke him. A woman he could not touch, specifically because he'd married her. *No good . . .*

She seemed to wait breathlessly to discover what he would do. Hugh had no idea either. When he eased his hips between her thighs, she began trembling. He was learning that her skin was sensitive, her entire body so damned responsive. *Taking her would be like handling a firebrand.*

What if he sought to make love to her, and she *let* him? He swallowed hard, his breaths coming fast from the mere thought.

To finally possess her.

With a defeated groan, he leaned forward to briefly catch her sensitive earlobe between his lips, flicking it with his tongue. She hissed in a breath and shivered. With one hand flat on the small of her back, he tugged at her hair with the other, making her arch till she rested back with her elbows on the table.

Dazed with intent, he leaned down to press his mouth to her silk-covered nipple.

Eighteen

———— •◆• ————

$\mathcal{A}$s Hugh moved his lips down her breast, he rasped harsh words in Gaelic against her skin, seeming lost, as if he was so absorbed in what he did that he truly had no comprehension of it.

She threaded her fingers through his hair, cradling him to her as she sighed with pleasure.

This was what she was missing with Freddie. And, no, she could *not* live without it.

It wasn't only that he'd made her desire him; she sensed he *needed* her, or needed something from her. She was desperate to give him whatever that was.

Thoughts of the future and memories of the past all dimmed before the hunger she'd seen in his eyes.

Still gently tugging her hair to make her arch, he nuzzled her hard nipple, rasping against it, "Damn it, you're supposed tae tell me tae stop." After a hesitation, he closed his mouth over the aching peak, then began languidly circling his tongue around it.

"*Oh, my God,*" she whispered in wonder.

He glanced up, eyes dark, measuring her responses, studying her. "You like that?" At her helpless cry, he moved to her other breast. "You think that I'll react the same way to your teasing as I did years ago." He repeated the same tender exploration, saying against her breast, "You're going to push until I finally break."

"B-but in the past—"

"In the past, I was young and honorable. Now I'm old enough to know what I need and dishonorable enough"—he softly tugged on her nipple with his teeth, making her gasp and arch harder into his mouth—"*to take it.*"

"Hugh," she murmured, "Hugh, please."

"Do you want me to take it, lass? Push me more, and you'll soon feel me sinking into your soft body." He pulled back, met her eyes. Whatever he saw there made him recoil from her. Stabbing his fingers through his hair, he opened his mouth, then closed it. Finally, he bit out, "Stay here. Lock the door behind me and doona leave this room."

"Why?" she whispered.

"I never thought you would be like this," he grated. "No' with me." Then he stalked out and slammed the door behind him.

She wasn't supposed to be like *what* with him? *How* was she wrong?

He remained outside, leaning against the door. He would have to wait there before going downstairs—she'd seen his thick erection bulging against his trousers and knew he'd have to get his body under control. Hers was just as ungovernable.

As Jane sat panting on the edge of the dinner table, a fork parallel to her thigh and a glass of wine perilously close to the hand she'd thrown back to support her, she realized something dire. The kiss in the carriage hadn't been an anomaly.

She and Hugh were going to be like this every time they were together.

She'd known Hugh would be a skilled lover—he was accomplished at everything he did, and whenever he'd assisted her from a carriage or into her saddle, he'd handled her as if she were made of glass. But she'd never imagined that the towering Highlander would be so . . . *erotic.*

He'd made her *burn* for him, made her wet and aching between her thighs. Again.

His kisses were slow and devilish, his lips firm and carnal. Could he guess that his threat to, oh, dear Lord, *sink into her soft body*, made her yearn for him even more? She'd almost cried, "Yes, do it!"

She thought he hit something outside their room, then she heard him finally leave.

She hadn't wanted to charm and cajole Hugh into staying married, because she knew that he likely would leave her behind again, married in truth or no. And she'd been so angry with him for putting her in the position to be hurt all over again, and had vowed that she would protect her *still* raw emotions.

Now she reasoned that they were both hurting at this moment. Though she didn't want to *stay* married to him—she hadn't wavered that much—she didn't want to be separated from him right now. Not so soon. She half-expected him to disappear for another ten years, and wasn't nearly ready for that to happen again.

Get him back here. . . . Give him what he needs.

Decided, she smoothed her gown, pulled her wrapper closed, downed a glass of wine in one unladylike gulp, then made for the door. She glanced out, but he wasn't on the landing.

Looking both ways, she hurried down the landing and

peeked over the railing, down into the boisterous common room. Hugh sat at a table draining some liquid, his hand white from clenching the mug.

She exhaled in relief. She wasn't alone in this feeling— she'd affected him just as much as he had her.

Perhaps he'd never returned for her because of his dangerous occupation. Her eyes widened. Perhaps he'd always wanted to but couldn't—

Her lips parted when she saw Lysette saunter up to him, draping her arm around him. The woman drew in close, whispering something in Hugh's ear as she ran her hand up and down his back.

He pushed her away, but Jane saw to her shock and horror that he did so only to follow Lysette to a back room.

Nineteen

———◆———

"*M*acCarrick, it's been too long," Lysette said, closing the door behind them.

"Do you have information about Grey, or no'?" Hugh's voice was still rough from the pleasure of kissing Jane, his mind still in turmoil.

When Jane had been pleading before, Hugh had looked into her eyes and seen something he'd never expected. She hadn't been pleading with him . . . to *stop*. She'd wanted him to take her, had been *asking* him to.

Never. Never was it supposed to be a variable that Jane might desire me back.

He strode to the whiskey decanter and helped himself, then stared down into the liquid. He'd counted on the fact that even if he lost control, Jane would remind him with a stiff-wristed slap that she would not welcome his attentions. Without that check, he was doomed.

"No pleasantries?" Lysette said. When he turned an unbending look on her, she asked blithely, "Why would I have information about Grey?"

Women and their games. Hugh was sick of them. "Because you slept with him for years. And I know you've been keeping tabs on him since he left you."

Her look turned calculating. "If you want to know anything about Grey, then tell me who *she* is."

"You owe this to Weyland regardless." Weyland arranged loans for people like her—information gatherers—to open shops and taverns and inns at crossroads all over Europe, like nets. Lysette was good at her job—she was observant and intuitive—and in exchange for information, she made a good living.

"Doesn't Weyland have a daughter named Jane? One who is reportedly lovely?"

He swigged, knowing he wouldn't drink more than a glass. "One and the same."

"Now it all makes sense. Everyone expects Grey to strike out at Weyland, and you show up here married to his daughter, taking her out of London. You'd do just about anything for the old man. Apparently, you'll brook a marriage in name only."

"So sure it's a marriage of convenience?"

"Yes, when I find you here in *my* room—away from your new bride." When he only drank again, Lysette said, "Grey told me once that you were in love with her."

Who *hadn't* Grey told? How many people pitied him his feelings for Jane Weyland? Christ, Jane *MacCarrick*. Hell, he pitied himself for how much he liked the sound of that. "Grey said a lot of things that were no' true. You of all people should know that."

"It's obvious she's playing with you. That one cares nothing for you."

"And why would you say that?" he asked, striving for an uninterested tone.

"When I was flirting with you earlier, she looked at me as if she was amused. The last thing women regard me with is amusement, especially when I'm draped over their husbands."

"Perhaps she's confident."

"Arrogant."

Possibly.

"You reach too high with that one."

"Lysette, you are the third person today to express that exact sentiment. It's ingrained." Ethan, Bidworth, Lysette. Hell, even Jane's servants recognized the divide between him and Jane.

Lysette approached him, running her finger down his chest. It left him cold, and he drew her hand away with an expression of distaste, but her other hand was busy easing his shirttail from his trousers. "You should be riding a woman tonight. Even if the arrogant English chit would let you, she still wouldn't be woman enough for a man like you."

Lysette had no idea. He'd had a glimpse of Jane's unfettered passion just moments ago, and it had staggered him.

Hugh exhaled and took her wrist, removing her hand. "Doona speak badly of her in front of me. We were friends long before this. Besides, I took a vow." Until their marriage was annulled, he'd keep it.

She pouted. "You'd deny yourself for a marriage of convenience? When I've been attempting to seduce you for years?"

Hugh had noticed her flirtations. Might even have taken her up on it. She had all the qualifications—in other words, she looked nothing like Jane. But she'd been sharing his friend's bed, and Hugh had never needed it badly enough to lose his head as some did.

"Let me give you what she won't. Or can't." Her voice went low. "I can do things to your body that will make you wonder how you've lived without me for so long."

Here he had a willing, attractive, and, apparently, wicked bed partner who'd gladly accept a night with him. And the only desire he had was that Jane would give a damn if he did it. Lysette ran the tip of her tongue over her bottom lip, gaze locked on him.

Knowing what he'd just come from, he felt vaguely insulted at Lysette's interest. He still had Jane's taste on his lips and could almost still feel her warm, soft flesh against his tongue. Hugh had learned long ago that it was of little use trying to find a substitute for her.

He set the glass down. "If you're no' going to give me information on Grey, then I've no other reason to be back here."

"Where are you going?"

"Back to my arrogant English chit. Who could teach you a thing or two about seduction."

"You're still in love with her," she said stiffly. "You're different. Already." She gave a humorless laugh. "You're satisfied with the mere *idea* that she is yours." When Lysette cast him a pitying look—yet another to add to the count today—Hugh wanted to roar that Jane had wanted him, too.

He turned to the door.

"Oh, Hugh. You stupid man! People like her don't want people like us. I know this. Your Jane Weyland might flirt, she might even desire you. But you'll *never* have her heart."

He bit out over his shoulder, "Jane *MacCarrick*." For however long.

"And what happens when she finds out you're a cold-blooded killer?"

He slowed.

"What will she think of you then?"

He couldn't imagine. Killing as a soldier was a celebrated thing. Even the mercenary she thought him sounded better than an assassin. Assassins hid and struck from the shadows. That's what people believed. Generally that was true, but Hugh had also had to fight for his life more times than he wanted to remember.

He feared that even if she could get past all the killing he'd done, fierce Jane still might find his means . . . cowardly.

"Even if she wanted you, you can't go back to a life like the one she lives."

Lysette was right. The odds were against Hugh ever settling back into society, finding those day-to-day rhythms. They called it *reverting*—when battle-weary soldiers or assassins too long in the field went back to civilian life and somehow made a go of it. It was extremely rare, especially for someone like Hugh, who had always been adrift in social situations anyway.

Just as he'd made it out of the doorway, stabbing his shirttail into his pants, she said, "Hugh, wait!" She hurried over to him, putting her hand on his chest to stay him. "Grey reached France this week."

He shut the door behind them once more. "How do you know?"

"Because the woman I solicited help from to keep tabs on him showed up dead there."

"Does no' mean—"

"Her throat was slashed so violently, her head nearly came off."

Grey. No doubt of it. "He's out of his mind."

"Even so, he's still lethal. And he hates you and Ethan for what you did to him."

"You were right in league with us," Hugh was quick to remind her.

"But something else happened that night. What did you do to him?"

"I've no sodding idea," he lied, finding it easy with her.

"If he's coming after Jane, it's just a matter of time before he finds you two."

"He'll seek you out as well, Lysette. You canna reason with him, and he's beyond saving. I hope you're prepared."

"I will be." Her expression resigned, she said, "Aren't we a pair? A coquette about to be taken down by an assassin, and an assassin about to be taken down by a coquette."

When Hugh returned to their room, Jane lay curled up in bed with nearly all the lamps out, though he could tell by the tenseness of her form that she was still awake.

He sat and watched her for more than an hour, and eventually she fell asleep, but it wasn't long before she grew as restless as she was during waking hours, tossing and turning. Her eyes moved rapidly behind her lids. He wondered what it would be like to see her utterly relaxed.

A real husband could join her and pull her to his chest, pet her, soothe away whatever dream gripped her. He wouldn't fear that she might want him to make love to her for comfort, or that he'd need to for the same reason.

Hugh wasn't a real husband. No matter how badly he wanted to be.

He reached for his bag and drew out the *Leabhar*. Ethan was right. Reading it would strengthen his resolve. It would remind him of the consequences of his actions and keep him from musing about what it would have been like to take Jane right on this table.

Walk with death or walk alone. What more did Hugh need to see?

The three brothers all walked with death, just as had been predicted. Court was a mercenary, and somehow Hugh and Ethan had met the one man in England who could guide them into their current occupations—Ethan, a jack of all lethal trades who was called in to deal with *unpleasantries*, and Hugh, an assassin.

Hugh had been fortunate. He'd only been dispatched to kill grown men, and on each mark, he'd agreed that they'd needed to be taken out. Still, the faces began to accumulate. The grueling hours of preparation and the innate loneliness of the job took their toll.

Always, in the back of his mind, he imagined the look on Jane's face if she found out.

On his first kill, he'd hesitated, knowing that if he pulled the trigger, he would cross a line and could never go back. But he had done it. He'd killed in cold blood, purposefully, determinedly. How dare he think to entwine his life with hers in any way?

The idea flashed through his mind that there was still time to summon Ethan to come take her away—from himself. He dismissed the idea. Hugh wanted Jane protected—not terrified.

Lost in thought, he barely heard her soft moan. She

still slept, but she'd turned onto her back. One arm slowly fell over her head, stretching her gown taut, outlining her breasts in cool silk.

Another soft murmur and a very sensual shiver accompanied her quickened breaths.

This was not happening. She couldn't be dreaming of something erotic, but her body and her movements told him otherwise. Could she possibly be dreaming of him? Of the way he'd kissed her earlier? No! He couldn't let himself think like that.

No good can come of this.

Yet, as he looked from the book back to her, he realized his resolve was already faltering. *She would need an outlet for all that passion. Like handling a firebrand. . . .*

She raised her other hand and her ring glittered in the lamplight as her fingers brushed the side of her breast. He swallowed hard. He could give her an outlet, provide her release. His hands were fists as he fought not to touch her. If he were truly married to her, he could wake her by sliding his shaft into her. He'd find her already wet, already close, and he would slowly rock her to orgasm. But she wasn't his to reach for in the night. All he could do was spy on her from the shadows.

She turned her face into her auburn hair spread over the pillow, nuzzling the curls as if she desired to feel them against her skin as much as he did. A lock tangled around her pale neck, and he rose, reaching down to tug the thick strand free.

Unable to help himself, he carefully lay beside her. As ever, he had to gnash his teeth against the pain that stabbed at him whenever he finally let his body be at rest. Everyone believed rising in the morning was hell on old injuries, but relaxing for sleep was just as bad, especially after what he'd put himself through over the last few days.

At length, once the pain had subsided to bearable, he levered himself up on an elbow to gaze down at her. Surrendering to the need to touch her, he brushed the backs of his fingers over her cheek. She stilled, but didn't wake, her breaths growing deep and even.

I could take care of you, he thought. *In all ways.* Some part of him had always believed that if he worked hard enough, he could give her whatever she needed. If things were different, he could try to win her, to prove that he was the man for her.

He marveled at the sweep of her dark lashes, the gentle parting of her lips. Even after all this time, he was still fascinated with her, still filled with affection for her.

Nothing would ever change that.

Hugh had known she was the only one for him since that night all those years ago when he'd returned to the lake and had seen her after more than a year away. Her eyes had sparkled as though from some secret amusement, and her hands held the doorway behind her as she rocked her hips up and back. Playful, bright, smiling. Everything a man like him would crave like air.

"Why, Hugh MacCarrick, do my eyes deceive me?" she'd asked.

"Jane?" he'd bit out incredulously.

"Of course it's me, darling." She'd sauntered up to him and touched her pale, soft hand to his face.

With her touch something passed over him, shocking him, calling him.

"Jane?" he'd repeated in a strangled tone as he tried to

assimilate all the changes in her. Her voice had grown sultry, would forever be that way. Her breasts were lush. She'd become a woman, the most beautiful one he'd ever seen. His heart had thundered in his chest.

"It looks like you're leaving," she murmured. "That's a shame, Hugh, because I've missed you so."

"No' goin' *anywhere*," he'd growled, and his life had never been the same.

Twenty

———— •◆• ————

Jane had heard him return to the room last night and wondered if that was how their situation would work. All done? Passion spent with Lysette? Go back to protecting Jane?

When she'd seen him leaving Lysette's room, tucking in his shirt—only to be coaxed back inside once more—Jane had lurched back to her room. Berating herself as a fool, she'd clutched the basin, close to being sick.

This morning in the carriage, which now seemed far too small, Jane kept her eyes averted so he couldn't see how much his betrayal had hurt her.

But what had he betrayed? The vows of a sham marriage—a marriage he'd made clear he couldn't wait to discard.

So why did it hurt so badly?

Even knowing what he'd done, she'd dreamed of him last night. She'd dreamed he'd done exactly as he threatened—taken her, sinking into her body.

Though she was still a virgin, she could imagine how he would feel thrusting inside her, how his big body would flex and move over hers as she wrapped her legs around him. In her fevered dreams, he'd fondled her breasts in his hot palms and sucked her nipples.

Instead, he'd probably been doing those things earlier to Lysette. She turned away and put her knuckles to her mouth.

What a bewildering position to be in—and she wasn't particularly steady and clear-thinking in the best of situations! She knew her own weaknesses. She was impulsive, often saying and doing things without thought. She had emotions that swung from one extreme to another like a pendulum, and she felt things too strongly.

Worse, all her faults seemed to be exacerbated when he was around. Her emotions ran high, and actions and words that seemed undeniable at the time made no sense in retrospect.

She'd always been like that to a degree, but she'd endeavored to better herself. She'd learned that whenever she got into a temper, or whenever she was inundated with what her cousins labeled Bad Ideas, she needed to step back from the situation, perhaps leave the room to compose herself—to give herself a chance to see things rationally, reasonably.

Stepping away had always helped her; now here she was, trapped in a coach.

She let out a weary breath. She *wished* she were a reasonable person, wished that inexplicable urges and impulses didn't goad her.

Why was it that everyone could see these faults in her, but no one bothered to suppose that she didn't *want* to be so flawed?

Jane could imagine what it would feel like to be reasonable. She imagined she could do something as simple as donning spectacles to see the world more clearly. She would peer at her relationship with Hugh, and see a very simple equation.

Hugh equaled pain.

By the second day after they'd left the inn, Hugh had decided he would welcome Jane's games.

She'd ignored him with an ease that would bruise any man's sense of worth. As their coach rolled through another sleepy town, he glanced over at her by the open window, watching as the sun and the breeze streamed in, toying with her loosened hair.

Over the past day, she'd silently read *A Gentlewoman's Apprentice*—or whatever book was behind the false cover. He hoped it wasn't a novel in the same vein as the one he'd skimmed in her room in London. Especially since her eyes had been riveted to it as she ate an apple, or nibbled on a piece of hay she'd plucked when they stopped for food at midday.

He should be glad that she'd left him alone. So why did he hate it when she ignored him, if the alternative was enduring her teasing?

How many more days—and nights—can I take?

For the tenth time that day, he silently willed his brother to work fast. Ethan had an uncanny way of finding people, and the best case scenario would be for Ethan to locate Grey and stop him before he even reached England. The worst case was that Grey could evade him for months. . . .

Hugh thought back over his and Ethan's last conversation. He should have pressed him about what had happened with the Van Rowen girl. He should have given Ethan the benefit of the doubt and asked if his brother might be searching for something more. Hugh had, Court had—why had Hugh never considered his older brother would have the same needs?

When Hugh saw him again, they would split a bottle of scotch and discuss this situation like men. If Ethan truly wanted the lass—even after discovering who she was—Hugh could share strategies for putting her from his mind.

Strategies to share? *Smug once more, MacCarrick?* When he could think of little but Jane?

Eyes wide, she gasped and flipped to the next page.

At least she was in better spirits now than yesterday. Then she'd appeared deadened—not sullen, just lacking her usual animation. Jane generally exuded energy, but she had stared out the coach window, seeming to see nothing.

He'd feared he had startled her with his attentions. Or that she even felt guilt for allowing his kiss because of her relationship with Bidworth. Perhaps she'd been appalled with herself for . . . enjoying it.

As much as he couldn't comprehend it, she *had* enjoyed his lips on her. He kept recalling how she'd appeared—breathless, pupils dilated, her skin flushed. But if she'd been like a firebrand that night, the next morning, she'd been like ice. . . .

Jane was clearly unhappy—a condition Hugh had never been able to handle well. "Sìne, I want to speak with you about the other night."

She didn't glance up from her book. "So speak."

"Lass, I am fallible," he said quietly. "And I'd asked you no' to taunt me like that."

She raised her face to him in a flash, eyes glittering with fury. "So what you did at the inn is *my* fault?"

Taken aback by how strongly she felt about this, he said, "No, I should have been able to govern myself. It will no' happen again." Of course she felt strongly. She'd thought she could play without repercussion. She'd never expected him to kiss her like that.

"Why do you care how I feel about your . . . your behavior?" she asked. Had her accent ever sounded so proper?

He hesitated, then admitted, "Your opinion of me is important."

"Is that why you won't talk about your profession?"

He said simply, "Aye."

"Silly, Hugh." Her slow, unexpected smile in the sunlight was spellbinding. "I can't think less of you than I do right now."

"*Lysette*," Grey whispered at her ear, stroking her blonde hair from her forehead. "Wake up."

She did in an instant, shooting up in bed. Her jerky scream into his hand turned to a whimper when he placed his knife against her pale throat. The polished blade reflected the light from a nearby lamp, glinting when she began to tremble. "You've got so many men watching the place, I'd started to think you were expecting me," he murmured. "Don't tell me you've missed me." He eased the pressure of his grip on her mouth, but increased the pressure of his knife. "I don't have to remind you how short your scream would be, do I?"

When she cautiously shook her head, he grinned in the face of her fear, of the tears beginning to fall, before finally removing his hand. "Yes, you must have suspected I'd visit, since you have your inn guarded like a fortress.

But you of all people should know I can get past anyone you've brought in."

"What do you want from me?" she whispered, easing the bed covers up to just below her neck.

"Hugh and Jane stayed here on their journey north. I want their destination."

"You know he wouldn't trust me with that information."

Grey raised his brows. "And you discovered nothing in all of your customary prying while they were here?"

"Hugh's cautious, and I don't believe the girl knows."

"I have a good idea anyway," he said honestly. "I merely was hoping to confirm. So it seems this might have been a wasted trip." He removed the blade. Just when her big blue eyes began to fill with hope, he said, "Of course, since I'm already here, I plan to make you pay for selling me out to Hugh and Ethan."

Her shoulders slumped. "They wanted to help you."

"*Help* me?" He remembered Hugh in a terrible rage, his bone-crushing blows raining down so quickly that Grey hadn't had a chance in hell of defending himself. Then the two brothers had forced Grey into a murky basement where his muscles had curled and tightened, until he'd screamed with pain. For day after day, he'd suffered hallucinations in the dark, interrupted only by his vomiting.

Even now, shadows passed before him as he remembered how those haunting faces with their glassy, sightless eyes had descended on him. He hadn't been able to escape them. Because of her duplicity.

"I only told them because I wanted you back with me," she cried. "I wanted you to get well."

"You wanted me to get well, or you wanted to ingratiate yourself into the bed of a strapping young Highlander?"

She looked away. "What are you going to do to him?"

Grey spotted a bottle of scotch—fitting, he thought—beside her bed. He helped himself to a glass. "Take away what's most precious to him."

"The girl is innocent in all this."

He nodded. "Which is lamentable, but, in the end, incidental."

"Hugh will die before he lets you hurt his woman."

Grey sipped, savoring. "So I'll likely kill him within minutes of Jane."

"His brothers would hunt you to the ends of the earth."

He shrugged. "Ethan's already on my trail. With all the subtlety of a charging bull." That was how Ethan had always operated. No sneakiness, just annihilating his enemies with relentless pursuit. He would wear them down until they got sloppy—or grew too wearied of looking over their shoulders expecting to find his gruesome, scarred visage in the night.

Ethan was incredibly effective in his occupation, a legend of sorts. Not famed like Grey, of course. "He nearly found me three nights ago. Apparently, he somehow knew about my London loft," he said in a chiding tone. That was his Lysette, selling out to the highest bidder. Not a drop of loyalty.

Luckily, Grey knew all of Ethan's hideaways and properties as well.

"I didn't tell anyone about it"—she shook her head, her blonde tresses dancing about her pale shoulders—"I swear it."

Deciding that she was actually being truthful, he said, "Don't worry, I believe you. I can admit that Ethan's good." If information was as valuable as coin, then Ethan had amassed a fortune from others like them who secretly worked in service to the Crown—outside the law. "And I realize now that he must have been keeping tabs on me ever since he deigned to free me from his basement." Grey's fist tightened on his knife handle.

Lysette saw it and flinched.

"I'll take care of Ethan, though his life's so bloody miserable, it's almost not sporting to relieve him of it." Which would be more cruel, to make him live or to kill him? Didn't he himself have an affinity with Ethan? Ethan was a man who had nothing left to lose. Wasn't there power in that?

"And Courtland?" Lysette asked softly. "Do you think he won't seek retribution for the rest of his life, if it takes that long?"

"Lysette, I'd be more worried about your own survival right now." He gave her his most affable grin. "Or you can just relax and accept what's inevitable." He would finally sever her from his life . . . slowly.

That got a fine Gallic rise out of his little Lysette. Her tears stopped, and her eyes narrowed. "Hugh's going to win. And I just wish I could be around to see it."

Grey threw his glass to the floor and lunged across the bed. "I try to avoid allowing last words." He grabbed her chin, skimming the knife up her body. "And I don't normally tolerate last-minute confessions, but I'll make an exception for you."

Hatred burned in her expression. "My last words? You'll lose—because Hugh has *always* been better than you. Faster, stronger. Even before your affliction you were a pathetic shot—"

The knife flashed and blood sprayed over him.

"*You clever girl*," Grey said wonderingly with a cluck of his tongue. "You got me to do it quick."

Twenty-one

—————◆—————

Jane slammed the door on Hugh hard enough to make him grit his teeth just before the impact. The pictures on the walls were still rattling when she locked it behind her.

After two days trapped at Ros Creag, the MacCarricks' depressing lakeside manor, with Hugh's curt surliness as company, she was ready to march up to Grey and say, "Do your worst. I defy you."

The only reason she hadn't hied herself off to a cousin's estate was that members of her family were due to arrive at Vinelands any day now. Not that Hugh knew that. "At this season, there will no' be many around," he'd said, defending his decision to take her here. But her family sought out the quiet fall season when there weren't *many around*, since it was the only time they could be themselves. . . .

"Jane, I've warned you about locking the door," Hugh grated outside her room. "Open it, or this time I'll break the goddamned thing down."

"As you said yesterday—"

The door burst open.

She gaped, as much from the wildly swinging door and splintered doorframe as from Hugh's lethally calm demeanor—he wasn't even out of breath.

"I'll be damned if I can figure out why you've been angry," he said. "But I've about had enough of this."

"As have I!"

"You know, I always wondered what it'd be like to live with y—with a woman."

"And?"

"It's a wee bit like hell, with your carrying on."

"What do you construe as carrying on?" she asked, indignant. "When I avoid you because you've cut me off at every attempt I've made to start a conversation? Why would I *want* to be around you when talking to you is like pulling teeth?"

"And how's that?"

"I asked you why your brothers haven't married, and you snapped, 'Drop the subject.' I asked you why none of you have any children, and you said, 'Enough of this.' I asked you if you've ever considered adding a trellis and a rose arbor, *anything* to soften the grimness of this place, and you just walked out of the room! I've never met a surlier man."

"If I am, it's because you've ignored everything I've asked of you."

"Like what?"

"I asked you to avoid the windows, yet I continue to catch you in the window seat in the upstairs parlor, staring out at Vinelands. I've asked you to pick up things in your room, and you tell me it's your 'horizontal system' and that if I canna discern it then I must be stupid."

Everybody who knew Jane knew she was untidy—her lady's maid played solitaire and read gothic novels all day because Jane wouldn't let her straighten much—but untidy worked for Jane. Without her system, how would she ever find anything?

"And you refuse to let the maid clean up here," Hugh finished.

"I don't wish to cause any extra work for anyone, and the servants are only here for a few hours a day. If it bothers you so terribly—and, really, Hugh, when did you get to be so exacting?—you can keep the door closed."

"You know I canna do that."

She sighed and trudged across the plush rugs to peer out the window. Ros Creag, which meant "stony promontory," was as forbidding and no-nonsense as its name, just as it had been in the past. But then, the appearance did exactly what it was meant to—it kept people away. Had this place been welcoming, the Mac-Carrick brothers would have been overrun with Weylands borrowing fishing gear and foodstuffs, dropping off pies. . . .

Everywhere she looked outside, the gardens were freakishly orderly, as though a gardener had laid out the shrubs and flowers to the inch with a ruler, then ruthlessly checked any undue exuberance. The manor was stately but imposing, its bricks made of dark rock, like the craggy, lakeside cliff it clung to.

Though separated from Vinelands by just that small cove, this place was a world away from it. Whereas Ros Creag was stern and solitary upon a cliff, Vinelands occupied an expanse of lawn rolling down to the water and a swimming beach, and looked like a quaint country cottage, though it had eight bedrooms. Arbors and follies dotted the property, and a small dock crawled lazily from the shore into the water.

And Hugh wondered why she'd always preferred her own home to his.

"So you truly doona like it here." His words came from just behind her, but she hadn't heard him approach. She frowned, recalling that he'd done that in London, too. He used to stride loudly, his boots booming across the floor. Now he was all sneaky silence.

With a shrug, she turned and headed for the door. One good thing about Ros Creag? It was big enough that they need never see each other.

Damn, she'd been nettled since the night he'd kissed her. Apparently, Jane agreed with everyone else that Hugh reached too high in wedding her.

As he watched her walking away, he told himself yet again that it didn't matter. Once Grey had been killed and she was completely out of danger, Hugh would leave her just as he had before.

And go where? Do what? If the list went public, he would have no profession. He'd thought about joining up with Court's crew of Highland mercenaries, but had dismissed the idea. Hugh was a loner, always working solo. Always on the periphery.

Except with Jane. She was the only person on this earth he'd ever been able to be around constantly. Hell, he'd never been *able* to spend enough time with her, had always yearned for more.

Now that he'd gotten his wish, he wanted to take it back.

No, he could tolerate this. The situation was only temporary.

Yet it wasn't only the clutter or even her continued

pique that bothered him. It had finally hit him that he would be *living* with her, under the same roof, appearing as man and wife. She was so mysteriously feminine, and never having lived with a woman, he found himself a shade overwhelmed.

With a grated sound of frustration, he strode after her, picking his way around piles of clothing. Hugh was uncomfortable with disarray, having come to crave order and structure in everything. Without order, came randomness; Hugh hated random. He felt he'd been chosen at random for his fate, and he resented the lack of control.

Weren't women supposed to be fastidious, organized creatures? More unfortunate for him, much of Jane's disarray came in the form of her fascinating undergarments. There were garters he hadn't seen in her room in London, and even stockings with designs in them.

"Wait, Jane." He caught her elbow just as she reached the hallway. "Tell me why you doona like it here."

"I'm used to being around family and friends, everyone talking and laughing, and you take me away from all that to stay in this *depressing*—there, I've said it—manor. And even then I could tolerate it, if you were fit company."

"What is so bad about this place?" he asked, glancing around with an incredulous expression. "You never liked coming here in the past, either. Why?"

"*Why?* I would have to leave my house—where there was whistling, and my uncles chasing their giggling wives, and happy children running about like wild creatures—to come here, where the curtains were drawn, and it was as dark and silent as a tomb."

"I was just as uneasy at your home."

"Why on earth?"

He doubted he could ever convince her that her family's behavior might make outsiders uncomfortable, much less someone as solitary as Hugh. But her locking the door on him rankled on so many levels, and he was just irritated enough to say, "Your aunts ran about with their skirts hiked up, fishing, smoking, passing a bottle of wine between them. And sometimes when your uncles *caught* your aunts and swooped them upstairs, they weren't as quiet as they could have been with what they were doing."

"And how would you even know that, from the collective fifteen minutes you spent with them over five years?" When he said nothing, she asked, "Do you deny assiduously avoiding everyone but my father?"

He couldn't deny it—he'd never wanted Jane to see how awkward he was around groups of people. "You ken I've usually preferred my own company."

"At least my family was kind to you. Unlike your brothers' treatment of me."

"My brothers were no' unkind to you."

"Are you jesting? One entire summer, Ethan crept about like a frightful ghost in his lair with the entire side of his face bandaged from some mysterious injury— which you would never talk about. And if anyone happened to glance at his face, he'd roar with fury and run them off."

Ethan had been a harrowing sight that summer. And every summer after. "And Court?"

She gave him an incredulous look. "My God, I think he's the angriest man I've ever encountered, always simmering. You never knew when he was going to go off.

Being around him was like sidling around a bear trap. And it wasn't a secret that he wasted no love on me."

No, Court had never liked Jane. Hugh supposed Court had resented the girl who tagged along with them everywhere and was frustrated that Hugh didn't mind at all. That last summer, Court had despised her teasing treatment of his brother, never considering that Hugh woke every morning impatient to return for it, day after day.

But Hugh hadn't known Jane felt as strongly about Court, and about Ethan, as well. "I dinna realize it was so bad."

"You never seemed to notice these things because you were so used to them." She adjusted a vase on a shining end table, as if she couldn't stand its perfect placement. Seeming to calm herself, she said, "Hugh, rehashing all this will help nothing. When I ask you questions, you don't have to answer them, and you can be as dismissive as you please. That's your prerogative. My prerogative is that I don't have to be around you when it's avoidable."

"The subjects you brought up are difficult ones."

She raised her eyebrows, waiting for more.

"If I answer one question, you'll ask a dozen more about my answer, no matter if I doona want to talk about it. You're no' happy until everything's laid bare."

"I do apologize for wanting to know more about a man I used to be friends with, who disappeared for years without a word, who has now returned to be my husband in an odd marriage of convenience."

"Damn it, I told your father to tell you good-bye."

She glared at that. "Don't you think I deserved it from you? It's becoming clear to me that we *didn't* have the friendship I'd imagined. I must have been like a gnat in your ear, a silly little girl who followed you around when you only wanted to hunt or fish with your brothers."

"We *were* friends—"

"A friend would have told me good-bye when he knew he was leaving and had no intention of returning for years."

Could she have thought of him? Could she have *missed* him? "Are you angry about that?"

"I'm puzzled. I would have told you good-bye."

"I dinna believe you would even think of me much after I'd gone. I dinna think you would care overmuch one way or the other."

She didn't deny it or confirm it, just continued, "But now you've come back and we're in this confusing situation, and I'm trying to reason it all out, but I don't have enough information. Papa told me this might take months. Are we to be like this the entire time, with you cutting me off or getting angry when I ask questions?"

"I doona want to be that way. I just . . . I just doona know how to handle this as well as I should."

"What do you mean by 'this'?"

He pinched the bridge of his nose. "Jane, sometimes you throw me. And I'm unused to being married—even if it's only temporary."

"Very well, Hugh. Let's start with an easy question." When she raised her eyebrows, he nodded grimly. "Why would my father ever find occasion to associate with someone as deranged and violent as Grey?"

That's an easy question? "Grey was no' always like this. He came from a wealthy and well-respected family. He had strong connections."

"And he was your good friend?"

"Aye."

"Did you try to help him with his affliction?"

Hugh chose every word carefully, knowing he owed her more of the truth, but unable to divulge his own dealings without revealing everyone's. "I attempted to reason with him, bully him, bargain with him. Nothing worked."

After that, Hugh and Ethan had decided to take matters into their own hands to wean him from opium. They'd captured Grey and carted him back to one of Ethan's estates.

Grey had been furious, frothing at the mouth, spouting insults. Either he had always been a sick bastard—and opium, like liquor, magnified his faults—or his entire personality had been altered.

He'd vowed that if Hugh couldn't "muster the ballocks to finally go fuck Jane Weyland as she so clearly needs," then he'd make short work of her. Hugh barely remembered lunging for Grey's throat and raining blows on his face. Ethan had scarcely been able to haul Hugh off. Afterward, all three of them had seemed shocked by Hugh's utter loss of control.

But after two weeks in a basement, Grey had emerged, seemingly cured. For a year, Hugh had believed he'd maintained an even keel. Ethan, however, suspected Grey only waited for a chance to strike out, and he'd been right.

"I thought for a while that he'd gotten better. But the last time I saw him, his pupils were like pinpricks even in the night. . . ."

Seeing Hugh's disappointment, Grey had self-consciously smoothed his soiled jacket and given him a half grin, and with it a glimpse of his old self. His accent had been clipped and proper, even as he looked away and said softly, "I didn't want to be like this, you know."

"Then why?" Hugh had asked.

"Not quite the way I'd planned things, as it were," he'd continued lightly, but when Hugh said nothing, Grey finally cast Hugh a look that was raw, unguarded. "I woke up one morning, and I was nothing but that number." He averted his face again as if embarrassed. "Good-bye, Scot." Then he'd walked away. . . .

Hugh shook off the memory. "He was lost for good."

"Do you miss your friendship with him?"

After a long hesitation, Hugh nodded. He did, even as he now burned for Grey to die—and even as Hugh knew his brother was out in the world, seeking to kill him.

Twenty-two

"*H*ugh! It's me."

He blinked his eyes open. He was clutching Jane's wrist as she leaned over him, her expressive face full of worry. He released her and fell back onto the bed. "Jane?" He ran his hand over his brow, finding it damp with sweat. "What're you doing in here?"

"I heard something. I thought you were having a nightmare."

"Aye." He was often plagued with nightmares, murky scenes of targets who refused to die. He had always strived to make clean shots, to make it quick. But sometimes at great distances, in inclement weather, he'd failed to do so. When the shot was off the mark, they often writhed; some screamed shrilly. "Did I say anything?"

She shook her head. "What was the nightmare about?"

"No' important." It was then that he noticed her night-dress. Clinging, sheer white silk. His gaze dropped to her breasts—and she noticed, nibbling her lip.

At once, he sat up and snatched a bundle of the cover over his sudden erection. "Damn it, you canna come in dressed like that." His voice was hoarse.

"I rushed in when I heard you. I didn't stop for a robe."

"When will you learn, Jane? I've told you, I've a man's needs. And when I see you like this . . ."—he shook his head hard—"it affects me. I doona want to do something we'd both regret."

She quirked an eyebrow. "You're saying the sight of me in a nightgown is so irresistible it might make you, a man of the world, lose control?"

"Aye," he said simply, then added, "I've been long without a woman, Jane, and you are verra beautiful—"

"What do you mean, *long*?" She angrily crossed her arms. "As in four days?"

He frowned. "What're you speaking of?"

"I saw you go into Lysette's room. And come out with your shirt untucked."

His eyes narrowed. "You would no' have seen that if you had stayed locked in the room."

Her voice was cutting. "That is of no matter."

"She tried to seduce me."

"Tried to, or succeeded?"

"Are you jealous?" He didn't dare hope she could be. Didn't dare hope she felt the blistering envy that clawed at him when he thought of her with another.

She put her chin up and sniffed, "You spent our wedding night in the arms of another woman. I hardly felt complimented by it."

"So it's your vanity that's been injured." Disappointment settled over him. In a deadened tone, he said, "I dinna sleep with her."

"You *didn't*?" Her arms fell to her sides as if they'd gone boneless.

"Why do you sound so disbelieving?"

"It was clear she wanted you."

"I took a vow to you, and until that vow is annulled, I'll keep it. Now, go back to your room."

Her hand fluttered to her forehead. "I see." Strangely, her face had paled. After a moment, she nodded. "I'll try to straighten my room. And don't worry about me 'carrying on' anymore."

"And what's brought about this change?" Hugh demanded, about to bellow with frustration. "Because now your vanity's intact and you lost no competition with Lysette? So you can go back to being decent to me?"

She seemed to flinch at that. "It wasn't competitiveness or vanity. And I'm sorry for how I've behaved." She looked as though she genuinely meant it.

His ire eased somewhat, and he softened his tone. "Then what, Jane?

Twining her hands, she said nothing.

"You're making me crazed, lass. I know you're unhappy, and I doona know how to change that." He rubbed his forehead, and exhaled. "Tell me how to change that."

At length, she whispered, "I was unhappy because I was jealous."

Jane left him with his lips parted and brows drawn, and withdrew to her room, easing the door nearly closed.

She stood trembling against the wall with her hands flat against the rich wainscoting. Though she'd wanted to stay in his room, she'd *stepped back*. She was proud of herself and felt mature for her decision, especially since she'd been flooded with compelling impulses—along with many Bad Ideas on how to handle them. She was a mix of roiling emotions.

It was possible that Jane could have been more awful to Hugh over the past few days, but she couldn't conceive of how. "*I know you're unhappy, and I doona know how to change that,*" he'd said, sounding so weary. Immediately, Jane had remembered her father's words—*Hugh tries. . . .*

She squeezed her eyes tight, embarrassed at her cutting behavior, even as she was so *pleased* with him, so relieved that Hugh hadn't touched that woman. Of course, a major deterrent to her feelings for him had just been eliminated. Which brought about *her* revelation.

Was she right back where she'd been at the inn as she sat on the table? When she'd feared letting him out of her sight?

Yes—

Jane's eyes shot open when Hugh's hand wrapped around the back of her neck. He'd pulled on his pants and entered her room silently, giving her little warning before he dragged her to his naked chest. Leaning down, he slanted his lips over hers, groaning at the contact. He broke away only to ask, "You were truly jealous?" then set back in.

Telling him the truth could open her up to hurt, could accelerate the rate at which she dropped off that cliff. And still, between their licking, seeking kisses, she whispered, "I didn't want you kissing her. Because you should've still been kissing me."

At her admission, he tensed, hesitating for only a heartbeat before he lifted her in his arms, striding with her back to his bedroom.

"Hugh?" she murmured in a daze. "What are you doing?"

"I've something on my mind," he said, setting her on the bed, following her down. As he leaned above her, his dark hungry gaze flickered over her, and his voice broke low. "Something I need tae see."

He rubbed an unsteady hand over his mouth, looking like a man in agony. His body seemed to thrum with tension. Frowning, she brought her palms up to cup his face, but he shuddered, even at that slight touch. What was happening here?

For all the books she'd read, for all that she'd heard from her cousins and learned in London, she'd *never* imagined a man behaving like this—as though he were about to die from desire. The erotic books she'd read never had accounts of men's bodies *shuddering* with lust, pained with a need so great they could scarcely speak and could barely stand to be touched.

He reached forward to brush her nightdress straps down her shoulders, then dipped a kiss to her collarbone. Just as she felt cool air on her breasts and belly, he hissed something in Gaelic, and sank back on his haunches to stare. She felt his gaze on her bared skin like a touch and arched her back for him.

Leaning forward once more, he rasped, "*Mercy.*"

She thought she would scream in pleasure with the first wet flick of his tongue to her aching nipple. He cradled her breast with his whole hand, holding her in place as he sucked her between his lips.

"Hugh," she moaned, threading her fingers through his thick hair. "It feels so good when you do that."

His other hand was easing upward between her legs, his fingers caressing as they slowly ascended. "Tell me tae stop this," he said against her breast.

She shook her head, body quivering when he kneaded her inner thigh, coaxing her to spread her legs wider. The rough texture of his hand abraded her tender skin, but she loved it.

"Tell me now." His palm rubbed upward. She shook her head again and whimpered, afraid she was about to climax. She didn't want this ever to end.

"Ah, God, I canna stop." His fingers passed the thatch between her legs. "I need tae stroke you here."

She cried out when he slipped the pad of his thumb against her clitoris, rubbing it sensuously. Another finger delved to her slick sex. "*So wet.*" He lowered his head, and against her damp nipple, he said, "*You'd be ready for me, would you no'?*"

When he spread the moisture and continued his slow, agonizing strokes, she writhed helplessly to his touch. "Please, Hugh," she said, panting. "Don't stop."

He raised his head, studying her face. "I will no'." His voice sounded hoarse, lost. "I want tae make you . . . make you come for me." He stroked more firmly. "Tae *see* you—"

She gave a strangled moan—she was already there.

Twenty-three

——— ◆ ———

*H*ugh gazed in awe as she suddenly arched her back, hands clutching the sheets.

Without thought, he set four fingers on her, cupping and rubbing her sex fast, mouth sucking greedily on her nipple to make it stronger for her. With his other hand, he snatched up her gown so he could watch her body twisting with pleasure.

She gave a breathy cry that made his cock jerk painfully in answer, and her knees fell wide open. In utter abandon, she rocked her hips against his hand, over and over, until the tension left her.

Trembling, she fell back onto the arm he'd draped behind her, lying docile and open as he slowly continued to pet her flesh.

He couldn't catch his breath. The sight of his fingertips against the wet auburn curls at her sex . . . He was going to lose his seed right in his trousers.

She leaned up to bury her face against his neck. To his disbelief, she whispered how much she loved his touch. *His* touch. After a decade fantasizing about it, he'd made her come.

And it was the most incredible experience he'd ever had.

Her breaths were warm and quick, and between her words, she gave his neck little licks that made his cock grow impossibly hotter and harder.

At that moment, spending in his pants did not strike him as a bad idea.

He inwardly shook himself and pulled away, but she'd looped her soft arms around his neck and eased a knee up beside his waist.

"Hugh, what about you? Won't you stay with me?" She tugged gently, until he allowed himself to settle his hips between her thighs.

She wanted him to come as well? Could he drag himself away? Not when she undulated her bared sex against him. Impossible. He was burning to free himself and sink into her slick heat, desperate to ride her mindlessly, finally taking what he'd needed for so long.

Instead, when she did that sensual roll of her hips again, he tentatively thrust back against her. She sucked in a breath.

"*Dinna hurt you?*" he choked out.

When she said, "No, darling, no," he leaned up and found his hand shooting between them to rip open the fastening of his trousers. He shoved his pants down to his thighs, baring his cock, so that it hung down over her.

They were both breathing heavily, staring at where their bodies almost touched. Their flesh was so close. Her eyes were half-lidded as she stared at his shaft, at the slick head. As if in a dream, he watched as she rolled her hips again, seeking him. He put his straightened arms on each side of her, holding himself up, sweating with the effort not to take her.

He knew he couldn't have her, even when it felt so right to be here with her like this. He was awash in how right it felt. Yet, unable to stop himself, he pressed his own hips down. Lower, so slowly, until his shaft grazed against her swollen little clitoris.

His eyes rolled back in his head.

She gave a cry and another undulation that nearly put his cockhead inside her, ending everything. One of his hands shot to her hip to pin her down, then he pressed his shaft harder against her mound. He stayed there, letting it throb against her. Where his control came from, he had no idea. He only knew he had to stretch out every second, to make it last the rest of his life.

But when she reached eager hands forward to grasp him, he grabbed her wrists, knowing he'd come before her last finger had wrapped around his shaft. "Put your arms over your head, Sìne." She let them fall above her. "Keep them there for me." She nodded, as if she understood his struggle.

Soon the urge to thrust grew overwhelming. He obeyed it, pushing slowly over her sex, slipping up to her flat belly, then back, a near-constant groan rising from his chest. With his position and the movement, he was close to being inside her, as close as he would ever allow himself to get. Her cries would be the same—as would the way she was gazing up at him when she spread her legs wider and whispered, "*Oh, God! Yes, Hugh!*"

He savored even this agonizing pressure. Another slow push over her sex.

"*Jane*," he groaned. Each time his shaft slid over her, he

could feel his sack tightening until it ground against her wetness too. She made some unintelligible sound at the contact.

The pleasure was too great. He was going to come, and he was going to come hard.

He dropped his head and rasped, "Arch your back for me. Have tae taste you again." When she rushed to do so, he sucked her nipple between his lips, then tugged it with his teeth until she moaned.

Was she telling him she was about to come again? He'd make her. He'd hold on until she did once more.

The pressure had nearly turned to pain when she cried out his name and thrashed beneath him in her orgasm.

Lost, he ground himself determinedly up and back against her. "Ah, God, Sìne, I have tae . . . come," he groaned, beginning to ejaculate. He gave a brutal yell each time the hard spurts lashed across her belly . . . over and over until he'd finally emptied his seed.

His body wracked with after-shudders, he sank onto his elbows with hoarse exhalations of breath against her damp neck.

He couldn't believe he'd been thrusting over her like that. He closed his eyes in shame—he'd spilled his seed on her.

Drawing away, he tucked his sensitive shaft back into his pants, then rose to grab a towel. When he returned he couldn't bear to look at her, even as he wiped her skin and pulled her gown into place. He tossed the towel away and sat on the edge of the bed, head in his hands. Never had he felt so ashamed, so low. How was he going to face her tomorrow? Didn't matter, he'd have to.

No matter how badly he needed to leave, they couldn't be separated.

"Jane, I doona know what happened. I'm sorry." He should be humiliated to be near her, and yet it was she he wanted to be with in the face of his shame—so that he didn't have to take it alone. It was enough to drive any man mad.

"There's nothing to apologize for." She sat up on her knees behind him. "Nothing."

"No, I should have had more control."

"Hugh," she murmured, rubbing his back, "it's just me, remember? It's just your Jane. We were always comfortable around each other."

"This should no' have happened," he insisted.

Just when he'd decided to rise, she said, "Stay. Sleep with me, please." She coaxed with light touches and soft words until he somehow found himself out of his pants and in bed with her. When he'd resigned himself to staying like this, he drew her back to his chest, his arms smoothly crossing over her as if he'd locked her against him thousands of times before.

As he'd imagined that last summer again and again, she was finally naked in his bed. He'd stared at this very ceiling and fantasized about touching her, kissing her. He'd dreamed of holding her as she slept.

The reality was so much more. He'd known he would love the scent of her hair. He hadn't known he would want to groan and shove a handful to his face. Or that he would realize her hair was long enough to brush his legs if she threw her head back while she rode him.

He'd known he would love the feel of her, but he hadn't realized how round her arse would be or that it fit like a puzzle piece to his lap.

"No more nightmares, Hugh," she whispered drowsily. "Or we'll have to do that again."

He already wanted to do *that* again, was even now growing hard against her bottom. When she sighed in contentment, he frowned as he tried to recall how he'd ever thought living with her was bad.

Twenty-four

————◆————

When she woke the next morning, Hugh was sleeping soundly. She lay staring, fascinated with the man before her.

With his jaw unclenched, his face looked changed, younger even. The gashes on his cheek were healing, giving him a roguish look. That made her smile. He *was* a rogue—a mercenary—but he wasn't a *rake*.

She skimmed the pad of her forefinger over his bottom lip, remembering how he'd kissed her last night—deeply, desperately, like it was the last kiss he'd ever take from her, and he had to make it last.

Everything in her had responded, and she'd let herself go. She shivered just recalling how he'd rocked his massive body over her, sliding his shaft against her sex until he'd brought her twice to orgasm. And then to see him take his pleasure as well, to see him spending over her flesh . . . wondrous. Though judging by his discomfited reaction last night, she doubted she'd ever be seeing it again.

Which was a problem, as she'd all but decided Hugh MacCarrick had to be her first lover.

If she'd ever needed her cousins' advice, it was now. Today. Surely, today they would arrive.

When she tenderly brushed a lock of black hair from his forehead, his gorgeous dark eyes eased open. Seeming still half-asleep, he reached his hand up to stroke her cheek. When she smiled, his brows drew together in puzzlement.

Then he shot away from her.

After stabbing his legs into his pants, he paced for long moments, the muscles in his upper body growing more and more tensed. "This should no' have happened, and it canna happen again," he finally said.

His tone implied that they were discussing a tragedy, something akin to a death in the family—not the most mind-boggling pleasure she'd ever imagined. She couldn't help but feel insulted, and sat up, drawing the sheet up to her chest. "Honestly, Hugh, you're making a mountain out of a molehill." She waved her hand dismissively. "We . . . trifled a bit."

Instead of being grateful as she'd expected—after all, she could have called him a cad and pressed to stay married—he appeared furious. "If we'd 'trifled' an inch lower, there could be dire consequences. Have you forgotten that we both agreed no' to do this? We agreed at the outset. Do you want to get stuck in this marriage?"

"I wish you would stop living in terror that you might get trapped in marriage with me. We didn't make love. Now, it's very simple. We put this behind us and never speak of it again."

"I've never met a woman who could skewer a man's sense of self-worth like you can. Whoever marries you in truth will need to be a better man than me."

She glared up at him. Skewering had never been her intention, but at that moment, she didn't regret the outcome. "You are making too much of this," she insisted.

"Why are you so angry when nothing permanent occurred? You're acting like a provincial."

"Maybe you can easily put it behind you, but that *trifling* affected me." Suddenly his eyes narrowed as he lunged forward to grab her elbow. "You're no' a virgin, are you?"

She drew back her head in bewilderment. "Why would you ask *that* question?"

No, no, Hugh. Don't be like this. For ten years, he'd been out sowing his wild oats; yet he probably expected her to have been waiting for a husband. Of course, she *was* a virgin, but, as was often the case, right now she wished she weren't.

Such a narrow-minded expectation was galling.

"Answer me."

Her tone cold as ice, she said, "Darling, I've been as celibate as *you* have been since we last saw each other."

He released her, but kept his hands raised as he backed away, as if he couldn't believe he'd touched her.

"Why would you care if I bedded a dozen men?" she asked in confusion.

He raked his fingers through his hair. "Because women like you doona get 'easy annulments.' No' based on lack of consummation."

Women like me.

He hit the wall, making her jump, then turned to her with the air of some trapped beast who knew the end was near. He was that averse to having her as his wife?

"How in the hell did you plan to end the marriage?" he demanded. "How?"

"I'm sure my father can manage something—"

"It will no' bloody stop me, Jane. I dinna sign on for more. If our annulment does no' go as planned, I will still leave you."

Her heart went cold. Memories of loneliness and hopelessness washed over her.

He'd left her before without a warning. He would again, this time after telling her to her face that nothing would cleave him to her—even as she sat naked in a bed still warmed from him.

No longer would she open herself up to him. She couldn't. *Self-preservation, Janey.* Hugh MacCarrick was the only man who could ever make her cry. False smile in place, she said with all honesty, "Of course you will leave me, darling. I never expected anything else from you."

He shot her another disillusioned look, then strode away.

After his behavior the night before, this morning had already been grueling enough. But now to learn that Jane had definitely had at least one man was punishing for him.

He'd suspected she and Bidworth had been lovers, but to *know* . . .

The idea of Bidworth, or another man like him, taking her innocence made Hugh's stomach clench, made him want to roar with fury. He felt this even as he knew he had no right to, no right to hate the fact that she'd welcomed another—or others—into her bed.

He'd said those things to Jane out of jealousy and because he'd been furious with himself—for one foggy moment when he first awakened, he'd been about to start the madness again. Even now, he found himself wishing he'd just gone ahead and taken her last night, or even this morning, when she'd looked so tousled and well-loved.

He'd taken his frustrations out on her, sounding like some inflexible old-guard Tory, and she hadn't deserved it.

Jane was unique and independent, and she couldn't be judged by others' standards. She was twenty-seven and had a very healthy sexual appetite. Even as he understood this, the idea of her appeasing her needs with others maddened him.

Because he was obsessed with her. He wanted her to lavish that desire on him, wanted her all to himself. The idea of Bidworth trying to handle all her passion was laughable. After last night, Hugh knew that he was the man for it—even as he knew he could never allow himself to have her.

He'd given her a few hours to get over her pique, but now they needed to talk about what the hell they were going to do about their annulment. Hugh loped to her room, but found no sign of her. He made his way to the upstairs parlor. After dressing this morning, she'd sat in the window seat there for hours, gazing out at Vinelands as she had for the last two days.

He and his brothers used to do the same constantly. They'd first traveled down to this property at the suggestion of concerned relatives in the clan. Ethan had just received the injury to his face and would be able to heal in a more private setting; Court would have no one to fight. . . .

They'd been there only a week before the Weylands had descended on the area.

From the lofty vantage of Ros Creag, the three brothers had sat and watched the goings-on at Vinelands. Always a huge fire burned outside, people *danced* in the yard, and singing and raucous laughter carried across the water.

Hugh, Ethan, and Court had gawked in confusion. Their existence had been dour, their home in the north of Scotland dark ever since the death of their father. They'd rarely spoken to their mother, Fiona, who couldn't recover from the loss of her beloved husband Leith.

The day he'd died, Fiona had pulled at her hair, screaming at her sons, "*I told you no' to read it! How many times did I tell you? It always wins!*"

Hugh shook himself, preparing to face Jane as he entered the parlor—the empty parlor. She wasn't in the window seat. Excellent, she was avoiding him again.

Or would she have tried to leave, after his callous words this morning?

A sense of unease settled over him. He bellowed her name. Nothing. Just as he was about to go tearing through the house, some movement outside caught his attention. He glanced out the window, saw bairns piling out onto the front lawn at Vinelands, with some harried woman running after them. Adults alighted from carriages. Weylands were here? *Now?* Brows drawn, he strode forward to peer out.

And spotted a glimpse of Jane's green riding skirt on the shore path to Vinelands.

He bounded down the stairs, then outside onto the terrace, disbelieving his eyes. As though she sensed him, she turned back, gave him a sarcastic salute, then turned away dismissively. Sprinting for the stable, he vowed he'd tie her arse to a chair before she did this again. He looped a bit on his horse, not taking time for a saddle, before charging hell-bent along the path.

As he neared, Jane began racing for Vinelands as if for a friendly country's border. But Hugh dropped from his horse to the ground and snared her around the waist in one fluid movement.

Swinging her around to face him, he snapped, "Never, never leave like that again!"

"Or what?" she asked, panting.

He clutched her slim shoulders. "Or I'll tie your arse to a bed." When had *chair* become *bed*?

"Not likely, you brute—"

"Brute? This brute's tryin' to protect you, yet you treat all this like it's a game."

"How can I not when you tell me nothing? You've given me nothing truly tangible to worry about! You and Father both said Grey isn't in England, so how could he have followed us here?"

"Why take that risk?" Hugh said, loosening his hold on her shoulders. "Why're there Weylands here now?"

"They like the quiet season."

"You knew they were coming?"

She nodded. "Hugh, I need to go there. It's important to me."

"Why did you no' just ask me to take you?"

She rolled her eyes. "I knew you wouldn't let me. But I'm asking you now to come with me."

Go with her? To the other side? *No' bloody likely.* "I canna keep an eye on you among all of them." He was so unused to being around groups of people, it made him constantly wary. Much less around *these* people. "And how would you explain us?"

"I'd tell them the truth." Her chin went up. "We're married. That's all I'd say, for right now. In the future, I'll explain what happened."

"Too many people," he insisted. He had no wish for Jane to know how utterly inept he was in social situations.

"This is my family. They'll never say a word. You've never seen such a loyal family."

"Jane, you've got to understand that your life is on the line."

"Look me in the eyes and tell me that a day at Vinelands will put my life in more danger than staying at Ros Creag."

Hugh opened his mouth to speak, then closed it directly. If Grey had somehow made it past the net into England, then he would have Ethan breathing down his neck long before he ever thought to approach Ros Creag. And if he somehow got past Ethan, Grey would have to traverse the lake by ferry, which could be seen from Vinelands.

Technically, Hugh deemed it safe enough. But the last social event he had attended as a participant, not just skulking in the shadows, had been the festivities the night before Ethan's ill-fated wedding, and Hugh had never seen any of those guests again.

His next attempt was to be a day at Vinelands? A trial by fire? Damn it, he'd avoided this all those times in the past—yet now she expected him to voluntarily walk among the mad, carefree Weylands. He'd be more comfortable walking into a hail of bullets.

And God help him if Jane told her cousins about his behavior the night before. He shuddered at the possibility. A trial by inferno. "Does no' matter. I've told you we're returning. So that's what we're going to do."

She bit her lip and gazed up at him with those big, green eyes. When he realized she was about to ask in a way he hadn't yet figured out how to deny, he cut her off, snapping, "No' a chance," and dragged her toward the horse.

He was biting out Gaelic curses, she slapping at his grip on her elbow and kicking at his shins, when a voice cried, "*Jane?*"

They both faced forward and froze.

Twenty-five

———•◆•———

"*O*h, bloody hell." The seventh circle of hell. That's what Hugh looked like he'd ventured into as more and more of her family filed out of the house and approached them. Belinda was here with her husband and children, and Sam and her family had arrived as well.

She had to laugh evilly. "Too late to run. You're snared, I'm afraid."

"Aye, and you'd best enjoy it," Hugh muttered. "You go back to a locked cellar."

"Jane!" Samantha cried again, her russet curls bouncing. "What are you doing here?"

"Aunty Jane!" five children called as they besieged her, trampling her to the ground as she laughed.

Belinda clapped her hands in delight. "But you said you couldn't come this week!"

Then they noticed Hugh behind her, and everything went silent while jaws dropped. The children stared up at the towering Highlander in wonder. To break the awkward moment, Jane held up her hand, and as expected, Hugh shot forward to help her to her feet.

"What's *he* doing here?" Sam asked, never one to mince words.

Hugh gave Jane an expression as if to say, "Indeed."

"Well, he's . . . we're married."

Sam's jovial husband, a physician named Robert Granger, murmured to Sam, "Not four days ago, you told me she was marrying Bidworth."

From the side of her mouth, Sam answered, "That's because she *was*."

"Well, obviously *that* did not happen," Jane said blithely. "So wish us well and meet my new husband."

Hugh knew her cousins—barely—so she introduced Hugh to Robert, and they shook hands. If Hugh's threatening look hadn't deterred him, Robert would likely have bear-hugged him a welcome into the family.

Then she presented Hugh to Lawrence Thompson, Belinda's husband, a prankster and a considerable wit with a ready laugh, who cradled his hand after Hugh shook it.

Seeing all of them lifted Jane's spirits and made her realize how much Hugh's awful words had hurt her. *I'll still leave you.*

Hugh eyed everyone with such a leery demeanor, so noticeably out of his element, that she couldn't resist. She knew she had a diabolical gleam in her eyes when she faced Hugh and said, "I absolutely must catch up with my cousins and show off my new ring. In private." He was subtly shaking his head. "Hugh, why don't you get to know *the other husbands*—they like to drink scotch and sit on the lawn about this time of morning. Talk about the stock exchange and such."

She hadn't missed his wary glance at the children either. "Oh, and, children, your new uncle Hugh loves to buy presents and treats. You've only to tell him what you want!"

•   •   •

"Off of him now!" Robert exclaimed as he shooed bairns off Hugh. "Run along and play!"

Hugh wanted to fall down with relief when the last one made yet another request, released his leg, then scampered away. Jane really was going to do this—she truly was leaving him to deal with these men. She and her cousins had gathered up bottles of wine and strolled out on the dock without a backward glance.

"Don't know what Jane was thinking, to set the hounds to you like that!" Robert flashed him a sheepish grin. "But, finally, it's just men." He led them over to a set of wicker lawn chairs and, once seated, began pouring a round of drinks, though it was not nearly ten.

"So, what do you do, MacCarrick?"

Hugh reluctantly sat and accepted the glass, not knowing his way around this. "I'm . . . retired." He'd never been forced to make conversation. Never spoke unless something needed to be said. In more than one way, he'd been perfectly suited for his occupation.

"That's the way to do it, my boy!" Robert raised his glass—then drained it. "Retire, take a beautiful bride, and enjoy life."

Lawrence worked on his drink more slowly, but not by much. "Are you and Jane starting a family straight away?"

Hugh shrugged. After seeing her happiness when all those bairns waylaid her, he had never been more keenly aware that he could never give her children.

Robert sank back with his second drink on his knee. "We waited, Sam and I, nearly three years to start."

Waited? So odd to hear these upper-class gentlemen speak of topics like this. "Waited" meant contraception.

Robert and Lawrence then mused on how their wives had behaved and looked when pregnant ("quite lusty" and "pleasingly plump"), how children changed a man ("didn't know what I was about before them"), and other things Hugh tried his damnedest to block out.

He kept glancing over at Jane and her cousins deep in conversation, knowing she was telling them everything about last night. Each time she closed in to whisper to the two women, he cringed, feeling his face flush violently.

After a grueling hour of conversation Hugh barely heard, Lawrence suggested that the men target-shoot. Hugh ran his hand over the back of his neck, knowing he would have to miss. Though he had a powerful desire to impress Jane, to shoot as these people had never seen, he stifled it, aware how unwise it would be to demonstrate exactly what he excelled in.

A quick glance told him that Jane had shaded her eyes with her hand to see. Would she remember that he could shoot? She used to tag along with him on hunts all the time, had tromped with him over every inch of woodlands in the area.

Hugh recalled one of the first times Jane had accompanied him. Afterward, she'd bragged to Weyland about Hugh's shooting: "Papa, you wouldn't believe how he can shoot—so calm, and steady as a rock! He hit a duck at seventy yards at least in a stiff breeze."

Weyland had eyed him with new interest. "Did he, then?" Hugh hadn't understood why at the time. He'd had no way of knowing that Weyland was sizing him up for a lethal profession—one that had provided wealth to a second son who'd had none, and laid out the path to walk with death. . . .

Twenty-six

———— • ◆ • ————

"So how is your Scot in bed? As good as you've always dreamed?" Sam asked.

Jane rolled her eyes. Of course, the conversation had wended its way to this topic, and Sam was going to needle for details until the entire truth came out. So Jane related everything—well, almost everything.

She told them of her stunned hurt over Lysette, and her subsequent relief when she'd found out Hugh had been true to her. She admitted that they'd been intimate last night but hadn't consummated the marriage, and she related their last conversation—or, more accurately, fight. She confided her suspicion that Hugh was a mercenary of some sort.

Sam said, "I can't imagine what Uncle Edward is up to, forcing you to marry MacCarrick."

"And Hugh being a mercenary?" Belinda glanced in his direction. "Does sort of fit."

"But, marriage of convenience or not, why haven't you rendered it very *inconvenient* already?" Sam asked.

Jane surreptitiously rolled down her stockings, discarding them and her shoes to dip her feet in the water. "Hugh doesn't want to be trapped and will do whatever it takes to get out of it. He's made that abundantly clear. I believe his words were, '*I will still leave you.*'"

Belinda had pre-opened the cork on the second wine bottle, but still couldn't get it open. She handed it to Sam and said, "Jane, I can see why you wouldn't want to chance this, but I don't understand why he is so averse. Does he have a lover?"

"No, he said he is 'between.'"

Sam took out the cork with her teeth, then spat it into the lake. Recorking a bottle was something of a crime at Vinelands. "Does he make any money as a mercenary?"

"Father told me he had some. But then, Father also neglected to tell me his true occupation."

Sam asked, "So sure he's a mercenary?"

Jane nodded. "His brother is. And Hugh was just down there on the Continent fighting with him. That's how he got those marks on his face."

Sam handed Belinda the bottle. "Which brother?"

"Court. Courtland. The *angry* one."

After they both flashed expressions of recognition at that, Belinda said, "At least he wasn't as bad as the oldest one."

"The one whose face was all cut up! He used to give me night terrors," Sam admitted.

"Oh, me too!" Belinda said. "One morning I was out berry-picking with Claudia, and we met him on a foggy lane. We froze, and he scowled as if he knew what was about to happen. When we dropped our baskets and ran, he roared curses at us."

For some reason, Jane felt a brief flare of pity for Ethan. He would have been only twenty or so.

"Later we felt awful. Silly." Almost as an afterthought, Belinda muttered, "But we didn't go back for our baskets."

"So what the devil is MacCarrick's hesitation?" Sam frowned. "He's got enough money to support you, he doesn't have a woman, and he's completely lost for you."

Jane gave Sam an unamused expression, then turned so Hugh couldn't see her take a gulp of wine. After his rant this morning, Jane figured he'd be displeased to find even a temporary wife stockingless and passing around a bottle. "He's so lost for me, he tells me twice daily how our marriage will end."

Sam waved her comment away. "I'm merely saying what I see. It is a puzzle. I do so love puzzles."

"Maybe he's got a lusty Scottish lass waiting for him back in the clan," Belinda offered, taking a more ladylike taste of the wine. "Someone with ample breasts and wide hips, someone who can cook."

Jane's brows drew together. Suddenly, she found the idea of traveling to his clan's seat decidedly less appealing. Jane would be the outsider, not speaking the language, not understanding exchanges between Hugh and his kinsmen, or between him and any lasses he'd left behind.

Sam said, "At least Jane has the lusty part down pat."

Jane didn't bother contradicting that. Her cravings before had been an irritation, but now with Hugh—and after last night—they seemed to consume her. "I swear"— she leaned in as Sam's two daughters ran by the end of the dock, chased by a heaving nanny—"I swear, sometimes I believe that I think about making love as much as a twenty-seven-year-old male. There are people obsessed with all things carnal. Maybe I'm like them."

Sam rolled her eyes. "This, coming from the twenty-seven-year-old virgin."

"Samantha, you mustn't judge," Belinda chided in a prim tone. "Jane never asked to be a virgin." She snapped her fingers for the bottle. "So what happens if you don't consummate the marriage? What happens at the end of this adventure for you?"

Jane put her hands behind her and leaned back, inhaling deeply. The air was redolent with the scent of wild roses, not yet checked by the autumn's first frost. "Our marriage is dissolved. Hugh goes back to mercenarying or marauding or whatever his secret endeavors are."

Then Sam asked, "Janey, just a thought. Do *you* want to stay wed to him?"

Jane had wondered if Sam and Belinda were tiptoeing about Jane's past fixation on Hugh, focusing only on his motivations. They most likely feared Jane would cry over Hugh yet again.

As she contemplated the question, she watched Hugh purposely miss yet another shot, even with Lawrence slapping his back and elbowing him. Hugh could have embarrassed the two men, but he hadn't. And she'd seen him eyeing the way Robert held his rifle and knew he badly wanted to correct it, but he'd said nothing. He really was trying to rub along with her odd family.

Jane sighed. After their encounter the night before, she knew she could spend the rest of her nights with that man. Even after their row today, she knew he'd make a good husband.

At an early age she'd discovered his personality and temperament were devastatingly attractive to her. She'd set her cap at him, and after he'd left, she'd never met his equal.

She gave them a tight smile. "Doesn't matter, does it? He couldn't have made it more clear that as soon as this is over, he will leave and not come back. I swear, you should have seen the look on his face when I told him I hadn't been celibate."

"To be fair," Belinda began, "an easy annulment was one of the terms of the deal he agreed to. Without it, this could get tricky. He might even fear you'll have to divorce. Which cousin Charlotte can tell you is nasty business, after all the hours she's spent at the courthouse."

Sam was shaking her head. "No, he's jealous. He reacted to the thought of you with another man, or men."

Belinda covered her mouth with three fingertips, stifling a hiccup, then snapped her fingers for the bottle again—this time from Jane. "Jane, I'm actually going to have to agree with Sam on this one. He does look at you like he's been starved and you're a feast."

"You've only seen us together for the shortest time!"

Sam said, "But he keeps looking over here at you. Watch for it now. Give it five seconds. Five, four, three—"

Jane tugged one of Sam's russet curls, but Hugh did, in fact, turn to look at her two seconds later. "He might appear a bit possessive," she allowed. "But he should. He's protecting me."

"Come on, haven't you ever seen a Highlander madly in love? No?" Sam jerked her thumb over her shoulder toward Hugh who was staring at Jane with a smoldering expression. "Behold!"

"Madly in love. That's ridiculous." Yet her heart had started knocking hard in her chest.

Belinda frowned. "Jane, where's your famed confidence?"

"Embattled. Running screaming for the hills. Which happens when one's husband regards his marriage as a sprung bear trap. When he appears determined to gnaw off a paw to escape, well, that never helps, either."

"Maybe he doesn't think he's rich enough or good enough for you," Belinda said. "After all, you were about to marry an exceedingly handsome and wealthy earl."

"She's right," Sam said. "This smacks of self-sacrifice to me."

"So you think he's here, ready to risk his life for me, because he's in love with me and couldn't stand to see me hurt?"

Belinda nodded. "Why, that's it, precisely."

Why *was* Hugh doing all this? Yes, she knew he owed her father for his livelihood. But surely this was above and beyond repayment. "Any ideas on why he'd leave before and be furiously resolved against marrying me now?"

"No, but in your place, I'd be finding out," Sam said. "And I'd develop a strategy."

"A strategy for MacCarrick," Jane said, tapping her chin. "Why do I have a sense of history repeating itself?"

Sam shrugged. "True, our last plan wasn't utterly successful—"

"Utterly successful?" Jane asked with a laugh. "We endeavored to get him to marry me, and instead, he disappeared for a decade."

"Well, then, what are you going to do?" Belinda asked.

Brows drawn, Jane said, "Wait until an answer comes to me from nowhere, then act impulsively and inappropriately?"

Sam rubbed her chin thoughtfully. "It might just work."

Twenty-seven

*T*oward sundown, Hugh caught her just as she was leaving the house through a side door. "You canna avoid me all day." He eased her against the wall, and she let him.

"I stayed within your eyesight," she said, surprised when he rested a hand beside her head and leaned over her. "Besides, I thought you were enjoying spending time with Robert and Lawrence."

He narrowed his eyes. "Oh, aye. Today, I've shot, fished, and smoked, and because I've had to keep my eye on you throughout it all, they've ribbed me without cease for being 'wrapped 'round the old finger.'" He sounded so gruff, she almost smiled. "Did you tell your cousins about last night?"

"Of course I did."

"You told them how I . . . how we . . ." He trailed off with a groan, bending down to rest his forehead against hers. "Jane, you dinna."

"Have you been worried about this all day?"

He pulled back his head. "Christ, yes."

She studied her nails. "Well, you deserved to agonize over it, after how hurtful you were this morning."

"Likely, but I doona want our private business bandied about by your cousins. After one day's post run, all seven will know."

"I did tell Sam and Belinda, but I didn't give details. I merely told them we've been . . . intimate but haven't, well, made love."

"That's too much still," he said, but he relaxed a fraction, leaning in again. "I dinna think you would voluntarily speak to me after this morning."

"I'm going to make myself forget what you said."

"I'd appreciate that—"

"If you make a deal with me. Every time you brood over the next two weeks, you have to give me a hundred pounds."

"A hundred? Why do you want this?"

"I've realized today that just because we're forced to spend this time together, it doesn't have to be miserable. I want to enjoy myself—with you—and it's impossible when you're mired in thoughts of something else."

"I canna just change myself—"

"Make the deal, Hugh, or I *won't* forget what you said this morning, and I *will* divulge everything to my cousins, right down to the exact words you were saying when you were above me."

He looked away, jaw clenched so hard that she thought he could chew metal, and gritted out, "I'll make the deal."

"Good. But be warned, those pounds will add up rapidly."

"I think I can handle it."

"The expense or the not brooding?"

He was saved from answering when Sam's daughter Emily appeared.

"Come on, Aunt Janey," the girl cried, grabbing Jane's hand and pulling her toward the lawn.

Jane caught Hugh's hand, and over her shoulder, she explained, "Emily's like I was when I was little—running wild all day until I dropped where I stood."

"When you were little?" Hugh raised his brows. "You were still like that at thirteen."

She chuckled, which seemed to surprise him. When they reached a blanket on the lawn, Jane sat and tugged Hugh's hand until he dropped down beside her. Emily crawled into her lap.

"Aunt Janey," Emily whispered loudly, "is he the rough Scot you married?"

Jane saw his face grow cold immediately. "He is."

Emily eyed him suspiciously. "Am I really to call him uncle, then?"

"Um, yes, sweeting, he's your uncle Hugh."

"Is he really going to buy us presents?"

To Emily, she whispered loudly, "You should ask him."

Emily tilted her head. "Are you going to get me the dollies I asked for?"

Hugh looked at Jane briefly before answering. "Aye."

"You won't forget?"

When he shook his head, Emily flashed him one of the beatific smiles that, in the past, had gotten Jane to promise her—and deliver—a brown-spotted, white pony that Emily could name Freckles. Hugh merely gave Emily a nod, like a man greeting an acquaintance at a club.

Before Emily scampered away, she said, "Bye . . . Uncle Hugh."

Jane frowned at him. "You act like you've never been around children before."

"I have no'. No' in years." Then he tensed. "What should I have done?" He seemed to be waiting intently for her answer.

Hugh tries. . . . "Well, you could have said, 'Yes, sweet, but only if you are good all week long,' or something along that line."

He seemed to be filing that away. "Dinna know you liked bairns so much."

"I *love* them," she said, glancing over at the children playing, getting grass stains all over themselves. "I love everything about them. How their hair smells like sunshine at the end of the day, and how they feel everything so strongly and they're so quick to laugh. . . ." She trailed off at his darkening expression. "Did I say something?"

"Why have you no' gone about getting your own?" he snapped.

She drew back. "Alas, there's an intermediary necessary for 'getting' them—he's called a husband."

"Seems like you should no' have been so stringent about your 'qualifications' for a husband, then."

"You make it sound like it's too late—I'm only twenty-seven! My mother had me when she was twenty-nine. There is no reason for me to settle. Or there *was* no reason to settle—oh, I'm confused. I swear, it'd be so much easier if I was either completely married or completely single."

"But right now, you're half-married to a *rough Scot*?" he grated.

That had really gotten to him. "They don't mean anything by it."

He looked away and plucked a piece of grass as he asked, "Were you . . . were you shamed to have me here as your husband?"

"Oh, heavens, no!" she said, then wished she'd been a little more poised—and a little less exclamatory—in her answer, even as his grim expression eased somewhat.

She didn't care what her cousins said. She'd always found Hugh's rugged looks handsome. He dressed simply but well, and he had good manners for all that he didn't talk much—and for all that his handshake was a "bit excruciating," as Robert had told Sam, who'd told Jane.

"Besides, rough Scot is a lot better than what they call Robert." When Hugh raised his eyebrows, she said, "They call Robert the laughing quack. He thinks the two of you are fast friends, by the way. He told me he got a good sense about you, though he couldn't wrangle more than two words out of you. He's usually right about these things."

"Good sense, huh? Then why. . . ?" He never finished the question, as he'd caught sight of Lawrence starting the bonfire. "There's to be a fire?" He eyed his surroundings warily. "Here?"

She nodded. "We eat supper out here whenever the weather's this nice."

"I ken that." His gaze was watchful as Belinda and Sam began setting out food and wine.

"We will stay, won't we?"

He swung a look at her as if she'd just asked him to drink from the Thames.

They intended to sit out here. All of them. Together. Oh, no, no.

"No, we canna stay." He rose, pulling her up with him. This, Hugh would not do.

He and his brothers had been invited to attend those fireside dinners, but they'd never accepted, all of them too uncomprehending of the strange behavior of this family. Men drank readily and smoked cigars in front of their wives, trilling laughter sounded throughout the night, children slept draped over their parents wherever they'd fallen asleep, not waking even at the loud laughter.

How many nights had the three brothers sat out on their terrace, listening, giving each other looks of bewilderment?

Now he was to be on the other side of the cove, for the fire?

He must have shown how dismayed he was, because she sidled up to him, a smile playing about her wine-reddened lips—the lips he'd burned to sample when he'd pressed her against the house just minutes ago.

"I'd really like to eat here tonight," she said.

He shook his head sternly.

"Please?" she asked in a soft voice, making him wonder which was worse—that she could manage him, or that they both knew she could.

She took his hand, easing them back down to the blanket. "We'll just sit here." He knew she was manipulating him, but he was also aware she would clasp his arm and mold her body to his as they sat. Withstand the fire; get this attention.

He would win this one.

Leaning close, her breasts soft against his arm, she trailed her hand up to the back of his neck, then made slow, lazy circles with her nails. "This is not so bad, is it?"

Not with her, but the others had all convened—from nannies to bairns to couples—all lazy on blankets around the fire, with delicacies spread about on china dishes.

Though Jane prepared him a selection, and the food smelled delicious, he had no appetite.

Once the children had dropped off—with the wee lass Emily bundled in a blanket and curled over Jane's ankles—and the nannies had retired, more bottles of wine surfaced. The talk grew lively and the language turned frank, even in front of the ladies, even *by* the ladies.

Hugh glanced up when he heard Robert say, "At least Hugh knows what she's like. Imagine if he'd married her without having known her for so long."

Samantha said, "Well, I'm sure he knows that Janey's the wildest of the Eight."

"I am not!" Jane cried.

"Does Hugh know about the Russian prince?" Samantha asked, and Jane gave a self-satisfied smile.

Hugh's no' sure he wants to know about the Russian prince. . . .

But Samantha had already begun. "Just this spring at a ball, a horrid old lecher of a prince stuck his hand down Charlotte's bodice. Little Charlotte was so mortified! So we all went on the offensive, spreading rumors about his eleventh toe of a male appendage." Samantha's eyes were glinting with amusement. "But Jane merely watched from the side like a tigress sizing up prey, waiting for the right moment. I saw the whole thing happening. As he strolled past her, she flashed him a come-hither smile. His attention was so fixed on her that he never saw her foot sweep out from under her skirts to trip him. He crashed face first into the gala-size punch bowl."

Hugh felt the corners of his lips quirking. Fierce lass.

Belinda added, "Jane sauntered up to us, brushing her hands off, and remarked"—she mimicked Jane's sensual voice—"'Darlings, all men bow before the Weyland Eight. Or they fall.'"

Hugh raised his eyebrows at Jane, and the words slipped out: "They bow, do they?"

"Weren't you listening?" she asked with a saucy grin. "That, or they fall. And the big ones like you fall *hard*."

No bloody kidding.

Everyone laughed. After that, the conversation devolved into a dirty limerick contest. When Hugh found himself on the verge of grinning, he grew guarded. He forced himself to draw back. That's what he did—he was always on the outside, looking in. Always. It wasn't difficult—he was so different from these people, it was like night and day.

Everyone here was so bloody comfortable in their own skin, so settled and sure in their relationships, affection displayed openly, unconsciously. Samantha laughed with her lips pressed to Robert's neck. Belinda and Lawrence held hands to walk ten feet to go retrieve her shawl.

What would it be like if he belonged here, if Jane truly were his? What would *he* be like without the constant shadow of the *Leabhar* over him? How he envied this life.

One family so blessed, one cursed.

When he exhaled, Jane absently stroked the back of his neck with her nails, as though she sensed he needed it.

He stared into the fire. Just weeks ago, the woman his brother loved—the only one he'd ever loved—had almost died. Because of Court's brash actions, the two of them had been hunted down by the Rechazado.

Two had followed Annalía's brother to the MacCarrick home in London, and had seized her, dragging her outside. When Court had charged after her, one shoved a gun against her temple so hard she'd been bruised. Court could do nothing to help her, could only grate out a strangled plea to Hugh, who, as usual, had been on the periphery and able to back away.

Hugh had made it upstairs to his room, snatched up his rifle, and drawn a bead from the second-story window. Never had a shot meant so much—he knew his brother would be destroyed if the girl died.

Hugh had succeeded in killing the target in a way that prevented the man from firing, but Annalía had had to crawl away from the dropped body that still clenched her. Before Court could get to her, she'd slipped in the pooling blood, crying softly.

And as he'd seen Court rushing to her, Hugh had been shamed to feel relief—that he himself had never risked Jane. He remembered thinking, "I'll die before I expose Jane to something like this."

But he was. . . .

Jane kissed his ear and murmured, "A hundred pounds and counting. Care to make it two?"

Twenty-eight

———•◆•———

Grey felt the hairs on the back of his neck stand up just before the tavern went silent.

He shook his head, grinning into his cup. The unrelenting bastard had just entered the very lakeside tavern where Grey had reposed during the day—and the one he was departing from by ferry as soon as darkness fell.

Grey had already determined his means of a swift exit and slipped toward the side door, but he hesitated in the shadows to get a closer look at his pursuer.

Ethan MacCarrick. Ah, the fiend that fiends feared.

That made Grey want to chuckle.

Ethan's eyes were intent, surveying the scene for threats. His face was set in a scowl, his scar bone white. Grey had always hankered to know who'd dealt Ethan that blow, but Hugh wouldn't speak of the subject and resented being asked about it. Yet Grey knew that whoever had done the job had had skill—Ethan's scar whitened with any expression—and he had done it when Ethan was still a young man.

Backing to a wall, Ethan continued searching the crowd, no doubt for drunken patrons who looked like regulars. Grey knew that they were the gatekeepers—the ones with all the information—because drunks could be remarkably perceptive, and no one was guarded enough around them.

Under Ethan's watchful glare, a patron suddenly bolted toward the door. Within the space of a heartbeat, Ethan had the man by the hair, hauling him outside.

Grey skulked out the back, trailing as Ethan pulled the man into a foggy alley. From a distance, Grey watched him slowly strangling the man with one hand, then allowing him to gasp out words in violent intervals. Grey rolled his eyes. Ethan's style had always been blunt and dependent on power.

When the mark yelled a name that was actually a roundabout lead to him, Grey supposed Ethan had had *some* success with it. After knocking the man flat, Ethan returned to the tavern, inadvertently trapping Grey—the bloody ferryman was *inside*, guzzling ale, waiting on Grey to give the word to depart.

Damn it! Although Grey was only a half-hour ferry ride away from Ros Creag, he felt he needed to move quickly. He suspected that Hugh wasn't planning to remain at the lake much longer. Hugh must know Grey would eventually discover his den.

If Ethan didn't withdraw from the tavern directly and ride from this small town, Grey would have to kill him tonight. Grey hadn't planned to—at present; he wanted to murder Jane. He'd always found it prudent to prioritize these things lest one overextend oneself, and yet already he'd deviated from his plan by pursuing Lysette.

In this matter, however, Grey might not have much choice.

But Ethan wasn't exactly an easy target. To strike without detection, getting close enough to the man to gut him, would take hours of work—hours Grey didn't have.

After a quarter of an hour passed and Ethan remained inside, Grey realized he was going to have to *shoot* Ethan. . . .

Assessing the area for a serviceable vantage, he found a balcony that faced the tavern's front entrance with a view of the side alleyway as well. As he climbed up one of the balcony's iron filigree supports, each old bullet wound in his chest screamed in protest.

But once he'd set up his position, time crawled by as he waited for Ethan to emerge. He watched people strolling on the street, or entering and exiting the tavern's groaning front door. Was Ethan eating in there? Interrogating? Grey knew he wasn't likely buying a woman. Ethan took no pleasure in life, not even pleasure in women any longer.

After well over an hour, Ethan exited from the side door. Grey aimed his pistol, though his hand shook wildly. With his other hand, he slipped medicine between his lips to ease it.

Immediately, Grey knew something was different about Ethan. In the light of a flickering street lamp, Ethan looked distracted, off his game.

Grey knew of only one thing that could make the man look like that, because he'd seen a similar expression on Hugh's face many a time.

Ethan MacCarrick had a woman on his mind.

In the past, Ethan had put on a good show, seeming uncaring about his appearance. But now, when two boys stopped and stared at his face, his brows drew together, as if he were only just comprehending how people saw him.

He glowered at them, but evinced no satisfaction when he made them flee. Instead, he ran the back of his hand roughly over the scar.

Grey wouldn't pity him, though. Not when he remembered sweating with pain while locked in that dank basement. A flare of rage began to burn inside him, until it overrode even the most assiduous chewing of his medicine.

When Ethan had finally released him, Grey had acted as though he were grateful and on his way to wellness. Hugh had appeared so bloody relieved—and so guilty for hitting Grey. "Ach, it's good to have you back," Hugh had said. But Ethan had given him a look that said, "I'll be watching you."

Now Grey watched him. Again, he took a bead with a tremulous hand, willing it to grow steady.

Though Ethan couldn't have heard the sound from his distance away, the instant Grey cocked his pistol, he froze. He either sensed Grey at last or realized how careless he'd been, walking into an alleyway with vantages all around, without so much as a cursory scan of the area.

Ethan gazed upward and spotted Grey. His expression was disbelieving; so was Grey's—he'd never thought he would take out the great Ethan MacCarrick so easily. Then Ethan's face became a mask of rage. He yanked his gun free and fired.

When the bullet merely whistled through a deceptive billow in his bagging clothing, Grey pulled the trigger.

Blood spurted straight into the air from Ethan's chest, then cascaded over his fallen body.

A pathetic shot? Not tonight. Grey had aimed true.

Twenty-nine

———— •◆• ————

*H*ugh rode back to Ros Creag with Jane dozing in his arms. She'd fallen asleep tucked against his chest in front of the fire, with the girl still slumbering over her legs. Once Robert had scooped up Emily, Hugh had gently lifted Jane, then quietly refused offers to stay the night.

Now Hugh found himself almost grinning as he imagined the looks on his brothers' faces when he told them he'd endured an evening at the Weylands'. They'd never believe him.

Yet it hadn't been that bad. No, he admitted to himself, it was one of the most enjoyable times he'd had in years. And now he was holding Jane again, and the moon was out, and she was . . . *nuzzling his chest*? He drew back his head. "Jane, are you awake?"

"Only just," she murmured, sliding her hands up to clutch his shoulders.

He frowned down at her. "Then are you drunk, lass?"

"No, I feel very clear."

In a voice gone hoarse, he asked, "Why're you unbuttoning my shirt?" There was no way she could miss his instant reaction, seated as she was. Grabbing her upper arms, he shifted her until she wasn't directly on his stiffened shaft. "No, Jane, you ken we canna—" Sweet Christ, had she just touched her lips, her tongue, to his chest? He threw his head back and stared up at the moon. All of the vows he'd reiterated to himself today grew indistinct in his mind, and he shook his head hard. "You continue to treat this like it's a game."

She blinked open her eyes as if she'd just woken from a dream. "I don't treat it—"

"You knew better than to go anywhere without me."

"I had to talk to my cousins. I needed their advice. Badly," she said cryptically.

Though he knew she'd never answer, he asked, in a deadened tone, "About what?" Excellent. Yet another secret that would taunt him.

"About the fact that . . ."—she leaned up to press her lips tenderly to his—"I want you to make love to me."

He almost slid off the horse and took her with him.

Her light touches during the day had goaded him, stoking his need for her—which had only burgeoned after last night—to a fever pitch. And all day, he'd played the part of her husband. Despite himself, he'd begun to feel like one.

Tonight, he wanted to demand a husband's due.

"You want me tae take you?" His voice roughened at the thought.

When she nodded against his chest, he exhaled a breath he hadn't known he'd held. He found himself positioning her on his lap, turning her until she was astraddle him. Once her legs hung over his, he ruched up her skirt high in the front and back. As he kissed her neck, one of his hands clutched her nape, the other rubbing far down her back to dip inside her silk pantalettes.

Squeezing her bottom, he lifted her up against his erection, rocking her to it, making her whimper, and him curse in agony. When he set her back down, she sucked in a shocked breath, because he'd cupped her between her legs so her sex rested in his palm. Her flesh was warm and wet in his hold, and she moaned in delight at the contact. But her moan turned to an anguished cry when his finger eased inside her.

Her sheath was incredibly tight and gripped his finger hungrily, making his cock ache to replace it. "I will no' be able to stop myself," he grated. "It will no' be like last night."

His thumb and forefinger played, and her head lolled, but he retained his firm hold on the back of her neck to make her face him.

Eyes heavy-lidded, she nodded.

"Do you understand me?" He rubbed her sensuously, and she began to undulate against his fingers.

"Hugh, oh, God! Yes, I do."

As soon as she'd panted the words, realization hit him and his entire body stiffened. "*I'm going tae be inside you tonight.*" After so long. "You want me tae be." Another thrust of his finger to punctuate his words.

"Oh, I do!" She was close. He could feel her body quivering, her thighs tightening and relaxing around his hips in seeking intervals until he thought he was going to explode.

Inevitable. He ached to possess her, and she wanted him to do the same. Why had he ever imagined that he could fight this? At her ear, he rasped, "*Come for me first.*"

"*Hugh, I will . . .*" She kissed him fiercely when her orgasm began, giving a wild cry against his lips. Her nails dug into his shoulders, and her wet little sheath clenched around his finger, again and again. His cock grew slick at the tip in anticipation of that tight heat.

When she sagged against his shoulder, he moved his hands from her sex to cupping her bottom. Once they'd reached Ros Creag, he kept her in the same position with her legs locked around his waist, even as he dismounted and tossed the reins in the vicinity of the tethering post.

By the time he'd bolted the front door behind them, she'd gone from resting her forehead on his shoulder to kissing him, clutching his arms, her hand colliding with his as they grasped each other.

Desperate to bury himself inside her, he hastened toward his bed, bounding up the stairs two at a time, breathing hard against her damp neck. Inside his room, he laid her back on the bed, then shrugged from his jacket and pistol holster, tossing them both aside. After he'd yanked his shirt over his head, she reached her arms up to him.

He had one knee in the mattress to go to her. After wanting her for so long—

Hugh froze.

Outside, the gate to the terrace creaked on its hinges.

Hugh's head whipped up, his dark eyes flickering over her face. He bolted to his pistol.

"Hugh? What's happening?" She felt so dazed from her recent pleasure that she could barely form words.

"Stay there," he snapped, striding to the windows, yanking the heavy curtains closed. "Doona move, especially not in front of the windows."

"I-is Grey out there?"

"It could be nothing." Hugh cautiously peered out one side of the drawn curtains.

"I thought he hadn't reached England yet."

"I doona want to take any chances."

She was startled by the idea of Grey being just outside, but she wasn't afraid. She was too reassured by Hugh's presence. "Should I have my bow?"

"No, lass, you doona need your bow."

"How long will you stay there?"

"Till dawn," he answered.

"What? Why don't you come to bed? You bolted the doors—he can't get in."

"If he's out there, I might catch sight of him."

She asked slowly, "And what would you do if you found him?"

His voice was quiet, cold. "Kill him."

"But he was your friend," Jane said. "I always believed we were more or less absconding, not, er . . . executing."

"He's killed before."

"No, you're not serious. . . ." She trailed off when he caught her gaze, his eyes locked on hers.

"Men. And women."

"Why? What's made him do that?"

"I've told you, his mind is damaged. His affliction is worse than it's ever been."

Her eyes went wide. "Is he like Burke and Hare, or Springheeled Jack?" she asked in a breathless voice. "One of those compulsion killers that I've read about in the *Times*?"

"I'm sure he has much in common with them."

"Why didn't you tell me?"

"I didn't want to frighten you needlessly," he said, then added in a distracted tone, "And I never thought he would even get close to us."

"If you knew he was such a horrible killer, why did you agree to this? You could be risking your life."

He said nothing.

"Hugh, you wouldn't, um, risk your life for mine?"

"What kind of question is that?"

She made a sound of frustration. "Oh, just answer me, won't you?"

His body seemed to tense, and after an obvious struggle, he gritted through his teeth, "Aye."

"T-truly?" Her voice went higher.

"Just try to get some sleep."

As if that was going to happen. After a few long moments, she asked, "How does he kill them?"

"With a blade."

The blood drained from her face, leaving it cool. "Grey . . . *stabs* them? Even women? Would he do that to *me*?"

Hugh hesitated. "I doona know that telling you—"

"I have to know, Hugh," she interrupted sharply. "I need to know what he plans."

Hugh's gaze flickered over her face. Finally he said, "He slits their throats—"

A violent pounding on the door boomed through the silent home.

Thirty

Jane jerked with fright, then whispered, "Who in the devil would be knocking?"

"Ethan." Hugh relaxed a fraction, stowing his gun in his pants waist. *It has to be.* "My brother is supposed to meet us here. Jane, lock the door behind me, and doona come out until I return."

When she followed him to the door, he strode from the room, pausing outside only long enough to hear the lock click into place.

His brother's timing was as impeccable as ever—just when Hugh had decided to take Jane, just when he hadn't had a doubt in his mind that he would . . .

Hugh hurried down the stairs, then crossed to a front window. When he glanced past the curtain, unease crept up his spine. It was one of Weyland's messengers—not his brother.

In that instant, he realized something had happened to Ethan. Hugh yanked open the door and snatched the missive from the grim man. "Do you know anything about my brother?" Hugh asked, though it was unlikely since most messengers weren't privy to important information.

The man shook his head, then turned away directly to set off and confirm that the missive had been received.

Locking the door again, Hugh ripped open the letter and read the one line. Disbelieving what it said, he crumpled the paper in his fist, then turned and charged up the stairs.

As soon as Jane opened the door to him, he shouted orders. "Pack your smallest bag with clothes, essentials only. You can take your bow but no' thirty bloody books. We leave in ten minutes."

"What's happened?"

"Grey's in England. Has been for days." If Grey could control the Network like this, deceiving and manipulating so many in the field, then his addiction wasn't impairing him mentally as they'd suspected. It seemed the man had lost nothing, and was *playing* with them. "He could have followed us directly here."

Hugh had been so intent on getting into Jane's skirts, he hadn't been concentrating on protecting her from a man whose entire life centered on killing.

Grey could attack in so many insidious ways. He could poison the well, or burn the house with a mixture of turpentine and alcohol, then pick off anyone who escaped. Toward the end, burning had become a particular favorite of his.

Swooping together piles of clothes, she said, "How do you know he's in England?" She must have sensed that he was about to hedge his answer, because she snapped, "This is no time to be secretive! I'm in the middle of this, too!"

Hugh ran his hand over his face. "He killed Lysette."

She gasped, dropping the bag she'd been filling. "If he could be near, then what about my family at Vinelands?"

"Grey has never gone out of his way to kill indiscriminately—only people he hates, or who fit his agenda. But to be safe, I'll leave a letter for Robert explaining that they should make haste to leave."

"Only people he hates? Then why would he kill Lysette?" She resumed packing. "You said they were lovers."

"They had been, but it ended badly. He thought she betrayed him."

"Hugh, if he's really out there right now, he could shoot us."

"He does no' like to shoot," Hugh assured her. "He was never verra good at it, even before he was afflicted with tremors."

"But why don't we stay here? Stay locked in—"

"He'll have no qualms about burning the house down around us." He strode up to her, grasping her shoulders. "Lass, I'm going to keep you safe, I vow it, but you need to trust that I know what I'm doing."

She gave him a shaky nod.

"Now, dress to ride in the forest. Something dark if you have it."

"We're leaving the coach?"

"The driver's off the property. Besides, Grey can track a coach, but he'll never follow our trail on horseback," he said as he scanned her suddenly empty floor. *Was* there a bloody system to her clothing that he couldn't discern? "Remember that rocky trail up by the waterfall to the north?"

"Yes, you wouldn't let me ride it when I was younger."

"Well, we're going to ride it tonight, and until we're well away, we're going to do it really bloody fast."

• • •

Fifteen minutes later found them riding in the woods through fog so thick, it seemed to swirl like an unctuous current in the moonlight.

Hugh had her reins fisted in his hand, and Jane held on to her horse's mane as it charged up and over the harsh terrain. Branches snatched at her clothing and at her hair until it came free, streaming behind her.

At the first sign that her horse stumbled, Hugh brought her mount forward beside his own, and dragged Jane behind him. Making sure she was holding on tight, he took up a breakneck pace. His surefooted horse proved up to the task, her mount bustling along behind.

Nothing in London could compare with this thrill—her arms around the torso of a Highlander as he rode faster than she'd ever ridden a horse, much less at night.

Though it all felt dreamlike to her, Hugh was very purposeful and alert. All night, like a chess player anticipating his opponent's moves, Hugh guided them north. Oftentimes, he would ride in one direction, then slow, cock his head, and turn back around.

"How are you doing, lass?" he asked periodically, patting her leg.

Now that she realized the danger she was in, she was overwhelmed by how much Hugh was doing for her. The image of him at the moonlit window, body tense, eyes watchful, ready to do battle, was seared into her mind.

He'd admitted he would risk his life for hers. With that, she knew for certain that he couldn't have left her before out of callousness, or neglected to tell her good-bye out of indifference. No, Hugh was so much more than what she saw on the surface. And she planned to investigate all the layers.

She hugged him tighter, and all of a sudden she was seventeen again, riding behind him just as they'd always done when they'd explored new places.

"Do you need to stop?" he asked over his shoulder.

"No, I'm fine. I-I'm excited to go to the Highlands at last."

After a hesitation, he answered, "It's no' always like it is in English ballads."

"What do you—"

"Duck," he commanded. She did, just in time to skim under a limb. "There are brigands and reivers who are no' as heroic as you read about."

"Oh." Long ago, she'd looked up Carrickliffe on a map, and she remembered it was far to the north on the coast. "Are we going to your clan?"

"No' that far. No' yet."

She stifled a sigh of relief. After all these years of yearning to go there, now she balked.

"We'll go to Court's."

"Where's his home?"

"Southern Highlands. If it seems all right, we'll stay there instead. I warn you, it's no' going to be luxurious, but I think it will be the safest place."

"Is Court going to be there?" *Please say no.*

"No, he's probably in London by now. Or he might have decided to stay on the Continent and go on a job to the east with his men." He muttered something that sounded like: "As long as he didn't go back for her."

"What's that?" she asked, clasping her hands on his hard torso, fighting the urge to rub her face against his back.

"Nothing, lass. Try to get some sleep if you can."

When he placed his big, rough hand over both of hers and warmed them, a realization hit her like a thunderbolt: she hadn't been pushed off a cliff. She'd dived, and the ground was approaching, had *always* been approaching.

She'd just had her eyes closed.

Thirty-one

———•◆•———

$\mathcal{A}$s Jane bent down to the crystal-clear creek, cupping water to her mouth, a branch cracked behind her. She whirled around, but saw no one in the dying light of the day. She knew Hugh would have announced himself, and he wouldn't have been finished unpacking the horses for the night. It must be an animal—the forests they'd been traveling through were teeming with roe deer.

She sat on the bank, pulling her skirts up to dip her stockingless legs and a cloth into the chill stream. As she brought the cloth to her face, she reflected over the last four days, during which Hugh had taken them racing through thick woodlands and over craggy rock plains.

The scenery continued to grow more and more breathtaking as they passed ancient Celtic fortifications and sweeping vistas. The leaves were staggering in color—shot through with scarlet, gold, and ochre. Now that they were officially in the Highlands, everything seemed crisper, sharper. Even the air was sweeter. London was dingy by comparison.

Late each night, they'd stopped to camp beneath the trees. Each morning, she'd watched Hugh rise in stages, wincing in sympathy as he clenched his jaw against what must be marked pain. And still he'd set to work, quickly readying them so they could make their way—as he'd told her—toward his brother Courtland's property.

Over each mile, as she rode beside him, she'd watched him study the land, much as he had done when he'd taken her hunting years before. He used every amazing skill she'd ever seen him demonstrate as a hunter, and she'd realized she was as awed by him as she had been at thirteen.

And now he was her *husband*.

His intense, focused expression drew her eyes again and again, reminding her of how he'd looked at her those last two nights at Ros Creag. Unfortunately, he'd made no move to touch her since then.

She knew he would deem their last encounter a close call and be thankful they'd dodged a bullet. She deemed it an *if at first you don't succeed* encounter.

As she brought her wet towel to her face, she contemplated her future, wondering, as ever, if it would include him. The facts: He found her attractive, and he'd wanted to make love to her. He would die for her. That first night he'd returned to London, he'd been so dirty because he'd ridden for days to reach her.

So why wouldn't he desire her for more—

Footsteps over crackling leaves sounded just behind her. Before she could whirl around, a hand covered her mouth; other hands seized her, dragging her away from the water and deeper into the shadowy woods.

She dug her heels into the ground, furiously biting at the hand over her mouth, clawing wildly. The man holding her grunted and cursed. Just as his hand moved, she twisted around to see her attacker; cold metal pressed against her throat and she stilled in terror—

"Get your hands off my wife," Hugh said with a steely calm.

The men froze. Jane frantically blew hair from her eyes and saw Hugh with a rifle, raised and steady, his eyes as cold as ash in the dying sun. He had it aimed at one of the two men who'd grabbed her, the one who had a hunting knife against her neck and a soiled bandanna hanging down around his own. The second man trained his pistol on Hugh. "Let her go, or I'll kill you."

Raw fury emanated from Hugh, but somehow he controlled it.

These two must be bandits, some of the very unheroic ones Hugh had mentioned. Why weren't they hiding their faces with the cloths they wore?

Because she and Hugh weren't only to be robbed.

Rattled by Hugh's killing look, the man holding her swallowed audibly, his bandanna rising with his Adam's apple, and pressed the blade harder to her skin. When she felt blood dripping down, she gasped.

Hugh's eyes narrowed, but he said nothing, just waited. Jane realized that she'd seen him go utterly still like this before—when he'd been hunting and had a target in sight.

Time seemed to slow. How many times had she seen this uncanny concentration just before his forefinger smoothly pressed the trigger? When she saw Hugh's thumb brushing his rifle, she realized these men were about to die.

The one clutching her began dragging her away. The knife wasn't so tight at her neck as they stumbled back. She should hit him . . . kick him . . . give Hugh his chance to shoot.

Jane felt the bandit's rank breath waft over her as he said to Hugh, "Yer bonnie wife's about to be my—"

The boom of the rifle made her jerk with fright, but the knife was gone. The man lay crumpled to the ground behind her, blood oozing from a hole between his sightless eyes.

She glanced back at Hugh.

Never taking his gaze from the second man's shaking pistol, Hugh emptied the cartridge from his rifle as if he had all the time in the world. "Pull the trigger, then," Hugh demanded, *impatiently*.

Jane screamed when the bandit shot; a bit of dark cloth flew up, but she couldn't tell where Hugh had been hit. When the man saw Hugh was still standing, he paled and hurled his gun at Hugh before spinning around to run.

Jane tottered on her feet. *So close.* But Hugh must have been unharmed, because he tossed his empty rifle to the ground and caught the man in three long strides, his movements contained, lethally silent.

Everything's as silent as he is. The woods hushed by the shot. Or is my hearing weakened from the report? Then she heard a whimper, and didn't know if it came from her or the wide-eyed man struggling to free himself. But his thrashing was useless—Hugh's grip was unyielding, his massive hands and forearms clamped around the man's head.

How can Hugh move so quietly? What an odd grip he's got on the bandit—

Jane flinched as Hugh's strong arms twisted in different directions. Suddenly, the thick pop of breaking bone was deafening. The man dropped to his knees, head lolling at an unnatural angle, before his body slumped to the ground.

After a heartbeat's hesitation, Hugh turned to face her.

Thirty-two

———— •◆• ————

Jane's slim body shook with ragged breaths. Her pupils were dilated and her lips were pale and parted in shock.

A trail of stark crimson crept from the slice at her neck, and alarm flared in him. "Sìne, I need to look at you," he said as he cautiously eased closer, fully expecting her to run. He knew what he must look like, and he knew that what he'd done to those two would terrify her.

No response.

"Jane, I dinna do this lightly," he explained slowly, approaching her. "Those men would have killed you." *Eventually.*

Nothing. Her face was drawn, white with fear. When he stood before her, he prayed she wouldn't run. *Doona flinch from me. . . .* He couldn't take it if Jane feared him.

He eased a hand to the slash on her neck, brushing his fingertips to it, then nearly sagged in relief to find it was a mere graze. Before he could stop himself, he put his arms around her. As he clutched her to him and lowered his head to hers, he groaned at the feel of her, warm and *safe* in his arms, but her body was quaking. "Shh, lass," he said against her hair. "You're safe now."

"Wh-what just happened?" she whispered. "I don't understand what just happened. Were they bandits?"

"Aye, of a sort."

"Are you hurt?" There was a burn mark and a small hole through the outside of his pants leg.

"No, no' at all. Do you think you can ride tonight?"

"But what are we going to do with the b-bodies?"

"Leave them. They will no' be found for some time, if ever." He drew back so he could look down into her eyes. Running his hands up and down her arms, he said, "We must leave this place immediately. Can you get dressed while I see to the camp?"

She nodded up at him, and he forced himself to release her, knowing he had work to do, and quickly. Keeping a close watch on her as she dressed and daubed a wet cloth to her neck, he packed up their gear and re-saddled their horses.

When Jane was ready, she said, "Can I . . . can I ride with you?" She glanced down as if embarrassed to ask.

Without hesitation, he lifted her into his saddle, then swung up behind her, wrapping an arm around her. He exhaled a long breath, pleased she still wanted to be near him.

"Try to rest—I'll ride through the night."

She gave him a shaky nod.

Eager to get her away from this area, he redoubled their already punishing pace. After an hour of hard riding, they reached a craggy, dry creek bed. When they had to slow to cross, she murmured, "Thank you. For what you did back there—for what you're doing."

"Say nothing of it."

"Apparently, you're more of an expert at this than I'd imagined." When he was silent, she continued, "Which makes me wonder, in light of this and Lysette's death, how much of an expert Grey is."

He ground his teeth.

"You're not a mercenary, and he's not a businessman."

"No."

"Care to explain?"

Finally, he answered, "I canna tell you, even if I wanted to."

"Do you want to?"

"I . . . doona know." Part of him did—to get her look of disgust over with.

After long moments passed, she asked, "Are you angry with me?"

"God, no, why would I be?"

"Because I got you into this situation."

"Lass, you are no' at fault here. I am. I should have been more aware—"

"No, I wasn't saying I thought *I* was at fault—*neither* of us is. I was saying that I'm sorry you had to kill because of me. I fear you'll feel badly about it."

"Should I no'?"

He felt her shoulders stiffen. "I will truly have my feelings hurt if you regret doing something noble and necessary to save my life."

Noble? He felt a deep welling of pride, and discovered then that noble was exactly how he wanted to be around her—exactly how he hoped she might see him.

She'd watched him kill with his hands, but she understood he'd had no choice. *Necessary.* The thought came from nowhere: *She could accept that I've killed. Without judging me.*

But could she accept the way he'd done it?

In the papers and in literature, assassins were regarded as cowardly and were universally reviled—even those from one's own country. In the last three major Continental wars, every army that captured snipers executed them summarily—there were no prisoners, no exchanges. Not that there would have been bargaining for gunmen like Hugh anyway. . . .

None of this mattered. Hugh couldn't tell her of his involvement without divulging others'.

"Hugh?"

"I could have let the second one run for his life."

"What if there were others in his gang? Or h-he might have wanted revenge for the death of the other. Or he could have caused a commotion, and then Grey would know we've been here."

Hugh might have considered these factors, but he hadn't. There'd been no thoughts in his head when he caught the second man—nothing but the need to kill him for daring to touch her.

"You don't feel guilty, do you?" Jane asked.

"It dinna exactly improve my mood."

She twisted around, wriggling over his leg and against his arm so she could face him. Irritation was clear in her expression. "You act as if you'd had to shoot orphans and kittens! You killed *killers*." She frowned, her voice growing soft. "Do you regret having to do that to save me?"

His arm tightened around her. "No, lass, never." *I relished it.* "I just would rather . . . I dinna want you to see that."

She blinked at him. "To see how brave you are? To see you just stand there while the man shot at you?"

"It was no' bravery. The odds were slim that he could have hit me in a place that would put me down before I could get to him. And I meant that I dinna want you to see blood and death. I doona want that memory to follow you. To hurt you."

"*If* it was a memory that could hurt me, I simply wouldn't allow it to pervade my life. I don't want you to think I'm glib, or cold." She seemed to be choosing her words very carefully. "But I believe when the load gets too heavy, we have to shuck some weight from our shoulders. And Hugh"—she gently laid her hands on his forearm locked across her middle—"it really seems that you need to lighten your load."

What if I did? What if he just refused to feel guilt over his deeds and stopped dwelling on all he'd done? The temptation to do so was great.

Another mile passed in silence. At length, she murmured, "Hugh, when you called me your wife like that . . ." She trailed off.

He briefly closed his eyes. "I know. It will no' happen again."

"Th-that's not what I was going to say." She was trembling against his chest, her wee hands tightening their grip on his arm.

"Then what?"

Her next words made him sweat for the first time that day. "When you called me your wife, I found I really . . . like it."

If Jane had been curious about Hugh's life before the attack yesterday, now she was desperate to know more.

Though they'd finally slowed their pace to ascend a slippery embankment, she wouldn't question him now. She glanced over at him riding beside her in the morning sun, and her heart ached at how exhausted he appeared.

He'd been ever wary, so vigilant to protect her—and they'd ridden hard.

The attack had demonstrated yet again how stalwart a guardian Hugh was. When she'd had the knife at her throat, she hadn't believed she was going to die—not then—but she had comprehended how her life would end if it came down to Grey.

Jane wouldn't take another minute with Hugh for granted.

"We're almost there, lass," he said then, with an encouraging nod. "I ken how hard this has been for you."

"For me? What about for you?" He and his horse looked much like they had that night in London.

He shrugged. "I'm accustomed to days like this."

"Of course," she said absently as she tilted her head to study him.

Hugh was a powerful protector, ready to unleash a chilling violence; yet, with her, he was tender and passionate. He had secrets, but she knew he'd be a faithful husband. He'd always desired her happiness above his own.

Just then, a breeze blew a lock of his thick black hair over one of his dark eyes. . . .

She swallowed hard. Recognition took hold.

The Scotsman is . . . mine. As she gazed at him, she realized he was still *her* Hugh. Jane wanted him, always had, but now she felt an abiding respect for him—a deeper, more mature . . . *love.* Oh, lord, she didn't love Hugh as much as she had before.

She loved him much, much more.

Yet she'd barely survived his leaving *before*—now what would happen to her if she lost him again?

She had decided he would be her first lover. Now she

knew that this quiet, wonderful man had to be her last. *How can I get him to stay wed to me?* she thought, feeling panic rush through her at the thought of being forced to part from him. *No! Calm down. Think!*

"Jane, what's wrong?" he asked.

"N-nothing." She eked out a smile for him as a plan evolved in her mind.

No teasing. Only seduction. And only for keeps.

He frowned in return, and once they'd reach the rise, he increased their pace again. She was glad of the time to think.

Obviously, she needed him alone to prove that living with her wouldn't be a "wee bit like hell." So, she was pleased anew they weren't going to Carrickliffe.

Unfortunately, the only thing more undermining than a clan of strangers would be *Courtland MacCarrick*—who'd always hated her.

Hugh had said he didn't expect Court to be at his secluded home. *Perfect.* And barring Court's presence, *nothing* could keep them from staying there.

Thirty-three

———— •◆• ————

A bit of work, my arse. Hugh stifled another curse.

Upon reaching the border lands of Beinn a'Chaorainn, Court's property in the wilds of Scotland, Hugh had had his first sense of unease. The long, winding drive was overrun with fallen trees, strewn across it at irregular intervals. They were rotting, meaning no one had been here in ages, not even a caretaker with a work cart.

By the time the house came into view, rain clouds had gathered, casting the manor in an ominous light. At the sight of it, Jane seemed to wilt in her saddle. The estate where Hugh had planned to hide Jane for possibly the entire fall . . . left a lot to be desired.

With a sinking feeling, he surveyed the tangled, stunted gardens, the front door hanging askew from one rusted hinge, the windows either broken out or matted with dirt and dead ivy.

At that moment, something wide-eyed and furry careened out of the front doorway.

He glanced at Jane. Her lips were parted, her breaths little puffs in the cold air. Dark circles were stark against her pale face. Their pace had been furious, but Hugh had reasoned that they could rest and recuperate at Beinn a'Chaorainn. Yet even under the strain of their travels, she'd been trying to cheer *him* up, keeping her mood buoyant for him, sweetly scolding him for brooding.

Now, Jane's expression was guarded as Hugh dismounted and helped her from her horse. Without a word, he strode inside with his shoulders back, as if taking her here hadn't been a colossal error. The next viable alternative was to go to the clan, and he'd wanted to avoid that at all costs.

Hugh crossed the threshold, took one good look around. *And so the clan it will be.*

Feathers and nests from grouse and pigeons littered the hall. It appeared that red squirrels, maybe badgers or even foxes denned here, and Hugh could *hear* teeming in the chimney. As if standing in sentinel, a pine marten was poised upright in the entry hallway, front legs bowed aggressively.

"Look, Hugh!" Jane cried, showing genuine energy for the first time today. "It's a ferret. Or part cat? I can't tell." She eased past Hugh, cooing, "It's the most adorable wittle thing."

Hugh reached for her arm. "No, Jane, doona—"

It hissed at her and scuttled away—back inside. Jane looked crushed, mumbling something about never liking "ferret cats" anyway.

She followed him further inside, batting at the cobwebs that drifted in his wake, spitting frantically against one that brushed her lips. Freed of it, she gazed around the great room, her eyes wide with dawning horror.

His face flushing, his tone defensive, he said, "This is the last place anyone will look for us." He reckoned the manor had been broken into, and once the front door was lost, nature had moved in. Still, Beinn a'Chaorainn had never, by any stretch of the imagination, been habitable in recent memory.

There wasn't a stick of furniture to be seen, apart from three damp, pitted mattresses slumped against a wall. When Hugh's further exploration found the kitchen empty of pots and dishes, Jane said, "It appears that I'll be forgoing a bath." Her tone was strained.

He opened yet another cabinet—nothing. "I saw a loch out back." He might even have spotted steam from a hot spring, adjacent to the rocky banks—hot water ready for the taking. "If I could just find one sodding bucket, a pot to bring water up—"

He broke off when some unseen creature upstairs thundered into a run, crashed into a wall, then darted back the same way. Jane turned away, covering her face with her hands.

Crossing to her, he muttered, "Ach, Jane, I dinna know." He tentatively laid his hand on her shoulder, frowning as he pulled free a few feathers that had settled in her hair.

He'd done it—he'd finally pushed her past her limit. As they'd neared the property, he'd again warned her it would be far from luxurious. She'd replied that as long as there was a bath, she would be fine. In fact, she'd dreamed aloud about soaking for hours—and that was before they'd been covered with dust, feathers, and spiderwebs.

She was exhausted, she'd been attacked, and not only was there no bath, there was no bed and no fire, and the areas where there were precious stretches of intact windows seemed to be precisely where birds had nested.

Hugh couldn't believe he'd brought his lass to a place like this. How could she not cry?

She bent over, and when her shoulders began to shake, Hugh vowed silently that he was going to beat Courtland to within an inch of his life.

"Jane, I never would have brought you here if I'd known. And we will no' stay." He turned her toward him and gently drew her hands from her face.

Jane was . . . *laughing.*

"I'm sorry," she said, biting back a snicker, holding up her palm. "Our situation is *not* funny." With an expression of concentration, she tapped her temple and said, "*Dire,* Jane, that's what it is. Not amusing."

She was likely delirious—Hugh's expression indicated that he certainly suspected so. He was peering at her as if she'd just been released from Bedlam and would be returning forthwith. *But then the accommodations would be sublime compared to this. Many fewer grouse.*

And she lost it again.

Of course, this was where Courtland MacCarrick lived. She didn't know which was worse: Court owning a place like this—or the fact that her determination to stay here was still unfaltering.

"Jane?" he said slowly. Poor Hugh. He'd been so discomfited when they'd entered—his broad shoulders had been jammed back—and now his worry was evident. "Lass, what're you laughing about?"

When another feather wafted down to stick jauntily out of Hugh's hair, she snickered some more. Wiping her eyes, she said, "It's just that this is so much better than what I'd expected Court's home to be like."

"And how's that?"

"It's *above* ground."

Hugh's eyes briefly widened, then he half-frowned, half-grinned.

Jane inhaled, forcing herself to continue in a dry tone, "And I had no idea Courtland was such an animal lover. Look at all these beloved pets."

"Aye," Hugh agreed, his tone as dry as hers, "since he was a lad—never could keep enough of the wee beasties. Names them, every one."

She gave a burst of laughter, surprised and delighted with Hugh, but reined it in to observe, "And Court's quite clever with his menagerie. I never would have conceived of utilizing the chimney and the mattresses as pens for them."

Hugh nodded solemnly. "Makes it easier to feed them their steady diet of dirt and cotton. Look how they thrive."

Wrestling with laughter, Jane observed, "And the décor is quite fetching." She tapped her chin. "Early hovel, if I'm not mistaken. Only the most studious and dedicated neglect could achieve this."

"Aye, this level of hovel is rarely seen. He's been hard at it for *years*."

She did laugh then, having more fun bantering with Hugh in this awful place than she could remember. "Hugh, I think you're enjoying yourself with me."

He looked at the wall to her right as he said, "When you can refrain from teasing me, I like being around you." When he glanced back at her disbelieving expression, he added in a gruff voice, "Always enjoyed your company."

There was something in his expression, the smallest hint of vulnerability, as if he expected—or only wanted—her to make the same admission. "I enjoyed being with you as well," she murmured.

"And by *enjoy*, you mean that you liked having someone at your beck and call to retrieve anything you could no' reach and to bait hooks." Had the tight lines around his eyes relaxed somewhat? "Admit it—you never lifted a paddle to row around the lake when I was near."

"And you liked having me run my nails down your back, and filch for you whatever pie was cooling on the kitchen windowsill, and give you peeks of a transparent linen shift when we swam."

His eyes went half-lidded. "Christ, I did like you in nothing but wet linen."

Her toes curled in her boots, as much from his admission as from his sudden hungry expression. But then he seemed to grow bewildered by what he'd just said, and strode outside toward the lake. She was right behind him.

At the edge of the water, they turned back to face the manor. Sidling next to him, she butted his arm with her head until he grumbled but lifted his arm to put it around her shoulders.

"I truly dinna know, Jane," he said, his tone weary. "I welcome your humor, but it does no' erase the fault. This has added at least two days' riding to get to Carrickliffe."

Even if she weren't bent on staying here, the idea of more riding made her feel ill. "This was a fine property once," she offered, planting the seeds for a later request to stay here. If she came out and asked now, he would think she'd completely lost her mind. But, in truth, the place had probably been incredible at one time. Nicely situated on a hill overlooking the crystal-clear lake, the manor consisted of two wings. But the wings weren't connected at a right angle—they flared out so that all the rooms in each had a view of the lake and the glens unfolding behind it for miles.

"Aye. Once."

"Just pulling down the dead vines covering the brick would make a big difference in the façade." A hovel it might currently be, but the manor house had been designed in the much-lauded baronial style. The massive stones at the foot and the ancient beams inside shouldering the ceilings in that great room were all the rage in England.

Most important, Jane could be alone with Hugh here. In her eyes, that meant it was perfect.

Except for one thing, she thought, running her hand over the back of her neck and gazing around. She'd just gotten the eerie feeling that they were being watched.

"Perhaps so," Hugh said. "But that does no' help us for tonight."

"Cheer up, Hugh," she said absently. "Things can't get worse—"

Rain thundered down, like a loosed bucket of freezing water.

Thirty-four

———— • ◆ • ————

"Well, the good news is that I got my bath," Jane murmured in a drowsy tone. She lay on her side, her head resting comfortably in his lap as he sat back against the wall.

Where her fortitude sprang from, Hugh had no idea.

This afternoon, after they'd run for the manor in pounding rain, he'd settled their horses under a portico for the night, and then they'd investigated most of the interior.

Dodging streaming leaks from the ceilings, they had finally stumbled upon a tiny bedroom off the kitchen, likely a servant's quarters. It had only one window, and the panels, though cracked, were intact. The room was free of feathers, and no scrabbling sounded from its undersized fireplace. The chimney was only partially obstructed—the smoke from their small fire crept in flagging tendrils, but always up.

After eating a dinner of biscuits from a tin, tea steeped in heated rainwater, and apples liberated that morning from some farmer's orchard, they'd settled down for the night.

"Hugh, why did Court let this place get so run-down?" she asked.

"Now that I've seen it, I think it was probably neglected before Court even bought it." After that, his brother had had no time to improve it. Court had been on the Continent with his gang, working to pay off this place, which he'd bought for pennies on the pound.

Though the land was rich, and there was an astonishing amount of it, the manor was occupied by its own demolition crew. Hugh was amazed that Court had considered bringing Annalía, a rich and cultured lass, here to live. Annalía was a brave girl, but Hugh thought even she would have swooned at the state of Court's home.

Yet, hadn't Hugh done the same? He'd brought a rich and cultured woman here.

Lightning flashed outside, and when thunder rattled the structure, the creatures outside the room began to mew and tussle with renewed vigor. Hugh pinched the bridge of his nose, but Jane only chuckled.

"I'll take you to an inn tomorrow," he said quickly. "There's a village a few miles north of here, and they might have a place for us to stay. You can have a proper bath."

"Hugh, you're brooding so hard, I can *hear* my money piling up. And you already owe me five thousand pounds, at least." She sounded lazily comfortable and amused.

"Five thousand, is it?" He stroked her damp hair, and they settled into companionable silence. But as ever, worry for Ethan weighed on his thoughts. Hugh was cut off from communication with London and daren't leave Jane anywhere while he went to search for Ethan or hunted for Grey.

Hugh had to assume that Grey was still loose, which meant Hugh and Jane could be together indefinitely as they waited for the bastard to be captured or killed.

Indefinitely? Hugh gave himself ten days before he was in bed with her—and that would be drawing on every reserve of discipline he possessed . . .

"Hugh, tell me something about your life, something exciting you've done since I saw you last."

Anything exciting he'd done fell firmly into the category of *classified*. He finally answered, "I bought a home in Scotland."

She turned on her back, gazing up at him with interest. "Oh, do tell me about it."

He ran his free hand over the back of his neck. "I stumbled upon the estate on the coast in a place called Cape Waldegrave." She had to tap his hip to prompt him for more. "The waves are relentless and so lofty that you can see the sun set through them." He admitted, "I could no' rest until I owned it."

She sighed. "It sounds breathtaking. I think I'd like living in Scotland."

He berated himself for imagining the look in her eyes if she saw the cape. It was of no bloody consequence that she would love its wave-tossed cliffs, or that when he'd chosen the property, he'd specifically thought of her there, of wanting to impress her. . . .

Since leaving Ros Creag, he'd tried his damnedest not to think about how close he'd come to having her after all these years. He recalled how inevitable it had felt to be with her, as if resisting the need to be inside her was senseless. Especially since she seemed to desire it just as much.

The idea that this stunning woman, who laid her head trustingly in his lap, had been willing—eager—to make love to him made him crazed. And the more time that passed, the less embarrassed he was about his actions those nights at Rose Creag—and the more aroused he became.

Ten days? Mayhap a week.

Doona look down . . . just doona look. . . .

Hugh hissed in a breath when he did look, glimpsing her naked body as he helped her from the hot spring into the cool morning air. He threw the towel around her as though she were on fire, but the image of her standing wholly naked, with water sluicing down her smooth flesh, was seared into his mind.

A week without touching her? That had been an absurdly optimistic estimate.

"This was such a wonderful surprise!" She gazed up at him as though he was her hero, her eyes sparkling with pleasure. She showed no visible signs of fatigue from their demanding journey, or from last night's bleak accommodations in what was, in essence, a closet. Resilient lass.

In a breathless voice, she asked, "Hugh, how did you find the spring?"

"Yesterday, I thought I saw steam rising from this cove of the loch, but dinna want to get your hopes up until I explored it."

"I wondered where you'd gone this morning."

"I had no idea the water would be this clean." He frowned. "Or that you'd be willing to shuck off your clothes and dive in." After making sure the towel was firmly tucked in, he swooped her up into his arms for the five-minute walk back to the manor.

She laughed, throwing her arms around his neck and clinging to him so sweetly. "I woke thinking I'd find you beside me, but that ferret cat was there instead. When it hissed, I tossed my boot at it, which it appropriated. I want to stay here. Can you help me find my boot?"

"You've thrown me again, Jane."

"Well, I've been thinking, and I've concluded this place is not half bad." When he gave her a stern look, she said, "I'm not jesting, Hugh. If I'm to be in Scotland for an indeterminate time, away from all my family and friends without any town entertainments, I'll need something to do. This is actually the perfect opportunity. Since this tumbledown place needs work, we might as well see it done." He said nothing, so she continued, "Together, we'll compile a list of materials we'll need, and you can fix and I can clean."

"You? Doing the cleaning?"

She blinked up at him. "How hard can it be?"

He opened his mouth to explain, then closed it. Jane had decided that cleaning wouldn't be difficult; Jane would not be moved from this opinion until she'd tried it.

"Why would I want to do this?"

"It needs to be done. It's your brother's home. He can pay you back."

No, he couldn't. Court was taking in a much larger income now, but overhauling this manor would be costly. Still, Hugh was warming to this idea. For one thing, setting this place to rights—to order—had a definite appeal.

"And don't you think we'd be safe here, surrounded by all this land?" she asked.

Even safer than with the clan. If he could protect her here, provide her with something to occupy her, deaden his body with work, and be doing Court a favor, why not?

She gazed up at him. "Can't we stay here? Please, Hugh?"

And so it's settled.

So he wouldn't look like the easy mark he was with her, he waited until he'd deposited her back in their closet room before saying, "Aye, then. We'll do it. But only if you stay near the manor and do as I ask you—to keep you safe." He gently clasped her chin. "We canna let our guard down. Even here."

"I promise."

As he turned toward the door, he said, "Call for me when you're dressed, and I'll come help you reclaim your boot."

When she nodded happily, he strode outside. The morning fog had dissipated. As the sun rose higher, illuminating the front elevation of the house, he was better able to assess how much work would be required to make this place livable.

In the morning sun, refurbishing it looked *possible*.

Hugh believed he could do a lot of the work himself. Perhaps this wasn't such a daft idea. Yes, work like this could deaden a man's body and burn off a woman's energy. This place might just be his salvation—

Jane shrieked.

Not a heartbeat later, Hugh was sprinting for her.

Thirty-five

———— ◆ ————

*J*ane hiked up her skirts and dashed out of the house, bent on nabbing the Peeping Tom she'd caught spying on her through a cracked windowpane.

She turned the corner and found Hugh steadying the peeper after he'd apparently run into him. The miscreant's hat flew off, revealing a spill of long black hair. A girl? Yes, dressed in a bulky hat and clothing. She was likely eighteen or so, short, with a strong build and incongruous freckles.

Jane pointed her finger. "She was watching me dress."

"I was no," the girl lied.

"You most certainly were." Jane was furious. She'd seen the peep's jaw drop and they'd met eyes—Jane had clearly caught her red-handed—then she'd hied away. Jane had sensed a presence for some time, but had thought *Hugh* was watching her.

The girl had seen a show indeed.

"Why would I be looking at ye dress? I'm a girl, can you no' see?"

Provincial, she mouthed to Hugh, but he scowled at her. After steadying and releasing the girl, he asked, "What are you doing here?"

"Been using the land, since no one else was." She hiked a thumb over her shoulder toward the dilapidated stables. "Those are my chicken coops beside the stable and my turnip patch in the back. My horse, too," she said. Jane spied a swaybacked pony, pulling weeds with very long teeth in a broken down corral. *Corralled?* As if it was going anywhere. "I'm yer neighbor of sorts, or as close as ye can get with this estate."

"What's your name?"

"Mòrag MacLarty—stress on the Mac, if it pleases ye. Are ye kin to Master MacCarrick?"

"I'm his brother, Hugh MacCarrick. My wife and I are staying on for the fall. We plan to fix up the place."

She nodded slowly. "My brothers have the windows Master MacCarrick ordered last year stored in our barn. And they've got a fine share of lumber they'd likely be willing to sell before winter."

"That's good news."

"And ye could hire them to help around here. Six of them, all strong as oxen." The girl gave Jane a once-over, then said in a pert tone, "And ye'll be needing help with the housekeeping?"

That little peeping witch . . .

"Aye. Are you interested?"

Mòrag nodded, and named her price for daily cleaning, cooking, and laundry. He countered, and they settled.

Without consulting her, he'd just hired a maid. Jane knew how to run a house, and knew that hiring servants was firmly in the woman's sphere of the home.

Hugh added, "But you'll need to ride over every day for at least two weeks. And I expect you to work as hard as we do."

She snorted at Jane. "Should no' be a problem."

"Why, you saucy little—"

"Jane, a word with you." As he grabbed Jane's elbow, he said, "Mòrag, what are the odds that we'll have a hot meal tonight?"

"If ye can get the hearth flue cleared of the squirrels, ye can count on it."

He nodded, then dragged Jane across the weed-clotted yard. Jane glanced back, just in time to see Mòrag stick her tongue out at her before turning toward the manor. "I don't want her, Hugh. She's impudent."

Hugh glared down at her. "Why have you taken such a dislike to her? For watching you dress? She's probably never seen anything like your Parisian silks and laces. And *believe* me when I tell you that anyone would have stopped and stared. She would have to be curious."

Jane couldn't put a finger on why she bristled around the girl. Perhaps it was because Mòrag—or whatever her name was—clearly didn't like her. "She stuck her tongue out at me," she said lamely.

"The last owner to live here was a verra foolish *Englishman* who was hard on all those around here. Keep that in mind." When she remained unconvinced, he said, "Once we get the inside habitable, the outside is going to keep me busy from sunup to sundown. Do you truly want to haul water and pluck chickens? Surely, you canna cook?"

Haul, pluck, cook. Not her favorite verbs, and not ones traditionally associated with Jane. Her idea of turning the house around by herself suddenly seemed very daunting and not quite as adventurous as she'd hoped. At that moment, they heard banging in the kitchen. The girl had found the cookware! Jane rolled her eyes at Hugh.

Hugh pressed his advantage, saying, "She can buy us supplies in the village as well."

Jane put her chin up. "It might be nice to have someone around—but only to help me as *I* work." She marched toward the manor, with Hugh following her. Inside, Jane made her manner brisk. "What can I do?" she asked the girl.

"I'm thinkin' no' much, by the look of ye."

Jane gave Hugh a meaningful look, but he just squeezed her shoulder. "Is there a ladder anywhere around here?" he asked the girl.

"In the stable, just behind my saddle and gear."

Taking Jane aside, he said, "You stay right in here. I'll be back directly," then set off for the stables.

While Hugh was gone, Jane attempted to help the girl—who, she admitted, got things *done*—but Jane was under the impression that she only got in the way of Mòrag's cleaning. Her first clue was when Mòrag snapped, "Git yer scrawny arse out o' my way, English."

The squirrels sensed something was afoot with their chimney community, and began chattering their fury.

When Hugh returned with firewood and a damp blanket, Jane frowned. "You're not going to start a fire directly under them? There could be baby squirrels or injured ones or older ones—"

"Squirrel stew is *mighty* tasty," Mòrag interrupted.

Jane gave her a horrified look, then whipped her head around to Hugh. "Squirrel st-stew?"

He checked a grin. "Jane, I'm going to start a verra *small* fire, with damp wood that will smoke more than anything. Then I'll drape a wet blanket over the hearth opening down here. It'll give them enough time to run up to the roof."

When she still appeared unconvinced, Mòrag said, "Enough with the bluidy squirrels, English. Now, which do ye want to do? Dress chickens or scour pots?"

When Jane merely bit her lip, Mòrag said, "Pots it is." She nodded at an open closet full of them. "You can take all of them to the pump in the back and wash them. There's soaps and brushes in the shed off this kitchen."

Though Hugh wanted to help, Jane waved him away. "I can do it by myself," she said firmly.

"Doona go anywhere but to the pump and back. Agreed?"

"Hugh, really." At his unbending look, she muttered, "Agreed."

When she began hauling pots out to the pump, he moved to a window where he could see her. "We're going to need supplies," he told Mòrag. "But I doona want anyone to know we're here, nor any visitors out here."

"Why no'?"

He'd thought about telling her something ridiculous, like they wanted to surprise his brother with the renovation, but the girl was smart and, he sensed, trustworthy. "There's an Englishman who might come looking for us. A dangerous sort of man, and one we'd rather avoid."

She eyed him, knowing he was being less than forthcoming. He didn't care, as long as they understood each other.

"The sundries storekeeper will know ye're here, and that means the whole village will know. But no one outside of it will."

He added another piece of wood to the small fire he'd started. "The villagers doona like strangers?"

"Nay, no' at all. Strangers are met with a tight lip and a surly expression anyway, and if an outsider asks any of the townsfolk about yer whereabouts, I'll hear word of it directly. And I'll make sure everyone knows ye're honeymooning and are no' keen on receiving any visitors just now."

Hugh raised his brows. They might as well have dropped off the face of the earth by coming here. Hugh and Mòrag understood each other perfectly. He nodded, finished draping the blanket over the fireplace, then strode outside. He chanced his tottering ladder all the way to the second-story roof to clear debris from the top of the chimney.

From the higher vantage, he could keep an eye on Jane as she worked. When she disappeared inside, he took in the views, comprehending more and more what had possessed his brother to buy Beinn a'Chaorainn. A breeze rippled the loch, then stilled, and the water reflected sunlight in a perfect mirror. On a fine day like this, he could see twenty miles away to the rounded spine of mountains at the far edge of Court's property.

For the next half hour, Hugh dodged the exodus of fleeing squirrels and marked damaged spots on the roof to fix when Mòrag's brothers could help with the major repairs. All the while, he checked on Jane, hard at work on her task.

The pots were heavy and unwieldy, but she seemed content to transport only two or three at a time to the pump. Back and forth she went, again and again, until she'd finally collected a mound of pots, handles sticking out in every direction.

At the pump, she rolled up her sleeves, then drew down on the lever—

Black sludge exploded out of the faucet, splattering over the front of her dress and her face like paint from a dropped tin.

"Oh, bloody, hell," Hugh muttered, hurrying to climb down, snapping two rungs on the descent.

Jane froze for long moments, then sputtered, wiping her face with her forearm.

The girl had done that on purpose, no doubt of it. Mòrag could have told Jane to take the pots to the loch. Before Hugh reached her, Jane swung her gaze to him and raised one finger, her eyes murderous.

"I will handle this," she said between gritted teeth. "Don't you say a word to her."

"Jane, this will no' be tolerated—"

"Precisely why I'm about to take care of this. If she wants to toss down the gauntlet, then I'll pick it up." After carefully filling the largest pot with sludge, she lugged it toward the stables. The weight was so heavy it dragged her arm down, skewing her balance.

When Jane returned from the stables—where Mòrag's saddle and bags were—the bucket was empty and swinging at her hip, jaunty as a berry basket.

Thirty-six

———◆———

By the end of the first five days at Beinn a'Chaorainn, Hugh felt like a cauldron about to boil over.

This unfortunate state was attested to by the fact that the property was already turning the corner. Every time Hugh thought about touching Jane, he worked.

In his time here, Hugh had accomplished the labor of a dozen men.

This afternoon, he sawed boards for the entryway floor, while Mòrag and Jane cleaned upstairs. The days that were clement enough for him to work outside were the days Mòrag aired the manor. Through the open windows, he could hear Jane humming or laughing as she cleaned, or spy flashes of her as she strolled down the hall.

He found himself looking forward to those glimpses of her.

With the three of them toiling, his and Jane's living situation had improved dramatically. Hugh had selected the two best adjoining rooms in the manor for Jane and himself, and then Mòrag had gone to work like a dervish cleaning them, as if to embarrass Jane for her sneezing clumsiness with a broom.

On Mòrag's second day, she'd returned with a packhorse and a cart. She'd only purchased necessities for them—

linens, mattress rolls, kitchen and cleaning supplies, food-stuffs—but the shopkeepers in Mòrag's small village were quick to pile wares on her to take back to the brother of "Master Courtland." They all saw Court as a savior, the ruthless warrior Scot who'd reclaimed the land from a haughty English baron—a baron who had insisted on raising sheep, and running off tenants to allow them to graze.

Court had done nothing but capitalize on the baron's bad business sense, but Hugh wasn't going to enlighten the shopkeepers.

In fact, Hugh was becoming more and more confident that staying on was the right decision. Having Mòrag around was ideal because not only was she transforming the interior and reluctantly teaching Jane how to help, but her presence kept Hugh from trailing after Jane's skirts like a wolf licking his lips.

The one problem with Mòrag was that she and Jane bickered constantly. Jane was bewildered to be ridiculed for the way she talked or disliked simply for being a for-eigner. Hugh didn't want Jane to be miserable, but he wouldn't mind her understanding that "bloody English" was merely an equivalent to "rough Scot."

Sometimes Jane won an argument, and Hugh would hear her say, "No, no, I promised myself I wouldn't gloat." Sometimes she lost a spat and would sniff, "Oh." Pause. "Well, *obviously*."

And they competed at everything. When he'd dragged some old furniture down from the attic and repaired it, Jane and Mòrag raced to paint or stain it, looking more at the other's progress than their own. When he replaced the windows, they raced each other at cleaning them. In fact, Hugh feared Jane was working much too hard, toiling with an almost frantic zealousness. Hugh knew she was competitive by nature, but this seemed to be more than a mere rivalry.

To distract her, Hugh had crafted a target for her out of a dense hay bale with a sheet stretched taut over it, and she'd painted the rings. Yet she didn't practice in lieu of work; she woke earlier to do it all.

Every morning, on the terrace between the manor and stables, she donned her three-fingertip hunting gloves and her quiver. Her breaths would be visible in the cool air as she drew her bow, her expression intent. It was a thing of beauty to watch, and he secretly did so every morning.

Even Mòrag would pause at the kitchen window and stare in amazement.

Though Jane had been behaving herself, his want of her never relented. Even if she wasn't teasing him, she might as well have been. Jane exuded sexuality. Today, he'd passed her in a tight spot and had laid his hands on her waist. Her breaths had gone shallow and her cheeks had heated.

If he passed her room and spied her stockings and little garters strewn about, his gut tightened with want. Because their rooms were so close, each night Hugh drifted off to the intoxicating scents of her lotions and light perfume and to recent visions of her laces and silk corsets. In other words, he went to bed every night hard as steel.

On several occasions, Jane had approached him, nibbling her lip, appearing as if she needed to discuss something serious. He had no idea what she might be wanting, but always found himself relieved when she turned away without saying anything. Yet he knew soon she would broach whatever subject she wrestled with—and he sensed that this wouldn't bode well for him.

If he wasn't tormented with desire for her, he was wracked with concern about his brother and Jane's continued safety. And growing each day was a thick sense of foreboding Hugh couldn't shake.

Something had to give. . . .

As Hugh labored with his horse to haul debris away from the manor, Jane perched in the saddle, sitting backward so she could watch Hugh.

She *loved* to watch him work, especially when he was shirtless. Whenever he stood and ran his arm over his forehead, the sweat-slick ridges of his stomach would tense, and Jane's breath would go shallow. She didn't think she'd ever seen anything half as beautiful as his muscles covered with sweat.

Today was her first afternoon off since they'd arrived. Mòrag was harvesting kale today, so Jane was relaxing, which obviously pleased Hugh.

He likely believed she worked so hard just to compete with Mòrag, but Jane feared her cleaning skills would be forever eclipsed by the girl's.

No, Jane worked to prove she could be an asset to Hugh, that she was a good wife and one worth keeping. She tended the gardens, she painted furniture, and she arranged the beautiful homespun rugs Mòrag had bought from local artisans. The house was already becoming homey and comfortable.

If she lost Hugh in the end, it would *not* be from lack of trying. . . .

"Water, lass?"

She blinked, tossing him his canteen. He drank greedily, then ran his forearm over his mouth. She loved it when men did that. And by "men" she meant "Hugh." When he tossed the canteen back, she was so busy staring at him that she missed, fumbling the canteen twice before it thudded to the ground. She could barely contain her yearning—indeed, she'd ceased bothering to hide the depth of it—yet Hugh still hadn't touched her. Again and again, she mulled reasons why.

With a frown, he released the leather trace over his shoulder, then scooped up the canteen on his way to the saddle. When he dusted it off and handed it to her, she gave him a sheepish smile.

He backed away from her with a guarded expression, then took up the traces again. The horse strained forward once more.

She'd struggled to broach the subject of staying married to him, but his eyes always seemed dark with warning—just like now. She felt as if she would be all but proposing to him, and she could admit her confidence was shaken. Men were usually tongue-tied, stumbling over themselves to give her whatever she wanted. Hugh was distant, his countenance shuttered.

She inhaled, grasping about for courage. There wasn't going to be a better time than now. Before she lost her nerve again, she quickly asked, "Do you want to know what I've been thinking about?"

He shook his head emphatically, so she waited several minutes before she asked, "Hugh, do you think I'd make a good wife?"

After a hesitation, he slowly answered, "Aye."

"You swear?"

"Aye."

"You're not just saying that to spare my feelings?"

"No. Any man would be proud to call you wife—"

"Then why don't you just keep me?"

He stumbled over his feet, falling to his knee in the mud.

"*I* want to keep *you*," she declared, as if her seemingly innocent question hadn't just sent his body and mind reeling.

He rose, inwardly cursing. Why did she have to start with the teasing once again? Damn it, all in all, he'd been having a good day. The unseasonably mild weather had held pleasant, and he'd been enjoying her company, as usual. As she'd chatted and laughed about this and that, he'd been sneaking glances up at her, marveling at how much Scotland was agreeing with her.

Her cheeks were pinkened, her eyes appeared, impossibly, a more vibrant green, and her auburn hair was even shinier, seeming burnished with gold.

The lass was growing so beautiful that at times, she rendered him speechless.

"It's a reasonable question, Hugh."

Now he felt himself growing cold. "This is no' something to jest about."

Earlier, the expressions flitting across her face had gone from thoughtful to panicked to fearful, then to the determined mien she wore now. "I'm not," she said in a steady voice. "At all. I want to stay married to you."

He opened his mouth to speak, but couldn't quite manage it when he saw that she was serious. *Unbelievable.* His voice hoarse, he finally said, "It will no' happen, Jane."

She *wanted* to be his lover and his wife? Right now, he wished to God he were selfish enough to keep her.

"Why? If you give me a good reason, I'll desist from this. Otherwise . . ." She trailed off, as if in warning.

"I told you, I never wanted to be married."

"But *why*? Give me one reason."

"That is just no' the life for me," he said simply. "Never has been and never will be. You have to accept that some men are no' husband material."

"I think you are."

"You doona even know me anymore."

"Because you won't tell me anything," she countered.

"Take my word for it."

"Are you certain you don't want just to *try* staying married after all this is done? To see if we suit?"

"Aye, I'm verra certain," he said, making his tone cutting.

"Really?" she said slowly. *Raaaally.* As if she hadn't heard him, she slipped down from the saddle. "It's a big decision." She gave him a solemn nod. "I know you'll want to think it over." Before strolling off, she tilted her head and studied him, her bright eyes focused and clear.

It was, he thought, swallowing hard, the same way she looked at her arrow's target.

Thirty-seven

———— • ◆ • ————

*H*aving raised the subject of staying married, Jane returned to it over the next week with stubborn frequency.

As Hugh worked a Dutch block plane over a new column for the rickety portico, he waited for a glimpse of Jane and mulled over her latest campaign.

The night before, he'd been drinking scotch on a rug by the fire. She'd sat behind him, up on her knees to rub the sore muscles of his back, sharing sips of his drink. His lids had grown heavy as he'd relaxed against her.

The fire, the scotch, his wife easing his body after a hard day's labor. *Bliss*. He took a savoring sip—

"Any thoughts on our marriage, my love?"

He'd choked on his drink. She'd smiled innocently when he glowered.

This morning on her way out to the terrace to shoot, she'd said in a casual tone, "I noticed you didn't pack any reading material—except for that odd book—so I left a novel on your bed." As he stared after her, she tossed over her shoulder, "And I marked the scenes I *particularly* enjoyed."

He knew exactly what kind of novel she spoke of. As soon as she was out of sight, he bounded up the stairs, eager to see what she would like. Set on his pillow was a book with her false cover, and he tore it open. Five minutes later, he sank to the bed, running a shaking hand over his dazed face.

If these were scenes she enjoyed, then they would suit *perfectly*. . . .

No, damn it, this was just the latest battle in her insidious campaign. Her continual sallies never let him forget that every day, here for the taking, was the woman of his dreams. He was like a stallion around a mare in heat—he couldn't concentrate, couldn't keep his mind on anything but how her hair smelled and how her skin tasted.

His eyes followed her everywhere. When she worked, she'd taken to wearing a bandanna over her hair, and she'd begun unbuttoning her blouses to beat the heat of the kitchen or whatever chore she'd undertaken. It seemed to Hugh that her dampened breasts were always on the verge of spilling out. Jane, usually so elegant, looked like a lusty barmaid, and he loved it.

In fact, he couldn't decide which version of her he liked best: the clever beauty in London, the archer with her leather-tipped hunting gloves, or this carefree temptress.

His need for her was unrelenting. He wasn't thinking clearly. He was constantly hard during the day and couldn't sleep a night through without having to spend. The other night, after dreaming about her riding him, he'd awakened soaked in sweat—and precisely three quick strokes away from ejaculating.

She'd wrecked him, weakened him. And when she began staring at Hugh with a mixture of almost innocent curiosity and blatant yearning, only one thing kept him from answering the plea in her eyes.

The book. He kept it out now, staring at it often. It reminded him of what he was. . . .

He frowned when he realized that well over an hour had passed since he'd heard humming or seen a flash of her going by. Hugh hoped she'd decided to sleep for an hour or two, instead of her usual exhaustive toiling, even as he doubted it.

He laid aside his plane, dusted wood shavings from his trousers, then strode in the front door. He met Mòrag, returning to the kitchen with a basket of turnips.

"Where's my wife?"

She shrugged. "Saw English in the north wing last. Said she was going to wax the floors."

He nodded and grabbed an apple from a bowl, then dropped it as he caught an unmistakable scent.

The girl sniffed. "What the hell has she done now?"

"*Paraffin*, Mòrag," he barked over his shoulder as he took off at a run. "Think about it."

Mòrag gasped and dropped her basket to follow.

Paraffin wax was for floors.

And was easily confused with paraffin oil—another term for . . . kerosene.

He burst through the closed door and swallowed at the sight. Jane had coated thirsty mahogany wood with jugs of kerosene.

She tottered to her feet. "I wanted to surprise you and have this all finished." She rubbed her nose delicately with the back of her hand. "But I feel quite foxed." Shrugging, she picked up a chunk of sandstone and said, "I was just going to sand the dried area—"

"*No!*" he and Mòrag shouted at the same time. *One spark . . .*

Heart in his throat, he lunged for her just as Mòrag cried, "Are ye daft, English?"

Jane blinked, sputtering as he hauled her outside to the well. "I assume I did something wrong?" she said as he quickly stripped her of everything but her shift.

"Aye. I'm agreeing with Mòrag on this." He pumped a continuous stream of water all over her wee hands and arms, scrubbing the oil away. "You've taken on far too much for one person with this project. And that oil is flammable and usually used by"—*lanterns*—"by professionals. If one drop of candle tallow hit your skirt just then, you'd have gone up in a blaze."

"Oh." Jane bit her bottom lip. "You're angry."

"Concerned."

"Hugh, be patient with me."

"God knows I try, lass."

When he spied Mòrag preparing to leave for the night, he ordered Jane, "Scrub your legs and feet. I'll be right back," then strode to the stable to catch the girl. "Mòrag, I want you to keep my wife away from any and all dangerous and flammable substances that might be on this property. Lock them away if you have to. And I'll triple your wages if you can keep her out of the north wing till I can replace the boards."

Hugh turned back to Jane to bark, "Scrub!" and Jane jumped with fright, then dutifully scrubbed.

Mòrag made a disgusted sound. "You're no' going to scold English worse? After ruining the room like that?"

Hugh shrugged. "From now on, I'll make sure she understands some things are dangerous around here, but, no, she'll no' know she damaged an entire mahogany floor."

"I'd have been tarred." But then Hugh knew Jane had started growing on the girl when Mòrag glowered and threw her hands up. "English is no' *stoopid*—you ken we'll have to bluidy age the new floor, too?"

"It's time you told me why're you've been working so hard, lass," Hugh said when he returned.

She was feeling tipsy and cold, and yet delightfully shivery as Hugh's rough hands rubbed up and down her arms, checking for oil residue. She grinned drunkenly. "I'm endeavoring to impress you. So you'll keep me. And let me live in your seashore house."

When he gave up a shadow of a grin, she said, "Actually, that wasn't a joke."

His face creased into a scowl. "You bring marriage up? Again? You're as stubborn as a Scot! Do you know that?"

"I could make you happy," she insisted. "And you're in a position to take a wife."

"Damn it, lass, you would no' like being married to me."

"How would it differ from what we've been doing?"

When he'd agreed to this marriage, he'd anticipated her wanting out at the first opportunity. That was supposed to be the one constant. He'd never imagined he would be grasping for arguments against *himself*, as he stared at Jane's shift getting soaked with cool well water and clinging to her plump breasts. His hands on her arms began to move more leisurely.

He hadn't been concentrating well anyway, but how could he be expected to formulate an argument when faced with her little nipples stiffening under every spurt of water that hit them? He was in a bad way. He remembered that last time he'd kissed them, he'd *felt* them throb beneath his tongue. . . .

He broke away, removing his hands completely from her body. "Jane, forget this plan of yours. I'm no' a good man. And I would no' make a good husband."

"This makes sense to me. It's a logical move for us. We're already married, and we've done the formalities." She lowered her voice to say, "All you have to do is make love to me."

"Logical? You want this because it's logical? That's the one bloody thing it is no'."

Her brows drew together as she gazed up at him. "Hugh, what is so wrong with me?"

He'd never imagined a woman like her could fear herself lacking. He couldn't allow her to think that in any way. Which meant telling her the truth. At least, part of it.

"It's no' you. It's *me*."

Whatever he'd said had evidently been the worst he could have. Her face grew cold in an instant. "Do you have any idea how many men I've told that to spare their feelings?" She crossed her arms and eased away from him. "Oh, how the worm has turned. Now I'm the unwanted, unhappy recipient of platitudes."

"Jane, no." He reached out and laid a hand on her hip, tugging her closer. "You are everything a man could ever want in a wife." He caught her eyes. "The truth is . . . the truth is that if I were ever planning to marry, I'd have you or none at all."

She tilted her head. "None at all?"

"None. It truly is my problem. I have . . . difficulties that prevent me from marrying."

"Tell me *one* reason you don't want to marry."

"That will merely invite more of your questions. As I said before, you doona seem to be happy unless everything's laid bare."

"Hugh, this involves me, and I deserve to know more. I'm just asking you to be fair."

"Aye, I know. Believe me, I ken that. But you need to get inside and dry off."

"I'm not leaving until you tell me one reason."

Finally, after a long hesitation, he bit out, "I canna . . . give you bairns."

Thirty-eight

———— •◆• ————

"Oh," Jane said, letting out a breath she hadn't known she held. "Why not?"

"Just never have."

He was right. Now she wanted to ask a slew of questions. "I suppose you purposely tried," she said, struggling to disguise the hurt she felt. The thought of him wanting a child with another woman scalded her inside.

"Christ, no, I have no' tried."

She frowned. "Then how can you know?"

"My brothers canna either."

Her eyes widened a touch. A childhood illness. It would have to be. Her eyes widened even more—was this why he'd never wanted to marry at all? Never wanted to marry *her*?

It would explain everything! She swayed, and Hugh's grip on her hip tightened. Hugh wouldn't want to deny her children. He was always selfless like that. This made sense—this was the reason she'd wracked her mind for! She wasn't daunted by this in the least. If she had her Scot, she could go without children. After all, her cousins would continue to spawn at an accelerating rate, inundating Jane with children to play with.

If her heart had turned like a cart's wheel at the sight of her wedding ring, then this latest revelation made her feel like someone had lit the cart on fire and sent it careening down a mountain.

Her first impulse was to tackle him to the ground and kiss him, but she stifled that impulse, realizing almost immediately that it had been a Bad Idea. Surely he would be vulnerable after his admission, and she didn't want to appear pleased over what he considered a loss. Her second impulse was to scoff at what he erroneously thought was a major obstacle, but to scoff would mean she didn't respect his beliefs on the subject.

Men really cared about these things, didn't they? Did he feel he was less of a man because of it? She took a steadying breath. *Be rational.*

"I see. I appreciate your taking me into your confidence." She sounded calm, reasonable.

He nodded gravely. "I've never told anyone before. But now you understand why I would no' want to marry."

"I understand."

He nodded grimly.

"But it doesn't change my mind about us whatsoever."

"*What?*" he bit out, releasing her to take a step back.

"I don't know how to convince you that this wouldn't have a huge impact on my life."

"You told me you love children. Even gave me reasons."

"I love *other people's* children," Jane said with a wry grin. When he scowled, she grew serious. "If you think I've ached in my breast wanting my own, it just isn't true. I love the ones you saw me with because they are my family." She glanced away. "I hope you don't think I'm an unfeeling woman because I haven't experienced that need. That's something *I* haven't told anyone."

"Did you never think to have them?"

"If I got married and it happened—or didn't happen—I wouldn't have cried either way."

"This is no' how I expected you to react to this," he said, running his hand over the back of his neck.

"I'm sorry to disappoint you. But this changes nothing for me."

"Damn it, the only reason you want this is because you have to fight for it. And once the fight is over, the desire will be, too."

"That is *not* true."

"In the past, you've fought for things you dinna necessarily want—you did it only because you needed the challenge. Admit it!"

Well, maybe once or twice . . . But when she was younger she'd also believed she was all but married to Hugh—no challenge there, and yet she could think of little else but him.

"And what happens if I give in and your interest fades?" Hugh demanded. "When you get back to England among your friends and family and parties, your desire to stay with me will wane. This is obvious to me, Jane."

"It hasn't faded yet," she muttered.

He gave a humorless laugh. "Oh, aye, for the entire few weeks we've been together?"

She shook her head—*now, where's that cliff?* "I meant for the ten years we've been apart—or you can just round it up to half of my life."

He visibly swallowed. "Are you saying. . . ? You doona mean . . ." His voice broke low. "*Me*, Jane?"

Jane sighed. "Yes, you—"

He tensed just as she thought she heard horses down the wooded drive. In one movement, he turned, shoving her behind him, and ripped off his shirt to cover her.

After Hugh's trail vanished in Scotland, Grey's options hadn't been promising.

This was Hugh's country, and the wilds were his element—never Grey's.

Worse, Hugh would bloody *know* he was good enough to lose Grey. That galled him.

If Grey hadn't been dallying with Ethan, he wouldn't have missed Hugh and Jane's nighttime departure. He found it ironic that by taking the time to kill one brother, he let another one escape.

Though he knew the countries of western Europe and northern Africa like the back of his hand, he'd never worked in Scotland. He was fluent in four languages, but Gaelic was not among them. The farther north he traveled, the more closemouthed and hostile the people were toward Englishmen—even more so toward Grey, who was emaciated and appeared ill. And possibly mad.

He had thought about returning to London to torture Weyland, but he knew the old man wouldn't talk—and Weyland probably didn't know for certain where they were anyway.

Just as Grey had begun to wonder if he could ever find them, he'd remembered that it was standard procedure in the Network to stay as close to telegraph lines as possible—and that only the most vital information, coded, of course, was dispatched.

Hugh would stay within a day's ride of a telegraph

office, checking in periodically for word of Grey's capture or death, so he'd know when to return home. Even though Grey knew all the codes and possessed the keys, no message would be sent without his own defeat. Which was a conundrum. How could Grey get Weyland to telegraph?

Then he'd realized he didn't have to be defeated before a message was sent.

Word of Ethan's death would be considered critical.

Grey had suspected an urgent telegraph to Hugh about his brother would be sent to several stations throughout Scotland. In the end, Grey uncovered— through varying degrees of violence—that only four went out, and two of the receiving offices were located in this small area in the south central Highlands. Grey had combed every inch within a one-hundred-mile-radius of the first station and had almost completed the radius of the second. Hugh had to be around here somewhere.

Unfortunately, the people here were cold, as usual, and money had no effect on them.

He'd just decided to throttle someone for the information when he heard the nicker of a horse behind him. Glancing back, he spied, far up the road, a girl emerging from a path in the woods—one that he hadn't seen as he'd passed.

She was alone, leisurely riding a pony in the opposite direction, and she had no saddlebags. A day trip. Interesting. What was out in this wilderness? Perhaps Hugh's hideout?

This girl would likely be as closemouthed as every other Scot he'd encountered, but Grey just smiled, slipping medicine between his lips to ready himself. The wee black-haired miss obviously worked for a living. Grey's hand flitted to his blade, holstered at his hip.

Grey knew that women who worked for their bread were particularly keen on keeping their fingers.

Thirty-nine

———◆———

Jane rested her chin in her palm, staring out the window down at Hugh as he drank with the other brawny Highlanders.

The sounds they'd heard on the drive had been half a dozen towering Scots riding what looked like warhorses—Mòrag's brothers, come to arrange work on the last part of the roof.

Hugh had joined them for homemade scotch, but hadn't invited *her* to socialize. Which didn't bother her. Whatsoever. Nor did the fact that Hugh hadn't even seemed particularly interested in her earlier revelation, at least not more than he was in swilling mash with other Gaels well after sundown.

She was still reeling from *his* admission, and had dozens more questions for him, but he'd remained down there for hours. For someone who professed to being a loner, Hugh seemed to be getting along well with the men, and they treated him like one of their own. She frowned. He *was* one of their own. He was a tall and proud Highlander, and when he spoke to them in his low tone, these men quieted and listened. They already were growing to respect her steady, patient husband.

Jane twirled her hair at her lips, then sniffed. Lord, would she have to bathe in a vat of acid to get rid of that harsh wax smell? Barring a vat, she was having another bath—and she wouldn't be heating water for it. Hugh wouldn't miss her if she headed for the spring, and she couldn't go ask him to accompany her without being accused of "teasing."

Gathering her bathing gear and a towel, she exited the side door, away from the men. During the pleasant stroll, she gazed up at the nighttime sky and mused over the last few weeks with Hugh. She'd sensed she was wearing him down with each encounter they had, but did she really want a man she had to "wear down" to get him make love to her? A man who hadn't particularly seemed to care that she'd always had feelings for him?

When she reached the loch, she marveled at how beautiful it was here. The moon was full, yellow and ponderous in the sky, reflecting over the hint of fog enshrouding the surface. Steam rose in wisps from the concealed pocket of rocks containing the hot spring.

Breathtaking. Damn it, she didn't *want* to leave Scotland. Now London seemed so drab, sooty, and heartless. When Grey was caught, how could Jane go back there, knowing what she was missing both with Hugh and with this country?

With a sigh, she disrobed. The water looked too appealing to resist any longer, and she slipped in. After setting her soaps and oils on the small ledge jutting from the side of a cliff, she washed her hair thoroughly. She'd just dunked under to finish rinsing it when Hugh appeared.

For the first time, she actually heard him before she saw him. Glancing over her shoulder, she saw that his hair was disheveled and his demeanor was weary, but his eyes . . . they burned wild.

"You didn't have to come out here to coddle me," she said. "Go back to your new friends."

He was silent, just staring.

"Are you drunk?" She'd never seen him this way. Even at Vinelands, he'd had no more than a glass of scotch while everyone else imbibed heartily.

"Aye," he finally answered. "But it does no' help."

"Help what?" she asked, bewildered by this new facet of Hugh.

"Help me stop wanting you day and night. And I've come to realize only one thing will."

She stood waist-deep in the water, her hair streaming down her back, looking at him over one shoulder. Steam swirled all around her, and a hunter's moon glowed above, illuminating the pale perfection of her body.

Long moments passed as they both remained still, breathing heavily, as if gauging what the other's next move would be. Unless she'd been jesting earlier, this exquisite woman had admitted to having feelings for him—for *years*.

He'd rather not have known that.

He hadn't drunk with the MacLarty brothers only to make sure none of them got any ideas about his wife— especially after they'd all seen Jane in nothing but a wet shift and his shirt. He'd drunk because she'd absolutely staggered him—

She turned fully to him, arms by her sides. Something in him simply . . . snapped.

With a muttered curse, he snatched off his shirt, boots, and pants. He dove in after her, then yanked her naked slick body to him, pressing her close. Her hands trailed up his chest to twine behind his neck and her lush breasts slipped against him, making her moan softly.

"This was supposed to fade, but it has no," he slurred against her neck. "It's worse. How the bloody hell can it be worse?"

"I-I don't understand you, Hugh."

"You will," he said, then used a straight arm to sweep off her bathing oils from the rock ledge. He set her roughly atop the shelf, putting them face to face. She gasped, but he simply gazed at her, committing this scene to memory. Her dark hair was streaming over her breasts, over her tight, jutting nipples. The silky curls at her sex were stark against her pale, spread thighs. "So beautiful," he rasped. "You torment me. If you only knew . . ."

He shoved his hips between her legs, leaning in to softly suck her earlobe. She sighed, relaxing, allowing him to work her legs wider.

He grasped her breasts, molding them, covering them completely with his hands. Then, as she gazed at him breathlessly, he leaned down to suckle her as he'd wanted to do that afternoon.

She cried out, and he recognized that he couldn't stop what was happening, even if he wanted to. And he did *not* want to.

Switching to her other nipple, he sucked her hard, but she liked it, holding his head to her breast, arching her back for more.

Only after he'd made sure that both of the peaks were hard and throbbing did he pull away to move down her body, to her spread thighs. When his mouth was inches away from her sex, he let her feel his breaths before he pressed his opened lips to her, and slid his tongue out. She gave a strangled cry as he closed his eyes in bliss, delving at her folds, finding them deliciously slick with her own wetness.

He glanced up to gauge her reaction and found her wide-eyed, shamelessly watching him. If possible, that aroused him even more. He spread her flesh with his thumbs, kissing her so that she'd never forget the sight of it. Between licks, he rasped, "Have you had this done tae you before?"

She shook her head. "N-no, never."

He knew his expression was wicked. "I'm going tae make you come like you never have before."

She gasped. "Are you sure you want me to, Hugh?" she asked with a hint of nervousness. "While you're down there?"

"I want you tae come right under my tongue," he growled, taking her between his lips to suck her clitoris for the first time.

She cried out, threading her fingers through his hair, clutching him hard. "Hugh, *I will*, yes! *There*. Oh, God, yes!"

At that, he went mindless . . . felt her damp breast clutched in his hand, her soft, soft flesh beneath his tongue . . . licking, devouring, squeezing her. He pushed up against the backs of her thighs, pressing her knees wider to get to more of her exquisite taste. She gave a sharp cry, undulating her hips up to his greedy mouth, completely abandoned.

He broke away to say, "Now come for me," then returned his tongue. When she did, her long moan was broken only by her awed words: "It feels so *good*. Hugh, you make me *feel so good.*"

He licked her madly as she writhed, and his cock seemed to pulse in the warm water with her every word, her every cry. When she grew too sensitive, he finally eased up, then stood before her. "*I have tae be inside you,*" he groaned, desperate to sink into her glistening, plump flesh, still spread to him. Becoming frenzied, he used one hand to pin her wrists above her head against the rock.

Her half-lidded eyes grew wide and she quickly said, "Wait, Hugh. L-let me free. I need to tell you something." But her words sounded indistinct as he cupped her sex beneath his whole hand. "Hugh, please—"

"I am," he growled, keeping her wrists pinned. "I've waited too goddamned long, and I'll wait no more."

"But I'm—"

"No more talking." He was through listening. "*You've haunted me.*" He wanted to punish her as she'd punished him again and again. He wanted to take out ten years of pain on her and make her feel what he'd suffered. He shoved her legs wider, about to plunge into her and take her mindlessly, furiously. Finally.

With his free hand, he clutched her breast, feeling his cockhead straining against her, seeking to be inside her. "I've told you I'm no' a good man. If you would believe me, if you only knew, you'd no' want my hands on you. But you push and push."

"I know. I do." Her face went soft, and her body relaxed. "And I'm sorry. It's just that I need you, Hugh," she whispered, then leaned up to press kisses to his neck. "So much that I can't think of anything but you." The light touch of her lips and her panting words against his skin set him awash in that indescribable feeling of . . . rightness.

Her eyes met his. She gazed up at him with desire, but also with trust.

He released her wrists and lowered his forehead to hers. "*Damn you, Jane*," he whispered harshly.

Had he actually thought he could hurt her? The woman he'd been born to touch and to hunger for?

"Don't be angry, please," she murmured. "I want this, but only if you do."

He almost laughed at that—*if he did*.

"I do, Sìne." He was glad she'd made him come to his senses. Not because he was going to back out of this—no, their fate was sealed on that score—but because he'd be damned if he took her like a mindless, rutting animal. The first time.

He disbelieved what he was about to do, but he was resolved. For once in his life, he would have the woman he desired more than anything else on earth. He didn't deserve her, but he was a selfish bastard. He didn't deserve her, but God, he needed her.

He'd bring her pleasure again. He'd meant for her to come around his cock when it was thick inside her, but knowing how badly he wanted this, he'd probably embarrass himself, losing his seed with the first thrust.

He slipped his middle finger into her wetness, and she moaned, hips arching up to meet his hand. She was wet for him, but so tight.

"Hugh," she gasped out when he withdrew his finger and returned with two, preparing her, thrusting deep just as she arched up—

He froze. Staring down at her in confusion, he said in a strangled tone, "Jane? You're a virgin?"

Her eyes flickered open at his tone, and she bit her lip guiltily. "I-I was going to tell you."

He removed his fingers, shaking over what he'd been about to do. He'd been about to hurt her—had *wanted* to—never knowing how devastating it would be. "Why did you no' tell me?"

"I thought you'd be less likely to make love to me."

"You thought right!" His eyes narrowed. "But you and Bidworth?"

"Never even got close."

His relief staggered him, but then he realized that now there was no way he could have her. Just as he was about to pull away, she grabbed his hips, holding him to her.

"Hugh, I want *you* to show me this, only you. I've waited so long, and I know you'll make this incredible for my first time."

She couldn't have said anything more convincing, because he knew she was right. He'd imagined taking her virginity countless times, envisioned the care he would take to spare her pain if he could. He would do everything in his power to pleasure her. Would another man be able to give her what Hugh was dying to?

Forty

———◆———

"*I* will," Hugh vowed, returning his fingers to her. "I want tae show you this. And that means readying you." He began to tease and stroke her flesh again, making her melt for him, until she was on the verge of release. Mercilessly, he kept her just on the edge as he delved and rubbed, over and over.

She moaned with need, ready to beg. "Hugh, I'm ready!" she cried. "I ache so much inside . . . please . . ."

He was so gorgeous in the moonlight—his eyes were burning with intent, with possession. She swept her palms over his damp chest, reveling in the way the muscles in his torso flexed under her hands.

At last, he took his shaft and positioned it, clenching his jaw when the head met her entrance. "*So hot . . . so wet.*" His lips were parted, his breaths ragged. "It's everything I can do no' to come right now." When he began working the head inside her, she felt it stretching her—no matter how much he'd prepared her, the fit was still tight. "Tell me," he rasped, feeding his length into her, "tell me what you meant this afternoon, Sìne."

By the time he met the barrier, she was trembling, clutching his shoulders, and he was sweating with the obvious effort to go slow. He gazed down at her, dark eyes questioning.

"*I'm yours*," she whispered. "*To take*." She'd never been more certain of anything in her life.

He groaned, thrusting deep. She felt the tearing, hissing in a breath just as he groaned, "So *tight*." He shuddered, but remained still inside her as he gently smoothed her hair back from her forehead. "I dinna want to cause you pain."

"No, I knew there'd be"—she tried to conceal a wince—"a bit of hurting."

Even with this discomfort, the feeling of closeness awed her. This was worth the wait a thousand times over. She could feel him throbbing inside her, could see his anguished expression, but somehow he didn't move, wanting to spare her pain, wanting to please her.

She gazed up at him and couldn't hold back the words: "I . . . love you."

"What did you say?" he bit out, battling the frantic need to shove his hips at her.

"I always have."

Her words made him wonder if he was dreaming this entire scenario—this was exactly as he would imagine. Now, when he was buried so deeply inside her, the need arose to say the words that would bind her to him—a vow of self, spoken in the old language. Yet he couldn't. He didn't have that right.

Instead, he bent down and kissed her, with everything he felt for her, until she was panting. Her hands went from holding on to his shoulders, as though for dear life, to exploring touches over his body. When she tentatively rolled her hips, he withdrew, then eased back inside her, determined to make this good for her. *Concentrate. Slowly in . . . easing out. Again.*

He had to stop wondering why she had chosen to give this gift to *him*—to *love* him. He drew back to study her face. "Does it still hurt, Sìne?" he asked, rocking against her.

Her eyes fluttered open with a look of wonder. "N-no, not anymore," she murmured. "That feels so perfect. . . ." She leaned up to press her wet little kisses on his chest, driving him mad. "Does it for you?"

In answer, he shuddered again and couldn't help stirring himself in her, savoring all her wetness around him. When he thrust again, her nipples were hard points goading his chest. He bent to lick them, and she began meeting every thrust.

As soon as he slipped his thumb down between them and rubbed, she cried, "*I'm about to . . . You're making me . . .* Oh, God, *promise* you'll do this again to me. Tonight." She took his face in both of her hands. "Promise, *Hugh.*" His name became a cry as she climaxed.

Though he fought it, had even stopped thrusting, her hungry body demanded, her sex squeezing him, tight as a fist. He couldn't hold his seed. Defeated, he bucked between her thighs with all his strength, yelling to the sky. He came with a violent force, shuddering with each fierce pumping inside her.

As he leaned against her, heart thundering against hers, he said hoarsely, "You love me?"

Back in his bed, she curled against him, her breaths light on his chest, her body warm and soft with sleep. But

Hugh was wide awake, turning thoughts over and over in his mind.

Tonight, he had dared to put his rough hands on her delicate body—his hands, which had killed so many times before. He'd dared to take her virginity—had been about to do it in a crazed moment of anger. He'd almost hurt her without measure.

Yet he *hadn't.*

The only dire thing he'd done was to give in when she'd wanted him four more times. If he was destined to bring her pain, then why had she told him that what they'd done had *awed* her?

He wondered where the guilt was. He'd expected to be disgusted with his weakness; instead he felt alive, energized, optimistic. His body was relaxed, his muscles at ease. Throughout the night, she'd made him feel like the lad he'd been when he'd seen her last. He wanted more of that feeling.

Tonight, he'd made her his, and it had felt like it was his *right* to do so.

Because she wants me, too. She'd *always* wanted him. Before she'd slept, she confided to him about her feelings, and how long she'd struggled with them. The more she revealed, the more astounded he'd become.

She'd told him she compared all men to him—and found them all lacking. Compared to *him.* He pulled her closer with the crook of his arm. He could scarcely credit it, but knew she told the truth.

What if I just tell her about the curse? he thought again. She was intelligent. He respected her ideas and admired the way her mind worked. Maybe between the two of them, they could figure out a way.

Tomorrow, then. It would be done.

• • • •

The next morning, Jane stretched with a grin on her face, feeling sore and well-loved. She was also more *in* love than she'd ever been. Last night had been everything she'd always dreamed it would be—better than.

Her only regret was that they hadn't been spending the last ten years of their lives like this. But as long as they spent the rest of them this way, she was mollified.

Her eyes slid open, and she found Hugh was dressed in pants, seated on the edge of the bed. She took one look at his face and knew.

"Oh, dear God," she murmured. "I'm a regret."

"It's no' like that, Jane—"

"Then tell me you don't regret making love to me."

He raked his fingers through his tousled hair. "It's more complicated than that."

She gave a bitter laugh. "It's very simple. The man I gave my virginity to, wishes he hadn't taken it."

He flinched.

"You win, Hugh." She stood, wrapping the sheet around her. "I'm going to say three words I've never uttered to anyone in my entire life: I—give—up." She stormed out, striding into her room. After slamming her door, she locked it behind her.

Seconds later, her door was rocked from its hinges. With a gasp, she glanced up from donning her shift.

He was huge, filling the doorway. She was even more aware of his strength and the power in his body because she'd spent the night learning every inch of it, rubbing, cupping, and licking it.

"Stop doing that to my doors!" she cried.

"Then doona ever keep a locked door between us."

"I'm done talking to you!" she snapped, and darted past him, heading for the broken door.

He grabbed her elbow, swinging her around. "Will you no' just listen to me?"

They were toe to toe, both breathing heavily. His brows drew together as if he was confounded, then his hand shot out to clutch her nape, yanking her against his unyielding chest. His voice a broken rasp, he said, *"My God, I'll never get enough of you."*

His lips crashed into hers, slanting into a scorching, possessive kiss, making her ache anew. But she somehow shoved against him. "No! I'm not doing this! Not again. Not until you tell me what happened between last night and this morning."

After a hesitation, he took a deep, seemingly calming breath, then nodded. "Verra well. Dress yourself. Then we'll discuss some things," he said, looking for all the world like a man sentenced to the gallows.

Forty-one

Half an hour later, once Jane had washed and dressed, preparing for whatever he had to confess, she sat patiently waiting on the side of his bed.

Hugh hadn't spoken, just paced the room like a caged beast, appearing as if he were . . . *nervous*.

"Just say what's on your mind," she said as he passed. "Whatever it is, it can't hurt to tell me."

He slowed. "And how would you know that?"

"Is it a secret that someone would kill me for? That Grey would torture me for?"

"No."

"Does it embarrass you?"

"No, but—"

"Hugh, they're just words. Trust me with your secret, and you won't regret it." When he still resisted, she tried to make light. "Do you worry that I won't find you as attractive if you're not the brooding Highlander with his devilish secrets? Tell me."

"Hell, you won't believe me anyway," he muttered. "This is going to sound mad. I ken it's going to." He ran a hand over the back of his neck. "But my family was . . . cursed. I believe that I will bring you nothing but misery if I stay wed to you."

Cursed? What the devil is he talking about? Though her thoughts were wild, her tone was inscrutable when she said, "Go on, I'm listening."

"Ten generations ago, a clan seer foretold the futures of the Carrick line and recorded them in a book called the *Leabhar nan Sùil-radharc*, the *Book of Fates.*" He pointed to the old book he always had on the table. "My brothers and I are fated to be solitary, living our lives alone, and will bring pain to those we care for if we think to do otherwise. We will be the last of our line and can never have children. For five hundred years, the foretellings have all come true—every single one of them."

"I-I don't understand . . ." She inhaled and began again, "Do you care for me enough to stay with me otherwise?" she asked.

"Aye, Christ, yes."

"Then you're telling me that nothing stands in the way of us staying married except for a . . . *curse*?"

When he didn't deny it, Jane barely stifled the scream welling in her throat. *This just isn't happening to me!* How could she be rational in the face of this? Reasonable was impossible.

It was as if one of the foundations of her adult life had just suffered a fracture. Now everything built on it had gone askew. The quiet, steady Hugh she'd known for half her life was gone, and in his place was a superstitious madman.

"Hugh, people simply . . . people like us simply don't think like this anymore. Not with science and medicine. Mòrag is superstitious because she doesn't know any better. You've traveled the world, and you're educated. Beliefs like this belong in the past."

"And I wish I could put them there. But this has shadowed me for my entire life."

"You know me well enough to know I can't accept things like this."

"Aye, I ken that." He exhaled a long breath. "And I know that you scorn those who do."

"Naturally!" she snapped, then struggled for calm. "Are you telling me this now because you're willing to forget this, forget these beliefs?"

His expression looked hopeless—and resigned. "If I could have figured out a way to get around it, I never would have had to tell you."

When she realized that he wasn't revealing this to explain his past behavior, but to explain why he couldn't stay married to her, her lips parted. "You're really saying this? That a *Scottish* curse—and, my goodness, aren't those always the worst kind?—keeps us from remaining wed?"

All of the worry, the careful strategizing, the effort to win him—all of it was for nothing.

Because of a curse.

Frustration threatened to choke her. *No, Father, actually I* can't *cajole him into staying with me.* She'd never had a chance from the outset.

"Everything in the book comes to pass," Hugh said. "Everything. I ken it's hard to believe."

"I should have kept a tally of your excuses! You're not the marrying kind, you can't have children, and, oh yes, you are cursed. Anything else you want to declare to scare me away? I know! You *used* to be a eunuch? You've only two months to live?" Then, in a breathy voice, she said, "You're a *ghost*, aren't you?"

He clenched and unclenched his jaw, visibly grappling for control. "Do you think I'm lying about this?"

"Hugh, I sincerely *hope* you're lying—" She broke off as a thought arose. "Oh, dear God." A trembling hand flew to her forehead. "Does this mean that a five-hundred-year-old curse is the only thing you were trusting to keep me from conceiving?"

"I told you I canna get you with bairn." His eyes narrowed. "But you said it dinna matter either way."

"I said it didn't matter, so long as we were married! Right now, all I know is that you're still leaving. And, yes, you told me you can't have children, but I'm having trouble with the source of your information."

He strode to the table, flipping to the end of the book. "Just read the words, and let me explain."

She shook her head. "I can't listen to this. I would no more listen to this than I would hear an argument that the sun is blue."

"You've wanted to know, and now I'm telling you—the first person I've ever told—but you doona want to hear it?" he demanded. "Read the words."

She yanked the book out of his hands. "This is the root of the *curse*?" At his nod, she tossed it back to the table and flipped through, not bothering to be careful with the pages, though she could tell it was very old. Some of the text was written in Gaelic, some in English. Her brows drew together as she flipped toward the end. Now it all seemed to be written in English.

"Why're you frowning? Did you feel something—"

"Yes!" she cried, swinging a wide-eyed gaze at him. "I'm feeling an overwhelming urge to toss this into the lake."

Ignoring her comment, he moved beside her and turned to the last page. "This was written to my father."

She perused the passage. *Not to marry, know love, or bind, their fate; Your line to die for never seed shall take. Death and torment to those caught in their wake . . .* "You said all of this has come true?"

"Aye. My father died the day after we read this the first time, the verra next morning, though he was no' much older than I am now. And years ago, Ethan's intended died the night before his wedding."

"How?"

He hesitated, then said, "She either fell. Or jumped."

"Is this blood?" Jane scratched her nail against the copper stain at the bottom. At his nod, she asked, "What's under the stain?"

"We doona know. It's never been lifted."

She peered up at him. "What if it says, 'Disregard the above'?" At his scowl, she said, "Hugh, I don't think this is a curse—I think this is *life*. Bad things happen, and if I made myself a template of future woes, I could pick and choose from everything that might have happened to match it. Now, I admit, your father's death was strange. But there are physicians in London who posit that the mind can make the body do anything—even shut down. Belinda told me about it. If your father believed strongly enough, he could have effected this."

"And Ethan? The death of his fiancée directly before his wedding?"

"Was either an accident or his intended wasn't well and couldn't take the idea of marriage to someone she didn't love."

Again and again, she brought up points, calling on everything she'd ever learned about science or just plain human nature.

Finally, he undermined all her efforts by saying simply, "I believe it. I *feel* it."

"Because you were raised to, and you grew into this curse, grew to fit it. You are the epitome of a self-fulfilling prophecy. You believed that you would walk with death, that you weren't supposed to have joy in life." She reached out and tentatively touched his arm. "But Hugh, I'm not expecting you to simply turn this off. It's been with you for thirty-two years—it will take time to let go. I'm willing to work at it if you are." His silence actually made her more optimistic. "In time, we'll get you to start believing that you *will* have happiness—that you deserve it." She cupped his face. "Tell me you'll at least try. For me? I'm ready to fight for us if you are."

The moment stretched interminably. Her whole future hung in the balance—but surely he would make the right choice. She couldn't be this in love with someone who would throw away what they had.

When his gaze left her face to flicker uneasily to the book, she realized she'd lost.

Jane didn't lose well.

Releasing him, she snatched the book, then stormed out of the room and down the stairs.

"What're you doing?" He was right behind her as she marched out of the house into the thick morning fog. "Tell me what you're aiming to do."

She hurried through dew-wetted grass toward the loch. "To get rid of the problem."

"The book is no' the problem. Just a reminder of it."

She had the lake in sight and didn't take her eyes from it when she said, "Then I'm ridding you of the reminder." She drew the book to her chest with both arms around it. She suddenly felt a sheen of cold sweat over her body, and inwardly shook herself.

"No, lass, it's no' that simple. Pitching it into the water will no' *do* anything."

"It might make me feel better." She turned to go to the first rocky rise, farther up the water's edge. It was deeper there, and she wanted this tome to sink to the bottom, never to touch another life again.

"It will no' matter if you cast it in the loch. It always finds its way back."

"Are you mad?" she snapped over her shoulder without slowing. "Listen to yourself!" When she reached the spot she wanted, she changed her grip on the book, readying to lob it, but hesitated.

"What are you waiting for? Do it, lass. I've done it enough."

She raised her eyebrows in challenge. "You think I'm jesting? I'll do it!"

He waved her on, and she flung it with all her might. They both stood silently watching it sink, the pages fluttering until it disappeared.

"Odd. I don't feel any different." She faced him. When he evinced the same grim, resolved expression, she didn't bother to hide her bitter disappointment in him. "You were right—it didn't *do* anything. You're still going to throw away what's between us. We must *still* be cursed."

"If I risked only my life, this would be done," he grated. "I would no' think twice. But if I were to cause you any kind of hurt, I could never forgive myself."

Tears began spilling from her eyes. "Any kind of hurt?" She threw her hands up. "*This* hurts right now, Hugh. It hurts worse than anything I've ever known." She futilely wiped her eyes with the backs of her hands. "Of course, you'll just see that as proof that the curse is in effect, right?"

"I would no' have had you feeling even this." He looked as if watching her crying was torture. He seemed to want to touch her but only clenched and opened his fist. "I would no' have come back if no' for Grey and would never have seen you again. I managed it for years—"

"You . . . you *purposely* sought not to see me?" He'd been avoiding her? When she'd been begging her cousins to ride with her past his London home, praying for a mere glimpse of him? "This just gets better. Well, understand that the last ten years have been unbearable without you. So by staying away, you hurt me. By abandoning me, you devastated me."

"Abandoned? I never made you any promises."

"I thought we were getting married!" Her tears streamed without check. "I thought you were just waiting until I was eighteen. I didn't describe my wedding ring to someone I *didn't* believe would be my husband."

His lips parted, but then he shook his head. "Even if none of this had happened, even without the curse, I still would no' have offered for you. I dinna have anything to offer you. I had *nothing.*"

"I wouldn't have cared as long as I was with you."

"That's bullshite!" he roared, finally reaching the limits of his control. "You liked wealth and made no secret of it. And every time you made that clear, you dinna see me tensing at yet another reminder that I was no' good enough for you. You described that ring for a reason, Jane—because you expected it!"

"The only thing I expected was *not* to be abandoned without a word. And I'll tell you right now that it's so much worse to be left behind than to do the leaving."

"*You have no bloody idea*," he bit out, his tone seething. "You want to know my secrets, Jane? Know that at twenty-two, I went out in the world and did a cold-blooded thing. And I did it for *you*. Because I knew if I did such a heinous act, I would never dream of entangling my life with yours. So doona tell me it's easier to walk away—it's no'. No' if you can possibly go back."

"But you're still going to do it again. When Grey's caught."

"Aye. I know that I will," he said, staring down at her. "Even if I doona know how."

Forty-two

———— •◆• ————

*L*ater that morning, when Hugh felt he had calmed enough from the morning's fight, he found her on the terrace shooting her bow. With her face cold and expressionless as marble, she drew back her bowstring and shot, drawing one arrow after another from the quiver at her back with incredible speed.

She'd long since shredded her target.

"Jane, can you stop for a moment?" he asked, falling in beside her when she retrieved her arrows.

Angrily yanking them out, she collected them in the quiver. "Can you not see I'm busy?" She didn't even glance at him, just returned to her line to nock another arrow. In one fluid movement, she raised her aim to the target, pulled and released the bowstring, hitting dead center.

"I need to speak with you," Hugh said.

"And I need some time alone."

Noting the drawn expression on her face and her arms beginning to shake, he said, "You've been at this for hours, lass."

"There's nothing to talk about, since I understand the situation perfectly. I've all but *begged* you to remain married to me. I've confessed my unwavering feelings for you and offered to do whatever it takes to get us past this. But there's a rub. You can't, because you're *cursed*."

At last, he'd revealed his weighty secret, and she'd brought up the strong arguments he'd anticipated from her. But what had he expected—that he could be talked from something that had pervaded every corner of his life? Hell, even if somehow he could come to disbelieve the curse, he'd had it hanging over him so long, shaping him, that he was suspicious of happiness, was uncomfortable with it.

He knew he shouldn't have told her, if he wasn't capable of even trying. "So what do we do about this marriage? We need to decide something."

"We can decide this very easily. You let go of this curse absurdity. If you swear never to mention it again, I'll vow to wipe this memory from my mind. Then we'll live happily ever after. Or, if you insist on this tripe, then we will end in one of two ways—divorce or separation."

"If I could let this go and stay married to you, I'd give my right arm for it."

At that, she hesitated in the middle of a shot, and hit just wide of the center.

"But you can't," she said softly.

He gave a weary exhalation. "No."

Making her manner brisk once more, she said, "Then we've made our decision."

"Jane . . ." When she wouldn't look at him again, he turned from her, but didn't know where to go, what to do.

Work. Work would take his mind off her, off scenes of the night before. Yet the only thing left to do on the property, after weeks of ceaseless labor, was to clear the trees from the drive. He crossed to the stables, entering the darkened building. His mood must be palpable—the horses seemed startled by him, though they never had been before.

Yes, getting lost in exertion would dull his desperate want of her. Who was he deluding? *Nothing* would dull it. It'd bloody gotten *worse,* now that he'd been foolish enough to think he could slake himself inside her—

Blinding pain exploded through his head. The side of his face slammed against the hard-packed ground; warmth seeped down the back of his neck.

Grey.

Another blow connected with Hugh's temple. Two hits, placed just as Grey had been taught to do—if he wanted to keep a victim alive but immobilized. The booted kicks to Hugh's gut were solely for Grey's enjoyment.

Grey clucked his tongue. "Damn, Hugh, you could've made this a little more challenging."

Jane had watched Hugh amble down the hill toward the stables, looking as if he carried the weight of the world, and felt a pang, then grew more angered than before. He never allowed her to just *step back,* to lick her wounds a bit. And if she'd ever needed to . . .

She felt as if she'd been slapped and was still reeling.

He didn't want to stay with her, even after they'd made love and she'd easily concluded that it was the most wondrous thing that had ever happened to her. It was bad enough that she'd given her virginity to someone who regretted taking it, when she'd waited so long, waited so impatiently. But rubbing salt in the wound was the fact that Hugh regretted taking it because of a sodding *curse.*

This was so fantastical as not to be believed.

Give his right arm, he'd said. Though all signs pointed to his caring for her much more deeply and for much longer than she'd imagined, she actually prayed that wasn't true. If he'd felt *half* of what she had for all these years and denied them a marriage because of this . . .

She thought she might begin to hate him.

If Hugh had been honest and forthcoming about his superstitions all those years ago, she would have gotten over him. She would have understood there was no chance for them, and she would have married someone else. But he hadn't been forthcoming, and she was done letting her feelings for Hugh "Tears and Years" MacCarrick eat away at her life.

It was time for Jane to be practical. She could never compete with a five-hundred-year-old curse. She was never going to have a life with Hugh, so what would she do after Grey was caught? Though she'd told Hugh they could divorce, the idea of it made her cringe. Perhaps she could still get an annulment.

Based on Hugh's insanity.

Or they could stay married but separated. She tilted her head. Yes, that was the better option. She would demand her dowry from Hugh—and her father had better be prompt to pay it, after he'd forced her into this *farce* of a marriage.

With that money and as a married woman, she could be independent. She could travel, sponsor the arts, finally found the Society for the Expression of Vice! She could write dirty books for Holywell Street, take lovers like there was no tomorrow and have ten children by them. Yes. This could work—

A thought made her heart sink and her blood boil. Hugh might believe in a curse as contraception, but Jane did not.

She could be pregnant from last night.

How could he do this to her? He expected her to accept this madness, and vowed to leave her, when she could very well be carrying his child!

Before she had any real idea what she was doing, she was marching down to the stables. This was probably a Bad Idea. She'd impulsively tossed that book, but throwing it away hadn't made her feel any better—well, not *that* much better. It had gone differently in her mind and such.

But what did it matter how she behaved now? What else could be hurt by releasing the tirade bubbling inside her?

Nothing.

Because things couldn't possibly be worse than they already were.

Forty-three

———◆———

*H*ugh cracked open his eyes, wincing with pain, and found himself staring into the barrel of a pistol.

He struggled to rise but almost lost consciousness. Though he knew he couldn't dissuade Grey from this course, he had to try—because he understood exactly why he'd been kept alive, and his gut roiled with dread.

"Doona do this," he bit out, laboring for breath against the stabbing pain in his ribs. "Kill me, make it slow, but she has no place in all this."

"Why waste your breath?" Grey asked. "I just don't *think* that way. In case you never noticed, I don't think like you at all. I'll kill her as easily as an insect."

"You were no' always like this."

"Precisely why I'm here, Scot. To redress wrongs."

"How did you find us?" Hugh grated, trying to stall.

"It was the oddest thing. I was stalking this young lass, not far from here, planning to remove her fingers, when she met up with a band of six riders. Big bastards on massive mounts. They set off onto a path into the woods, but left a trail so deep that a blind man could follow them, a trail straight here. . . ."

Out of the corner of his eye, Hugh spied a flicker of white. Raising his gaze, he saw Jane poised at the stable entrance, face stoic as an angel's. An avenging angel's—she had an arrow nocked in her bow, pointed at Grey's back. The string was pulled so tight with her leather-tipped fingers, Hugh thought the bow would snap.

Hugh dropped his eyes, but Grey must have followed the direction of his gaze. He twisted around to fire at her, but she let her arrow sing without hesitation. She'd obviously aimed for his heart, but she'd caught him too quickly. Grey hadn't finished whirling around when her arrow struck. It only pierced his gun arm—through the forearm, pinning it to his chest. Hugh couldn't see Grey's face and reaction, but saw Jane's.

Her eyes were stark and wide, her lips parting in shock.

A monster. The man she'd known as Grey was gone and in his place was something she could scarcely comprehend. His face was drawn tight over his prominent cheekbones. A wide coal-black hat shaded his wasted face and darkened teeth.

Before she could nock another arrow, he lunged for her. Swinging his free arm out, he backhanded her, sending her spinning into the wall. She heard Hugh's roar of fury just before her head hit and snapped forward. She slumped, sinking inch by inch to the ground, as she fought to keep her eyes open.

Even though Hugh had been lying on the ground with blood coursing down his neck and temple, now he somehow lumbered to his knees, but Grey turned. With a yell, Grey reared back his leg and kicked him across the side of his head, making Hugh's body jerk in recoil before collapsing once more.

Jane bit back the hysterical scream clawing at her throat and crawled to her bow. She snatched it up just as Grey turned, setting those crazed eyes on her. Scrambling backward, she clumsily tore another arrow from her quiver.

The movement made her vision blurry . . . couldn't stop blinking . . . even while taking aim. On a prayer, eyes closing, she pulled back the bowstring and shot again. She heard a meaty thump. *Hit him . . . In the shoulder.*

Not a kill shot. Try again. Fight. Another arrow.

Grey closed in and ripped the arrow and bow from her with his free hand, tossing them both away. "Jane, I'm afraid you're just being tedious now," he said, his tone gently chiding and utterly out of place with the maniacal expression on his waxen face. "If you cooperate, I might make this a bit less agonizing."

Blood poured from his wounds; his right arm was still raised against his chest, the hand that clutched his pistol useless. When he attempted to remove the first arrow, he rocked on his feet. Finally he just broke the shanks of both arrows at the middle, then dropped his gun, catching it with his left hand.

"Grey, goddamn it, there must be something," Hugh bit out, laboring to speak, "something you want more than this."

"We aren't going to do this, are we?" Grey asked, as though exasperated. "Hash out old ills and slights, revealing things never revealed before in the hopes of a final understanding? If we did that every time you and I killed, we'd be wise men indeed. Besides, you know there's never been any reasoning or bargaining that has moved me—*or you*—to mercy."

What is he saying?

Grey stowed his pistol and unsheathed his blade,

making her freeze with fear. *Grey slits their throats*, Hugh had told her.

When he turned to her with the knife, she tried to meet his chilling gaze. "W-why?" she whispered.

"*Why?* Because your father ordered my death, and he almost succeeded. Four bullets in the chest in return for nearly twenty years of murder for the old bastard. And because, once, when I was in a very bad way, your husband beat me to within an inch of my life—over you, incidentally—then left me to rot in a dark basement. I'm going to kill you to punish them for their slights. It's nothing personal, you see."

"My *father*? What are you talking about?"

"You didn't know any of this?" He cast a glance at Hugh, and tsked. "That's not very forthcoming of you. And now that I think on it, it's arrogant. You never told her, because you didn't expect me to last long enough to be a threat. Take me out and she never has to know? But here I am." To Jane, he said, "Your father deals death for a living, and Hugh is his most prolific assassin. Your father, Hugh, Rolley, even Quin have all lied and hid their real faces from you. How much you must have trusted them all to protect you. I bet you feel more foolish than frightened right now."

She spat the words, "They knew well enough that *you* needed to die."

"Yes, Weyland sought to destroy what he'd made."

"He didn't make you like this—your addiction did—"

"Wrong! When your father was doling out jobs, he made sure I took the brunt of the bad, the ones that really twist a man. *My* sacrifice made your husband what he is. Know that Hugh could so easily have been like me."

"Never," she hissed.

"Why not? Hugh's a cold-blooded killer too, creeping about in the night and taking lives—just as I do." He drew his lips back from his dark teeth. "But he's not ruined, not yet. Because your father made sure he preserved Hugh for *you*."

She blinked in confusion.

"Did they tell you *nothing*?" He gave her a pitying smile. "Dear girl, Hugh has yearned for your heart so badly and for so long that I'm finally going to give it to him. Still warm from your chest."

Forty-four

————— •◆• —————

As he gathered the last of his strength, Hugh was forced to do nothing but listen as Grey revealed what Hugh was. He saw Jane's face, stark with confusion, her gaze darting to him as if waiting for a denial.

But when Grey took the merest step closer to her, Hugh lunged forward, tackling Grey's legs. They plunged forward and struck the ground.

Hugh rolled away. Grey's body lay poised, propped at a grotesque angle by the remains of the arrows—until with a sickening rush, the tips pierced his back.

At once, Hugh struggled toward Jane. Over his harsh breaths, he barely heard the faint gurgling sound coming from Grey. When Hugh reached her, he drew her up in the crook of his arm, gently touching her face, but she couldn't seem to focus on him. "How badly are you hurt, Sìne?"

"Hugh, you got . . . hit, kicked."

"He pulled the blows. Wanted me to see."

She gave a weak cry. "Oh, God, I feel his blood." It was seeping outward from Grey, soaking her skirts.

Hugh swooped her away, moving her into the sun.

"Is he d-dead? Make sure he's dead, please."

Hugh gently laid her back against the wall, then bit back

pain as he closed the distance to Grey. When Hugh turned him over, the man's eyes were open. He lived still, but the arrow through his chest ensured it wouldn't be for long.

Leaning in so Jane couldn't hear, Hugh hissed, "Goddamn you, where's the list? Did you release it?"

Grey made a small movement as though he'd tried to shake his head. "*Have it,*" he said with a gasp, blood bubbling up from his lips.

"Did you do something to Ethan? Tell me!"

Grey's face split into a gruesome grin. Just before he died, he rasped, "*Ethan . . . was . . . my last number.*"

Through a haze, Jane felt Hugh lifting her in his arms, though he had been injured as well. She felt him shuddering as he clutched her, but she wanted to walk on her own, to take care of him. Yet every time she made a move to free herself, he squeezed her to him like a steel vise.

She frowned when her skirts dragged down, then remembered they were wet with Grey's blood. As Hugh walked, the material made sickening smacks against his legs. Nauseated, she fought to keep her heavy eyelids open, but it was impossible. . . .

When she cracked open her eyes once more, she found herself in Hugh's bed, already stripped of her bloody clothes.

"You're awake." Hugh was gazing down at her with an agonized expression.

Well, of course she was. She only had a bump to her head and a bruised jaw. *He* was the one who was hurt, with dried blood tracking down his face and neck. When he began washing her off with a wet cloth, she said, "Hugh, stop this . . . let me get up to see to you." He continued on as if she hadn't spoken, and she couldn't summon the strength to rise.

Just when he'd finished and had slipped a new shift on her, Mòrag entered the room, took one look at the pile of bloody clothing, and began firing questions.

"Go downstairs," he ordered, talking over her. "There will be a saddled horse somewhere near the main house. Secure it outside the stable." Then, seeming to rethink the matter, he said, "The Englishman who'd been aiming to hurt us is dead in the stable. Doona go in there."

"Well, if he's dead, he will no' need his horse!"

"Do it!" Hugh barked. "And doona read anything in his bags."

"I canna read," she called over her shoulder as she hurried from the room.

Jane reached a hand to his temple. "We have to see to your head."

"It's nothing." He knew from experience that he would be foggy and would sleep more for a couple days. His ribs would hurt like hell for weeks, but he'd recovered from far worse than this. "I'm a hard headed Scot, remember? But you . . ." He studied her jaw, touching the tender area, and she couldn't prevent a wince. "The bastard meant to break it." His voice thrummed with cold anger when he said, "And would have, if he'd been stronger."

"What did he say to you in the end?"

"He said he . . . killed my brother."

"Oh, Hugh, I'm so sorry."

Mòrag bustled into the room again. Between breaths, she said, "I've secured his horse."

"Good." He rose unsteadily and told her, "Stay here till I return."

"Hugh?" Jane whispered, not ready for him to leave her sight. She was shaken to her bones, in pain, and still afraid, even though Grey was dead.

"I have to check on something," he answered, not looking any happier that he had to go. "I'll be right back." To Mòrag, he said, "Stay with her."

The girl replied, "Fine horse o' his, with such high-class tack. *My* saddle was ruined by English with the sludge—"

"Take it," he barked. "Just doona dare leave this room, in case she needs anything."

Mòrag nodded, and as soon as Hugh had left, she said, "What the hell is going on, English? Did you shoot that man full of quills?" She appeared almost admiring.

Jane nodded, feeling no regret for helping to kill a man, so she was surprised to find tears tracking down her cheeks. Her mind was a tangle of thoughts and questions.

How much of what Grey had said was true? He was either a madman speaking lies—or her life was not at all as she'd thought. Was she surrounded by deceivers, by killers? Did Hugh truly lurk around in the dark and kill unsuspecting people?

Could Hugh have wanted her to the desperate degree that she'd wanted him?

Grey had been as dangerous as they'd said, but now he was dead, and the threat was gone. Even after this, she sensed nothing had changed with Hugh—which meant soon she'd be going home.

To live among people she didn't even know anymore.

Hugh found the list in a sealed, waxed tube in Grey's saddlebag, and burned the paper, watching until nothing remained but the finest ash.

Jane was safe from Grey, and this other danger would never touch her or her father. They'd come through unscathed. But Ethan hadn't.

No. Hugh refused to believe it. He didn't think Grey would lie about this, but maybe the man had been mistaken. He might have hallucinated.

Wouldn't Hugh feel it if one of his brothers were dead?

Hugh would write and request information about Ethan. Yes, he'd get Mòrag to ride to the telegraph office this morning. Grey's death needed to be reported, as did the recovery of the list.

He wished he had an idea of what he would be writing about Jane—other than the fact that Grey had told her so much that Hugh would now be forced to explain the rest.

When he returned with the message and sent Mòrag off to post it, he found Jane was sleeping, her cheeks still wet. How could the events of the day—and of their long night before—not have left her exhausted?

He washed himself, gritting his teeth against the pain as he removed the dried blood from his beaten body. After he'd wedged a chair against the door, he crawled into bed beside her.

When he woke, he found her on her side, watching him. It was night, but the moon was firing light into the room.

"How is your head?" she asked sleepily.

"Doona worry about me, lass. I'm concerned only with your jaw."

She brushed her fingers over it. "It'll be sore. And it's already starting to bruise, but I'll be fine."

He touched it too, needing to make sure.

"Hugh, I want to understand what Grey was talking about. What did he mean about you, and about my father?"

She'd heard too much—she'd have to know the rest. And didn't he owe her the truth after what had happened with Grey? She'd tolerated so much, had coped with all that had been forced onto her. Hugh knew this, and yet, still he hesitated.

As many times as he'd imagined making love to her, he'd imagined the look on her face to learn of this. "Jane, I worked as . . ." He trailed off.

"Go on. Please."

"I was a gunman."

"What is that?"

He swallowed. "I . . . I killed people for the crown."

"I don't understand. I thought you worked with Courtland. And how could my father be involved in that?"

So Hugh explained that Weyland headed an organization that dealt with *situations*—ones that couldn't be resolved diplomatically. He revealed what all of their roles were.

"Quin and Rolley, too? Why didn't I ever discover this?" she asked.

"Most family members don't. And your father never wanted this to touch you. That's always been his worst fear. Lying to you sat ill with him."

Her voice soft, she asked, "Did lying to me sit ill with you?"

"Never lied to you."

She bit her lip, frowning as she clearly thought back. Then she said, "My father did try to have Grey killed?" At

Hugh's hesitant nod, she asked, "Was Grey right to say that you were favored over him?"

He ran a hand over his face. "I dinna believe so before. I thought Grey got the jobs he did because he was a bloody decade older than me and had years more experience. Now . . . I think unconsciously, Weyland might have."

Her eyelids were getting heavy though he knew she was burning to ask dozens more questions. "And what about Grey's comment about . . . you and me?"

After a lengthy hesitation, he grated, "True."

His answer seemed to hurt her more than anything. "How long, Hugh?"

"Since that summer. Same as you."

She met his eyes. "Do I know all your secrets now?"

"Aye, lass. Every single one of them." When she fell silent, he said, "Jane, will you no' tell me what you're thinking about all this . . . about me?"

She answered his question with one of her own: "Will what happened today change anything for us?"

He finally made himself shake his head.

"Then nothing will." She turned away from him, murmuring, "So it doesn't matter what I think."

Forty-five

—◆—

*H*ugh shot up in bed, wracked by a nightmare worse than any he'd ever had. The piercing pain in his ribs and head was still unfamiliar, momentarily confusing him when he woke. He frowned at his surroundings, rubbing at his eyes. It was well into the afternoon. Had he slept through the entire night and morning?

His body was still shaking; his sheets were soaked with sweat. He'd dreamed of Ethan's fiancée on the cold flagstones, head framed by her blood shining in the moonlight. But instead of seeing her glazed, sightless eyes, Hugh saw Jane, cold and still in death. He shuddered just remembering it—

Where the hell is she?

When he heard her in her room, getting dressed, he let out a relieved breath. After rising in stages, he staggered to the basin, wetted a cloth, then ran it over himself to wash the chill sweat from his body.

Her light footsteps sounded in the hall outside his room as she made her way downstairs. He dressed as quickly as his injuries would allow, then followed. When he eased down the steps and into the kitchen, he found her motionless, staring blankly.

The first thing he noticed was that her bruise had darkened and spread since yesterday, and he flinched to see it. Then his gaze landed on the object of her rapt attention—the *Leabhar*.

He crossed to her side, silent. Even after all this time, the mysteries of the book still stunned even him. He wondered again how many of his forefathers had futilely tried to burn it or bury it in a locked chest, desperate to rid themselves of it. But the *Leabhar* was tied to his family like a disease passed down.

"It can't be the same," she said softly. "I threw it in the water."

"It is the same."

"S-someone must have dragged it up from the bottom. You got Mòrag's brothers to retrieve it."

"It's dry, Jane."

"This is a jest. It has to be," she insisted. "There's more than one book."

He opened to the last page with the distinct blood stains.

She gaped at it in horrified wonder. "I don't understand."

"This is why I dinna care if you threw it in. The *Leabhar* always finds its way back to a MacCarrick. Do you still think this is naught but superstition?"

She rubbed her forehead. "I . . . I don't . . ." She was saved from answering when the loud nicker of horses sounded down the drive.

When he strode to the window, she asked, "Who can that be?"

A coach pulled to a stop at the front entrance. Hugh

spied a man stepping out, and panic rioted in his chest. "It's . . . Quin."

Hugh knew his telegraph would have arrived at Weyland's yesterday morning; Quin must have set out at once, taking the daily rail to Scotland, then crossing the distance from a station to here by coach.

Quin could only be here for one of two reasons. He'd come to collect Jane—though Hugh hadn't asked him to, not yet.

Or he'd come to deliver news of Ethan.

Hugh turned to her, but she was already ascending the stairs, her back ramrod straight, no doubt thinking Hugh had telegraphed her cousin to rush up here and collect her at the first opportunity.

Before Quin could make the front steps, Hugh threw open the door and met him. "Why're you here?" he demanded. "Have you heard anything about Ethan?"

Quin answered, "We were just receiving the latest dispatches in London when I got your message." His expression was guarded. "We haven't been able to find him. I do know that witnesses heard gun report and saw two men yanking Ethan's body into an alley."

"To rob him or aid him?"

"We don't know—only that he'd definitely been shot."

Definitely been shot. Hugh stepped back to keep himself from pitching forward. He'd blindly held on to the belief that Ethan lived.

"He could still be alive," Quin said. "We're combing the area, and Weyland will let you know if anything breaks."

Hugh didn't trust others to look for his brother—he

needed to be out there searching. His brows drew together. "But why are *you* here?"

Quin answered, "Weyland wants the list destroyed or delivered into his possession."

"It's destroyed. Then why're you in a coach?"

"To retrieve Jane."

"I dinna send for you to do that."

"No, but you also didn't tell us that she was staying with you, just that she was safe here and had heard a great deal from Grey. As Weyland observed, your message said more than was written. Was I wrong to come for her?"

In the fall morning air, Hugh had begun sweating again, reminding him of haunting scenes from the night. . . .

When he didn't answer, Quin snapped, "Goddamn it, man, make a decision and quickly. You're affecting others' lives now. And I won't watch you toying with my cousin any longer."

"No' toying with her," Hugh said quietly.

"Maybe not on purpose, but the end is still the same—and it's been going on for years!" Quin was the only male in Jane's generation and was like an older brother to all the cousins, but especially to Jane who was an only child. Hugh understood Quin's anger and didn't begrudge him for it. "I'm sure she's been too proud to tell you this, but Jane's been in love with you since she was young."

"I ken that." Unbelievable as it seemed to Hugh.

Quin didn't hide his look of surprise. "Then what is it? Is it because you think she can do better? I hate to tell you this, MacCarrick, but she can. I know what you are and what you've done." He lowered his voice. "Now that the list is destroyed, you're going right back to work. Would you leave her behind each week as you sneak off to make a kill? What kind of life would that be for her?"

"She knows about me. And if I kept her as my wife, I would no' *continue*," he said, as if he was arguing to keep her.

"So you'll stay at home with her? Try to be domestic?" he asked, his voice full of derision. "How will you fit in with her friends and family, when you simply don't know how? My God, you couldn't sit a gathering before you turned killer."

He was right. Hugh had been too long in the field, and was so *different* from the people in her life anyway.

"If you can't make a decision," Quin said, his tone low and seething, "I'll bloody make it for you!"

The dream, the ominous reminder of the book, Quin's arrival—what more did Hugh need to see to realize he had to let her go...?

Apparently, Hugh needed to see Jane at the door with her bags packed, her mien stoic, and jaw battered. Hell, after the events of yesterday and the sight of the book this morning, she likely wouldn't have stayed with him anyway.

Quin sucked in a breath at the sight of her face. "My God, Jane. Are you all right?" When she nodded, Quin shot Hugh a black look.

Jane was dressed for travel, her bags at her feet. She was truly leaving. Today.

"You're goin' with him?" Hugh asked, his voice breaking a pitch lower.

"What else would I do?" She smoothed her skirts. "I'm glad you sent for him when the threat passed. Very forward-thinking."

"I dinna—"

"I thought so as well," Quin interrupted. "Doing the right thing for both of you. Jane, we need to get on the road if we intend to catch the train in Perth. Say good-bye and come along."

When she nodded absently, Quin collected her bags, then strode to the carriage—because they were leaving. Now.

Hugh had known he and Jane would part, but he'd thought he would have time to prepare himself. He turned back to Jane, staring down at her. "I was going to see you home."

"You don't think Quin can keep me safe?"

"Aye. Now. But I wanted to get you settled in, before—"

"Before *you* leave again?" She shrugged, her face cold. "We knew it would come to this. No reason to prolong it unnecessarily."

He exhaled, running a shaking hand over his face.

"We both have to get on with our lives," she continued. "This is what you want, isn't it?"

"I doona want you to go yet."

"Yet."

"What do *you* bloody want?" Was he sweating more? He couldn't stop seeing that dream before him.

Her voice quavering with emotion, she said, "We're back to the simple choice. We put the curse behind us. Or you refuse, and once I leave here today, I will never want to see you again."

He couldn't promise her he would disregard or forget something that had molded him and he couldn't easily give her loss, which was all she would have with him. But he had to know . . . "You'd be willing to be with me, even after everything you learned?" he asked, wishing she would say no. To find the one woman who could accept him, and to find her in *Jane* would be too much.

"I'd be willing to *try*, to see," she finally answered. "To maybe understand everything better."

"And after seeing the book?"

"That's something I don't think I will *ever* understand." She shivered. "Yes, when I look at it, I fear it—but I also know we could be stronger than anything written there."

Jane was here for the taking, ready to face hell for Hugh—and it humbled him. But shouldn't he be ready to do the same for her?

"Jane, come along!" Quin called from the carriage. "We have to make a train."

She turned back to Hugh. "If I leave here today, it's over. Forever, Hugh. I must move on from this." Her voice dropped to a whisper. "If you don't choose me now, you never will. But the sad thing is that one day you'll realize what you threw away." When he was silent, her eyes watered. "And I promise you, it'll be too late to get it back." She turned toward the carriage. Just as she was about to climb in, Jane stopped and strode back to Hugh.

She'd seen reason—she would stay with Hugh for a week more, a *day* more.

The cracking slap to his face took him completely off guard. "That was for the last ten years." She slapped the other side of his face, even harder. "And that's for the next!"

Forty-six

———— •◆• ————

"*I* never thought I'd say this," her father began, as he nervously regarded Jane's face, "but perhaps you ought to just cry."

Quin had suggested the same thing repeatedly on their journey back to London, right up until he'd deposited her in her father's study. She'd been home for an hour—long enough for her father to finish explaining what he and Hugh and everyone else did.

"I'm fine." *I'm numb.* When had her voice begun to sound so tinny?

She took a sip of her iced Scotch, defying him to say anything about her drinking so early.

"I'm sure this has all been a blow to you."

"Are you competing for the most patent understatement?" She rolled her eyes. "I mean, really, Papa, *imports*?"

He shrugged helplessly, and she sighed. He'd finally been totally forthcoming with her—she thought. She'd been markedly less so about Hugh's reasons for letting her go. "Who knows what he's thinking?" she'd said to him and to Quin. "He made comments like he thought he wasn't good enough for me. . . ."

"Jane, you keep saying you're fine, but you don't look it."

No, she'd been on the verge of crying since she'd first comprehended that Quin was there to retrieve her. In fact, she'd been as close to it as she'd ever been, without actually spilling tears. As she'd absently packed her things, she'd somehow prevented herself because she'd known that with her first tear, she might start something she couldn't stop.

"You're right." She gingerly touched the chilled glass on her swollen jaw, but the pain made her wince, and her father flinch—again. "This has all been a lot for me to digest. I see you and Quin and even Rolley, and I feel like you're strangers." She'd tried to put on a strong front when facing each of them, but for right now, all she could seem to manage was a wary indifference. "And Hugh? I had an idea of him for half my life. Now that's . . . changed."

She wasn't angry about Hugh's role in deceiving her. He had a job to do, and after talking to her father, she better understood the seriousness and significance of what he did. One of his bullets could spare a million of them in some needless war, and yet his job was lonely and grueling and he would never receive credit—or support if he'd been captured. She'd forgiven Hugh—for this, at least—but her father? "As for you, well, perhaps you might have provided a bit more warning about all this, and a lot less pressuring me to marry an assassin. Just a thought."

Her father couldn't meet her eyes—and she'd noticed that for the last hour, he'd avoided looking at her mother's portrait as well. "I regret what I did. But I swear that I believed Hugh would come around and do the right thing.

The man has been in love with you for so long, and he's always been honorable. But then, you understand that—you've always understood that. Jane, do you know how proud I was of you for choosing a man like Hugh? You saw things in him others couldn't. I thought the two of you were perfect for each other."

We almost were.

"Are you sure that you made it clear you were in love with him? And that you wanted to remain married?"

She made a sound of frustration. "You—have—*no*—idea."

He briefly raised his palms in the air. "Yes, yes, very well. I won't ask again."

"Well, what do you propose I do now?" She rotated the glass against her cheek to the cooler side and added, "With all the money from my dowry that you'll be giving me."

He quirked a brow, but wisely said nothing.

"I really have no idea what a woman in my situation does."

"Jane, I know I promised you I could smooth this over with Frederick, but"—he tugged on his collar—"he's not precisely available any longer."

"How's that?" she asked without interest.

"He's engaged to Candace Damferre. Her husband expired with no heir, leaving her everything. Bidworth's, uh, quite beside himself that they're both free."

What would Jane have done, weeks into marriage with Freddie, when his true love became free? Hugh might not have been able to give her a love-filled marriage, but he'd helped her father save her from a completely loveless one. "I'm happy for him."

"Are you truly?"

"Yes. I couldn't have gone back with him anyway."

"I know, but I promised you something I wasn't completely sure of because I was positive it would work out with you and Hugh."

She shrugged. "Don't feel guilty on that score, at least. You told me you could work all this out with Freddie," Jane began with a careless flick of her hand, "if the marriage to Hugh was unconsummated." She glanced up and frowned. "Your face is an interesting shade of red, Papa. Really remarkable."

His fists were clenched. "I'm going to kill him."

"Now, it seems"—she glanced both ways with exaggerated slyness and hushed her voice—"that I have to clarify if you mean literally."

For the last week, Hugh had combed the small lakeside village and all the surrounding areas for word of his brother. After days of doggedly chasing down every lead, Hugh was no closer to discovering anything to indicate whether Ethan was dead or alive.

As Quin had said, many had heard gunshots, and some shopkeepers saw two men dragging Ethan's lifeless body into an alley. One might have spied a very slim man loping down the street. The bottom line was that Ethan had disappeared, and Hugh had no more leads to follow.

Nor had he any idea where to go or what to do.

Without Jane, nothing held appeal.

In the past, his life had at least had some purpose, but he didn't know if he could go back to his occupation. Yes, the odds had been against Hugh reverting to a normal life—but, damn it, he *had* changed. Jane had changed him, and he had to wonder if he could return to that same existence. Besides, if it was true that Weyland always knew everything, then he now knew that Hugh had compromised Jane—and then all but kicked her out. He feared Weyland had washed his hands of Hugh.

In his place, Hugh would have.

Hugh's official missives to Weyland were responded to promptly, but coolly.

If not having Jane in his life had been painful before, now it was agonizing. Hugh knew exactly what he was missing. Worse, he knew how badly he'd hurt her. The more he thought about that morning, the more he regretted letting her go. But what choice did he have?

Where to go? He hadn't been to Cape Waldegrave for almost a year. He should go check on his estate and see if any improvements needed to be made—then do them all himself. Beinn a'Chaorainn was on his way there. He could pay Mòrag in advance to oversee the property. He could pick up the rest of his things and close down the house for good.

To go there and not hear Jane's laughter? Hell, who was he fooling? He just planned to go there to do eighty thousand pounds' worth of brooding.

Jane's cousins were hovering.

Claudia had basically moved in, and Belinda and Samantha visited as often as they could between time with their husbands and children. Today, Claudia and Belinda were flipping through fashion plates, smoking French cigarettes, and raiding Jane's clothing.

During the last two weeks, Jane hadn't had an hour to herself. Apparently, when Jane had returned home, she'd worried her entire family with her mottled jaw and insouciant demeanor. But now the bruise on Jane's face had healed, and her headaches had disappeared.

She often wondered if Hugh had completely recovered.

When she reflected over her time with him, she could think of only one thing she'd have done differently, even after all that had occurred between them. "*Trust me with your secret and you won't regret it,*" she'd told him. She felt a flush of guilt, knowing he would have to regret it. She'd demonstrated no understanding or compassion, but then she'd never felt such fury, such strangling frustration.

Jane had comprehended that she was losing the only man she'd ever loved—and that all the fight she had in her wouldn't change that fact. Because she was losing him to something that didn't truly exist. . . .

"Janey," Claudia began in a scolding tone, "are you thinking about Tears and Years again?" She shook her head slowly. "We don't think about him any longer, do we?"

For obvious reasons she hadn't told them what Hugh's profession was. For some unknown reason, she hadn't confided to them about the curse. Though telling them about it would actually have made Hugh more sympathetic to them, she knew Hugh wouldn't want them to know. As it was now, they suspected he let her go out of shortsighted stubbornness or, taken with his past behavior, inconstancy.

She *had* told them she'd made love to Hugh, and they'd all counted down the days together until she could determine whether she was carrying.

Jane had been relieved that she wasn't, of course. But she'd also felt a confusing pang. . . .

"Jane, I don't believe I've reminded you today," Claudia said, flicking her mane of raven hair over her shoulder, "that you spent a *decade* of your life pining for him." She gave Jane a piercing look. "You can't get those years back. Gone. Spent."

The first time Claudia had made this observation, Belinda had chided her, saying, "Jane needs to look to the future, not dwell on the past." Now she said, "Claudia's right. It's been two weeks, Jane. You've got to at least *begin* to get over him."

Claudia made a sound of frustration. "My Lord, Jane, I think you'd take him back—"

"Don't you dare think that!" Jane snapped. "I'm not a complete idiot. Getting thrown over by the man I've loved—not once, but *twice*, mind you—destroyed any hopes for a rekindling."

"Then what is it?"

"Things remind me of him. And every time I look at my father's guilty expression, it kills me inside."

With a firm nod, Claudia said, "Right, then. I think getting over him would be more easily done while traveling, perhaps to Italy, where gorgeous, virile men abound." When Jane raised her brows at the idea, Claudia continued, "Haven't you ever heard the old saying? The best way to get over a man is to get under an Italian."

Forty-seven

———•◆•———

"Courtland, you made this place sound awful!" Annalía Llorente MacCarrick said as she skipped along the winding walk to Beinn a'Chaorainn. "It's beautiful—I can't believe this is my new home!"

"Woman! Slow down," Court grated, limping after her. Now that she was feeling stronger after two months of illness, he always seemed to be slowing her down, chasing after her bright skirts. With his still-healing leg, he was scarcely able to keep up—which made him a nervous husband.

What if she stumbled, and he wasn't there to catch her?

Yet once he'd taken her gently by the hips and glanced up, Court could do no more than stare past her. *Whose home is this and what did they do with mine?*

Squatters. Of course. Squatters with good taste clearly had taken over here.

The shutters and front door, which had been barely hanging on by their hinges, were new and painted. A shining brass knocker beckoned visitors, the gravel walk was free of weeds, and greens were planted in intricate, immaculate beds. The roof seemed to have been completely repaired, and through the spotless new windows he could see furniture and carpets. Had his mother done this? Who else would it be?

When he unconsciously squeezed Anna's hips, she laid her hands over his and gave him a flirtatious smile over her shoulder. "Again already?" she purred, her accent giving the words a lilt. "My lusty Scot."

He raised his eyebrows at her clear invitation, and just like that, the house was forgotten. His voice grew husky. "I dinna give you enough at the inn last night? Or this morning?"

She turned in his arms and whispered, "I don't believe I can ever get enough of you." She cupped his face with her wee hands. "Courtland, why did you tell me your home was so awful, when it's grand? Why did you say we'd have to live at the inn until you got it *inhabitable*? I remember the words you used: *decrepit, dilapidated*, and, um, what was the other? Oh, yes—*sty*."

"I . . . it was no' like this when I left it." He dragged his gaze from her face and pondered his home once more. He'd known one day it would be beautiful, had vowed to make it so, but he'd never imagined this.

And he didn't even know who to thank.

"I can tell you now that I was so uneasy," Annalía continued, "not knowing what brutal Scottish wilderness you were bringing me to. And with the baby . . ."

Court had been dreading this, especially now that they were starting a family—albeit unintentionally. Even had she not been carrying, he had cringed at the thought of bringing her here. But then, he didn't have a lot of options.

To keep her, he'd had to give up his life as a mercenary. Without doing that work, he had little money. It had been a conundrum that had crazed him. His inability to keep her in the style to which she was accustomed had been one of his concerns in marrying her, a wealthy and regal—literally—beauty. And after that first time she'd tried, she knew better than to offer money to him.

He'd planned to fix one room, then do his damnedest to keep her in it until he could afford to do more. Now Court felt like a weight had been lifted.

Anna tapped her chin, frowning in the direction of the freshly painted stables. "Courtland, isn't that the horse my brother gave to Hugh?"

Court followed her gaze. It was indeed. Aleixandre Llorente had given Hugh that stallion for bringing his "unique talents" to Andorra to help rid his country of the Rechazado. Even Court hadn't known Hugh could blow up a mountaintop, or that he'd do it, killing thirty men, without blinking.

Hugh had come here and done this for him? This was where he'd been? Court had scoured London for him and Ethan and sent messages through a dozen channels to tell them about the *Leabhar* and the curse and the future—as in, now the brothers all *had* a future. He'd gone to Weyland to ask about Hugh's whereabouts, but the old man was cryptic, as usual.

And here Hugh was in the one place Court had never thought to look for him.

Court shook his head, remembering how indebted to Hugh he already was. First, Hugh had invested Court's money, giving him a steady income that freed him from having to ride with his gang. Then he'd come and renovated this property completely, knowing Court couldn't pay him back, at least not for a while.

Christ, he already owed his brother for something he could *never* pay back.

Hugh had also saved Annalía's life—

Something caught his attention from the corner of his eye. Turning, he saw a panicked young woman lurching from a side door, fleeing the house followed by some indistinct bellow. That couldn't be his brother's voice. Hugh didn't *bellow* unless there was a sodding good reason.

When Hugh yelled once more, tension shot through Court. He drew out the pistol holstered at his back and pulled Annalía into the house, then straight to the stairwell. "Anna, get in there. Now! And doona come out until I return."

Eyes wide, she climbed into the closet tucked beneath the stairs.

He turned back with a glower for good measure. "Woman, I bloody mean it this time."

Once she nodded, Court made his way up the stairs quietly—thanks to a plush carpet runner and the absence of groaning and loose boards. He followed the sound of his brother's cursing, punctuated by slamming and crashing. Was he fighting someone?

Court lifted his gun, and with his other hand he cracked open the door.

His pistol hand dropped, in time with his jaw. Not only had someone replaced his house, but they'd replaced his brother as well.

Even-tempered, steady Hugh was unshaven, dead drunk, and regarding him with crazed eyes.

Hugh pointed at the door, and the movement made him stumble. "That little witch took my goddamned whiskey."

"Who?"

"Housekeeper."

Court applauded the girl for having the ballocks to do so, and then the sense to flee. "Aye, and it looks as though you'd be lost without it."

"Go to hell," Hugh said, but his tone was more tired than angry. He sank down on the edge of the bed, elbows to his knees as he hunched forward. "What're you doing here?"

Court stared at his brother. "This is my home. Or it was. Why'd you fix it up?"

"Because Jane wanted to. Never could deny that lass."

"You were with her here?" Court couldn't fathom her reason for wanting to fix up *his* home, but he knew it wasn't out of any concern for himself. "I think it's time you explained everything," Court said, then listened in amazement as his brother recounted the threat from Davis Grey, the man's subsequent death—and Hugh's hasty marriage to Jane Weyland.

". . . I sent her away, and now she hates me," Hugh finished. "But hell, you made the sacrifice for Annalía, so I could for Jane." He exhaled with a measure of weariness Court had only ever seen in Ethan before.

He reckoned this was probably not a good time to mention that as soon as Hugh had left him in France, Court had seemed to lose all reason and had sped back to Andorra to win his wife back—the wife presently stowed under the stairs.

In fact, after weeks of searching for his brothers, and now that he finally had the opportunity, Court hesitated to tell Hugh about Annalía's pregnancy. Once Hugh sobered up, Court would break it to him.

"I was on my way north to my place and found myself here for the last week," Hugh said, then looked away to mutter, "Miss her." Seeming to shake himself, he said,

"You can have your house back directly. No' good for me to be here any longer." Then he frowned. "I thought you'd go east with your men."

"Changed my mind," Court said shortly.

"Seems you're reactin' to the loss of your woman better than I am. Damn, Court, you looked like hell when I last saw you. Got over her so quickly?" He ran his hands through his disheveled hair, then winced and swayed—no doubt from a healing head injury. The movement must have worn him out, because he rested his forehead in his hands. "Tell me how to go about that. And be smug about it."

"What the hell happened to your head?"

"Grey knocked me a good couple of hits."

"At least the bastard's dead."

Hugh nodded, his expression grim. "Court, I have to tell you something. About Ethan."

Court exhaled. "What has he done now?"

"He . . . Ethan is—"

"Courtland," Annalía said softly from the doorway.

Hugh's wild eyes got wilder at the sight of Annalía, but they seemed unfocused. He shot to his feet and roared, "*What the bloody hell have you done?*" He pointed a shaking finger at Court, advancing on him. "You vowed to me you would no' go back for her."

In her nervousness, Annalía fluttered her hands to her rounding belly—a gesture she'd assumed in the last couple of weeks—and the movement drew Hugh's gaze. Court saw when realization took hold.

He rocked forward, the heels of his palms shoved to his eyes.

Then he plunged backward to the ground.

Forty-eight

———— • ◆ • ————

*A*n hour later, when Hugh shot up in bed, he reeled once more.

Court caught his shoulder. "Drinking while concussed! You bloody know better. What are you trying to do? Kill yourself?"

His voice hoarse, Hugh said, "It is no' yours?"

Court ground his teeth. As much as it infuriated him, he had expected this question, and when Hugh had appeared to be rousing, Court had made sure Annalía was out of earshot, leaving her downstairs with the recently returned housekeeper.

"It's my child," Court answered. "I know why you ask, know you doona want to hope. I trust Anna with my life, but for your benefit, I'll tell you that I was with her every hour, day and night, for weeks." He struggled to rein in his formidable temper. "I'll say that once. Doona ask again."

"But, she's . . . you canna. What about the goddamned curse?"

"It's no' what we'd thought. The last lines must qualify the others, cancel them out. The general consensus is that it's about finding the right woman."

"*Consensus?* Who else bloody knows?"

"Annalía's family and . . . Fiona."

"You're speaking to our mother?" Hugh gazed at him wordlessly for a moment. "I canna believe this."

"Aye, I know. But she regrets her actions so much, and she wants to talk to you. Now that I'm married, I see . . . I can see why losing someone you love would make you crazed."

And Fiona and Leith had been deeply in love.

"When did you figure all of this out?" Hugh asked.

"After you left, I replayed the words from the book in my mind," Court explained. "*No' to know love.* But I did. I was lost for Annalía."

"I thought that meant no' to know love from another."

Court shot him a guilty look. "I was no' thinking. Bit desperate. I was ready to convince myself of anything. Then, when I got there, she told me she loved me, too. And that she was having my babe. The curse is wrong, Hugh."

Court knew exactly when Hugh felt a glimmer of hope, because he grated a harsh oath. "Ah, God help me. I might have gotten Jane pregnant."

"Best hope you dinna," Court muttered.

"What? Why's that?"

"Imagine your new wife delivering the babe of a six-and-a-half-foot-tall Highlander, and tell me if that is no' enough to keep you up nights for nine months. If I'd had any idea I could get a babe on Anna, I'd never have done it. *Never.*"

Hugh's brows drew together at the warning. "If it's no' already too late." Rising a shade more slowly this time, he bit out, "Going for her."

Court pushed him back and assured him, "There's plenty of time for that." Now that Court knew what it was like to have a good woman's love, he wanted it for his brother as well. And certainly there were better women out there for him than Jane Weyland. "Hugh, how can you be sure it's *her*?"

Hugh's grip on Court's wrist was shockingly strong. "Are you . . . are you *jesting*?" Hugh cast him an incredulous look. "I've wanted her for a third of my life, I'm presently married to her, and I'm so bloody in love with her it pains me."

Lost for that woman! There was nothing to be done for what Court was seeing now. "You will no' make it to the property line in your condition," Court said. "So you'll sleep this off and leave when I think you can ride."

Hugh stubbornly shook his head, rising once more.

"Do you really want to face Jane coming off a drunken bender and still recovering? And I doona like to say this— but what makes you think she'll welcome you as her husband, just because you slept together? You said that you sent her away and she hates you now."

"Aye, and I know I hurt her. But the lass told me she loved me. She did. She has since she was a girl." Hugh glowered. "Doona look at me like that. I ken how unbelievable it sounds." He walked unsteadily. "She believed we were to be married, then thought I'd abandoned her."

Court whistled through his teeth. He had never seen that one coming. "*That's* why she teased you? Then, brother, you've got an uphill battle ahead of you, I fear."

"Tell me something I doona know," he mumbled as he began scouring the room for clothes.

All the clan thought Court was the volatile one. Ethan was considered cold as ice. Hugh was supposed to be the even-tempered, logical—and neat—one. If they could see him now, grumbling about his injuries and sniping complaints as he quickly dug for clothing from haphazard piles on the floor, they wouldn't recognize him.

"You're no' up to this yet," Court insisted. "Just do me a favor. Stay here until dawn."

"No' a chance."

"Then for a meal and coffee? You need to sober up." He gave Hugh a pained expression. "And, brother, a bath would no' go amiss. You do know there are hot springs out back?"

Hugh stumbled over a boot, then coughed into his fist. "That so?" he said, flushing for some reason.

Forty-nine

———— • ◆ • ————

$\mathcal{A}$s Hugh neared London after a day of rail and riding, he fought a sense of urgency so strong it knotted his gut. After struggling against his feelings for so long, to give them free rein now was nigh overpowering.

And the crushing presence of the curse was . . . gone. Hugh finally believed he could have a future with Jane. He had seen Annalía, and he trusted his brother's judgment. On the subject of the *Leabhar*, Hugh trusted his mother's as well—and Court had said she believed as he did. At last, Hugh could reconcile that sense of rightness, of inevitability when he'd been with Jane.

A storm was whipping up to match his turbulent mood, but he didn't care—he'd still reach her on this very night. All he had to do was get to her and win her back.

One mile down, another mile closer. He leaned into the wind, frowning to realize that the only thing that stood in the way of his keeping Jane was how well he could persuade her.

Hugh had rarely had need of that skill. He usually got his way by intimidation or force.

He'd have to convince her that he would make an effort with her family, and that he could fit into her life. If he took it slowly, instead of a sudden immersion like he'd endured at Vinelands, he could get used to them.

He'd bloody figure it out.

Though she'd promised not to take him back, right now, anything felt possible to him. In fact, he hadn't even told Court about Ethan because, for some reason, Hugh had a strong sense that his older brother still lived. He would continue to search for Ethan, unleash runners to investigate, then make a determination one way or another before he heaped more apprehension onto Court's plate.

Court was already dreading the upcoming birth—Hugh had seen him eyeing Annalía's belly guiltily, even as she was unmistakably delighted.

Hugh had never thought about worrying for a wife in labor before—he'd never believed he was meant to have a wife or children—but now the idea of Jane going through that made him shudder.

Even as he reassured Court that women had bairns all the time, Hugh was promising himself he'd be talking to Robert, the laughing quack, and asking him exactly what the best way was "to wait" to have bairns—if she wasn't already pregnant.

By the time Hugh reached London, the rain had let up, but he hadn't. His horse's hooves clattered as they raced down the wet streets of London. A life with Jane, free of this constant dread, depended on his skills of persuasion. He swallowed.

Hell, Weyland might not even let him in the house.

Hugh owed the man yet another huge debt. Weyland was the only bloody one who'd seen so clearly that Hugh and Jane needed to be together that he'd taken steps to see it done. He'd forced Hugh to confront his feelings—and, Christ, he'd prevented Jane from becoming *engaged* to another man.

Hugh had repaid him by sending his daughter packing.

As more guests continued to arrive, Jane smoothed the silk of her new emerald green gown and pasted on a fake smile. She was preoccupied, restless, and bored at this party her father had manipulated her into hosting—her and Claudia's own going-away celebration.

Though she and her cousin had decided weeks ago to take a trip to Italy, her father had stalled them at every opportunity. Finally, they were departing by steamer in the morning.

Though her father was furious with Hugh, she knew he still had hope for them, believing Hugh would return for her. Yet without receiving a word from him for weeks, Jane knew better.

When Freddie and Candace arrived, Jane's smile turned genuine. Not only was she happy for the laughing and obviously adoring couple, she also experienced a renewed sense of relief that she hadn't wed him. Once she'd greeted them and they'd moved on to speak with someone else, she breathed a sigh.

"Why the serious look, Janey?" Claudia asked, handing her a glass of champagne. "You always liked elegant parties."

"I know." She loved the scent of the rose arrangements all over the house, the glitter of their chandelier fully ablaze, and the tinkling of crystal flutes kissing champagne bottles.

"Has anyone said anything about your marriage?"

She shook her head and took a sip. "No. Everyone's been tiptoeing around it." Most everyone here—a crowd of family and good friends—had heard rumors of Jane's hasty marriage, and just as hasty separation, but no one except her London cousins had dared to ask her about it.

"Well, then, cheer up! Tomorrow begins the adventure. We're actually going to leave this sodding little island."

"Claudie, won't you be sad to leave your groom behind for months?"

"His eyes watered today," she admitted, glancing away. "And I had a moment when I thought about backing out. But we're not getting any younger, Jane."

Jane exhaled. "That's too true."

When Belinda and Sam joined them, Claudia resumed taunting them. "Admit it, you old matrons, you're jealous of our trip. We leave *tomorrow*, sailing toward sun, cuisine, and virility. . . ."

From across the room, Jane caught her father's glance, and he gave her a quizzical look. She smiled at him in answer—she'd made an effort of late to be cheerful again, to get on with her life, but he'd been keeping a close eye on her tonight. He was continually worried, had been since she returned, and it showed. He'd barely agreed to let her go to Italy, until she'd reminded him that she didn't need his consent.

Suddenly, his face broke into a wide grin—which he immediately checked. His expression grew stern just as the crowd went silent.

She heard a commotion in the hallway—a banging, then arguing, then the booming: *"I'm here for my wife."*

Loud, striding steps echoed down the hall behind her. No. It just wasn't possible.

"My God," Belinda murmured. "Janey, what did you *do* to your Scot?"

Jane turned slowly to find Hugh at the doorway, seeming to fill it. Her eyes went wide at his appearance. He was soaking wet, his boots covered with mud, and his neck was bleeding readily from shallow lines where a branch must have struck him as he rode. He'd lost weight and his wet hair whipped across his face—his unshaven face.

But his eyes were what held her attention—they were black as night and burned with intent. He caught sight of her and his body tensed, like he was about launch himself at her.

Everyone was silent or gasping. Hugh just continued to stare at her as if he couldn't do anything else, his brows drawing together.

At length, when he finally dragged his gaze from her, he surveyed the crowded party in progress, swallowing because everyone here was dressed to the nines.

Except for him.

His expression turned grim, and his shoulders went back.

He'd just walked into a room full of people—normally punishing enough. But to look like hell washed over—*and to be clearly embarrassing her*? He swallowed again, wiping the rain from his face with his sleeve.

An older woman tittered. "*That* is Jane's new husband?"

Jane swung her gaze on the woman and snapped, "Oh, shut up."

So it's to be another trial by fire?

Didn't matter. Hugh was prepared to do anything. He strode toward Jane, past speechless guests, who stared at him so hard he could feel it.

He held out his hand for Jane. "Come, Sìne. I need to speak with you."

Her cousins were glaring at him, urging Jane to demand that he leave, telling her *not* to go with him. She didn't appear to be in any danger of the latter.

"I am sure this can wait," Jane said. Had her accent ever sounded so crisp? "Come back *tomorrow*. Afternoon."

When some people nervously laughed at that, Hugh glanced around, brows drawn.

He met Weyland's gaze, trying to read the man—who was clearly trying to read Hugh as well. "I just want tae speak with her, Weyland." His brogue had never sounded so thick.

But then he spied *Bidworth* strolling into the room. Hugh gnashed his teeth, having never considered that Jane might take back up with her suitor. He'd also never imagined that Bidworth wouldn't heed Hugh's warnings to stay the hell away from Jane. The man caught sight of Hugh, blanched, and made a strangled sound.

If Bidworth had dared to touch Hugh's wife . . . With his fists clenched, Hugh strode forward.

Bidworth backed up to a wall. "Bloody hell. He's going to hit me again, isn't he?"

Fifty

—◆—

"*This is not happening to me,*" Jane muttered.

"Will he really harm Bidworth?" Belinda asked, eyes wide as Hugh stalked poor Freddie.

"Yes," Jane hissed desperately, casting her father an entreating look. He wasn't going to do anything! He only studied Hugh and her, back and forth, eyes watchful.

"Fine." Jane glared at her father over her shoulder as she hurried toward Hugh. "*I'll* handle this." Once she'd reached Hugh, his hand shot out to clutch her elbow as if he feared she'd flee from him at any second. "If you'll come with me to Papa's study?" He hesitated, so obviously wanting to thrash Freddie. "Hugh, if you want to speak with me, I won't do it here." He finally allowed her to lead him from the room.

In the front hallway, Hugh slowed and grated, "Why in the hell is Bidworth here?" She saw him glance at her bare ring finger, and his tone went lower. "Have you . . . have you taken up with him again?"

"Not that it is any of your business, but he's here with his new intended," she answered calmly, letting him relax an instant before adding, "to wish me well on my travels."

"*Travels?*"

"Yes, you just ruined the party my family threw for Claudia and me to see us off to Italy for the winter."

"When are you supposed to sail?"

"On the morning's tide—"

"No."

She rubbed her temples. "I clearly misheard you. For a moment, I thought you had just dared to insert yourself into my life once more. You gave up any right you had to do that."

"No, I dinna. I'm still your husband. We're married, and we're staying that way."

She blinked at him.

"You heard me, lass."

Perfect, Jane thought with a sigh. *I can get this man to keep me, but first I have to wear away his will for weeks, and then he must be pistol-whipped, bludgeoned, and concussed. It's a formula.*

"What brought about this change of heart?" she asked.

"There's been no change of heart."

Behind Hugh, she saw her father ordering her cousins away, barring them from coming to her rescue. He probably thought he was buying Hugh time to apologize—when that notion hadn't seemed to have occurred to Hugh at all.

There was no apology, no flowers, not even a preamble. In fact, he hadn't bothered to take the time to *shave* before he'd barged into her party, threatening servants and frightening guests—after she'd thrown herself at him for weeks. "How dare you show up here like this!"

She couldn't understand him. Something had changed in Hugh—yes, he wasn't known to assail genteel soirées like a crazed Highlander—but this change was beneath the surface, a drastic shift in his whole personality. She sensed it. She . . . feared it. Maybe his head injury had been worse than he'd let on. Maybe it had altered him.

"I dinna mean to embarrass you like this, God knows I dinna, but what I have to say canna wait."

"Yet you couldn't tell me during all the time we were together?"

More titillated guests peered around the corner, and Hugh looked over his shoulder, seeming to snarl at them.

She gave the group a pained smile, and said in a confiding tone, "He's just about to leave, you see—"

"No' a chance of it," Hugh interrupted, telling her softly, "No' without you."

Under her breath she said, "What could you possibly have to say to me now?"

He opened his mouth to speak, but saw her glance past him once more at the gathering crowd.

Hugh's brows drew together. "This will no' work."

Her gaze snapped back to his face. "That's what *I'm* saying."

"You're coming with me."

"When hell freezes— Oh!"

Before she had any idea what he intended, he'd picked her up and easily lofted her over his shoulder. Her cousins gasped.

"Hugh!" She kicked futilely. "What in the devil are you thinking?" Jane felt her face flushing from humiliation—and probably from being upside down. She didn't deserve this treatment, and she didn't have to tolerate it. She was a woman who had bloody steamer trunks by her door!

Her father strode forward, and to him she snapped,

"How many times are you going to let Hugh act this way with me?"

"I swear to you, this will be the last," he said, his tone steely. "Is that correct, MacCarrick?"

"Aye, it is."

"That's good to hear, son. My carriage is outside—you can take her to Grosvenor Square in it."

Hugh nodded, then strode straight out the front door. More guests were arriving as he descended the stairs with her. She closed her eyes tightly in mortification.

When Hugh placed her in the carriage, she was breathless, speechless, and dizzy. As soon as they were rolling forward, Hugh dragged her across his lap, his hands flying to her face, cradling her cheeks as he pressed his lips to hers.

She froze, stunned.

"Sìne," he rasped. "Ah, God, lass, kiss me back." He brought his mouth down over hers, kissing her in that desperate way, as if it was the last he'd ever take from her. And like a fool, she felt herself responding to his need, to the urgency of it. He groaned, deepening the kiss as he clenched her in his arms.

She was so close to getting swept up, missing him so badly, all but forgetting the pain he'd caused. *No, no, no!* She forced herself to break away, pushing at him. "You said you wanted to *talk* to me. And I didn't even agree to that. You haven't given me any explanation."

After several moments, he released her, just as the carriage eased to a stop. When a footman opened her door, she hurried out, but paused when faced with the grand façade of the MacCarrick town house.

Her anger and hurt came back redoubled; a light mist began to fall, making her blink as she stared.

All those times she'd ridden by, praying to see him—and he'd been avoiding her all along. Had he seen her from the window and closed the drapes? She felt her bottom lip trembling to remember how badly she'd ached, how terribly she'd yearned to see him.

And that had only been the first time she'd lost him.

Fifty-one

———•◆•———

"Jane?" he bit out in a strangled tone to see her eyes watering. His one chance to win her back . . . *And all I've done is make her cry*. Of all the reactions he'd anticipated, her crying was not one of them. He clasped her hand in his, pulling her inside out of the damp night. He could tell she wanted to resist, but she didn't seem to have the energy.

He took her directly up into his room and sat her on his bed, curling his finger under her chin. She'd closed her eyes, but the tears were spilling out. He felt as if a knife was being plunged repeatedly into his chest with each tear. "My God, lass, did I hurt you? Was I too rough with you in the carriage?" His breath left his lungs in a rush. "Christ, I was." He remembered little of that mind-boggling kiss—he'd probably squeezed her with all the strength in his body. "I've wanted this for so long, and to be so close . . . I could no' control myself."

When she said nothing, just continued to cry, he murmured, "This played out badly, I ken that, and I am sorry for it. Ach, Jane, this is killing me."

"Then take—me—back," she said, biting out the words.

"You doona want to go back like this with all those people there."

She pummeled his chest. "Then take me to Claudia's!"

"I canna do that either, lass."

How could he have bungled this so badly? He hadn't been thinking clearly after everything that had happened and the mad journey here. But then to see her like a vision in the candlelight? The realization that this stunning, brave woman was *his* wife had hit him like a punch. He *was* the lucky bastard who got to dine with her each night and wake up beside her each morning. All he had to do was win her.

Then he'd seen Bidworth. And assumed the worst.

"I've much to tell you and could no' wait any longer. I wanted to stay married to you. But you know why I believed I could no'."

"Because of the *curse*." Her eyes glittered, and her tone was cold. "I would be *very* careful bringing that up to me."

"Aye, but since then I found out my brother's to be a da." How odd to say that. Hugh liked saying that. "He's married, happy—"

"So are you saying that the curse has been lifted?" She put her chin up. "Perhaps a magical charm was used to combat it? Will I be expected to wear a MacCarrick talisman around my neck?"

"I'm saying we misinterpreted the words. I knew when I saw Annalía was pregnant—"

"Listen to yourself! There's this curse that's prevented you from accepting me as your wife, but since some woman that I don't even know named Annalía conceived, now *we* can be together. Do I have it right?"

"It sounds mad. But today, for the first time, I realized I could have a future with you—without fear for you."

"Not good enough, Hugh. What if something else happens to make you think you'll hurt me again? You didn't believe in us before—why should I now? What if you find out what the book says under the blood, and it's even more devastating?"

"Court and Annalía think the last two lines qualify the ones that came before—that they're about each son finding the one woman he's supposed to be with. I believe that."

"And I'm the one woman for you?" Her tears were easing.

He drew his head back. "I have *never* doubted it."

"So you think you can get me with child now?"

"Aye." His voice gruff, he said, "I dinna, did I?"

"No, you didn't." At his relieved expression, she said, "Is the idea of children with me such a dread prospect?"

"No, but the thought of you in labor, in pain, at risk . . ." He stifled a shudder. "I dread *that*. And lass, I would no' share you well, no' even with my own bairns."

She tilted her head at his admission, her eyes seeming to soften as she gazed at him. "But you didn't get me pregnant. Will that change your mind?"

"No, nothing will."

"You said over and over that it wasn't just about the curse. You gave me reason after reason why we wouldn't suit."

"No, they were just excuses—"

"Are you saying you lied to me, then?"

"No, I've never lied to you. And I made those excuses to myself as much as to you." At her raised eyebrows, he said, "The reasons were true, but they doona matter anymore—because I will be whatever you need me to be." He brushed away the last of her tears with his thumb, and she sniffled, but let him.

"You can't change that you're a loner. I'm not, and I

won't live a solitary existence. Would you keep me from my family?"

"No, never. If that's the only thing standing between us, I'll bloody move in with a houseful of them."

Her eyes went a shade wider. "Really?" she said slowly. *Raaaally.* "You would do that?"

"Lass, none of what I've found out will matter if I canna have you. My future's with you, or I might as well not have one."

"But I'm . . . afraid, Hugh. Something else could change your beliefs, and then I'd lose you a third time." She briefly looked away when she admitted, "I couldn't do it a third time."

"Do you know how badly I wanted to seize on *any* of your arguments at Beinn a'Chaorainn for why we could be together? But I could no'. And even then I struggled no' to let you go. It was selfish of me, but I never sent for Quin to come for you."

"You didn't?"

He shook his head, gently laying his hands on her shoulders to rub up to her neck and back. "I've always been searching for a way I could have you, and now I've got one. If you accept me now, you will no' be able to get rid of me."

"So you came for me tonight because you want to be completely married?" Jane said, nibbling her lip. "To live together?"

"Aye, Sìne, if you'll have me." He swallowed, then enfolded her in his arms, but she was stiff, silent. Moments passed. . . .

When she at last wrapped her arms around him, too, he exhaled, realizing he'd been holding his breath.

He drew back and cupped her face, gazing down at her.

"Jane, I've told you before that I'm no' a good man—"

"But won't you be good to *me*?"

"Oh, Christ, yes. Always."

"Will you love me?"

His brows drew together, and his voice went hoarse. "Till my dying breath," he said, the words sounding like a vow. "And you? Can you love me, even knowing what I've done?"

"Hugh, I understand more about your profession now. I know that you saved soldiers' lives, but you never got any recognition. You might not get credit for your grueling job anywhere else, but I, for one, am so proud of you."

"Proud?" he choked out the word. "Do you know how often I dreaded ever having to tell you about this?"

"I always have been proud of you, and that hasn't changed." Then she eyed him. "Though I do want you to understand that if I'd been a son, I would have had your job."

"I doona doubt it," he said, his lips tugging into a grin, but then he grew serious once more. "You ken what this will mean? So think on this, because I swear to you, lass, I'll never let you go again."

Gazing up at him, she said, "Never let me go? I like the sound of that."

He blinked as if he didn't really believe this was happening. She understood the feeling. But she sensed they'd crossed a threshold—finally.

The antsy feeling was . . . gone. Because she was right where she was supposed to be.

"I have money for you now," he said, like he was trying to *convince* her to be with him. "I can spoil you. And we have that estate by the sea in Scotland."

"I get to live with you in your seashore home?"

"*Our* home. And you should, especially since I bought it with you in mind—"

"You *did*?" she asked, both surprised and delighted. When he'd told her of it weeks ago, she'd dreamed about being there with him, never knowing he'd done the same about her.

"Aye, I think you would be proud to call it yours. I'll take you there straightway, if you like. We can leave tonight."

She bit her lip and murmured, "Or we could stay here for tonight . . . and finish what we started in the carriage."

"My vote's for that," he said in a rush, making her laugh, but it turned to a delicious gasp when he pressed his lips to her neck. His tongue flicked out with wicked kisses until she was shivering and clutching his shoulders. Against her damp neck, he said, "I need to take you again so badly . . . dreamed of it . . ."

"Me, too." She moaned softly as he laid her back across the bed, pressing her skirts to her waist.

"After so long," he began, his voice a husky rasp, "finally I'm free to claim you for my own." He tugged her lacy undergarments from her, baring her to his gaze. Her knees fell open with his first hot touch between her thighs, and she watched in fascination as his eyes slid shut with pleasure. "I'm warning you now," he said, biting out the words. "I'm going to be so damned greedy for you, lass."

She eased her arms up to him, reaching out in welcome. "I'm yours for the taking."

At that, his expression turned fierce, his eyes burning with feeling as he stared down at her. "After tonight, love, you will no' ever doubt it."

Fifty-two

———— •◆• ————

"Are you ready to see our home, Sìne?" Hugh asked, as they stood near the end of a hedge-lined walk at Waldegrave.

She nodded, breathless. "I'm *beyond* ready." There were only so many minutes left until dusk, and they'd just arrived. "I've been dying to see it for the last week!" It had taken them that long in London to resolve certain concerns. If Jane hadn't been utterly in love with him already, then she would have been when he'd asked for help to fulfill his promise of toys to his new nieces and nephews.

He'd gruffly explained, "It's simply good strategy to get on with your family. I'll bribe the youngest generation directly before the holidays and ensure their cooperation."

Biting back a grin, she'd answered, "Toys: you're positively Machiavellian."

Jane had also taken the time to make up to Claudia for canceling their trip, and to thank her father repeatedly for, as he called it, "his brilliant marriage coup." Hugh had spoken with Dr. Robert, returning home from his meeting with a red face and a box of various . . . supplies. She and Hugh had decided they would reevaluate the question of children in a year or so. After all, she was greedy to have Hugh all to herself, too.

Now he clasped her chin and brushed her bottom lip. "If you doona like it here, you've only to tell me."

"I'm positive I'm going to love it," she assured him. Then she narrowed her eyes. He didn't look nervous whatsoever. She sensed he knew she would love it as he did—and that meant he was only increasing her suspense. She lightly cuffed his chest. "If I can ever *see* it. I promise I'll love it, even if it looks like Ros Creag."

"It's a wee bit grimmer. But I ken how you like that." He grinned, reminding her of how heartbreakingly handsome he was when he smiled. She'd be seeking out his smiles as if they were her target.

Though he'd offered to take her anywhere in the world for their honeymoon, she'd wanted only to come here. Undoubtedly, they would travel in the future, but they needed to be within a day's train ride of England because they were confident Hugh's runners would soon pick up a lead on Ethan. Jane also wanted them to be near Beinn a'Chaorainn for the birth of Hugh's niece or nephew in the spring—even if Courtland was going to be there. If Hugh could make the effort with her family, she'd do the same for him. . . .

"And we can change things here, too," Hugh said with deliberate slowness. "The color or—"

"Please, Hugh, I can't stand it anymore!" she said with a choked laugh. "I want to see our seashore home."

"You know I canna deny you." He took her hand and led her past the end of the walk and out into the open.

She gasped at the sight, feeling light-headed. When her eyes watered, he squeezed her hand. "Say something, lass."

"It's like . . . a dream." The manor was stunning both in beauty—and in size. Built of dark cream-colored brick, it had classic black shutters and marble balconies fronting the sea side. The grounds were picturesque, rolling down to majestic cliffs. *And the waves . . .* When she caught her breath, she whispered, "You really can see the sun set through the water."

At her words, he looked so proud, as though he felt ten feet tall. "I'm glad you like it," he said simply. "Ready to see the inside?"

"Can we just watch the rest of the sunset?" she asked.

"Of course." He drew her back to his front, wrapping his arms around her and resting his chin on her head.

As they gazed out together, she said, "But, it *is* a shame that it obviously won't need any improvements."

"Oh, aye." He chuckled, a low, rumbling laugh that was still rare, but came more often each day. She adored hearing it. "Still glad you married me?"

"A *bit*," she said, and he turned her in his arms. "I've only been waiting for this since the first day I met you, when you called me 'poppet' in your brogue."

"I recall that day. I remember thinking that when you grew up, you'd lead some man on a merry chase." He tucked her against his warm chest. "Ah, lass," he rasped, pressing his lips against her hair, "I just dinna know it would be me."

POCKET BOOKS
PROUDLY PRESENTS

IF YOU DECEIVE

KRESLEY COLE

Available now
from Pocket Books

Turn the page for a preview of
If You Deceive. . . .

If Madeleine van Rowen was ever going to lose her virginity outside of a collateralized, signed marriage contract, it'd be with the towering man she spied in the black domino. He'd just descended from the second story of "The Hive," the gaudily extravagant warehouse in which she found herself tonight.

From her spot on a raised dais, decorated with swans and lusty satyrs, Maddy studied the tall one over the rim of her second glass of punch. She was growing lightheaded and suspected the drink was spiked with more than rum—the spirit du jour—but she didn't particularly care. She wouldn't mind getting foxed after the day she'd just endured.

Today Maddy had learned that she'd failed to secure the man she'd journeyed from Paris to London to marry. *"Madeleine, I'm just not the marrying type,"* he'd said. *"I'm sorry."*

Preferring to drown her sorrows in private, she'd wandered off from her group of friends, the Weyland girls: Maddy's childhood friend, Claudia; her sister, Belinda; and their cousin, Jane. The three Londoner Weylands were sensation-seekers, always craving the next forbidden thrill, and the Hive was supposed to be . . . thrilling.

Jane Weyland, the de facto leader of their group had told the younger Maddy not to wander off again. After all, gentlewomen needed to *stay together at all costs* when out in London at night. Maddy rolled her eyes even now.

Please, innocent girls, Maddy had wanted to say. Though

this masquerade was packed to the rafters with prostitutes and their lecherous patrons, thieves and swindlers—it still paled in comparison to her everyday life.

Her *secret* life.

Maddy told everyone she lived in a wealthy Parisian parish with her mother and stepfather, but she actually lived alone in a slum called *La Marais*—translated as *The Swamp*—and every night she drifted to sleep to the music of gunfire and brawls.

She was a sneak thief and a pickpocket—who would steal a diamond as easily as an apple—and she wasn't above an occasional burgle. In fact, if Maddy hadn't considered the Weyland women her friends, they'd do well to be wary of *her*.

After adjusting her sapphire cape behind her and then her blue glacé mask, Maddy relaxed back on the dais bench, settling in to enjoy her view of the tall man. He stood well above most everyone in the room—six and a half feet in height, at least—and he had broad, muscular shoulders filling out his black jacket.

The black domino he wore had a fluttering drop in the front, and though she could see his brow and lips and strong chin, the rest of his face was covered. He had thick, straight jet hair, and, she'd bet, dark, intense eyes.

He was clearly searching for someone, striding with aggression, his head turning this way and that, fighting the crush of what looked like thousands of people. When a gaggle of bare-breasted tarts blocked his path, angling for his attention, his brows drew together—with consternation or aggravation, Maddy didn't know.

What she wouldn't give to bed a strapping man like that for her first time. After all, she was an aficionada of male beauty. Her friend Claudia would chuckle each time Maddy tilted her head and peered at a passing man on the street. Maddy grinned into her glass. Making men blush as she so clearly sized them up was one of the things she lived for.

But if today was any indication of her luck, her husband and first lover was to be the Compte La Daex, an obscenely wealthy, but aging roué, who was more than three times her age. In a last effort to avoid marrying that man, Maddy had journeyed to London, calling on her childhood friendship with Claudia, specifically to snare her brother Quinton Weyland. Unfortunately, Quin—with his curling hair, laughing green eyes, and robust finances—refused to marry. . . .

To distract her thoughts, she focused once more on the tall one as he made the perimeter of the building. His methodical and determined hunt, even the way he moved, entranced her. He finally stopped, raking his fingers through his hair, turning in a circle in the crowd. She felt sad that he couldn't find the paramour he sought so urgently, and drank to him, wishing him luck—

He raised his head up to where she sat, and his gaze locked on her. At once, he turned that aggressive stride toward the swan and satyr dais.

Frowning in confusion—*she* was the only one seated here—she lowered her glass. He must have mistaken her for someone else. She wondered if she should let him think it and enjoy a few kisses with him. How delicious that would be. Just to squeeze those muscular shoulders while his lips brushed hers . . .

As he neared, his gaze held hers until she was captivated—everything else dimmed. The drunken men were unseen; the high, false laughter of the courtesans below her were silenced.

He took the steps to her two at a time, and when he stood before her, she slowly raised her head. He stared down at her, silently offering his big hand to her. His eyes *were* dark—and she'd never seen such intensity. She inhaled a shaky breath.

Le coup de foudre.

Bolt out of the blue. No, no. *No bolts for me!* Maddy was ever practical, never fanciful. She had no idea why that thought had arisen—because *le coup de foudre* had a second, more profound meaning. . . .

The urge to take his hand was overwhelming, and she clutched her glass in one hand and her skirts in the other, finally saying, "I'm sorry, sir. I'm not who you seek, nor am I, er, one among these other women."

"I ken that." He took her elbow—gently, but firmly—and helped her to her feet. "If you were like these other women, I would no' be seeking you at all." He had a marked Scottish accent and a voice so deep and husky, it gave her shivers.

"But I don't know you," she said, sounding breathless.

"You will soon, lass," he answered, making her frown. But before she could say anything, he took her glass and set it away, then caught her hand to pull her from the dais into the crowd.

For Maddy, two flaws warred with each other for the title of which would prove her ultimate downfall: an overly developed sense of curiosity and a marked pride. She imagined the traits to be in a race like two horses in the *mutuels* she occasionally gambled. Right now, curiosity took the lead, demanding she hear what the Scot had to say—even when she realized he was taking her toward the back rooms lining the wall of the warehouse. She quirked a brow. The rooms where prostitutes more fully serviced their patrons.

He opened the first door they came upon. Inside the dimly lit area, a woman was on her knees before a young man, taking him with her mouth while he leaned down and pinched her swollen, rouged nipples.

"Out," the Scot ordered with quiet menace. "Now."

The woman obviously sensed a threat better than her

patron, and she pushed the drunken man back to tug up her bodice and scurry to her feet.

The Scot swung a glance at Maddy as the pair lurched out, no doubt to gauge her reaction to what they'd just witnessed. She shrugged. One of her best friends and across-the-hall neighbor was a *popular girl*—a euphemism for "prostitute"—and scenes like this took place constantly where she lived. Turn any corner and find a different vice on display.

At twenty-one years of age, Maddy had seen it all.

As soon as they were alone, he closed the door and retrieved a chair to wedge against it. Where was her alarm? Where was her well-developed sense of self-preservation in a place like this? The room was dominated by a massive bed—twelve foot square, at least—draped in glaring, scarlet silk; no one could hear her scream back here, and would ignore it even if they could, thinking a prostitute gave a good show.

Yet, for some reason, she sensed this man wouldn't hurt her, and she possessed unfailing and proven instincts with men—a priceless gift to have in La Marais.

In any case, if things played out badly, this wouldn't be the first time she'd kindly introduced her knee to a man's groin and her fist to his Adam's apple. He would be shocked at how dirty and fiercely this dainty mademoiselle could fight.

When he returned from securing the door, he stood before her, far too close to be polite. She had to crane her head up to face him. "As I told you before, sir, I'm not one of these women. I don't belong back here, nor should you be . . . collecting me as you did."

"And as I told you before, had you been a courtesan, lass, I would no' have collected you at all. I know you're a lady. What I doona know is why you're in a place like this."

I'm trying to forget that soon I'll have to return to hell. . . .

She shook herself and answered, "I'm here with my friends. We're out for adventure." At least the others were. She planned to pick pockets once the punch was flowing freely.

"And by 'adventure' you mean *affair*." His tone seemed to grow irritated. "A bored young wife looking for a bedmate?"

"Not at all. We're merely here to be scandalized so we'll have something to write in our little diaries." As if she could afford either the diary or the time to write.

"Is that why you allowed me to lead you back here? Because you thought I'd make good diary fodder?"

"I allowed you because it would have been fruitless to resist," she replied. "I've seen intent like yours before—would anything have stopped you from taking me to one of these rooms?"

"No' a thing in the world," he said, catching her eyes.

"Precisely. So I figured instead of being hauled over your shoulder and carried, I might as well follow you to a quiet place so I could explain to you that I am not interested in this."

He stalked closer to her, forcing her back to a narrow table along the silk-papered wall. "My intent was no' only to get you alone, lass. And it has no' waned."

Her demeanor was surprisingly composed, her brilliant blue eyes calmly measuring behind her mask, as if a six-and-a-half-foot-tall Highlander accosting her in a darkened room made for sex was commonplace.

Up close, Ethan could see that the lass was probably no more than twenty, but she was possessed of herself—and even more impossibly lovely than he'd believed when she'd passed him on the street outside.

"And what is your intent?" she asked. Her breaths might

have shallowed at his undisguised attention, especially when his gaze dropped to flicker over her breasts. She was slim, too much so for his customary taste, but her small breasts were expertly displayed, her cleavage plump above her tight bodice. He wanted to rip off his mask and rub his face against that creamy flesh.

"My intent is to"—*have a woman beneath me for the first time in three years*—"*kiss* you."

"You'll have to get your kisses"—she stressed the word as if she doubted that was all he wanted—"from one of the hundreds of courtesans out there."

"I doona want them." When his gaze had met hers in the crowd and her pink lips had parted, Ethan had been stunned to find himself growing erect. Now as he leaned his face in closer to her hair—a mass of white-blond curls, swept up to bare her neck—he smelled her light flowery scent and shot harder, his shaft straining hotly against his trousers. He savored the rare feeling, wanting to groan at the unexpected pleasure. "I followed you in here from the street."

"Why?" Her tone was straightforward, and he silently thanked her for not being coquettish.

"I saw you outside under a street light. I liked the way you smiled."

"And you just happened to have this with you?" She reached up, brushing her fingertips along the edge of his mask, but he caught her wrist, lowering it before releasing her.

"I liberated it from a passing patron when I saw you enter." The drop of his mask fluttered above his upper lip, and he'd quickly determined that no one could discern the extent of his scarred visage because courtesans had sought his attention. When they'd hindered his progress, he'd been tempted to lift his mask to frighten them away.

"Truly?" Her lips slid into that mysterious half-grin, and the need to see the rest of her face burned in him. "So the entire time I saw you searching the crowd, you were looking for *me*?" Her accent was unusual—English upper-class mixed with a tinge of French.

"Aye, for you," he said. "You were watching me from your vantage?"

"Raptly," she said, again straightforward, again surprising him.

The idea of her noticing him gave him an odd sense of gratification. "You're no' from London, are you?" When she shook her head, he asked, "Why are you here?"

"Do you want the truth or an answer fit for a masquerade?"

"Truth."

"I've come to England to search for a rich husband," she said.

"No' unusual," he replied. "At least you have the bollocks to admit it."

"I have a proposal waiting in the wings at home," she said, then frowned. "Though I had hoped not to fall back on that one."

"How is your hunt going?"

"Not as well as I'd hoped," she said. "A few discountable proposals."

"Discountable? Why?"

"Whenever I ask them to qualify themselves, they back off."

"Is that so?" he asked, and when she nodded solemnly, he felt a completely unfamiliar tug at his lips. "And how would a man qualify himself to you?"

"A token that would actually be dear to him, like an expensive ring or a pair of matched bays, or something along those lines."

"You've given this a lot of thought."

"I think of nothing else," she murmured so softly, he scarcely heard her. Then she added, "I did almost secure one. A truly good man." Her blond brows drew together as she was clearly musing about him. "There might still be the slimmest hope with that one."

For the first time in his life and at the age of thirty-three, Ethan felt the unmistakable heat of jealousy.

What the bloody hell is wrong with me? "Then should you no' be working tonight on securing him?" he asked, his voice colder.

She blinked up at him. "Oh. Well, the man I mentioned went out for the evening. I'm his sister's houseguest, so I'm accompanying her tonight."

That generation of Weylands had only one male—*Quin.* Ethan ground his teeth. Quin had always been a favorite with the ladies.

She sighed. "*Ça ne fait rien.* It doesn't matter." Her voice was growing a bit slurred.

"No, it does no'." The hell she'd be *securing* Quin. Ethan would have to see her around London continually as their paths crossed—and if tonight were any indication, he'd have to continually cuckold Quin. "Forget him. He's no' here and I am."

She gazed up at him and tilted her head. "Take off your mask."

"That defeats the purpose of a masquerade, does it no'?" If he removed it, she would stop gazing at him with a growing curiosity glinting in her eyes and stare up in horror. "I can enjoy you just as well with our masks on."

"And what makes you think I'd allow you to 'enjoy' me?" A flirtatious note had eased into her voice, so subtly he might have missed it. Not coquettish—but amused, intrigued.

She was playing, enjoying herself, but she had no idea

what she toyed with. "I've a sense for these things, *aingeal*." He brushed the backs of his fingers down her cheek, below the sapphire silk of her mask, and she allowed it. "Tonight you're aching for a man."

At that, she glanced away. "You might be right, Scot," she said casually, and then faced him once more. Her voice a purr, she asked, "But are *you* the man I await . . . where I ache?"

He felt on the verge of grinning. Ach, he liked this excitement. This bandying. He liked that she flirted with him, even knowing she didn't plan to go further. Why hadn't a scarred man like himself been attending masquerades every bloody week?

"I am that man." He took her by her tiny waist and lifted her onto the table along the wall.

"Scot, put me down!" she cried, but he could tell she was excited, well past intrigued now. "Why did you do that?"

"I want to be face-to-face with you when I kiss you for the first time."

Finally, his words drew a small gasp from her plump lips. "Are you always so arrogant?"

"Aye, always." He wedged his hips between her legs.

"You need to let me down," she said, even as she hesitantly ran her fingertip over his arm. "I've no time or use for handsome rakes with smooth words."

His lips did curl then, tugging on the tight skin of his face, forcing him to recall that he didn't smile—and that he was no longer handsome. "How do you know what I look like? This mask covers most of my face."

"You have a powerful body and a seductive smile. Gorgeous eyes," she said in a sexy voice that made his shaft throb. "You said you've a sense for certain things, well, I appreciate handsome men. An aficionada, if you will. There's a reason I spied you out tonight."

"Is that so?" When she nodded, he said, "Tell me your name."

"That defeats the purpose of a masquerade, does it not?" she answered, repeating his words. She placed her gloved hand on his chest, and let it rest there, as if she couldn't decide if she should push him away or clutch his shirt and draw him to her. He caught her hand, rucking the glove up to bare her wrist, then placed a kiss on her satiny skin there.

She shivered, tugging her hand back until he released it. "Look at you, Scot. You're a practiced seducer, if I've ever seen one."

"Practiced?" For the last decade, his flirtations hadn't been practiced—they'd been nonexistent. And before that, he'd never needed to seduce.

Impulse had made him kiss her hand.

So where did the sodding impulse come from?

"Yes, practiced. That kiss to the wrist is a perfect communication. The brush of your lips demonstrates that you'd be gentle and sensual in bed. The firm hold on my hand as you placed it indicates that you'd be masterful at the same time."

Gentle? He thought back. Had he ever been *gentle*? Right now, he recognized he had no desire to be so with her. He wanted to press his hips against her, to rub his erection at the juncture of her thighs and proudly show her how fierce his reaction was to her.

"I've met a lot of your kind," she said. "Know that I'm invulnerable."

"I'll take that as a challenge, *aingeal*. I'm going to be inside you tonight, and I'll remind you of your words when I have your legs wrapped 'round my waist."

"Oh, Scot, that won't happen." She shook her head, and a few glossy curls tumbled free over her shoulder.

"You're obviously no' innocent." Which was odd, since he knew she was upper class. She must be a jaded thrill seeker like Jane Weyland and her crowd. "Why no' spend a night with me?"

"You don't think I'm untouched? Why?"

"You looked like you could have yawned at the scene we found in here. No' many innocents would be unfazed by the sight of a prostitute giving a man a below job."

"Well, whether I am or not is incidental. The fact remains that I'm here to find a husband—not a lover. And I've no time for dalliances."

"Make time. If you're in London to find a husband, seems like you might no' be so disdainful to an unmarried man like myself." *He* didn't have time for this. Tomorrow he would leave town to search for Davis Grey, and for the first time, the call of a hunt like that wasn't as strong as the call of a woman.

She laughed then, a seductively sultry laugh that made him yearn to kiss her. "You are so unreachable, you're not even a remote candidate."

He tensed. "Based on what little you know of me?"

All humor gone, she said, "I know enough to suspect that you would use me and never look back. And I'm not condemning, just stating a fact." Her guileless blue eyes were suddenly inscrutable. "I think we have a lot in common, you and I."

"In common? Then you're achin' for us to tup, too."

Maddy grinned then. She simply couldn't help it. "And just like that, you disarm me." There was something about his rough—markedly rough—around the edges demeanor that appealed to her. Who was she fooling? *Everything* about him appealed to her, from his rumbling brogue to his muscular body, to his peculiar fixation *with her*.

"I want to do more than disarm you."

Her smile faded. The Scot wasn't giving up, and she regretted leading him on. She was behaving foolishly like a normal girl of twenty-one might, when she didn't have that luxury. Ever practical Maddy felt herself closing down, the barbs sharpening, the walls going up. "My friends have probably begun to look for me by now. I need to get back to them."

His brows drew together. "You're truly ... *leaving*?" He sounded baffled, as if he had no idea what to do with this.

She tilted her head. "And you're truly not used to being turned down?"

"I'm no' used to being in a position to be."

"You never pursue women?" she said in a doubtful tone.

"Never."

"So I was the lucky first?" Normally she would roll her eyes at comments like these and take them for what they were—verbal attempts to get into her skirts. But there was something about the way he said them, as if they were significant to him, as if they were not only truths, but new and unwelcome ones.

And that he blamed her for them.

"Aye." He exhaled. "You are the first."

"It's a shame on your first sally, you're going to fail."

His dark eyes narrowed. "And you call me arrogant? What makes you think you can dismiss me?"

"Because *you* are the one who sought *me* out."

"And I dinna do it in vain." He placed his hands against the wall on either side of her head, and then leaned in as if to kiss her. "I'm taking you from here tonight."

Though she was dying to know what his lips would feel like, she pushed against his chest—striving to ignore how rigid and big the muscles there were. "Not a chance of that,